DREAM OF ME

Jennifer Froelich

ISBN: 1475143427
ISBN-13: 978-1475143423

For Michelle

I sleep, but my heart is awake.

I hear my lover knocking.

-- Song of Solomon

Chapter 1

Shannon inched toward the edge of the cliff and wiggled her painted toes. She took a deep breath, a last taste of life. Her face and arms were covered in angry scratches, evidence of the foliage she had passed through while making her escape. But she was numb to any pain. For a moment she focused on her pink toes, in that lucid flash remembering her daughter's visit yesterday. Had Erynne painted them? But the moment passed. As she looked away from her feet, she thought of nothing beyond the setting sun, melting like a dollop of raspberry sherbet along the watery horizon.

The wind picked up, carrying with it the smell of Eucalyptus trees and kelp. A distant sound jolted her senses: the sharp cries of a baby. For years her cries had haunted Shannon. She swayed and began humming the lullaby again, her fragile mind hoping that doing so might quiet the child. She resisted the impulse to look over her shoulder. Whether pursued by staff from the nursing home or the dark demon from her dreams, it didn't matter anymore. It would all be over soon.

"A long time ago, on a path that curved toward the sea…" She started to tell the story, but forgot the words as the tide finally reached the bottom of the cliff.

Why had it taken her so long to accept reality – to understand that the story was hers? Sadly, she knew that the truth was locked inside her now, never to be released by a mind that refused to obey her will.

Another half step and Shannon's toes were curling over the cliff's edge, dislodging a trickle of pebbles that dropped thirty feet into the tide below. She sighed and took a deep breath. It was time.

Stretching her arms wide, she closed her eyes. The wind embraced her body, throwing her tears back against her wrinkled face. How she wished she could explain everything to Erynne. Had she even tried?

A momentary seed of doubt crept into her thoughts. She opened her eyes and remembered her daughter. As if summoned by clarity, Erynne was suddenly in her peripheral vision, breaking through the trees with a look of utter horror on her beautiful face.

"Mother! No!"

It's too late, Shannon thought. *I'm too tired to fight anymore. Quiet will come now, and rest too.*

She stepped forward.

ೞ

Only a handful of mourners gathered at the cemetery on the day Erynne O'Keefe buried her mother. Most of them were not dressed for the unexpected Pacific wind moving swiftly over the

Santa Cruz hillside. They stood in huddles, sweaters grasped at their necks, their faces screwed up in discomfort. It was early March and had been typically overcast since dawn, but now at midday, the clouds were darkening and the temperature dropping. A steady trickle of headlights was visible weaving its way along Highway One in the distance, but the fog was closing in, at any moment threatening to obscure everything beyond the homes that dotted the adjacent hillside.

Erynne stood apart from the others, oblivious to the weather. A gust of wind lifted her dark hair away from her pale face, but she was otherwise immobile, staring at the mound of dirt beside her mother's grave. The casket was beautiful – as nice as she could afford – but she couldn't bear to look at it. When the rain began to fall, someone moved close and held an umbrella over her head.

The priest's solemn tempo decidedly increased as the rain began to come down in earnest. Erynne barely listened to his words, knowing his eulogy could hold little relevance. Her mother had been placed in the Catholic Social Services foster care system almost sixty years ago. She had never taken Erynne to church, claiming to have never set foot inside one since her mandatory confirmation, which explained why this soggy priest used words like "giving" and "caring" to describe her. He simply hadn't known her.

The priest abandoned his Bible. Shielding its leather cover from the rain in the folds of his robe, he was now quoting Psalm twenty-three from memory.

"...Yea, though I walk through the valley of the shadow of death..."

Erynne closed her eyes and saw the Shadow of Death standing beside her mother on the cliff's edge, whispering in her ear, encouraging her to take her last step. She opened them quickly and focused on the dirt again, watching each drop of rain join the others, find a path down the steep slope, and eventually pool at the bottom in a puddle of mud.

When she looked up again, she saw Mark Osborn watching her from across the casket, his expression filled with sorrow and guilt. For a moment, she felt her eyes begin to sting. She blinked rapidly and looked away, searching the crowd for distraction. Her mother's old friends tottered in the wind. Very few of them had visited her at the care center. Erynne wondered if they thought Alzheimer's was contagious.

Her eyelids began to close. She'd had so little sleep in the past few days. Staying awake had been her last line of defense against an onslaught of images too horrifying to recall. The only rest she'd had was filled with dreams. Some were nightmares, harsh reminders of reality. Others she could barely remember. From these she woke with little but the impression of a comforting presence. They made her feel worse than the nightmares. She had not reached her mother in time. She had no right to feel consoled.

Erynne forced her eyes open and focused again on the dirt by her mother's grave. She heard a baby crying and wondered idly who had brought an infant to the funeral. She felt numb. Numb to the rain and the wind, numb to the fears that had been coursing through her since her mother's nightmares had returned two weeks ago.

The priest was wrapping it up, giving her just a few minutes to prepare for the onslaught of sympathy. As she bowed her head for the final prayer, she succumbed to the memory of her mother's frail form on the rocky bluff, her nightgown pressed against her body, her white hair billowing around her face like a cloud. Her sad expression had been so lucid – so *knowing*. Erynne jerked her head upward and opened her eyes, but it was too late. She could still see her mother stepping over the edge.

Chapter 2

"You don't have to do this today."

Erynne looked up to see Mark standing in the doorway of her mother's room at Cypress Care Center. The tie and suit jacket he wore at the funeral had been replaced by a more familiar stethoscope and white doctor's coat. Less familiar was his untidy black hair, usually combed so neatly, and the dark circles under his eyes.

"There's no need to put it off," she said, returning her attention to the open suitcase in front of her.

Mark frowned. "I expected you to go home and get some rest after the funeral."

"People kept calling and dropping by with food."

She pulled another nightgown from her mother's dresser drawer and began to fold it, trying to ignore its familiar scent. Mark walked around the foot of the bed and stood close to her.

"You could go to my house. Turn off your phone, sleep a little."

Erynne didn't answer him. Instead she placed the nightgown in the bottom of the suitcase and moved away toward the bureau. Mark had been her mother's doctor for almost five years. A few months ago, Erynne had finally agreed to have dinner with him. Maybe there was a time when they might have been able to take things further, but not anymore.

Opening the top drawer she found a skein of yarn, an old journal and a pair of reading glasses that Shannon had given up on some time ago. "You'll have to read to me now," she had said. Erynne cleared her throat and gathered the rest of it, heading back toward the suitcase where Mark stood watching her.

"I saw a police cruiser pulling away as I came in," she said.

"Officer Mills," Mark said. "He had more questions for the staff. The nurses this time. Marianne is taking it hard."

Erynne shook her head.

"Mom stole a key card and passed through two locked doors. Marianne checked on her just ten minutes before she disappeared." She looked up at Mark and tried to smile, but her lips trembled. "It wasn't her fault. Or yours. It wasn't anyone's fault."

"We'll see what the investigators say," he answered quietly. "You know that if they find us negligent in anyway…"

"I know, Mark. You're the most responsible person I know."

"I have my own reports to complete too, Erynne," he said gently. "I can't help wondering if your mother's nightmares had something to do with her wandering away."

Erynne focused on the inside of the suitcase, focused on her breathing. "Alzheimer's patients wander, Mark. You know that better than anyone."

"Your mother never has. She was here for almost five years and never showed the slightest tendency for flight."

"Until three days ago." Erynne swallowed a hard, angry knot in her throat and moved to the closet where she grabbed several sweaters.

"Yes," he agreed evenly, "only a short time after her nightmares began. When I first mentioned her dreams two weeks ago, you turned white as a ghost, Erynne. I didn't push it at the time. I figured it was another one of those things from your childhood that you wouldn't talk about. But now I need to know if I was right to let it pass."

Erynne focused on folding each sweater, reluctant as ever to dredge up a subject that would inevitably pull her back to the blackest parts of her childhood. She had no wish to relive all those nights lying in bed, listening to her mother sobbing from beyond her closed bedroom door. She had learned not to try and wake her. Her bruised cheek and scratched arms had been difficult to explain to a concerned teacher. Instead she had squeezed her pillow tightly against her ears and tried to imagine happy things – birthday presents, butterflies, caramel apples and trips to Disneyland that would surely happen someday – Mom had promised.

"Erynne," Mark pressed. "Did your mother have a history of nightmares?"

"Almost nightly when I was a kid," she admitted quietly. "They went away about the time she was diagnosed with AD. I thought they were gone for good."

Mark sighed. "I wish you had told me."

"Mom would be alive today if I had – is that it?" Erynne asked sharply.

"I didn't say that. I might have used a stronger sedative, though. Something that would have calmed her enough to prevent..."

"I know my mother and her history of self-medicating, Mark," Erynne interrupted. She returned to the closet, grabbing the rest of its contents. "There's not a narcotic in the world that ever held her down."

"Did you talk to her about her recent nightmares? Were they similar to those from the past?"

Erynne closed the suitcase flap and sat on the edge of her mother's bed, the same place she had sat two weeks ago when she first learned about the returning nightmares. That day, her mother's sallow face had been full of fear, her eyes wide and red-rimmed. She gripped the sheet with shaking hands and eyed her daughter suspiciously.

"Mom?"

Erynne had reached out to touch her mother's hand, only to have it pulled sharply away. Long ago she promised herself never to be hurt by her mother's erratic behavior. Still, it had been a long time since she had done anything that reminded Erynne of the mother she once knew. They spent her visits playing gin rummy, crocheting and watching *Wheel of Fortune* together. Alzheimer's had been a blessing in Erynne's life. It had given her a mother who was more lovable.

It had taken only a few minutes for recognition to dawn in Shannon's eyes. When Erynne reached for her hand again, her mother did not resist.

"Oh! I'm so glad you came."

"I'm here, Mom. Dr. Osborn said you've been having bad dreams." Erynne had tried to ignore her heart, thumping against her chest. "Can you tell me about them?"

"Yes," Shannon whispered, looking toward the door before piercing her daughter with frightened eyes. "You see, he's after me again, that's what."

"Who is after you?"

"He left me alone for so long, that I thought, 'Well, he's gone forever and won't bother me again.' And it was so nice, wasn't it? These past few years with just you and me?"

"It's been very nice, Mom," Erynne agreed.

Shannon patted her hand. "And we've had good times, haven't we? You were always such a good girl, taking care of me..." Her voice trailed off as her eyes found an interesting spot on the floral bedspread. She reached out a gnarled finger and absently picked at one of the flowers.

"Mom, who was it?" Erynne prodded. "Who did you dream about?"

Shannon looked up, her face wary again.

"Was it Daddy?" Erynne asked.

"No, not him. It was never him."

"You're safe here, you know. Dr. Osborne, Marianne – they take good care of you."

"I thought so too." Her voice cracked. "But he's coming. He won't stop until he finds me."

Erynne had tried to reassure her mother during that visit and every one that followed, but Shannon had remained afraid – during her lucid moments, at least – that her nightmares would come to life.

Getting up from the bed, Erynne turned away from Mark and walked toward the window. She regretted it immediately. This view of the Monterey Bay had always taken her breath away. The raw beauty of the Pacific's pulse beating against the jagged shoreline was something she had missed when she was away at school in Europe. It was something Shannon had never been willing to leave. But now, as Erynne remembered her mother's frail form on the slippery cliff's edge, she felt bile rise in the back of her throat. She wondered if she would ever love the sea again.

"The nightmares, Erynne?" Mark prodded.

Erynne shook her head. Could it be true? Had her mother died because of a nightmare – because she could no longer separate reality and fantasy in her decaying mind?

"I think the dreams were the same in substance," she finally said, turning from the window. "He was chasing her again. It was always the man without a face chasing her."

"That's what she told me too."

Erynne and Mark turned to see Marianne standing in the doorway. Her eyes were red-rimmed and she was ringing a ragged tissue between her fingers.

"I should have watched her more carefully," Marianne said, her voice thick with tears. "I tried to reassure her. I told her she was safe – that it was just another bad dream. It usually only took a few minutes for her to calm down and forget she'd dreamed in the first place. It was almost like clockwork. Her expression would change and she would start telling me a fairytale. The same one she always told, over and over again until she fell back to sleep."

"The one about a baby who was kidnapped?" Erynne asked.

Marianne nodded. "Yes – the baby was a princess, right? And there was a prince too. Both had to be hidden from an evil magician. I had never heard it before."

Mark shook his head. "I've never heard that one either."

Erynne pulled another tissue from her mother's bedside table and handed it to Marianne. "I think it was something my grandmother made up," she said. "Mom told it to me when I was a kid. It doesn't have a happy ending."

"She would sing too," said Marianne, "a lullaby that seemed to calm her."

Erynne turned back to the suitcase and zipped it closed. She knew the lullaby, but Shannon had stopped singing it for her when her father left.

"Let me help you with that," Mark said, reaching for the suitcase. But Erynne shook her head and set its wheels on the ground, pulling it toward the door. She had been here too long.

"Are you heading home?" Mark asked.

"Mmmm." Erynne was intentionally noncommittal. "Or to the studio."

"I can give you a ride."

"No, Mark. Thanks. I have my car."

Erynne's eyes finally met his as she passed through the doorway. She wished she didn't recognize what she saw there.

Chapter 3

Colin took a deep breath, closed his eyes, and opened them again. The air around him was stagnant and hot like a kiln. He wore a Sun Devils ball cap low over his sunglasses, but the sun was still too bright, reflecting off the sand and dirt, making him squint. He looked toward the west expectantly, his eyes coming to rest on a blank place in the sky directly over Luke Air Force Base. For a moment, no traffic passed. Nothing moved but ripples of heat that pulsed above the asphalt.

Settling back into his lawn chair, Colin waited. It wouldn't be long. Images from last night's dream tried to push their way to the front of his mind, but he fought them, focusing instead on the shaved cotton field in front of him. Sweat began to make its way past his temple. He twisted in his seat, wishing for a breeze. Seconds later, the distinctive hum of the engines started, pulling his eyes back toward the base. His pulse raced and he adjusted his hat.

They came off the runway fast. One, two, three, four. Colin strained his neck, leaning back as far as he could without tipping over the lawn chair. Zoom! Four F-16 Falcons ripped through the air right over his head, maintaining their perfect diamond formation. In an instant they disappeared into the depths of the blue sky.

Spectacular.

Two solo jets took off next, each flying straight up, then turning to the east, preparing for the next maneuver over base. Colin craned his neck as the fighters rolled above him. They missed each other by inches before racing for the horizon with nothing but two perfect trails of smoke in their stead. He counted almost thirty maneuvers over the next hour. When the planes finally returned to base, he stowed the chair in his trunk and wished he had made time to go on base, see the full show and tour the exhibits.

Maybe next year.

Colin was a freshman in high school the first time he saw the Thunderbirds fly. He and his dad had driven from their home in Lancaster, Pennsylvania, to catch the air show at Andrews Air Force Base in Maryland. From the moment the Thunderbird pilots had turned over their engines, Colin had been dazzled by the powerful F-16s.

"Those are real tactical fighters, Dad," he had said on the way home from the show, reading from a flier. "They can be made combat ready in less than seventy-two hours. All they do is replace the smoke generating system with a 20mm cannon."

"Pretty cool, huh?" his dad asked, eyeing him speculatively. Colin had talked of little else in the weeks that followed, driving his parents crazy and promising to enlist on his eighteenth birthday. True to his word, he had joined the Air Force shortly after high school. An injured elbow and imperfect vision forced him to give up his dreams of becoming a fighter pilot. He took it in stride, accepting the restriction with cocky idealism, boldly seeking one of the coveted enlisted positions in the Thunderbirds squadron.

Colin smiled now, remembering the stern response he had received from the recruiting officer.

His disappointment had passed quickly enough, and he ended up learning some valuable skills as an Air Force paper pusher. He even spent time pushing paper in Kyrgyzstan when he was deployed with an expeditionary security team providing operational support for forces in Afghanistan. A long military career hadn't been for him – but the experience taught him a lot, providing tuition money so he could go on to earn his accounting degree at Arizona State. He now managed the tax division of a corporate firm in downtown Phoenix.

Colin pulled out a water bottle and took a long drink as he cranked up the air conditioning in his Subaru and headed east toward the city. The back of his neck stung with the beginnings of a sunburn. Usually he was well on his way to tanned by mid-March, but he had been stuck in the office more than usual this year. Merging onto the freeway, Colin impatiently clicked through the radio stations until convinced that nothing was worth hearing. Finally he gave up and let his dream from the night before return to his conscious thoughts. It had been nagging him all day, despite his efforts to beat it down to the forgotten recesses of his mind.

It's stress, he told himself again, *like the others*.

But the conviction wouldn't stick and that vaguely breathless feeling washed over him again, making his skin pucker.

He had tried to analyze the dream, looking for some kind of relevance, but there seemed to be no connection to his real life. Not that he was a psychology buff or anything, but he had learned a little from his required college courses. Dreams were usually filled with symbols. A crashing car or speeding train meant you felt out of control, falling off a cliff or being caught naked in public meant you felt vulnerable. He grimaced as he remembered some of Freud's more colorful interpretations.

I won't even go there, he thought.

But his dreams lately were mismatched – coming from nowhere. They were set in unfamiliar places that changed around him. His mood changed too, each emotion more potent than in real life – happiness was euphoria, calmness near inertia. Sometimes his sense of expectation was so powerful, it nearly overwhelmed him. Other times he was out of breath, running through murky alleys or abandoned buildings, looking over his shoulder with blackest dread. He awoke on sweat-drenched sheets, his heart racing as he looked around his dark bedroom, bewildered.

Colin shrugged his shoulders, trying to work out the tension. He fiddled with the radio again, settling on something by U2. He had thought the air show would be a good diversion but, honestly, craning his neck to see the jets probably hadn't been the best idea.

It took forty-five minutes to reach his home in central Phoenix, and as he turned onto his palm-lined street he felt some of his tension pass away. He loved his house. It was a 1920s Spanish bungalow built in a great neighborhood – close to work and far from the dreaded sameness of suburbia. A small courtyard entryway and natural stone fireplace had been its strongest selling points when he bought it three years ago, and even though he still hadn't done much to furnish the place, he was happy to walk through its echoing rooms, admire the wood floor he had stripped and refinished himself and dream about the pool he would one day add to the large back yard. As Colin parked his car and headed inside, he glanced at his Orchid tree and the driveway that needed sweeping.

Later, he told himself.

He grabbed a Coke from the fridge and headed out back to the patio. It was a beautiful evening. The sun was just setting beyond the mountains and the sweet smell of orange blossoms filled the air. Night was descending and with the darkness, Colin's dream refused to be pushed aside again.

He had been running from someone. With his heart pounding in his chest, he ducked through doorways, under scaffolding, up staircases – never reaching any kind of destination. In his arms he carried an old woman who wore a nightgown and looked at him with wild eyes. Time passed in strange, jerking intervals. His arms ached under the woman's weight and fear, clouding around them like poisoned gas.

Colin emerged from an alley onto a rain-drenched street, passing graffiti on brick walls as he dodged potholes and puddles. It was a cracked sidewalk that brought them both down. The woman tumbled out of his arms, hitting the pavement with a sickening thud. Colin rolled clear, crashing into a collection of garbage cans. His stomach turned over as he crawled back toward her, carefully lifting her head into his lap.

"Someone's coming!" he whispered urgently. "We need to keep going!"

He shook the woman gently, but when she didn't respond, he turned desperately from left to right. There had to be a means of escape – or someone who could help him.

The woman groaned, shifting in his lap and pulling his attention back to her face. Colin gasped. In the seconds he had been looking away, her appearance had changed. Her skin had tightened, wrinkles faded, eyes brightened. Her white hair had changed too, darkening to brown. Her features were the same, she was just younger. By at least twenty years.

She grabbed his hand and pulled toward him with more strength than he would have thought possible.

"Protect her," she whispered.

Immediately, she released him and fell back in his arms. He knelt there, holding her in the street until everything vanished into mist. He woke with her words on his lips.

Colin shivered. The warmth of the sunset was already a memory, the shadows in his yard long and dark. He rose to go inside, wishing he could avoid bed tonight. He didn't want to dream again – not if anything similar was waiting for him in the recesses of his mind. Instead he flipped on the TV and turned on more lamps than usual. But the chill stayed with him long into the night, settling in his bones like fear.

Chapter 4

EOK Design Studio was printed in modest silver letters on a single-paned glass door between *Harry Yorst's Birkenstocks* and a small eatery called *Pizza My Heart* in downtown Santa Cruz. Most people passed by without noticing it. By contrast, Erynne's boutique occupied prime real estate on the north end of the Pacific Garden Mall, and was known to turn the eye of every woman who walked past.

"*St. Genevieve's* store front is like an elegant wedding cake," a columnist in the *San Francisco Chronicle* had recently written, "and is equally tempting."

Erynne appreciated the praise. The boutique was already known to wealthy women from Nob Hill to Seventeen Mile Drive as one of the best custom clothiers in the Bay Area, but she had seen a definite spike in interest since the *Chronicle* piece. The appointment calendar was now booked three weeks in advance.

When Erynne first started out, she sold at expos, trade shows and kiosks while her studio only occupied the narrow mall-facing space above the pizzeria. When success allowed her to open the retail front, she also expanded the studio, renting the entire upper floor. Now her employees had ample space to work. A row of Industrial sewing machines sat under a bank of tall windows, while two long cutting tables were positioned under hanging task lights. Wire baskets filled with notions, thread, interfacing and cutting tools were stored under the tables and dress forms of various sizes stood nearby. A comfortable seating area, well-lit in one corner, provided a place for coffee breaks and hand stitching.

Erynne had retained the original space at the front of the building for her private studio and office, having grown attached to the two floor-to-ceiling windows on the west wall, which allowed natural light to flood the studio. Exposed brick walls were decorated with simply-framed sketches from Erynne's portfolio, while barrels of fabric bolts were stored in the corner. Her most productive hours were those spent in the studio. She visited her boutique almost daily, but was happy to delegate its day-to-day operations to a capable manager.

Erynne drove straight to work after leaving Mark at the care center, but she didn't end up staying long. She had just started pulling fabric swatches from catalogues and making rough sketches when Gretchen arrived. For a moment, the hum of sewing machines and muffled conversation followed her from the workroom across the hall, but she quickly closed the door, excluding normalcy. Sympathy marred her pretty features, like it had all week. Erynne looked away. She didn't know how much more pity she could take.

"Do you know what happened to the JLA invoice for our last silk screening order?" she asked.

Gretchen ignored the question. "I thought you were going home to rest."

Erynne fiddled with her pen for a moment and then returned to her drawing pad. "I went by Cypress instead."

The older woman pressed her lips together. "I don't suppose you have eaten today either," she said. When Erynne didn't respond, she pulled a brown lunch bag from her cavernous purse and laid it on the corner of her work table.

"Why don't you go home now? You look tired."

Erynne shook her head. "A little later. Thanks for the lunch."

"There's nothing that you need to do today," Gretchen persisted. "I can cover for you – I don't have much work to keep me busy anyway."

"Then you have time to find that invoice."

Erynne ignored Gretchen for another half an hour while she quietly searched, furtively glancing her way every few minutes. But after she found the invoice, Gretchen stood at the corner of her desk, wringing her hands or smoothing her salt and pepper hair until Erynne sighed and dropped her pen.

"Fine," she said. "You win. I'll see you tomorrow." Grabbing her handbag, she walked out the door.

Erynne had hired Gretchen as her business manager the year her small fashion enterprise went from red to black, only six years after graduating from the Heriot Watt Design School in Scotland. Leaving her hometown to study in Europe had been Erynne's way of rebelling – and escaping – her mother's theatrics and co-dependent nature. It also had been an incomparable learning experience. After graduation, she was offered several positions, both international and domestic, but by then, Shannon's deteriorating health was impossible to ignore. Erynne moved home, wrote a strict five-year business plan and then put in the long hours needed to build a loyal clientele. Her designs were diverse enough to please both younger and older women –

something Gretchen had commented on during her first week of work.

"It's almost unnatural, what you can do with a bit of fabric and a pair of scissors," she had said, admiring her reflection in the mirror as she modeled one of Erynne's designs. And despite her tendency to hover, Gretchen had proven indispensable, both as an employee and as a friend.

"I guess I won't fire her after all," Erynne muttered as she reached the parking garage.

ᘓ

Dusk was settling on the horizon by the time she parked in her driveway and shut off the ignition. For a moment she sat motionless, exhaustion bleeding into her bones. Moisture from the day's patchy rainfall clung to the air, creating fingers of fog that reached for her through the Jetta's windshield.

Her neighborhood was uncharacteristically quiet. There were no kids playing basketball at the end of the street, no skateboards bumping against the sidewalk cracks like a needle on vinyl. She could hear nothing but the beat of her pulse and the subtle settling noises from under the hood of her car.

It was tempting to stay where she was, to rest her head against the steering wheel and wait for other random noises to emerge. Anything rather than going inside the house.

Better yet, she should return to her studio. Next season's line still sat unfinished on her work table. *Gretchen will be gone by now,* she reminded herself. But the fog outside her windshield was now a dense canopy, stifling her. Erynne shuddered, took her purse and went inside.

As soon as she stepped through the back door, she smelled the flowers from her mother's funeral. She didn't want them here. She didn't want to be reminded. She wanted the anesthetic of work, the familiar feel of fabric, the smell of sharpened pencils and fresh sketchpads, the hum of sewing machines and chatter of happy employees. Work, plan, organize. Work harder. All her life, these were the tools Erynne used to resist her mother's drama. Surely they would help her deal with her death – if only she was left alone to use them.

Dropping her keys on the counter, Erynne surveyed her dim kitchen with a frown. A light had been left on over the stove, highlighting a plate wrapped in foil. Lying on top was a note written in Gretchen's familiar script:

Please eat! I'll come by tomorrow to check on you. Call if you need me. –G.

"Brown bag lunches and warmed up dinners," Erynne said with a frown. She scooped up the plate and slid it into the refrigerator, then flipped on every light on the way to her bedroom, determined to banish the gloom.

Erynne's house was a small Cape Cod that had once belonged to her parents, and before that to paternal grandparents she never knew. After placing Shannon in the care home, Erynne wanted to move, but her business plans hadn't allowed it. This house was paid for and moving was a luxury she couldn't afford, bad memories or not.

She made many improvements over the years: fresh paint, replacement fixtures, new furniture and refinished hardwoods. But since her mother's death, whenever dusk hit, it seemed as if every change she had made receded. The paint faded from the walls to reveal tired floral paper. The hardwoods gave way to worn shag and cracked vinyl, her furniture transformed into bland mid-century pieces left behind by her grandparents and neglected by her mom and dad.

Erynne quickly pulled on her pajamas and brushed her teeth, trying to resist the onslaught of memories – thoughts better left to the recesses of her mind. They were cunning, though, coiling in the shadows, ready to strike like a snake. The bathroom, more than any other part of her house, had remained the same since her childhood. Two-toned pink tile covered the walls and surrounded the tub, unchanged since the first time she shaved her legs and polished her toes, sweeping mascara over her lashes with confidence, sure that her reflection would soon move on. She would find kinder mirrors in foreign places, where the walls didn't scream at night, where mother and daughter were not turned upside down.

Erynne dropped her toothbrush in the sink and leaned against the porcelain with shaking hands. Sudden nausea swept over her.

Not now, she told the walls.

Escaping to the hallway, she braced herself against the doorframe, waiting for her heart to quit pounding. There was a time when listing her accomplishments would push the panic away – A successful business, a contented life, personal pride, even, for accepting the responsibility of caring for her mother, despite their difficult relationship.

The decision had been rewarding, hadn't it? She built something new with her mother, a brief time to cherish – something to help blot out old traumas. But it hadn't worked like she thought it would. The old wasn't replaced with the new, just buried beneath the surface.

Paint over it, sand it. Hide it under a new rug.

Erynne pushed away from the wall and opened a door that always stayed closed. This had been her mother's room, left unchanged from the day she left it to live at Cypress.

Tripping over shadows, Erynne felt her way to her mother's bedside table and turned on the lamp. Rosy light filled the room. Blackout shades hidden by heavy, yellowed curtains had always made it appear the same, day or night. Shannon had insisted upon them, often finding her only restful sleep during the daytime. Erynne coughed, overwhelmed by the dust and memories. How long had it been since she had even vacuumed in here?

Beaded necklaces hung on the mirror above an old dressing table, where dusting powder and lipstick sat abandoned next to Erynne's framed graduation picture. Postcards from Europe were stuck at angles into the mirror's frame. Across the small room, the closet door wouldn't close for the collection of old housecoats hanging over the top. Inside, her mother's dated dresses drooped on wire hangers, dusty and neglected, but not altogether free of Shannon's familiar scent – a combination of Rose Milk lotion and Avon perfume.

Maybe it was the fragrance that worked as a catalyst, reacting with the memories to drive Erynne to her knees in front of the open closet door. She wasn't strong enough to push them away this time. Tears that had only trickled for the past few days came now in a torrent of guilt and pain.

How could she have been so stupid? She had shut up this room with its memories and embraced the sweet woman her mother had become. But she had never faced it. She had never been willing. Proof enough were the nightmares. She had denied their power. For her own peace of mind, she withheld their importance from her mother's caretakers.

Erynne pressed her forehead against the dusty carpet. Mark would be too kind, telling her that she shouldn't blame herself –

that even if she had told him everything about her mother's history of nightmares, it would have made little difference. But she wasn't so willing to let go of her guilt. Pushing herself away from the floor, she sat up and swiped at her tears, staring at the floor of her mother's closet where boxes and bags were stacked haphazardly. So much clutter – so much she should have dealt with in the years that had passed. With one impulsive sweep of her arm, Erynne dislodged the mess, allowing the neglected collection to spill out across the carpet.

For several minutes she stared at the pile without focus. Eventually a subtle movement caught her eye – the tarnished shine of a gold chain that was dangling from an envelope. Leaning forward to examine it more closely, she saw that the envelope was one of several tied together with a piece of grosgrain ribbon and left in the bottom of an old shoebox with a handful of Polaroid snapshots.

Erynne gathered the stack, scooted backward and leaned against her mother's chenille bedspread where the dim lighting would better illuminate her find. Pulling the first envelope from the stack, she quickly took in the faded typewritten address and 1955 postmark. Ignoring the gold chain, she wrestled the letter free. It too was typewritten and worn from handling. Her eyes passed over the text quickly.

> *January 14, 1955*
>
> *Dear Mr. and Mrs. Marshall,*
>
> *We regret to inform you that the natural mother of your charge, Miss Shannon Kelly, has taken her own life. This tragedy occurred two weeks ago on New Year's Eve. We leave it to your discretion as to whether you inform the child of the circumstances of her mother's death. It is our opinion, however, that*

knowledge of a parental suicide can only bring harm to a child's natural spirit, good health and understanding of God's wisdom and Grace.

Vagueness rather than deceit is advised, though you must do what you deem appropriate.

The only personal belonging of any value left behind by Nancy Kelly is the enclosed necklace. Her last wishes, expressed in a brief note, were of passing it along to her daughter.

Our sincerest sympathy,

Sister Martha Bradford,
California Catholic Foster Care Services

Erynne dropped the letter in her lap and pulled the gold chain free of the envelope. The heavy pendant it supported was unusual in shape and was formed out of a dark green stone. After a moment, she decided that it looked most like a tree. Her mother had been only eight years old when the letter was written. Erynne fingered the other letters in the stack, knowing they needed to be read.

But not tonight.

Rising on unsteady legs, she headed for the door, the necklace still in her hand. The letters she left behind, abandoned on the floor by her mother's bed.

 લ

At one o'clock in the morning, Erynne pushed back her covers and swung her feet over the edge of her bed. The letter,

27

necklace and all they implied would not let her sleep, despite all her pillow pounding and counting sheep. From where she sat, she could see through the open bathroom doorway. The pink tile she couldn't face earlier that night was now bathed in moonlight.

Look at it, the moon told her. *No running away this time.*

Suicide. It was a word Erynne had not let herself consider. Her mother had died, yes. She had stepped off a cliff. But her mind was not sound. Premeditation or intent could not be assigned with confidence. That was what the police said. It was even what the reporter from the *Sentinel* had written.

Maybe it was true, but Erynne knew her mother's past – the police and reporters did not. Shannon had written countless suicide notes in years gone by, leaving them tucked into writing tablets or desk drawers where she thought Erynne wouldn't find them. Or did she intend for her to see them all along?

When Erynne was fifteen, she thought her mother had finally made good on her threats when she found her lying still and pale on the bathroom floor, her hair haloed by pink tile, her eyes glazed over and staring sightlessly at the undercarriage of the sink.

"Mama?"

Erynne ran forward, her eyes searching wildly for blood, razor, or knife. Instead, she found a bottle of sleeping pills in her mother's hand. Grabbing them, she quickly counted. The bottle was almost full – only three missing.

"Mama, what are you doing?" she asked, her voice trembling.

Shannon blinked and slowly pushed herself into a sitting position. Her nightgown was twisted around her thighs and her graying hair looked like it hadn't been washed or combed in days. When Erynne dropped to the floor, her slender shoulders shuddering with violent tears, her mother rose to her feet, leaving the pill bottle on the floor.

"I should never have become a mother," she said impassively before shuffling off to her bedroom and closing the door.

Erynne blinked back hot tears, angry that the memory could still affect her this way. Lowering her head back onto her pillow, she took measured breaths, willing it all away. The necklace she found lay bathed in moonlight on the night table in front of her. She picked it up and closed her fingers around it.

Until today, she had known nothing about her grandmother – only the fairytale she had passed along to Shannon sometime before child protective services took her away. But now she knew enough to change her outlook forever. Her grandmother had committed suicide and her mother, whether with intent or without, had taken her own life too. What did that mean for Erynne?

Chapter 5

Michael dressed carefully, keeping his eyes focused on his reflection in the mirror as he straightened his tie and brushed lint off his shoulders. Brahms played quietly from the stereo in his dressing room, calming nerves that had been sensitive all day. He was beginning to make out party noises from below.

He hoped he could cross several major PAC leaders from his list after the evening was over. This annual party at his opulent Georgetown home was popular, his campaign manager assured him, and necessary. Michael knew Markham was already downstairs, ensconced in the wingback chair in his study, scotch in one hand, his other tapping impatiently on the leather upholstery as he waited for Michael to make his appearance. But Michael didn't want to go down too soon. He practiced his smile in the mirror, checking for signs of artifice. This night had to be perfect. Nothing could go wrong.

Michael's headache from earlier had dissipated only an hour ago, but the aftertaste left him feeling drained. He blamed it on his dream last night. Once again, he had been hunting, driven by the scent of fear. For weeks, the dream had been the same. The frustration of waking too soon swelled every morning.

But last night's dream had positively unnerved him. Michael had finally caught a glimpse of his prey. Now when he looked past his own reflection in the mirror, he saw her wrinkled face, her watery blue eyes staring back at him, sometimes tortured, sometimes vacant. She was the same woman who had haunted him for weeks, he now realized. Every night he had pursued her through streets and alleyways, his urgency to find her raw and primal.

Last night had been different.

The woman appeared just like before, but as Michael gave chase, his pulse had quickened with fresh understanding. He was stronger this time – and finally gaining ground. His thirst to capture her constricted his throat, his heart pounded wildly as he reached for her, sure that escape was impossible. But that was when she had turned and looked at him with serenity – defying her former fear. With one step she had fallen away from him, disappearing through a luminous cloud that just as quickly engulfed Michael. He floundered, trying to escape the expanse that suffocated him from all sides, suddenly aware that he was no longer falling through air, but water – deep and blue, like the woman's eyes.

Michael woke with a start in the early morning darkness. He was drenched in sweat on a damp island of twisted sheets, still feeling as if he was thrashing against the waves. By the time his heart rate returned to normal, the gray shadows in his bedroom began to take form and Michael realized that the force that held him now was a pounding headache. He swallowed four aspirin with shaking fingers and then sat on the edge of his bed, glad that Margaret wasn't expected back from Connecticut until late this afternoon.

He had not been able to shake his sense of unease through breakfast and his morning routine, despite the full schedule that his secretary had placed in front of him when his driver dropped him at the Capitol. It had been a beautiful spring day in Washington with just a touch of crispness in the air. Under blue skies laced with wispy clouds, the cherry trees were in full bloom, providing a beautiful backdrop for the tourists who came out in mass each year to visit the national monuments. Yet Michael was unproductive, staring out of his office window at the treetops, wishing again that his father was still alive to help him.

It had only occurred to Michael late in the morning that the solution to his dreams might exist within his own mind, accessible by using techniques his father had explained long ago. Locked inside his private bathroom, Michael had squinted into his palm, studying this "seeing space" as his father had called it, hoping to find some semblance of an answer. But he had quickly abandoned the idea. Staring at his palm revealed nothing but pink skin lined with typical creases. Michael was no two-bit fortuneteller. The things that had been revealed to him in the past had come from a deeper place inside. Still, he regretted the way he had always dismissed his father's warnings. The Gift had always been strong in him. Youth had made him arrogant. Michael had never been able to see through the flesh on his palm to that inner truth, despite his father's insistence that he try.

But how could he when he knew he could be interrupted at any moment?

Michael was rarely alone anymore and couldn't afford to be the subject of gossip among his staff. He ran his hand under warm water, applying soap liberally, as if removing evidence of a practice he still found distasteful. Things might have been different if his father had not died so suddenly. Their shared Gift made them both aware of the cancer, but neither had seen how swiftly it would move through his body.

Meeting after meeting filled the rest of his day. Michael's secretary promptly ushered him away from the office at six o'clock so he could prepare for tonight's party. Finally able to focus again on his reflection in the mirror, Michael willed the party noises from below to take center stage in his mind. He couldn't be distracted by anything tonight, especially not something as vaporous as a dream.

Margaret slipped up behind him, running her hands tentatively over his shoulders. Through the mirror, he could see only her glittering fingers, manicured tastefully, covered in diamonds that he had purchased. The rest of her was completely obliterated by his substantial form.

He turned around and looked down at her, tilting her chin up so he could see her face clearly in the light. Margaret was a beautiful woman – blue eyes, aristocratic nose and white, even teeth, auburn hair, elegantly styled in a French twist. He preferred it loose, but agreed that this was more appropriate for the occasion.

When he completed his appraisal, he smiled in satisfaction. Not because her makeup was applied perfectly, and not because of her hair or jewelry. His pleasure came instead from the slight quiver of her lip. Her pale eyes spoke of an extreme desire to please him, to be everything he wanted – no, needed – her to be.

As Michael's eyes moved lower, they rested on the neckline of her dress, which plunged slightly, revealing the curve of her breasts. His lips twisted downward as his fingers traveled along the edge of the fabric, resting at last on her lace slip, which was showing from beneath.

"Who are you wearing this for?" he asked, his mouth suddenly a hard line of anger.

"I thought – I mean, the saleswoman said it wouldn't..." Margaret's breathless voice trailed off as she tried to straighten her dress. "I'm sorry."

Ignoring her pleading voice, Michael roughly moved aside her hands and grabbed the silk fabric, tugging violently until the garment ripped from neckline to waist. "Find something decent to wear or don't bother coming downstairs at all."

Margaret moaned as she turned away. Her hands shaking, she stepped out of the ruined dress and staggered toward the dressing room door. Michael watched her retreat with fascination. His desire flared in an instant, urging him toward quick pursuit. He grabbed her roughly, pushing her against the door frame and covering her mouth with his. Margaret's gasp of pain only increased his ardor. He held her in place with his powerful legs, bruising her slender upper arms as his mouth moved down her throat.

Suddenly she stilled. Michael felt the change. Her body was still there, but her mind had retreated toward safety. It was a new trick she had conceived, one Michael had not yet learned to counter. It did its job. As quickly as his passion had been kindled, it was gone. He released her and turned back toward the mirror, leaving her to stumble toward the darkened bedroom, where she would undoubtedly struggle to find a suitable substitute for her ruined dress.

Catching sight of his expression in the mirror, Michael smiled wickedly, for the moment not caring that it did not reflect a trace of the benevolent attitude that had helped him win his first senatorial election. With feral eyes and his wife's blood-red lipstick smeared over his mouth, he looked like a wild animal that had just attacked its prey.

He laughed, amused by his own behavior. Throughout his life, women had looked at him with love, desire, and respect. But tonight Margaret's eyes reflected the same look he had so often seen on the face of the woman in his dreams. And nothing affected him more powerfully than the look of fear.

Chapter 6

When Erynne finally fell asleep in the early morning hours, she dreamed. It began in her bedroom, where moonlight cast a blue glow across her pillow, coaxing her eyes open. She lay quietly for a moment, surveying her surroundings as if they were foreign to her. In part they were. She had fallen asleep under a green blanket, but now pushed back a white quilt. Her soft pajamas had been replaced by an old-fashioned white nightgown that she didn't own. Erynne rose from the bed, catching her reflection in a full-length mirror.

"This isn't mine," she said quietly, and yet she couldn't keep from staring – even swaying slightly as the ruffled hem grazed her ankles. The nightgown was beautiful, with pin-tucked pleating, tiny mother of pearl buttons and delicate tatted lace trim. Her grandmother's necklace rested at the base of her throat, gleaming in the moonlight.

A long time ago, on a path that curved toward the sea...

Maybe it was the crisp blue light that brought the old story to mind, encircling her like fairy dust, making the perfume bottles on top of her dresser sparkle. Erynne frowned, trying to make a stronger connection, but her bedroom door distracted her – left slightly ajar. Light from the hallway shone through.

When Erynne opened the door, she wasn't in her hallway, but on a cobblestone street, damp with fresh rain. Old gas street lamps lined the sidewalks and cast a glow across the cobblestones, drawing her eyes down to a footbridge that spanned the street in the distance. Dew sparkled on every surface. Ivy climbed the sides of the bridge and the field stone walls that flanked the street, rising well above Erynne's head. Trees peeked out from behind, creating a glittering canopy over the narrow street and obscuring most of the sky.

A breeze lifted her hem and she inhaled, enjoying the smell of rain. The brilliance of the street intrigued her. There were no signs or traffic signals – no noise except the gentle trickle of rainwater emptying into pristine gutters. She turned toward the footbridge, listening to the simple rhythm of her bare feet splashing along the wet pavement. When a second pair of feet fell in step beside hers, she was not surprised. It was a welcome harmony.

Erynne turned and looked at the stranger walking next to her. His face was unfamiliar, but his spirit wasn't.

"Have we been here before?" she finally asked.

"I don't know. It's nice though. And, yes – familiar." The stranger's voice moved over Erynne like a warm breeze.

For a moment he considered the trees overhead, then, turning back to Erynne, he smiled. "Nice nightgown," he said. "I figured you more for an old-nightshirt kind of sleeper."

"This is too beautiful to sleep in," she agreed. "Just for sleep walking, I guess."

And it certainly makes a better impression than my old pajamas, she thought.

"What about you?" she asked, taking in his dress shirt, which was unbuttoned at the neck and slightly crushed, as if he had been wearing it all day. "Is that what you're sleeping in?"

He shrugged, pushing a hand through disheveled hair.

"I may have fallen asleep while working."

"What kind of work?"

"Taxes."

Erynne wrinkled her nose.

"You're the creative type, right?" he asked.

"You could say that."

"And you like it? I mean, not really knowing whether you got it right or not?"

"Whoa – got it *right*? What does that mean?"

He considered his answer. "When I write a budget, it either balances or it doesn't. There's red and there's black – no guessing. But artists, writers, composers – they have to wait and have someone else tell them whether they got it right."

"No, that's not true," she said, shaking her head emphatically. "Creativity is a way of speaking. It's just who I am. I know I've gotten in right when I've expressed something I couldn't say any other way."

"That's sort of beautiful," he said.

Erynne smiled and looked at her feet, surprised to feel a rush of warmth in her cheeks.

"So, uh, were you the math nerd in school?" she asked.

The stranger laughed. "Not me. I grew up on the east coast. Played baseball in the street with my little brother every day until dinnertime. I was going to play for the Phillies someday – be the next Mike Schmidt."

"So what happened?"

He rubbed his elbow. "High school injury put me out of serious contention."

"Bad luck."

"Yeah, well, that's life." He shrugged. "Truth is, I couldn't settle between baseball player and fighter pilot, so ... you know, it all worked out for the best."

Erynne wrapped her hands around her arms and looked up at the canopy of trees. "My dad took me to a Giants game at Candlestick Park once when I was little. I don't remember which team they played – or even if they won. He bought me a hot dog and a bag of warm peanuts. I mostly remember it being cold. I think I wore his jacket all day."

"You miss him," he said. She didn't have to tell him her father was gone. Somehow he knew.

"I don't remember much about him," she said, "mostly just being on the road with both of my parents. We drove around in this old beat up van. That was before we moved into my grandparents' house. I heard an old couple call them 'hippies' once when we were parked on a beach. It was the first time I realized they were different."

He reached over and squeezed Erynne's hand.

"Different can be a good thing."

They walked on in comfortable silence, always toward the footbridge, but never reaching it.

"I've got a song stuck in my head," he said after several minutes had passed.

"Which one?"

The hours passed as they discussed music and movies, places they had visited, favorite foods and books. Erynne found herself laughing at his quirky sense of humor one moment and then arguing against his logic the next.

When the mist began to recede in the distance, she reluctantly recognized the inevitability of dawn. By unspoken consent, they stopped to watch daybreak emerged over the bridge, the black sky giving way to midnight blue and then gradually fading into pink streaked with gold. Erynne had never seen a more beautiful sunrise.

"It's breathtaking," she said. When she turned to her companion, his dark blue eyes were focused on her.

"Yes. Breathtaking," he repeated quietly.

In an instant, the softer shades of dawn were obliterated by the brilliant sun, thrusting its rays through the canopy of trees and forcing Erynne's eyes closed. In that split second, she knew she had made a mistake. It was already too late to go back to her dream.

Erynne opened her eyes. She was in her bedroom again and the cobblestone street was gone, taking the comforting stranger with it, banished by daybreak to the recesses of her mind.

Chapter 7

Reality set in too quickly. Lying still didn't help. Within minutes of waking, Erynne's mind was already refusing to return details from her dream. She remembered the street, but the conversations were fading, leaving her with little but the vague impression than she had shared too much and asked too little.

Breathtaking.

His voice spread over her, warm like the sunshine that crossed her bed. But it was no use closing her eyes again. Or holding her breath. Try as she might, she couldn't remember his face.

Erynne pushed back the covers and sat up, crossing her legs in front of her. It was all for the best, she decided. It was just a dream. Her mind concocting a story – and a great idea for a new line of sleepwear, she had to admit, but otherwise soon to be forgotten.

Her grandmother's necklace slid off the edge of the bed, reminding her that she had fallen asleep with it in her hand. She retrieved it and examined the stone more carefully in the sunlight. It was dark green and variegated in color. Marble, maybe?

"Definitely a tree," she mumbled, taking in the narrow bottom and the way it ballooned out in a cluster at the top. She wondered if it was formed that way by nature or by craft. The gold chain that supported it was drawn through a small hole drilled through the top. Erynne suspected that the stone was much older than the chain. Fastening it around her neck, she crossed to her dresser and examined it in the mirror. There was something about the necklace that pulled and repelled her, comforted and disturbed her at the same time. What was it?

The letters.

Erynne had abandoned them on her mother's bedroom floor, but now they came back to her – especially those she hadn't read. She crossed the hall to retrieve them, swiftly passing in and out of her mother's room, where the stale air was still thick with grasping sorrow. Another day she would face the task of cleaning. Not today.

Carrying the box to the living room, she left it on the coffee table and headed for the kitchen. Courage to read the rest of the letters would come with a strong dose of caffeine, she decided. As she watched the coffee pot fill, Erynne inhaled deeply, appreciating the familiar aroma. It felt normal, but only for a moment. Then she remembered the stranger from her dream telling her he liked his coffee black. She pushed the thought away – Alice shaking off Wonderland.

After pouring a cup and adding cream and sugar, Erynne went back to the living room with it and sat down. Pulling the stack of letters toward her, she took a deep breath and spread them out across the table. They were already sorted by postmark date, she noticed, and addressed in the same masculine script. The first one was dated seven years before her birth. She opened the envelope with shaking fingers and began to read.

Ↄ

August 1, 1972

Dear Miss Kelly,

I hope you won't think it's too presumptuous of me to write to you this way, but when we met in the hotel lobby, I saw that you were as startled as I was. I really had to take a second look to make sure I was actually seeing you.

I don't wish to interrupt your life in any way. I think it's apparent from what we know of each other that we've chosen different lifestyles. I don't want to change mine, and I'm sure you feel the same. Still, I had to track down your address. I had to write to you. Part of me needs to know that you actually exist somewhere.

If you will occasionally write and let me know how you are, I can somehow find a sense of reality in all of this nonsense. If this letter brings no response, I will know not to try again. I guess we both know that regardless of your decision, I will be seeing you again.

Regards, Sidney Green

Ↄ

February 25, 1974

My Dear Shannon,

I know it's been some time, but I had to write. I certainly hope this letter finds you – I know you move frequently. That's probably for the best, all things considered.

I've recently moved too. Not too far, but we needed the change. My address is on the envelope, but please don't write unless you absolutely must. My wife could never understand our situation. I don't think I would either if I were in her shoes.

I find myself constantly putting pen to paper and drawing a blank as to what I might say to you. Sometimes when I wake up, I'm so full of aching I think I'm truly going mad. Do you feel that way too? No one understands me like you, and so I finally give in and write, hoping that by doing so I might exorcise these demons within.

As always, I'll see your lovely face in my dreams.

Love, Sidney

☙

April 1, 1978

Dear Shannon,

I'll come directly to the point. You mustn't do what you're considering. You are not like your mother. And I won't let you, even if it means telling

Joy everything. You don't think they'd believe us? I don't care. I'll take that risk to keep you safe.

Move again if you have to. Tell your husband you want to visit his parents – whatever you can think of as an excuse. But please don't cause yourself any harm. You have more than just yourself to think about now.

With my love, Sidney

ᴄ⳾

February 2, 1986

My Dearest Shannon,

I think I understand the desperation you've felt over the years. I've been in the same place too long, I suppose. The nightmares just keep getting worse.

My wife thinks I'm reliving the war in my dreams. She wants me to go talk to a therapist. Can you imagine? If I told anyone, they'd lock me up and throw away the key.

I hope things have gotten better for you. I think if it weren't for our visits, I would completely lose my mind.

Please take care of yourself, Shannon. You can't know how much comfort you've brought me over the years. Memories of last night have lingered with me all day.

With my love, Sidney

ᴄ⳾

July 2, 1996

Dearest Shannon,

As hard as it may be, I won't be able to write to you again. Joy knows something, though she can't understand the scope of my feelings. I feel so disloyal to her, and I must admit sometimes I curse the connection we share. I didn't ask for this, and I know you didn't either. But the hold you have on my heart has scarred me deeply. It's a wound that will not heal.

I don't really know what I'm trying to tell you. Can I love you and Joy at the same time? I must admit, I'd choose her over and over again. But from the moment our eyes met, you've lived in my heart. You own it, Shannon. And, God help me, I can't get you to move.

Love, Sidney

Erynne stacked the last letter on top of the others, smoothing her hands over the paper as if that would help her absorb more information. Her coffee had grown cold before she had taken a single sip. The clock told her it was a quarter past nine and her stomach churned, reminding her that she hadn't eaten since yesterday morning. Still, she knew she couldn't eat. Not now.

Love letters.

She shook her head, a familiar heat of anger welling up in the back of her throat to reside with the knot of guilt and grief that had been lodged there since her mother's death. The dates on the letters spanned a period of time that included both her parents' wedding date and the date of her own birth. But should it really surprise her? Add adultery to the list of her mother's transgressions.

Erynne picked up her coffee cup and headed into the kitchen where she placed it next to the sink. With a shaking hand she filled a glass with cold water, hoping to displace the bitter taste in her mouth. By the time the glass was empty, she was telling herself to look at things more objectively. The letters did not truly reflect anything sordid, though they did imply a depth of feeling that was far more than casual. Sidney's sentiments had been sad, but strangely beautiful. This thought came uninvited, making her feel ashamed to the memory of her father.

But who was Sidney anyway? All of the letters but the last were postmarked in Pennsylvania. She wondered how he had come to meet her mother – how it was possible that they could have had an affair from such a distance.

Erynne returned to the living room and shuffled through the letters again, trying to settle on any fact that might conform to her mother's life. It was unsettling that he had spoken of having nightmares, and even more that he had written, *you are not like your mother.*

Was he talking about her suicide?

Notes Erynne had found in her mother's handwriting circled her thoughts too. *I can't take it anymore. I'll end it soon. Erynne will be better off without me.* Maybe the truth made Sidney a fool. How well could he have known Shannon anyway?

But Erynne took no comfort in the thought. Her neck prickled with a growing sense of unease. How often had she repeated those same words to herself? *You are not like your mother.*

Focus, she told herself.

Sidney had written something else that was bothering her. Sifting through the letters, she found it: *Regardless of your decision, I will be seeing you again.*

She shivered, remembering her mother's words from just weeks ago: "He's found me again."

Maybe Sidney had pursued her mother after only a brief affair, scaring her so completely that she had nightmares about him ever since. Erynne imagined for a moment that the letters were unsolicited, the prose of a lunatic who refused to recognize the end of a relationship. But as quickly as she had entertained it, she rejected the idea. Sidney's reference to nightmares could not be so easily dismissed. Even the sight of the word printed on his stationery made her stomach turn. Sidney had suffered from nightmares for years, just like her mother. That made him an ally, not an enemy.

Erynne wondered for the first time if Shannon really had been pursued by someone dangerous. Until now, she had always assumed that her mother's fears had been a reflection of her dementia, not a valid memory resurfacing. Was that why Sidney had suggested Shannon should keep moving?

If her mother had been stalked, the wounds ran deep, even affecting her more than twenty years later as the mysterious web of Alzheimer's dulled her memories. But was the return of that fear strong enough to make Shannon decide to step off a cliff?

Chapter 8

Michael's head hurt again. He blamed it on cross-country travel. His flight from Sacramento hadn't arrived at Reagan International Airport until nearly ten o'clock last night, getting him home much later than usual.

Margaret had already fallen asleep in the guest room, her own brand of silent defiance. He had been too exhausted to wake her, though he knew he would soon have to remind her of her obligations, both public and private. He had spent the week traveling from one tip of California to the other, exhausting himself with luncheons, speeches and rallies while she feigned illness and stayed home. Markham was less than subtle with his admonition.

"Next time, Margaret had better be clinging to your arm," he had said, "on every stop along the campaign trail."

This evening Michael arrived home just in time to catch her heading out the door dressed in a light blue tracksuit.

"Where are you off to?" he asked.

"I'm going for a walk."

He shook his head. "At this time of night? No. We need to discuss…"

Margaret held up a trembling hand to stop him, color rising in her cheeks. "Michael, please. I spent the morning at the hospital visiting sick children just like you asked." She paused, her voice husky and pleading. "You know how hard that is for me. And then to have to sit at that luncheon all afternoon, smiling politely while one senator's wife tells me about her five grandchildren and the other one tries to drink herself under the table… I've just had enough for one day. More than I can stand."

Michael's cell phone buzzed. Jerking his chin in dismissal, he watched her walk out the door as he dug it out of his pocket. It would be Markham.

"Yes," he answered curtly.

"Did you get any rest last night?" Markham asked. "You looked like cold death on *CNN* today."

"Never mind how I looked," Michael snapped. "How was the coverage? Are the numbers in?"

"Polls have you at plus ten."

"Ten? A week ago it was twelve."

"Georgia Cunningham is a tougher opponent than we banked on, Mike. I'll give her that. She looked well rested. That comes across as confidence."

Michael pinched the bridge of his nose. His head was now pounding.

"People like her husband too," Markham continued. "He's very supportive, always standing at her side."

"Markham," Michael warned darkly, "I'll deal with Margaret in my own time, my own way."

For a moment silence hung between them on the line. Markham had pushed too hard and he knew it.

"Get some sleep then, Mike," he said finally, his lighter tone forced. "We'll talk tomorrow."

Michael turned off his phone and climbed the darkened staircase with heavy footsteps, wondering if Margaret's ambivalence to his campaign was really going to be a problem.

"Ten points," he muttered darkly.

His father would have agreed with Markham. He would have pushed even harder, having never approved of Michael's marriage to Margaret in the first place.

"She'll be an asset or a liability, Mike," he had said on the eve of their wedding. "But can you afford to take the good with the bad?"

Michael had taken the risk, seeing into his near future quite clearly. Margaret was at his side, her charming personality bolstering his own appeal to the public, her elegance and good upbringing providing a rich and solid background from which to launch his campaign. Seeing the good had blinded him to the bad, which came quickly in the wake of Margaret's infertility and subsequent depression.

Walking through the dim bedroom, Michael snapped on the bathroom light and searched through his drawers for aspirin. His reflection in the mirror appeared haggard and pale, reminding him of Markham's admonition. He needed to stop worrying about Margaret's weaknesses and get some sleep. But if he slept, would he dream?

Undoubtedly.

Michael's dreams were becoming a major problem. He was avoiding sleep. When he did finally succumb to exhaustion, his nights were anything but restful. Every morning, he woke feeling physically and mentally drained.

I can't afford to lose focus right now, he thought. Not at this stage in his reelection campaign.

In the past, dreams had enhanced Michael's Gift. They had never left him confused. Or weak. But his mind was struggling against these new dreams, trying to harness them for his benefit. The harder he fought, the weaker he became. Now a new fear was setting in. What if the dreams portended something truly horrible? What if he was losing his Gift altogether?

Michael had spent as many years hating his supernatural skill as he had needing it. It was something his father had warned him never to reveal as a child, not even to his mother. Of course, she had seen around that. She had been watchful and increasingly wary as he grew. He was a teenager by the time he recognized the tinge of disgust that accompanied her fear. And, though he had always been popular in school, he began to imagine similar expressions on the faces of his friends. If they knew about the Gift, they would see him as a freak, he decided.

Michael's fear of discovery was paired with fresh appreciation for the Gift itself. After all, how would he know the threats posed to his popularity if he refused to use the skill he so desperately wished to hide? As Michael passed into adulthood, his father was there to help him keep his conflicting needs in balance. But his father was dead now. These dreams were something Michael would have to figure out on his own.

Splashing cool water on his face, Michael toweled off before running large well-manicured hands through his thick black hair. He studied his face in the mirror and saw his father's eyes staring back at him.

"Stay focused. The dreams will run their course," he told his reflection. It was his father's voice he heard.

Michael flipped off the lights and returned to his bedroom, determined to will himself into merciful, dreamless sleep. He usually took time to consider the orderliness of his immaculate rooms – whether the mahogany furnishings were gleaming with polish, the gray silk draperies drawn, and the navy duvet on his king-sized bed smooth and inviting. When he and Margaret had first married, she had teased him playfully about his obsession with neatness, but she had been determined to please him. Even eager to capitulate to his desires. It still gave him pleasure to see evidence that his authority had not slipped during their twelve years of marriage. If only his determination had the ability to invade her malformed womb and produce an heir.

Tonight, Michael ignored his surroundings and sprawled on the bed, consumed with nothing but the pounding in his temple. Despite the aspirin, his headache was getting worse, and he was beginning to feel sick to his stomach. He forced his eyes shut. Slowly, achingly, he fell asleep.

His dream pulsed. Strobe lights flashed. The colors were brilliant and offensive. Scenes repeated faster and faster, making his head swim. Unfamiliar city streets. A park. A beach. An abandoned building. A room with floral wallpaper and a hospital bed. Each view was fleeting, throbbing. Urgency built in his chest and suddenly turned to desperation. He needed to find something.

No. *Someone.*

As quickly as the lights attacked, they were gone, leaving deafening silence in their place. Michael stood in a park, ankle-deep in wet grass. Rolling lawns surrounded him, stretching out for acres until met with a dense line of trees. Concrete pathways curved through the grounds in several directions, disappearing into the dark fringes of the park. In the distance he saw a city with skyscrapers where countless windows twinkled in the night – man-made stars hanging in a foreign sky.

Michael's desperation was becoming acute. She was here somewhere. He turned in a circle, searching. On a hill behind him, he spotted a fieldstone wall that continued as far as he could see in both directions. Something as powerful as a Siren's song was calling to him from the other side.

Michael began climbing the slope. He searched for a gap in the wall – a stairway or gate that would lead beyond, but found nothing. The air around him was turning cold and the mist was thickening, threatening obscurity – or worse, oblivion. He ran the last few steps and clutched the wall while his feet sunk into the muddy ground. He had to scramble to keep upright, to pull himself high enough to look over the top.

A cobblestone street was laid out below him, deserted except for a woman, who stood on the far sidewalk in bare feet. She wasn't the old woman from his other dreams, she was much younger, with black hair that cascaded over her shoulders, brushing the edge of her white nightgown.

She turned and looked down the street expectantly. Michael's heart tightened in his chest, but no, she hadn't seen him. She was looking for someone else.

Michael let out his breath. Had he been holding it? It came now in short, ragged bursts. Sweat was forming along his hairline, despite the cold air. He watched her walk back and forth along the pavement. Time passed and stood still, all while he tried to quell the combating fascination and terror that were washing over him. Madness invaded his senses. He wanted to run his fingers through her hair. He wanted to squeeze them around her throat.

This final thought washed over Michael like a warm and thrilling explosion that also detonated his dream. And then he was gone, along with the woman. The strobe lights returned with a vengeance, pulsing against his eyelids.

Michael startled awake, the dark stillness of his bedroom a stark contrast to the blinding dream. He sat up and stared at the red digits on his alarm clock. It was three-thirty in the morning. Falling back against his sweat-soaked sheets, he struggled to control his breathing and ignore the film of sweat that beaded across his bare torso. His head was pounding with fresh vigor, the pain so intense he struggled to keep from crying out. Taking shallow breaths, he worked to block out all thoughts and images. If only he could get a few hours of sleep.

But Michael's mind refused to let go of the dream. The woman filled him with an odd craving. She had stood so still on the sidewalk. The longer he pictured her there, the more he realized that she had been taunting him, refusing to look his way, or grace him with a smile. The headache fueled his anger.

When it slowly began to ebb an hour later, he slipped quietly into a short restful slumber, imagining his next dream. Desire rumbled through his gut like hunger. Michael rolled over and vowed that next time, he would find a way over that wall. He needed to touch her, hold her . . . and then?

A smile crept over his sleeping face.

Chapter 9

"Let me think...how about the Eiffel Tower."

"You're not serious."

"Of course I am."

Her companion stopped in the middle of the cobblestone street and looked at her with astonishment. "The Eiffel Tower trumps Chichen Itza?"

Erynne put her hands on her hips. "Of course it does. It's iconic. And taller."

"But the pyramid is older *and* it's one of the new Seven Wonders of the World."

"You just said it was old and new in the same sentence," she said, her eyes dancing with laughter. "I think that disqualifies it."

He scowled. "Who made up this game, anyway? Me. So I get to make the rules."

"You're hard to take seriously when you sound like a fifth grader," she answered.

"Fine, we'll call it a tie," he conceded. "But I still win. My church tops yours."

"You cheated! You've never been to Istanbul."

"Have too."

"And I've never heard of the … something Sophia."

"Hagia Sophia. It's there. Google it."

They started walking again and after a minute, he reached out and took her hand.

"You know what would be great?" he asked.

"What?"

"We should meet at the beach sometime. I'm ruining all my socks on this street."

Erynne laughed. "You don't like it here?"

"Of course, but…

"You want to feel the sand between your toes."

"Exactly."

"I don't know." She smiled ruefully. "If you can't remember to take them off before you go to bed, it won't make any difference."

"That may be true," he said. "But it's a risk I'm willing to take."

"So, which beach would you like to visit?"

He looked puzzled. "I don't know. You want a name?"

"Oh, so there aren't any beaches where you live?"

"Plenty of sand. A little short on water."

☙

Erynne woke up laughing. The unfamiliar sound echoed off her bedroom walls and came painfully back to her as she fully regained consciousness. She shifted to a sitting position and pushed her tangled hair out of her face, feeling oddly guilty. It was morning again, time to reconcile dreams with reality.

Every morning this past week had been the same. The precious seconds before her eyes opened held the same peaceful joy Erynne felt in her dream world. The comforting stranger had been by her side again. But when full consciousness descended, her sense of alarm returned as well – usually in some multiple of its severity the day before. It scared her that she enjoyed the dreams so much. Logically, she knew they must be related to her grief. It didn't take a degree in psychology to figure that out. But it was disturbing to acknowledge that her mental state was so fragile. And why she would dream up a companion in such detail was beyond her.

"He cheated," she said out loud, remembering the game he had invented last night. What kind of figment of imagination would pretend he had been to Turkey?

She brought her fingertips to her lips, stifling a smile. But reality pushed through the window with the sunlight, chastising her. Tugging back the covers, she headed for the bathroom, repentant.

Maybe the dreams would go away if she didn't dwell on them, she told herself. Then again, maybe the problem was that she didn't want them to go away at all.

Whenever Erynne succeeded in forcing her thoughts from the dreams, they wanted to return to the letters she had found in her mother's closet, which now sat in an untidy heap on her bedside table. She had reread them so often she almost had them memorized.

If the letters were just evidence of an old romance, Erynne knew she should leave well enough alone. But for some reason, she had come to believe that the letters held greater significance. It was this idea that drove her back to the pile morning and evening. Yesterday she had even carried them to work and reread them at lunchtime.

But not today, she told herself.

She turned on the shower with conviction, determined to banish her dreams and the letters. Just for one day. She would go to the studio and bury herself in work, then tackle some housework and laundry when she got home. Maybe she would even start going through her mother's room. If that led her down roads best left untraveled, she would find some other diversion. Maybe she would take up jogging.

And tonight, she promised herself, *I will not go to bed early.*

ରୃ

An hour later, Erynne was leaving her parking garage and walking briskly toward her studio. It was Saturday and already busy on the Pacific Garden Mall, though it was not yet ten o'clock. Most of the shoppers were milling around the bookstore and adjacent pastry and coffee shops. *St. Genevieve's* would be opening its doors soon, but Erynne had checked in yesterday. She wouldn't visit again today.

Taking a deep breath of sea air, she felt good about leaving the house. Already several new design ideas had skipped across her consciousness and she was anxious to get to her drawing board and put them on paper.

The idea that her dreamtime companion was some kind of muse was something she quickly dismissed. Reaching in the depths of her purse for keys, Erynne reminded herself – again – that he was not to be part of her thoughts today.

"Good morning, Sam."

Sam was sitting under a tree near the entrance to her studio. He tipped his hat in greeting, but didn't say a word. He seldom did. Instead, he reached for his guitar and began to tune it. When Erynne was a teenager, she and her classmates had referred to the homeless in Santa Cruz as "mall trolls" for their tendency to spend their waking hours roaming the mall and their nights sleeping under the bridges that traversed the *San Lorenzo River*. The nickname, clever though it was, caused Erynne some guilt now – especially when she considered Sam, who was a favorite. He never asked for money, but didn't refuse it. Erynne often made requests and then opened her studio window to hear him play.

"How about some Simon and Garfunkel?" she asked today, offering him some folded bills. He tipped his hat again and took the money, starting in on the first bars of "America" by the time Erynne had climbed the stairs and unlocked her studio door.

She spent the next hour productively, sketching several new ideas and cataloging a new shipment of fabric swatches. She was just beginning to mock up a muslin pattern when her phone rang. It was Mark.

"Can you meet me for dinner tonight?" he asked.

Erynne set down her pencil. She had been putting Mark off every time he had called since the funeral but knew her excuses were running thin.

"Mark, I'm just not sure I'm up to..."

Mark quietly interrupted her. "Erynne, it's just dinner. I would really like to see you. Please."

You're being a coward, she told herself.

"Okay, Mark. Of course. Where would you like to go?"

cs

Leaving the studio shortly after Mark's call, Erynne grabbed a sandwich and then drove to the lighthouse, where she parked her car and sat staring out at the bay. It wasn't what she had planned for the afternoon, but her looming dinner date had made her too restless to go home and clean house.

She had once loved to visit the cliffs on an idle afternoon, but in the weeks since her mother's death, panic had seized her whenever she neared them. She wondered if she would ever again have the courage to go farther north, toward Natural Bridges and beyond, to the place where Shannon had stepped over the edge.

Erynne sat there for several minutes, listening to Roberta Flack sing "Bridge over Troubled Water" on her docked iPod. She remembered a time when her father had held her in his arms and danced around the living room while they listened to the same album under a dull needle. Erynne was very young at the time and had been lulled to sleep on his shoulder by the rhythmic pops and crackles that were inseparable from vinyl records.

She supposed it was fitting that she should think of her father so frequently since her mother's death. The morning after her first dream of the comforting stranger, she had felt embarrassed at having shared memories of her father – even in a dream. But Erynne was evidently less inhibited while asleep. As the nights passed, she had told him even more – things about her parents that she had not allowed herself to recall in years. The shared confidences were becoming more comfortable with each passing night, she realized.

She had dreamed up a good listener, then.

When the song ended, Erynne reminded herself that she was not going to dwell on her dreams today. Instead, her thoughts returned to Mark, who would be meeting her in a few hours on the wharf. She thought about the restaurant he had chosen and the sunset views it provided of the cliffs. A deep shudder ran through her.

Erynne got out of the car and walked to the end of the parking lot, determined to master her fear. When her toes touched the ice plant that curved over the cliff's edge, she stopped. This was far enough. Taking a deep breath, she looked out toward Steamers Lane, a favorite surfing area that ran between the lighthouse and wharf. She saw only a handful of boards against the dark blue water and remembered that the optimal swell and offshore breezes had passed with winter.

She stood still until her heartbeat returned to normal – a small victory. A bigger one followed when she turned and followed the line of the cliff toward the lighthouse. She reached the observation patio just as three small children ran by with their father in close pursuit.

"Look at them, Daddy!" said a tow-headed little boy as he reached the edge. "Seals!"

He pointed over the edge toward the lazy brown creatures that lay below, noisily sunbathing on top of a rock that protruded out of the bay just a stone's throw from the cliff. Erynne smiled as she watched the children respond with unrestrained joy each time one of the seals barked or roused itself from sun-induced sleep to squirm off the rock and into the water.

See? This isn't so bad.

Erynne could almost hear her dreamtime companion's voice, carried on the wind.

CR

Just before six o'clock, Erynne stood on the east side of the wharf watching a group of teenagers play volleyball on the beach below. Deep shadows were beginning to fall across the sand and she wondered if they would give up soon, finding it too dark to play. She fingered her stone necklace idly as she watched lights go on at the Boardwalk.

"Erynne." Mark approached so quietly, she jumped.

"Sorry!" She laughed and Mark kissed her cheek. "It's good to see you."

"You too. Lost in thought?"

She turned back toward the Boardwalk. "Just admiring the view."

He leaned on the railing next to her and pointed toward the Cocoanut Grove.

"It used to be a ballroom. Did you know?"

Erynne shook her head. "I should. I've lived here most of my life."

"It was built around World War I, I think, on the place where a casino had recently burned to the ground. Some pretty big acts came through here back in the day: Artie Shaw, Benny Goodman, the Dorsey Brothers."

Erynne smiled. "I didn't know you liked big band music."

Mark shrugged. "I wish I could have seen it that way."

"Instead of filled with videogames and miniature golf, you mean?"

He smiled. "Something like that."

"Listen. Can you hear the carousel?"

He tilted his head. "Maybe. I can smell the corn dogs and salt water taffy. Are you sure you want sea food? We could eat junk and ride the Giant Dipper instead."

Erynne laughed, but shook her head. Together, they turned to walk down the wharf.

A few minutes later, they were seated by the window at the Sea Cloud, their table providing a sunset view of the same cliff Erynne had visited that afternoon.

"You look lovely, as always," Mark said, taking in her coffee-colored linen dress. "Is that from your spring collection?"

"Shameless self-promotion," Erynne said.

They both turned to hear the waiter describe the evening specials. When he left, Erynne searched for something to talk about. She avoided looking at the tables around them. Everyone nearby seemed to be sharing a romantic evening.

"How are you really, Erynne?" Mark asked. "Are you holding up okay?"

"I'm fine. Trying to keep busy, but that's not difficult with my work load." She looked up again and tried to smile. She could see that he wasn't convinced.

"Are you sleeping okay?"

"Yes," she said. Her cheeks flushed. "That's not a problem."

Mark reached across the table and squeezed her hand. "Erynne, I saw you with your mother. You visited her more faithfully than most, even when her dementia was severe. I know you've got to be hurting. I just want you to know that I'm here. If you need me."

"Thank you, Mark." Erynne's voice was unexpectedly thick. She felt a surge of affection for him. "You're a good man."

Always focused on her career and her mother, Erynne had a history of ending relationships before they became too serious. She had rarely thought about what she would look for in a man when her priorities changed, but she knew now. She would have wanted someone like Mark.

Would have. So why didn't she?

The waiter delivered their meals and they talked about local news as they ate. Erynne could see that Mark was working hard to avoid discussing his job or Cypress. Erynne ate most of her red snapper and skewered shrimp, conscious that the doctor in Mark would be noticing her appetite. He seemed to relish the stuffed salmon and scallops he had ordered, swiftly emptying his plate.

"Do you want dessert?" he asked.

Erynne shook her head. "I'm too full."

When the waiter came to clear the table, Mark ordered coffee and settled back in his seat, his arms folded easily across his chest. Together, he and Erynne looked out toward the black cliffs, visible only because of the lights that twinkled along West Cliff Drive.

"Mark, do you think my mother's nightmares could have been an early symptom of Alzheimer's?"

Erynne was startled to hear her voice ask a question she had not consciously formed. She opened her mouth again, a reflexive drive to recall her words. But it was a vain impulse. Mark was already considering her question, a small frown furrowing his forehead. He turned away from the view and took a sip of coffee.

"No," he finally said. "I think she had emotional and psychological problems that went untreated for many years. If she had received help, she may have been able to come to grips with whatever frightened her so badly. She may have enjoyed several years of good health before the Alzheimer's set in. Unfortunately, it's the exception, not the rule, when someone seeks professional help."

Erynne nodded, uncomfortable for speaking her fears out loud. Mark's answer rang true, though. She clearly remembered her father's caustic words just before he had slammed the door for the last time.

"You're sick, Shannon. Get some help."

☙

Mark and Erynne headed back down the wharf a short time later, toward Beach Street where Erynne had parked her car. In the distance, the Boardwalk was brightly lit and she could see cars moving along the steep slopes of the Giant Dipper. The sharp cries of the roller coaster's passengers rose above the din like a crashing wave.

"It's cold tonight," Erynne said, fighting to keep her sweater on.

"Here, let me help."

Mark's arm felt warm around her shoulders, but caused Erynne's guilt to swell nonetheless. She should want this, she told herself again, so why didn't she?

She knew the answer just as she understood why the darkness of night was luring her to say goodnight and return to her bed. Her dreams were waiting, and with them the man she had been trying to banish from her thoughts all day.

When they reached her car, Erynne turned away from Mark to search through her purse for keys. If she didn't want him, it was time to let him know.

"I wasn't very good company tonight," she began. "I don't know when or if that will change."

Mark pushed his hands into his pockets.

"Good company for me, Erynne? Or for anyone?"

"Mark, I'm sorry. I don't know the answer." She hated this. "I'm just not where you are. I wish I was."

Mark nodded, a bleak smile forming against the wind.

"I hope we can…"

He cut her off, his voice gentler than she deserved.

"What? Be friends?"

Erynne looked away. A new sense of hopelessness made her suddenly very tired.

Mark took her keys and opened the car door. Erynne hesitated, wishing she could form words to make everything feel right again. But there were no right words in times like this.

There was nothing left to do but say goodnight.

Chapter 10

By the time Colin reached the summit of Piestewa Peak on Saturday morning, his breath was coming out in short bursts, reminding him of how long it had been since he'd engaged in any arduous physical activity. At just past seven o'clock, the April day was already warm, with the makings of a scorcher. Taking a long swig from his water bottle, Colin settled against a rock and surveyed the city below. Piestewa, known to almost everyone by its original name "Squaw Peak," protruded out of the middle of the Valley floor amidst several lower peaks, giving hikers who reached its summit the prize of a 360-degree view of metropolitan Phoenix. Nearby Camelback Mountain was striking against the clear blue morning sky, as were Shaw and Papago Buttes, other favorite Valley hiking spots for Colin, who had taken up the sport avidly after hiking the Grand Canyon a couple of times during his college days. Now he took every local opportunity to pursue the sport, especially during winter and early spring when temperatures were more forgiving.

On a clear day like today, Colin could easily make out the Valley's surrounding mountain systems in the distance. The Superstitions and White Tanks bordered the Valley on the east and west, separated by the 9,000-square miles that made up the vast valley floor. Today almost everything was visible between him and the soft blue and purple peaks, though during Phoenix's normal workweek, it would all be shrouded in a brown layer of smog. Much closer to the south and southwest were South Mountain and the Sierra Estrellas. He especially liked the three-mile hike up Quartz Peak Trail and was becoming more familiar with the many trails that weaved through the Superstition Wilderness and Four Peaks area to the east. But his list of trails yet to be hiked was still long and on days like today he wished for a more forgiving work schedule.

Colin wiped sweat from his face with the hem of his shirt. Humidity was high after last night's rain shower. A typical desert storm, the rain had first hinted its pending visit with dark clouds and a familiar zesty fragrance that permeated the air all afternoon on Friday. Colleagues in Colin's office had gathered at the twelfth story windows, watching the clouds and dust move in from the south and speculating on the potential for actual rainfall. Colin gave up on productivity goals for the afternoon, knowing that storm systems always created a restless energy among Phoenicians eager for overdue rain to drop on the parched Sonoran earth.

For the rest of the night, the rain had teased and the winds had blown, reminding Colin of monsoon weather more typical in late July and August. By ten o'clock, the channel five meteorologist reported scattered showers in various valley locations, but the storm had waited until two in the morning to hit the central corridor with its full force. Colin had seen several downed palm tree fronds when he retrieved his morning newspaper – the most telling evidence of a desert storm to those who had slept through it all.

But Colin had been awake, listening to the rain pound against his windows and wondering why it always rained overnight in Phoenix. He drifted in and out of sleep over the next few hours, but finally threw aside his tangled sheet and headed north toward Piestewa just as the sun crept over the eastern sky. His thoughts had not been with the storn, but with the woman he had been dreaming about for the past couple of weeks.

Colin rose from the rock and began his descent back down the mountain. It was his dream of the dark-haired beauty that had wakened him shortly before the storm broke, leaving him wide awake and pensive, wondering what might be triggering his mind to return to her each night. In his dream last night, the moon had illuminated the make-believe world around him as clearly as sunlight. While all of the other dreams had been on a cobblestone street, this time he was on a beach, sitting on the overgrown roots of a cypress tree. The bay in front of him had been magnificent. Blue water, dark and still, stretched out toward the horizon, lightened only by the yellow path of the moon. In his other dreams, he had always been immediately by her side, but last night he was scanning the horizon, waiting for her to arrive.

When he saw her in the distance walking along the shoreline, his heart contracted. The wind was pulling at her dark hair and she was struggling to keep it in place. With her free hand, she was holding up the hem of her nightgown, allowing the tide to graze her ankles. When she spotted him, she smiled. Still, there was an unreachable sadness in her expression. During their time together, Colin had tried to gently pry away her tough wall of reserve, but he had yet to reach the place where she hid behind her eyes.

They quickly closed the distance of sand between them.

"There you are," she said.

He squeezed her hand. "I'm here."

They continued down the beach together, hand in hand. Looking back to the place where his footprints had joined hers in the sand made Colin unaccountably happy.

"Were you humming?" she asked. A smile played across her lips.

"Humming?" he repeated dumbly.

She nodded confidently. "You were. An old song, I think. 'I used to walk with you, Along the avenue . . .' Maybe Nat King Cole?"

"'Somewhere Along the Way,'" Colin said matter-of-factly. "But I don't hum."

"But you know the song," she said accusingly.

"I have a vast wealth of useless knowledge."

She nudged him with her shoulder and they continued to walk in silence. Colin breathed in deeply, unaccustomed to the ocean breeze.

"Where are we? Do you know?"

She looked around briefly. "It looks like Carmel."

"Is Carmel always this deserted?" Colin asked.

She shrugged. "I guess it's just ours tonight."

The beach curved around the bay endlessly, and just like with the cobblestone street, they never made any progress along it. They talked for several hours before Colin was ripped rudely from the dream. Thunder rumbled overhead. He was back in his bed in Phoenix. The beach and intriguing woman were nowhere in sight.

Colin had pushed back his covers and shuffled to the kitchen for a drink, frustrated that his memory was already dropping details from their conversation. She had been on the brink of telling him something important, he was sure of it. But as his head began to clear, he wondered, was he annoyed by the interruption, or by the dream itself? Why did it matter what was said in a dream? No matter how strange or poignant, they were just dreams, nothing more.

All the way to the peak, Colin had tried to analyze his dreams, looking for some hidden meaning that could be attached to reality. But during his descent, he had abandoned the idea. His job was stressful, and left little room for imagination during waking hours. What he needed was more time on the trail. The dreams would go away on their own.

ॐ

Colin pulled into his driveway an hour later, juggling two bags of groceries and his car keys. As if on cue, Hector emerged from around the fence that separated their homes and took one of the bags off his hands. The two entered Colin's house through the kitchen door while Hector gave Colin a full neighborhood damage report from the storm.

Hector and his wife had been the first on the street to welcome Colin when he bought the house. When he told them about his plans for renovation, their faces had broken into wide smiles. An experienced electrician and handyman, Hector had proven valuable to Colin as each small project blossomed into something bigger. The two soon became friends.

"So, will you come for dinner tonight?" Hector asked. "Luz has a pot of chalupa on the stove." He tossed Colin a can of green beans. "My mouth is already watering."

"I wish I could," Colin answered honestly as he placed the can in his pantry and caught another one. "I already have plans."

Hector raised his eyebrows. "A date? What's her name... Cindy?"

Colin laughed. "No. Cindy moved to Atlanta two months ago. Her name is Andrea. She works in public relations on the floor above the firm."

Hector folded the paper grocery sack and handed it to Colin. "When are you going to settle down, my friend? Find a good wife like Luz?"

Colin rubbed the back of his neck. "You sound like my mother, Hector. Besides, you won't let me date your daughter."

"Ha!" Hector punched Colin playfully on the arm and headed to the door. "Well, if this Andrea turns out to be someone special, you bring her by so Luz and I can check her out."

Colin nodded and waved a reluctant goodbye, feeling a strong desire to cancel his date and spend a more relaxing evening with the Garcias. Luz Maria's kitchen was warm and inviting and always filled with the mouth-watering aromas of homemade tortillas, chalupa, tamales, chile rellenos or sopapillas. She had taught Colin to make fresh salsa and guacamole and usually invited him over to share their dinner at least once a week. Looking around his own dark kitchen, Colin struggled to remember a time when it had been filled with the smell of fresh food or the laughter of good friends. Somehow he knew that Andrea would be more comfortable eating gourmet food in a chic Biltmore bistro than throwing together a casual meal in his kitchen.

Colin pulled off his damp T-shirt and headed toward the shower, knowing full well that his date tonight would be like countless others before it – a pleasant evening with banal conversation that may lead to one or two similar evenings, but nothing more. Sometimes he wondered why he even bothered. But as warm water coursed through his hair and over his body, his thoughts returned to the beauty from his dreams last night, and the way her skin had looked under the moonlight – like satin, except for a small scar on her collar bone.

The clear memory of her scar sent a current of shock through Colin, raising goose bumps. Fantasy surely should not include such subtle details. If the woman was a creation of his imagination, wouldn't she be perfect? Airbrushed, like a model on the cover of a magazine?

"I must be out of my mind," he muttered as he turned off the water. But an uneasy feeling stayed with him as he dried off and dressed. Settling on the couch to watch the Diamondbacks game, he couldn't keep his mind from drifting back to the woman. Maybe she was a memory instead of a fantasy. But if that was true, who was she? And why was he dreaming about her now?

Chapter 11

Erynne moved quickly through the dark forest, her eyes turned toward the sky. She searched for the moon through a heavy canopy of trees but saw little more than her own icy breath, passing through her lips in tired bursts.

She had been on this path for some time, driven forward by a force she could not identify. Only in the last few moments had her senses begun to prickle. She didn't want to be here. When unease gave way to panic, Erynne tried to resist. It was impossible. Her arms were bound tightly against her sides and no amount of twisting or pulling could free them.

Pull away. Turn around. Stop!

Her mind could not obey.

Fear began to well up in her chest. She opened her mouth to scream, but no sound emerged. Instead, she heard the mournful wailing of an infant, startling to her ears for its nearness, but resonating from far away. Desperate to be free, Erynne tried to scream again, but found that her efforts only increased the pressure of the bindings around her arms. Her heart pounded in her chest as hot frustration enveloped her. Her silent screams continued to echo in her own ears, unheard, unanswered.

"Erynne? Erynne! Wake up, honey. Wake up!"

Erynne gasped and opened her eyes to find Gretchen hovering over her, deep concern etched on her face. Pushing herself up to a sitting position, she struggled to free her arms of the afghan that she had wrapped around herself earlier to take off the afternoon chill. The reality of her quiet living room rather than the cold forest was difficult to accept in her bewildered state. She looked around slowly, taking in the soft lighting, her mother's letters spread across the coffee table and Gretchen's anxious features as she moved to sit next to her on the couch.

"I'm alright," she said. "It was just a bad dream." Struggling to ignore her heart beating against her ribcage, she reached for her watch. "What time is it?"

"Almost five o'clock, Sunday afternoon," Gretchen said. "You didn't answer the doorbell, and then I heard you cry out. I was afraid something had happened to you."

"Sunday," Erynne repeated. She pushed her disheveled hair away from her face and sat up straighter, frowning. "Why are you here on Sunday?"

Gretchen's expression changed subtly, worry giving way to pity. "You always visited your mother on Sunday afternoon. I thought I'd just check in and see if you wanted some company. I promise not to stay long if you're not up to it."

Erynne nodded absently. She should acknowledge Gretchen's kindness, but her mind was still struggling to pull itself from the dream. Why had it been difficult for Gretchen to waken her?

Unwelcome images of the dark forest burst into her mind, and with them, the same sense of being bound and unable to scream for help.

Help me. I need to get free!

It was her mother's hysterical voice she suddenly remembered. She had dreamed of being bound too, and Erynne could not wake her.

A wave of panic swept over her. She stood up, looking for a way to escape her thoughts. Finding none, she sat back down, her head swimming.

"Now, Erynne, just sit there a minute," Gretchen pleaded, her voice pitched high with concern. "I'll fix you some tea and then see about making you something to eat."

Erynne nodded as Gretchen headed into the kitchen. After a few minutes, the everyday sounds of a whistling teakettle and clanking china broke through her consciousness and she began to feel more connected to reality. Gretchen stuck her head through the doorway frequently, her eyes sharp with concern. She chatted almost nonstop at a volume that would carry from one room to another – about local news, shop gossip and her husband, Len, who had dropped her off on his way to the hardware store.

"He thinks he needs another screw driver. Well, there are screw drivers all over the house, if he would just take the time to look!"

Erynne smiled. She could smell whatever food Gretchen was fixing and welcomed more ordinary conversation, even if it was exceptionally one-sided. The sky was growing dark through the window and she did not want to be alone.

"Here we are." Gretchen came back to the room carrying tea on a tray. "I'm warming some soup and bread. It should be ready in a few minutes."

"Thank you."

Erynne cleared a place for the tray on the coffee table, gathering her mother's letters into an awkward pile and pushing them to one side as Gretchen set down the tray and began to pour tea. Erynne took the offered cup, embarrassed that her hands were still shaking. If Gretchen noticed, she made no comment. Instead she leaned down and picked up another letter from the floor.

"You missed one," she said, placing it on top of the pile.

The letter was folded so that Sidney's final words of affection were clearly visible. Erynne didn't miss the way Gretchen's eyes rested on the words before politely focusing on something else.

"Apparently my mother was the recipient of several love letters," Erynne said with a trace of defiance. She looked up at Gretchen, forcing a tight smile. "Her life was messy – even messier than I realized, evidently."

"Was that who you were dreaming about? Your mother?" Gretchen's tone was careful, sympathetic.

Erynne shook her head. But the question triggered something in her memory – a possible connection she hadn't considered. Setting aside her teacup, she reached down by her feet and found the leather journal that she had been reading before she fell asleep. It must have fallen off her lap, forgotten until now. It had been among her mother's belongings at Cypress, one of the things Erynne had packed on the day of the funeral.

"I meant to clean Mom's old room today, but I couldn't do it." She rubbed the cover of the journal. "I thought going through some of her things from the care center was a fair compromise and I found this."

"Your mother's diary?"

Erynne shook her head. "Not exactly. It's a story, actually. One she told me when I was a child. It was like a fairytale." She tapped the journal with her fingertips. "I think I was dreaming about this story. This place."

Gretchen frowned. "It was hard to wake you, honey. That was some nightmare."

Erynne hated the word. She shook her head, wishing it away. But still, she could almost hear the crying baby, feel the forest closing in around her.

"It was rather dark for a bedtime story," she said, suppressing a shudder. "No once-upon-a-time. No happily-ever-after."

"What's it about?"

"An old woman who tries to save two royal babies from an evil magician. He kills her and takes them away, never to be heard from again."

Gretchen's mouth twisted. "It doesn't sound like a very good story for children."

Erynne shrugged. She could think of other scary fairytales: like Hansel and Gretel, or Little Red Riding Hood. Countless nursery rhymes were dark and violent too but she didn't argue with Gretchen. She had long ago stopped trying to justify her mother's actions.

"I didn't know she had written it down," Erynne said, "but her nurse told me she repeated it often, especially during the last few weeks."

When the nightmares came back, she added silently.

"I wonder why it was so important to her," Gretchen mused.

The back doorbell rang, making Erynne jump.

"That will be Len," Gretchen said, grabbing the tea tray and heading back toward the kitchen. "You stay put. I'll let him in and get your soup."

CB

Gretchen opened the back door and ushered Len into the kitchen. His sparse hair was wind-blown, sticking out in tufts of white around his bald crown. Together with his UCSC sweatshirt, plaid shorts and Birkenstocks, he presented quite an image.

Gretchen suppressed a smile. "Are you cold, honey?"

He kissed her cheek in response, nuzzling her with his cold nose.

Gretchen ducked away and pointed him toward a kitchen stool. While ladling soup into a bowl, she shared a brief account of her visit with Erynne.

"One thing is certain," she whispered, "I'm not going anywhere until her face regains some color."

She added two heavily-buttered pieces of bread to Erynne's plate, glad to finally have a chance to do something about her weight, which seemed to have dropped over the past two weeks.

"What's this?" Len asked.

He was holding Erynne's stone necklace. Gretchen noticed it earlier lying on the counter and remembered how pretty Erynne looked on Friday, wearing it with a green silk blouse and gray slacks.

"It's a necklace, of course," she answered, rounding the corner to look at it over his shoulder. "It belonged to Erynne's grandmother. She began wearing it after the funeral."

Len's brow creased as he turned the stone over in his hand and rubbed the edge with his thumb. "It looks familiar."

Gretchen shrugged as she turned back to Erynne's food. "It looks like a tree to me."

She carried the tray into the living room, where she found Erynne wearing a forced look of composure.

"Here we go," she said nonchalantly, setting down the food.

She knew how much Erynne hated being waited on, how she hated being at the center of any attention that didn't directly relate to her designs. But her heart broke at the stubborn set of Erynne's jaw, the barely-discernible quiver of her lower lip. This bright, beautiful woman had never looked so vulnerable, despite her best efforts to appear strong. Gretchen fought every maternal instinct she had by not taking her in her arms.

"Thank you," Erynne said, picking up her spoon. "I appreciate all you've done. Now will you two go home and enjoy your weekend? I really will be fine."

Gretchen shook her head dismissively, handing Erynne a napkin.

"Gretchen, I don't need a babysitter," Erynne persisted. "And what about Len? I can't believe he's content to hide in the kitchen while you spoon-feed me soup."

"Oh don't worry about him. I think he went back out to the car so he could listen to the end of the Giants game." She shook her head. "I don't know how he can get so excited about a baseball game this early in the season."

Erynne smiled. "If you're sure," she said.

"I'll just stay a while," Gretchen said. Her eyes fell on the journal that now rested on top of the letters. "You can tell me more about the story if you want to."

85

Erynne shook her head. "I think I've had enough of it for tonight. Maybe for a long time." She picked up the journal and handed it to Gretchen. "Here, you can take it and read it for yourself."

"I'm not trying to pry," Gretchen said, taking the book reluctantly.

"You would be doing me a favor," Erynne said. Her eyes swept the room, resting on the dark corners and black night beyond the windows. "There's a good chance I'll sleep better tonight, knowing it's not in my house."

Chapter 12

By the time Erynne walked Gretchen to the back door, the sky was deep blue and the first star was twinkling above the tree line. She wrapped her arms around herself, shivering against a cold wind that blew the smell of the Pacific into her face.

"I could stay the night on your couch," Gretchen offered.

Erynne smiled, but shook her head in response. She was feeling more like herself now and wanted nothing more than the quiet solitude she was accustomed to.

"Well, call me if you change your mind," Gretchen said as she stepped out the door. "Any time. Day or night."

"Thank you, Gretchen. Thank Len for me, too."

Turning to face her silent home as she closed the door, Erynne let out a deep sigh, relieved that her fear of being alone had dissipated. But as she entered the kitchen and began rinsing teacups, it occurred to her how rare it was to share tea – or anything else, for that matter – with someone in this house. She had indulged in the comforts of being alone too much perhaps, sheltering herself from the normalness of friends.

For Erynne, companionship usually seemed like more work than it was worth. She had never felt like a good friend to anyone. Her parents had certainly never shown her how to make love last. But in Len and Gretchen, she saw what a family should be: unconditional love, support, comfort, even a good kick in the seat of the pants, when justified. It was something she admired but couldn't feel part of. Gretchen honestly welcomed her into her life – even into her family – but Erynne wasn't ready for that inclusion.

Drying her hands on a dishtowel, she turned off the kitchen light and headed down the hall. Gretchen's suggestion of a warm bubble bath was too tempting to ignore. Erynne turned on the faucet and pulled out a fresh towel while the tub filled. Once settled into the deep, soapy water, she closed her eyes and allowed the subtle buzz of exhaustion to move along her skin, radiating upward along her body with the lavender oil she had added to the water.

But the water was a little too warm. Erynne lifted her arms out of the tub and rested them along the porcelain lip, adjusting her head against a rolled-up towel and relaxing again. She promised herself not to stay in the tub too long, just a few more minutes, until the water began to cool. Instead her weariness took over and she drifted off to sleep.

The sensation of bobbing up and down in the water forced Erynne's eyes open, which she immediately closed again, faced with brilliant sunlight that seemed too close and too hot. She pushed herself up and almost fell out of a canoe that was following its own course down a meandering desert river flanked by Mesquite and Palo Verde trees.

"Whoa! Careful, there. I don't want to have to go in after you."

Her companion was sitting in the forward part of the canoe, his hands casually resting on paddles that were unnecessary at the moment since the river seemed determined to keep the small craft to her middle and deepest section. The sun caught the tips of his cropped blond hair, turning it gold. He was shielding his face with a tanned hand and wearing a look of brazenly unconcealed amusement as he watched her struggle to right herself and then assume a comfortable position on the low bench. Erynne felt flushed with heat and annoyance. She wished, for one thing, that her dreams would give her something other than a nightgown to wear.

"Where are we?" she asked.

"I can't say. Do you like it?" He sounded proud, as if he was showing her his own backyard.

She looked wishfully toward the shoreline. "I'd like it better from over there."

The canoe suddenly lurched forward, interrupting his answer. Erynne gripped the edges as it began to pitch to one side in the foaming water.

"Hold on."

He sat upright and grabbed his paddles, but still didn't seem appropriately concerned, especially since he was traveling backward. Erynne opened her mouth and began to point him to the left, but he didn't seem to notice. With a brief glance over his shoulder, he navigated the canoe around a bend. In less than a minute they were passing into smoother waters.

Erynne breathed a sigh of relief and then hazarded a glance over the side of the craft. The water was not very deep and it was smooth, giving her a clear view of the rocks on the bottom. Some of them looked sharp, though. She wondered what would happen if the canoe hit one.

"Much better," her companion said. Sliding down in his seat, he laid his head back against the edge of the boat, closed his eyes and turned his face toward the sun. With one hand he steadied the paddles, leaving the other trailing lazily in the water by his side.

Erynne looked up and down the banks of the river but could make out no signs of civilization. Instead she saw breathtaking rock formations that dwarfed the trees in their immensity. She tried to find a word that described their color – varying shades between vermilion and terra cotta. Her eyes narrowed as she brought them back down to the fringes of the river. There she imagined snakes, scorpions or poisonous lizards sunning on rocks. Worse, they could be on the branches of trees overhead, just waiting for an opportunity to drop on her.

"I don't think I like this," she muttered, shifting her position in the canoe. The heat was oppressive and her hair clung uncomfortably to her neck.

"You know, for a creative type, you aren't very adventurous," he said sleepily, his eyes still closed.

Erynne bristled, finding his comfort with their location unaccountably irritating. She was considering a stinging retort when the river turned and dipped over a slight drop, forcing him to grab his paddles again. The bubbling water burst against the sides of the boat, spitting over Erynne's skin in a fine mist that was at once shocking and refreshing. They bobbed up, then down again and turned into an area that pooled against a curved beach, seemingly unaffected by the current of the water.

"Do you think you can keep this thing in one piece?" she asked sharply.

"It would help if you would just relax," he suggested.

Erynne took a deep breath, trying. She closed her eyes. For a moment, they floated peacefully, the canoe resting in place by the little beach, where gentle waves lapped at the shore. Erynne almost smiled, thankful for the cool breeze that was passing through the canopy of trees overhead and kissing her wet skin.

"Much better," her companion murmured as he settled back down into the canoe. He laid his arms across the side so that his fingertips rested on top of her hand.

"You really don't like it here?" he asked after a moment, searching her face with apparent disbelief.

"It's beautiful," she said grudgingly. "But I'd rather have my feet on solid ground." The breeze had stilled and she was beginning to feel hot again. She wished he would move his hand. Instead, he began drawing wet circles across the bridge of her knuckles with his fingertips. Erynne's breath caught in her throat, but she couldn't bring herself to pull away.

"So, it's a control thing?" he asked quietly.

When she didn't answer, he turned and looked up toward the trees. "Solid ground," he repeated thoughtfully. "You like to be able to walk away from anything that makes you uncomfortable. Or anyone?"

"Are you an accountant or a shrink?" she asked crossly, pulling her hand away.

His laugh shot across the river and echoed back from the cliffs. "Okay! I give up!" he said. "No more psychoanalysis. I promise."

Sunset arrived suddenly in the dreamland desert, bringing with it a drop in temperatures and long shadows. The water continued to gurgle around them and lap against the beach. Gray doves and meadowlarks cooed and chirped in the trees overhead, their chorus joined by crickets as twilight descended. The western horizon was painted in Maxfield Parrish hues, soft pink clouds fringed in lavender. Erynne saw Mercury twinkling between the branches in the washed blue sky overhead and felt an involuntary sigh escape her lips.

"Turn around," he said.

"What?"

"Come on," he coaxed. "Just shift in your seat and put your feet on the other side. You'll be more comfortable. I promise: I won't let you fall."

Putting his hand on her back, he steadied her as she followed his instructions then pulled her gently back against his chest.

"Better?" he whispered.

Erynne could not articulate a response, so she merely nodded. Dusk had not yet fully descended, but she could barely see the landscape around them anymore. She closed her eyes and took another deep breath.

"You're getting cold," he said, noticing her shiver. He wrapped his arms around hers, pulling her closer still.

Suddenly the water changed beneath them, jerking the canoe away from the peaceful beach and back into the current. Erynne opened her eyes and saw the river curve in front of them, winding its way around a bend and out of sight, swallowed by the shadowy walls of a canyon. She would swear those towering purple walls had not been so high a moment earlier.

Her companion had released her to devote himself to his paddles. She leaned away, giving him room to work. He pulled them briskly through the foaming water, his eyebrows furrowed in concentration.

"I'll try and get us to shore," he said. But his efforts were futile. The river continued to pick up speed, bouncing the canoe up and down and forcing her to hold on to its sides with white-knuckled alarm. Her companion was doubling his efforts but couldn't seem to make any progress. Instead it seemed like he was churning the river into its feverish pace with every strike of the paddle.

"Stop!" Erynne shouted. "Stop!"

She was yelling more at the water than at the man, panic beginning to well in her chest. Suddenly the canoe dipped up, then plunged down a sharp, rocky fall. Realizing her worst fears, she felt her slippery fingers give way as she was pitched over the edge. The sound of her companion's desperate shouts were the last thing she heard before succumbing to the water's surprising depth.

Erynne sputtered to the surface, back in her own bathroom.

During her sleep the water had cooled considerably. She shivered as she pushed it away from her face and blinked her eyes, trying once again to reconcile her dream with reality. Erynne had rarely fallen asleep in the tub and never to such a depth that she slipped below the surface. On shaking legs, she stepped over the side and reached for the comforting warmth of her bathrobe. Lowering herself to the bath rug, she hugged her knees to her chest, oblivious to the water that was dribbling down her neck from the dark, heavy cords of her hair.

Images from her dream moved across her mind with fleeting clarity before rushing away in a fog. Only her heightened emotions remained. She couldn't remember her companion's face. He had frustrated her, but she couldn't remember why. She remembered her fear of the water but didn't understand it. She had always been a good swimmer.

Erynne sat still until her breathing returned to normal, trying to piece together her memories like a puzzle. When her legs felt strong enough to support her, she rose and went to the mirror, automatically moving a wide-tooth comb through her hair as she examined her pale reflection. She stopped mid-motion,

93

remembering the way her companion had stroked her hand with his wet fingers. He had held her too, and whispered in her ear.

Erynne's face flushed. The warmth traveled the length of her body, rising again to rest deep in her chest like a dull ache. She closed her eyes and leaned against the sink, loneliness enveloping her like sweeping wind. She was being pulled into a dream world that made her feel more alive than she had ever felt. It was terrifying.

She pushed away from the sink and dressed hurriedly in cotton pajamas. How could she feel anything for a man she did not know – an imaginary man whose face she could not even recall?

Moving through her house, she mechanically began putting objects in order: straightening picture frames, picking lint from the back of her favorite chair. She wiped down the kitchen counter, though it was already clean, and turned off the light before returning to the living room. There, her eyes were drawn to the only items left rudely out of place – her afghan, crumpled on the edge of the sofa where she had risen from her earlier dream, and the detestable letters, shamefully pushed aside to make room for her dinner tray.

A sudden desire to grab them all and throw them in the trash threatened to overwhelm her. But she couldn't follow through on her impulse. Suddenly she knew why and it was like being slapped awake.

The letters were her only tangible clue, their writer the only possible link to understanding what her mother was going through.

What you're starting to go through too, a voice in her head suggested.

Looking down at the stack of letters, Erynne focused on Sidney's return address. It was a long shot at best. But when she closed her eyes, she could see herself back on the cliff, driven there this time by her own fears. Was it too much to imagine that descent? The fear and loneliness that would weaken her? The silent screams and wailing babies echoing in her mind until she was finally persuaded to the same hopeless edge?

"No. That's not going to happen."

Erynne had once left home – moved to Europe, in fact – just to escape her mother's fate. Yet here she was, in the same house, frightened by the same ghosts she had feared in childhood.

But I'm not my mother, she told herself.

Erynne reached for her laptop and began searching for a flight to Phoenix. She would face her fears head on. Whatever was happening to her, she would look for a way out. It might be her only chance of escaping the madness that had claimed her mother.

Chapter 13

Colin was not sleeping well. Almost a week had passed since he dreamed of losing her in the river. Every time he lay down and closed his eyes he saw it all again – the way she had slipped out of his arms and into the water. It had swallowed her whole, and he had done nothing to stop it. For the rest of the dream he searched the river and its shoreline, calling to her through the desert night but only hearing his own hoarse echoes answering back.

He had not dreamed of her since.

Instead, whenever he succumbed to exhaustion, he was plagued by disturbing dreams like those he had before they met: he was scouring strange cities, empty parking lots and abandoned buildings. Searching but never finding. By the end of each dream his frustration and sense of urgency were acute, awakening him with a sickening feeling of dread. They did nothing to erase her from his memory or lessen the ridiculous sense of worry he felt for her safety.

I promise. I won't let you fall.

That's what he told her just minutes before losing her to the river. She had been in his arms one moment and gone the next.

His broken promise gnawed at him, a failure committed by his subconscious that wouldn't fade – wouldn't let him sleep. Instead he sat up late every night, tinted blue in the reflection of the television. It was while sitting there with an idle remote control in his hand that his mind began to turn on him, offering implausible reasons for it all. He had been cocky and aggressive in the dream. He knew he was irritating her and yet he kept pushing. Maybe that's why she disappeared. He had pushed too far and ruined whatever was happening between them, just like he ruined relationships in real life.

His insomnia seemed like penance, the nightmares punishment. But Colin missed her. He worried he would never see her again and then his sense of reality kicked in, making him wonder if therapy was in order.

By Saturday he was a mess – a truth corroborated by his mother when he stopped by her Sun City home to complete a few chores.

"What happened to you?" she asked, taking in the dark circles under his eyes.

"Can't sleep," he muttered, passing through the back gate and heading toward the tool shed without further comment. But later that afternoon he finally succumbed to exhaustion and fell asleep in a shady spot on her patio. Mercifully, he did not dream.

Sprinkler heads popping up along the edge of the greenbelt woke him at six o'clock, joined promptly by the Shepherd of the Desert Church bells, which tolled at least three times a day and often more frequently in a place where funerals abound. For Colin, the interruption was jarring, especially as a sudden breeze had caught hold of the water meant for the golf course and pulled it across the chaise lounge where he lay.

He pushed away from the errant sprinkler and sat up, slightly disoriented. He had slept deeply it seemed – rare for him in Sun City. It was a place so consistently quiet that the silence became its own noise, heightening his awareness of every sound – the wind rustling palm fronds overhead, rabbits rummaging through the foliage or coyotes howling in the distant hills. He rubbed a hand through his hair, absently watching a mother quail lead four offspring under the canopy of a grapefruit tree, their miniature topknots bobbing along in rhythm behind her.

"Are you awake?" Colin's mother asked from the other side of the screen door.

"I think so."

"Well then, how about some lemonade?" She pushed the door open with her hip and stepped through, carrying a tray with a pitcher and two tall glasses filled with ice. Still slim and pretty, Joy Green spoke with a lilting Georgian accent, only slightly softened by her years away from the south. Colin shook off his sluggishness and rose to take the tray from her hands.

"Mom, you don't have to wait on me."

She gave his shoulder a squeeze. "It's no bother. I have to use the lemons before they go bad. They're dropping off the trees faster than I can squeeze them. I took a whole crate full to church on Sunday and another down to the women's shelter in Peoria. I don't know if they can use them, but I hate to see them wasted."

Colin puckered with the first mouthful. A little on the tart side, like Mom always made it, reminding him of his childhood in Pennsylvania where he and his younger brother had sold it on the street corner. Only five cents for a full Dixie cup.

Without bias, Colin had to admit that most of his childhood was similarly idyllic. He and his brother had gotten along well – and not – just like most brothers. They were still close, except geographically with Colin in Phoenix and Glen living in Lafayette Hill, a suburb of Philadelphia that was only a couple of hours from Lancaster. Colin was more surprised than anyone when his parents decided to move to Sun City several years ago. His dad had just reached the age of sixty when they made their announcement shortly after visiting Colin one winter. When Colin had flown back to help pack up their childhood home, Glen had been typically philosophical about their decision to move.

"They need the change," he had said, "especially Mom."

Colin wasn't so sure. Moving to a place where people die, but are not born seemed like a depressing step for people as young as his parents. He struggled to see the positive side of their decision, instead seeing their choice as an eerie declaration of finality – a thick, black period at the end of a sentence. Still, he wouldn't complain about having them nearby. And as he watched his parents adapt to the move and immerse themselves in the pleasures of retirement, he had to admit that Glen was right.

Situated west of Phoenix at the foot of the White Tank Mountains, Sun City was a planned retirement community complete with golf courses, pools, an amphitheater and enough shopping options to keep travel into Phoenix almost unnecessary. Most of the fifty-five-and-over residents were fierce supporters of the Maricopa County Sheriff's posse that protected their domain. Colin didn't blame them. They had lived through times of war and peace, now all they wanted was peace and quiet. Colin's parents fit right in.

During their first year in the Valley, Colin had sought to balance attentiveness with a respect for their privacy and sense of freedom. His parents did likewise, making a discerned effort not to interfere in his life. This was especially hard for his mom after Glen announced his engagement to Linda and embarked on a happy marriage that would soon involve grandchildren. Colin continued to avoid commitment of any kind, which amused his father, much to his mother's chagrin. For the first time in his life, Colin began to enjoy his father's company without reservation. They were both adults now. No lectures or reprimands, just tee times and ball games.

But Colin's initial fears about his parents' move to Sun City had seemed prophetic when his father died suddenly of a heart attack about a year after Glen's marriage. If he had lived just two more months, he would have been a grandfather.

His death had been a blow. There had been no time to prepare, no opportunity to say goodbye. Part of Colin wanted to buckle under his grief. It was so unfair to get his father back only in time to lose him forever. But Joy's grief had been so debilitating, he had been forced to lay aside his own.

Colin spent many nights lying awake in her guest room so that he'd be there when the tears returned, breaking into the stunning silence of her husband's final home. She had recovered over time, rebounding from her grief and learning to live life as a widow with grace. She returned to Pennsylvania for the birth of two grandchildren and came back from each visit with brighter eyes, looking more like the mother he had always known.

They had grown closer since his father's death. It was a bittersweet benefit. Colin was glad to be nearby whenever she needed him. He could never fill the void left by his father, but doing odd jobs around the house and taking her to dinner or a movie once in a while seemed to fill in the spaces left between her other social activities and volunteer work.

He only wished that she, like his father, felt no need to interfere with his personal life.

"So tell me about Andrea," Joy said, sitting down across from Colin to pour lemonade.

"Don't beat around the bush, Mom."

Joy shrugged innocently and handed him a glass. "I'm just curious."

Colin drained his glass and set it on the wrought iron table next to the chaise. "She's about my age, blond hair, blue eyes, tall. She lives in Tempe."

"Could you tell me anything that I wouldn't learn from her driver's license?" Joy asked dryly.

Colin scowled. "I just met her, Mom. Give me a break."

"And two dates is your limit, am I right?"

"Maybe I'm not cut out for more than that." Colin leaned forward and refilled his glass. "I seem to have a talent for irritating women lately."

"Women? You mean there's more than one?"

"Forget it."

Joy opened her mouth and then closed it again. She sat back in her chair and watched him as he moodily stared across the greenbelt. Sometimes he forgot how observant she was. He knew he had been abnormally quiet today, his somber mood setting in more markedly as evening fell. Night was coming and with it another round of insomnia and frustrating dreams.

And she wouldn't be there.

He set down his glass and leaned against his knees, his mother and her speculative expression forgotten for the moment.

What's happening to me?

He was standing on the brink of insanity, it seemed, caring way too much for a figment of his imagination. He should be glad she had disappeared and hopeful that his other dreams would soon fade to black as well. But somehow he wasn't. He didn't want to let go of her.

Melting ice shifted in Colin's glass, bringing him back to reality. When he looked up he saw that his mother's expression had changed. She was frowning now.

"What's bothering you?"

Colin shook his head. What could he say that wouldn't earn him a CT scan?

"I'm not sure I'll ever have what you had with Dad," he finally said.

Joy frowned. "Why would you say that? Why would you *want* that?"

"Isn't that what all the questions are about, Mom? You want me to find a wife – perfect love. Someone I can't live without. That's what Glen has, right? He met Linda and knew she was the one, right from the start. True, abiding love: a soul mate. Just like you and Dad."

"Colin, marriage is never perfect. You can't expect to find some kind of ...dream wife."

She had no idea how closely her words struck home, but Colin pushed passed them. He looked over her head at the empty house, remembering his father in those rooms.

"I know that, Mom. But Dad loved you so much. I bet he never doubted for one minute that you were the woman of his dreams. I just don't think..."

"Just stop it, Colin."

Joy's voice was brusque. She set her glass down with a little too much force, her jaw set tight. "Don't presume to tell me what your father felt for me, or how perfect our marriage was. It was true and real, but it was nothing magical. Yes he loved me. But I was never the woman in his dreams."

Colin sat frozen for a moment, stunned. Joy's cheeks were flushed as she stood and gathered their empty glasses, carrying them through the back door. He rose and followed her into the kitchen, his heart tightening as he considered her words.

"What did you mean: 'the woman *in* his dreams'?" he asked pointedly.

Joy was still for a moment. "Is that what I said? I didn't realize..." Her voice trailed off and she moved to sit on a bar stool.

"Mom?" Colin persisted.

"Calm down, Colin," Joy answered wearily. "Your father wasn't unfaithful to me, if that's what you're thinking. At least I don't think he was."

"I'm thinking there is something I need to know. Something I should have learned before now."

"Why?" Joy pushed back her hair with manicured fingers. "You can't have imagined that our marriage was perfect, Colin. Surely you know marriages have their ups and downs."

"Mom, please." Colin leaned against the counter. "You meant something by what you said. Don't leave it there."

Joy sighed. "Your father and I had only been married for six months when he left for Vietnam. By the time he returned, he was a different man, as you might imagine, coming home to a different life. His father had died in his absence, and you were born." She smiled weakly. "Can you imagine? Right from the horrors of war to instant fatherhood and the responsibility of his aging mother as well.

"He suffered from horrible nightmares during the last few months of his tour and then brought them home with him. I slept very little between caring for you and listening to him thrash about every night." Joy shuddered, looking beyond Colin's shoulder, into her own past.

"Those dreams frightened him horribly. They frightened me too and I wanted to help, but he wouldn't share them with me. I can only assume he was reliving his experiences from the war. I suggested some counseling. I even bought him a book about understanding dreams. I worried he was losing his mind."

Colin struggled to clear his throat. "A lot of veterans suffer from post-traumatic stress. Did he ever seek help?"

Joy shook her head. "He started a new job about that time, which took him away on sales trips so often that I never knew how much he suffered. When he was home, the nightmares became less frequent and his mood improved. I'm sure I would have gone on in ignorance if I hadn't been such a light sleeper."

"What made you think he was still suffering?"

"He wasn't suffering!" Joy said, her voice quivering. "Your father was dreaming about someone, Colin. I learned to recognize his nighttime movements, the murmurs he made in his sleep, the quiet sense of contentment he conveyed in the morning. This woman he dreamed up was comforting my husband in a way that I could not. I came to hate her."

Colin could not speak. An unidentifiable emotion washed over him. It seemed to come from far off and deep within at the same moment, mixing panic with relief and fear with understanding. Lowering himself to the kitchen floor, he rested his arms on bent knees and stared unseeing at the cabinets in front of him.

"Did the dreams ever go away?" he asked.

Joy rose from her stool and brushed imaginary lint from her pants. "I don't know how long he dreamed about the woman. When he realized that I was aware of his dreams, he did everything in his power to conceal them from me. My initial jealousy, in time, gave way to some amount of sensibility." She shrugged her shoulders, as if logic could dislodge the hurt. "He couldn't control his dreams – I know that. And the nightmares! They plagued him for years, with only a few stretches of good sleep in between. I thought he'd finally gotten over them when we moved out here. But they came back just a few months before..." Joy bit her lip. Colin rose to his feet and pulled her into his arms.

"Mom, you have to know that Dad loved you."

She nodded against his chest.

"And you're right you know," he continued. "Dad couldn't control his dreams. I'm sure he would have done anything to spare you that pain."

Finally pulling away, Joy squeezed his hands and forced a smile.

"Come with me."

Colin followed her down the hall and into the den, a room that had changed very little since his father's death. It was small and dark. The walls were lined with cherry bookcases and a single window was completely obscured by thick drapes. It had been an ideal environment for his temperament, Colin realized. Memories were already starting to click, like the fact that his father always had dark circles under his eyes and could be especially grumpy on those afternoons when he didn't nap.

Joy wrinkled her nose as she walked toward the curtains, opening them to let dull afternoon light into the dusty space. Colin figured she had rarely entered the den during the last few years, yet with the instinct of a lifelong homemaker, she was well acquainted with the room's inventory. She walked directly toward one of the bookshelves and found what she wanted.

"This is the book I bought for your Dad," she said, turning back to Colin. "He tried to read it, though it probably did little to help him."

Colin turned the book over in his hands, taking in the worn cover and dated, seventies style graphics that proclaimed: *Unlock the secrets of your dreams!* Catching amusement in her eyes as he looked back up, Colin began to laugh.

"I know what you're thinking!" Joy said, laughing at herself. "It's probably a lot of psycho-analytical garbage that has been debunked in the decades since it was written, but it was really popular at the time!"

Colin imagined his father trying to plow through the book, just to please his wife. He had been an avid reader, spending most of his life in the old leather chair that was now the centerpiece of this room, still showing the conformation of his father's shape. Colin lowered himself into it and was immediately enveloped by its memories. It still smelled of pipe tobacco.

Being here among his father's possessions brought everything back so clearly, the busy man who had been so distant when he was a kid. It was a tragic irony to learn now that they had more in common than he ever realized.

Looking back down at the book, Colin idly flipped through the pages, stopping when something that looked like an index card fell out and fluttered to the floor. Bending to pick it up, Colin flipped it over and inhaled sharply.

"What's wrong?" Joy asked.

Colin couldn't speak. His thoughts plunged through the images that had plagued his dreams every night for the past week: dark streets and strange buildings under red, smoky skies, to the same rain-soaked alley where he had held the old woman so many weeks ago while calling for help. Her anguished face came back to him now, pale and wrinkled, shrouded with damp white hair. But she had changed as he held her, turning younger until she became the face he now saw staring back at him from a snapshot.

Joy moved to a position over his shoulder, where she could see the picture clearly.

"So there was someone," she said blankly.

Colin could not argue against her assumption. He didn't try. It would be impossible for him to make a logical comment anyway while holding this photograph.

Who was she? Why did his father have a picture of her?

Colin knew there would be no neat answers. Examining the photograph carefully, he remembered her voice and the words she had whispered to him that night just before disappearing in the mist.

"Protect her," she had said.

But who needed his protection? And why?

Chapter 14

Michael was hunting again, drawn into his dreams every night by a heightened awareness of his prey. Zigzagging across a forest clearing bedded with pine needles and moss-covered logs, he passed from one grove of trees to another, never seeing or hearing the one he pursued. Instead, he could smell fear and confusion among the branches of the trees, as if she had just passed here not long ago.

It was this thought that propelled him, leaving him exhausted every morning. If only he could gain ground by moving more quickly, he was sure he would soon have her in his sights.

Michael was sure that the woman from the cobblestone street was his target. His reaction to seeing her there had been like nothing he had ever experienced, both fascinating and horrifying in a single moment.

Who was she and why was he dreaming about her?

Michael had rarely dreamed of someone he didn't know. The old woman was the only exception. Her unsettling disappearance had been pulling at the back of his mind for weeks. It wasn't until he first caught sight of the woman in the white nightgown that his uneasiness began to shift, becoming larger and indefinably more significant. His conflicting thoughts on the two women had leveled his concentration, seriously interfering with his campaign schedule.

Kendall Markham had been quick to comment on Michael's distracted air, cautioning him to pull it together before the press began to notice. His poll numbers had slipped over the same weeks, due largely to a television campaign that featured Californians who could not identify him as their senator or name a single piece of legislation that he had sponsored.

"Come on, Markham," Michael had snapped when seeing the ad for the first time. "People are phenomenally ignorant when it comes to politics. This is nothing new."

"No. But what is new is how Georgia Cunningham is able to capitalize on that ignorance in a way that makes you look bad!"

It had taken Michael a half hour to quell Markham's concerns. He wore a mask of contrition and promised a more attentive attitude during the coming week, knowing full well how difficult it would be to keep.

Public issues didn't honestly interest Michael. He wouldn't have even considered a career in politics if his father hadn't constantly pushed it. It had always been easier to capitulate than argue, the old man's ability for manipulation enhanced by the craft he had carefully honed. As a child, Michael had been encouraged by his mother to pursue a natural love for music, but his father had put those interests in their proper place. No pure joy should be found in a skill that did not provide an avenue to achieve power.

Michael had come to agree. His Gift beckoned him to a place of prominence. Over time, he had learned to love the power, feeling a rush of pleasure each time he felt the will of another bend to his own. Secretly he came to see the Gift as its own art form.

He was the composer, moving along from measure to measure, looking forward to the climax of the crescendo he was riding.

Before his first election, Michael's father had bombarded him with advice, all of it framed by a controlling use of his visions and threaded together with Machiavellian principles.

"Become first their hero and then their vice," his father had said.

Michael had done a good job of it.

Targeting a volatile issue in which community members considered themselves cheated, he had artfully thrust himself into the fray. It had been easy to mimic outrage and passion – and necessary. His charisma had quickly propelled him to the front of their grassroots movement. When his leadership eventually earned him his first political victory, Michael and his father had privately laughed about it. He could just as easily have championed the opposing viewpoint and won.

Once in power, Michael held on to his base by feeding their fears of the competition, fostering the idea that prizes won on their behalf might be lost in another's hands. It became easier all the time, especially because of his Gift. Michael had used the same technique in each election that followed, manipulating voters to be antagonistic toward his opponent. Division, he had learned, was a stronger ally than unity, which served only as a convenient uniform to be donned in times of emergency and then shed. For the most part, the public he so little cared for had only loved him more for these tactics, allowing his smile, his genial charm and soothing voice to remain in their minds instead of the harsh, vicious tone associated with the print and television ads run in his support.

But everything was different this time. Nothing about this campaign was falling easily into place. His opponent, Georgia Cunningham, was the epitome of class and grace. A no-nonsense attitude and fondness for straight-forward truths were foundations of her bastion, and a take-me-or-leave-me nonchalance about her candidacy made her especially appealing to the voters who paid attention. During the few face-to-face meetings Michael had shared with her in recent weeks, he had come away with his confidence shaken, acknowledging only to himself that she was the real deal.

"We need to dig up some dirt on her," Markham had grumbled.

Michael just shook his head.

"There's nothing there. Trust me."

He had used his Gift early in the campaign, looking for a Cunningham scandal to throw to the media. He had found nothing more disgraceful than a parking ticket.

And now he was distracted by the dreams. And his Gift was weakening.

But the dreams are important, he told himself stubbornly. *Perhaps even a test.*

It was the only explanation that made sense. Why else would he be plagued like this? Weak when he most needed his strength?

Tonight his dream told him he was right.

Michael emerged from the forest into a clearing. The moon shone brightly overhead, but he didn't bother using it to search out the woman's hiding place. She was gone, her scent disappearing like an ocean breeze that suddenly stills. But something beckoned him. He moved to the center of the clearing and saw it – his mother's house was just beyond the trees.

He moved forward with desperation. There was something there that he needed. Something his father had left behind that would explain everything.

The front door creaked on its hinges when Michael entered. It was dark and cold inside. Through a wall of windows he could see the ocean, inky black under a shrouded moon.

"Mother?"

His voice echoed back from the empty rooms. She wasn't home then, but off on one of her adventures.

The basement.

Michael stilled.

Yes, go now.

It was his father's voice, guiding him.

Moving by memory through the dark house, Michael found the stairs that led below. They were different from reality – narrow and lined with cobwebs, but he barely noticed. A glow was spreading from below, pulsing orange against the walls, welcoming him. Michael's breath quickened as he descended the stairs.

The room he found was different too. No wine racks or Christmas decorations stacked on metal shelves. No dusty Ping-Pong table. Instead he stood at the entrance of a round chamber flickering in red candlelight. A small table sat in front of an unlit fireplace with a leather journal in its center. Michael stared at it, mesmerized.

Listen, his father said.

The fireplace suddenly sprang to life. Flames like fingers from Hell reached across the hearth, turning the pages of the book.

Michael crossed the room in two strides. The heat of the fireplace radiated around him, burning his face, singeing his hair, but he ignored it. He needed answers. He needed whatever wisdom his father had written in this book. Feverishly he searched the pages.

They were empty. Michael sank to his knees.

Get up!

He quickly obeyed. His father sounded angry.

"What am I supposed to do?"

The fireplace roared and the pages of the book began to turn again, faster and faster. They whispered a message that only he could hear, speaking to him without making a sound. Suddenly he understood.

His father had dreamed of someone too. A woman who beckoned him, weakened him.

"Why didn't you tell me?"

The book shuddered and closed. His father hadn't understood his dreams either. He had hunted, like Michael. He had searched for answers and come up with more questions. The dreams had tortured him – *she* had tortured him.

But I almost found her.

Michael moaned. The very idea overwhelmed him. He licked his lips.

"Where? How?"

Keep searching. She'll be closer than you think.

The fire flared and then died. For a moment, Michael stared into its grate, his mind listening for more.

Behind you.

He turned around.

Nine cloaked figures stood in a half circle against the wall, chanting an unintelligible mantra. In the candlelight they seemed to be pulsing, like the flow of blood pounding against Michael's temples.

You're one of us, his father said.

Michael felt power emanating from them, surrounding and engulfing him. He joined their ranks, swaying to their rhythmic words. One came forward carrying a bowl of broth, which he pressed into Michael's hands. Another wrapped a heavy animal skin around his shoulders, all the while continuing to chant with the others. Their cadence increased in tempo as Michael lifted the bowl to his lips and drank.

The gamy liquid moved quickly through his body, filling him with power. He was stronger now. He knew what he needed to do. The bowl slipped from his hands as the walls of the chamber disappeared. Michael was alone in the forest again. He inhaled deeply, singling out the scent of his prey.

Moments later he emerged from a thicket of trees along the edge of a cliff. The ocean seemed endless. It stretched out below him in the darkness, black except for violent white peaks that pressed against sharp rocks. Michael stood for a moment watching, listening as the waves whispered instructions. He turned away, heading through the tree line into a swirling mist that obliterated everything.

But the mist was familiar.

His heartbeat quickened when he realized he was once again in the vast park where he had first seen the beautiful woman. Swiftly moving along the pathways, Michael found the familiar fieldstone wall and looked over it to the street below.

The woman was standing where he had first seen her. She swayed slowly and her nightgown swung against her ankles. Her lips were moving, but he could not hear her voice. He imagined she was singing. Now and again she looked down the street expectantly.

She's waiting for you.

Michael's heart pounded.

He closed his eyes, willing for himself a way to reach her. He opened them and looked one way then the other, finally making out a narrow stairway cut through the fieldstone wall just a few yards away. It hadn't been there before. The strength given by the cloaked figures still coursed through him. He would be denied nothing tonight.

Michael moved silently. The vapory air billowed around him as he reached the stairway and descended to the street below. What would he say? What would she do when she saw him?

His vantage was only obscured for a moment by the wall, but it was enough. By the time he could turn and look back to the place where she stood, his opportunity had disappeared.

She wasn't alone anymore.

The stranger who stood at the woman's side was fair-haired and tall. His back was turned so that Michael could not see his face, but he didn't need to. The rage he felt at his presence was already building.

Their voices carried to him as nothing but a murmur, blocked by the thick air. They were deep in conversation. The way the man's head was bent toward hers and the crease of concentration across her forehead spoke of intimacy. It was further confirmed when the woman suddenly turned away from the man, only to have him take hold of her hand and pull her back.

She gave in willingly, looking up at him with a tentative smile that spoke of renewed trust.

Michael slumped against the wall. The power he had gained just moments ago evaporated. The thick air closed in around him, heavy like the animal skin. But this didn't protect or empower. It stifled, it smothered. Perspiration began to bead along his temple.

Breathe!

It wasn't his father's voice this time. Michael had only his own inner warnings to guide him as the mist grew thicker still.

He could no longer see them, but he felt their bond as if he were somehow entwined in it. He closed his eyes, smelling her perfume, afraid of what he felt. Clenching and unclenching his fists, he fought to control his fear and turn it into more useful rage. She had made a fool of him, beckoning and then snubbing him, pulling him here only to push him away.

And what about the Intruder?

Michael's anger flared. Bursting out of him like a sudden storm, it obliterated the mist and the dream with it.

Sunlight poured through Michael's bedroom window, stabbing his eyes and pulling him violently toward reality. Drenched in sweat, he pushed away his constricting covers and sat up, holding one hand up to block the offensive light. His urgency from the dream had stayed with him, causing his heart to pound and bile to rise in his throat.

It was morning, time to focus on his campaign, ready or not. He looked at the clock. He had an interview with Fox News in two hours.

Moments later he stepped into the shower and let the stinging water pour down the contours of his hard body. His hand shook as he grabbed the soap. He leaned his head against the ceramic tiles, hoping the cold shock would remove the fear that engulfed him.

In the light of morning, the threat of his dream had only intensified. The conflicting emotions he felt for the woman alone had been bad enough. But the Intruder's presence compounded everything. Raw hatred moved through his bloodstream like a drug.

The reality of daytime and his full schedule frustrated him with its impotence, creating countless hours before his next opportunity to sleep, dream, hunt: to expel some of the violence that was building inside him.

The woman and her companion were a threat to everything he had worked so hard to accomplish. Michael knew this, but he didn't understand why or how. He remembered his father's empty journal from the dream and the scattered information he had gleaned from it. It wasn't enough. His father had dreams too, but they were not as dangerous as these. They had not threatened the political future they had both worked so hard to attain.

Keep searching.

His father had approved of the hunt. He had understood its necessity, a priority even during the thick of the campaign. Somehow Michael had to find her again. He had to take her, to separate her from the Intruder. Michael had been strong until *he* arrived. He would have reached her, if not for *him*.

Michael flinched in pain. Looking down, he discovered that his fists were clinched so tightly, his nails had dug into his palms. Half-moon cuts appeared on his wet skin and now blood mixed with water found its course down his forearms and dripped off his elbows, coloring the water that circled around the drain. Raising his hand to his mouth, Michael sucked the wounds, enjoying the metallic taste. He closed his eyes and imagined that it was the woman's blood in his mouth, her limp body trembling in his arms as the Intruder lay motionless at his feet, staring out of empty eyes.

Adrenalin coursed through his veins as he stepped out of the shower and dried off. Staring at his own reflection in the steamy mirror, Michael saw rage in his eyes that would not be abated. Behind him he saw movement in the bedroom and turned to see his wife step in from the balcony, unaware of his presence as she carefully balanced a brimming coffee cup in one hand. Michael approached her slowly, the taste of blood still in his mouth. She looked up just as he reached for her and the coffee cup crashed against the floor, splattering her bare legs.

Michael would have to wait until night to hunt for the woman from his dreams. But in the meantime, there were other ways to satisfy his lust for blood.

Chapter 15

Erynne watched the sun set over the Sonoran Desert from an airplane window. It was vigorous, fiery red bleeding to amber along the horizon and so different from the watercolor twilight she was accustomed to on the coast. Its warm golden glow blanketed the landscape below as her plane descended toward Sky Harbor Airport. In every direction, purple mountains encircled the sprawling city of Phoenix, while large red rock formations jutted out in clusters on the expansive valley floor. A broken vein of skyscrapers stretched through the middle of the city, reflecting back the golden sun like a million mirrors.

The old man sitting next to Erynne leaned forward, appreciating the view with her.

"I think of Marcos de Niza every time I land in Phoenix at sunset," he said.

Erynne nodded silently, wishing she could bottle the colors and have them woven into a tapestry. Just an hour ago, she wouldn't have been able to say who Marcos de Niza was, but her companion during the flight was a retired history professor from Arizona State University – one who, it seemed, couldn't easily set aside his love of teaching. He had introduced himself as Professor

Enrich while stowing a cowboy hat in the overhead compartment. His joy at learning this would be Erynne's first visit to the Grand Canyon State had been genuine. Before they rose from the ground in San Jose, he had begun his first lesson, much to her chagrin. It seemed he had hardly taken a breath during the two-hour flight.

It was the viceroy of Mexico, she learned, who sent Friar Marcos de Niza looking for gold during the mid-sixteenth century.

"Historians say that de Niza arrived in the Valley of the Sun at sunset to find hundreds of Indian dwellings made from adobe imbedded with tiny pieces of glittering mica. That's why he returned to Mexico City and reported finding a lost city of gold."

"Did the viceroy believe him?" Erynne asked. In spite of herself, she was enjoying his lesson.

"Of course! He immediately sent Coronado on an expedition to find it. He spent two years and two million dollars searching, but finally returned to Mexico City exhausted, demoralized and – more importantly – empty handed."

"I don't imagine anyone was too happy with the friar."

He shook his head. "He was summarily blamed for Coronado's failure and returned to Spain in disgrace."

"Imagine going down in history that way."

Professor Enrich shrugged. "Look on the bright side. Thousands of teenagers pass through a local high school named in his honor. Most of them remain willingly ignorant of his story, but they'll never forget his name."

Erynne shook his hand as they parted at the gate. She watched him walk away and then took a moment to gaze through the window at the closest mountain range, trying to imagine it as it had been hundreds of years ago with an Indian village rather than a bustling city at its feet.

As she made her way to the baggage claim area, she noticed Indian artwork displayed throughout the terminal – even the carpeting under her feet featured geometric patterns that were Navajo in design. She hoped to see similar patterns on Tuesday in Sedona when she was scheduled to meet the owners of a small textile company that created traditional Indian designs on fabrics suitable for garment making. Erynne had not originally intended to accept their invitation to visit, but she was too practical to make her visit to Arizona strictly personal. The appointment comforted her. Her trip couldn't be a total waste, she told herself, even if things didn't pan out with Sidney Green.

An hour later she was sitting by the pool at her hotel, which had been built on the side of a cliff in north central Phoenix. Gretchen had booked it for her, thrilled that Erynne was finally taking some time off.

"It features hacienda-style suites. Look at how beautiful it is!" Gretchen had pointed to her computer screen. "It's like being on the Mexican Riviera – right here in the states!"

"Without ocean views," Erynne added dryly.

But tonight she wouldn't complain about the view. She could see the lights of Phoenix to the west and south, twinkling beyond the palm trees and Saltillo-tiled roofs. A warm breeze passed over the patio and the smell of Mexican food from the resort's restaurant beckoned her to dine.

For the moment, Erynne was content to sip her ice tea. She was tired and glad to have some time to herself after spending so much time under Gretchen's watchful eyes.

It had been several days since she dreamed of the comforting stranger, but her nights had been far from restful. More often than not, she had simply awakened breathless, the scent of a seaside forest on the air, the mournful cries of a baby ringing in her ears.

The possibility that similar dreams had plagued her mother still festered in her mind, causing her to return again and again to Sidney's letters. It was a pointless exercise. She had poured over them so often that his words were now seared in her memory. Every letter conveyed a tone of urgency that Erynne found increasingly ominous.

Was it possible that Sidney knew about her mother's dreams? Would Erynne's dreams get worse, like her mother's, sending her down the same hopeless path?

It wasn't the first time the idea had crossed Erynne's mind, but it still brought her to her feet, as if she could walk away from it. Crossing her arms over her chest, she made her way down a steep staircase that led to a deserted patio on the edge of the cliff. Saguaros and ocotillo scattered across the dark hillside made stark silhouettes against the city lights. Something rustled in the bushes and Erynne took a hasty step backward.

Birds or lizards, she told herself, *not snakes or scorpions.*

But the dark desert still seemed wild and dangerous, reminding her of how she had felt in her dream with the river raging and the unknown desert creatures surrounding her.

A strong breeze passed over the patio, picking up the ends of her hair and causing the stone necklace to sway and thump against her chest. She didn't mind. Strangely it comforted her, like a heart beating on the outside, connecting her to her mother, her grandmother. She needed to find answers. For herself. For them. Erynne felt the pull of Sidney's letters tucked inside her suitcase.

But not tonight, she told herself.

She turned away and headed toward the restaurant.

అ

On Saturday morning Erynne woke early, parched with thirst and struggling under her sheets. Stumbling from her bed in the pitch blackness, she groped for the glass tumbler beside the sink and greedily gulped down tepid water. By the time she was satiated, the familiar cries of the desperate infant had faded into silence only to be replaced by a throbbing headache.

She headed for the shower, wondering about the absence of the comforting stranger. Had her nights been restful without him, it would be a good sign, she told herself. But replacing him with a disturbing forest and crying baby hardly seemed like evidence of a healing mind.

Her headache was gone by the time she had dressed, drained a cup of black coffee and headed downstairs to pick up her rental car. The concierge told her that Sun City was on the other side of the Valley, but not difficult to find.

With his written instructions laid open on the passenger seat, Erynne headed north toward the freeway that looped around the Valley, taking in as much of the unfamiliar city as she could while navigating. She had no specific plans before Tuesday, but was keeping her eyes open for places of interest. Today she wouldn't be anywhere near the Heard Museum or the Desert Botanical Garden that Professor Enrich had recommended, but she hoped to make time for them in the next few days, once the difficult part of her visit was accomplished.

Turning on to the westbound freeway, Erynne could see the city of Phoenix laid out below her to the south. Black, rocky hills flanked the freeway in clusters, scattered with Saguaro and creosote bushes. Her views were generally open on the north side to the desert, which was broken up by scattered subdivisions and shopping centers. She found the wide-open feeling of the desert

breathtaking. The clear sky was blue and fathomless as it stretched, unobstructed from horizon to horizon. Not too far from the freeway, half a dozen hot-air balloons floated in a scattered pattern above the desert floor and Erynne wondered what it would be like to ride in one.

There was a noticeable change in scenery when she finally exited the freeway and passed a sign welcoming her to Sun City. Erynne slowed down considerably to keep to the posted speed limit. She didn't mind. The drive had been too brief and her stomach was twisting in knots. She distracted herself by focusing on the houses she passed. Most were small block homes. Many were meticulously maintained but others showed the kind of soft neglect understandable with elderly caretakers. Within minutes, she turned onto a street that matched Sidney's address. The houses here were block too, mostly painted white with colorful trim. She spotted Sidney's house and pulled to a stop across the street. It was well cared for, with dark green shutters and lush foliage bordering a rock yard. The name "Green" was painted neatly on the mailbox.

Erynne smoothed her hair with shaking hands and opened the car door. Pushing her purse strap resolutely on her shoulder, she crossed the street.

No excuses, she told herself. *If you don't do this, you'll regret it.*

But halfway across the driveway she stopped, seeing a woman coming around the side of the house. She appeared to be in her early sixties and was wearing gardening gloves and a large straw hat.

Sidney's wife.

Erynne's heart sank. Her determination evaporated like the air of a deflated balloon.

Sidney is married. You knew that, she chastised herself.

But she hadn't thought it through. She had traveled all the way to Arizona without a plan, only the desperate belief that this was her last hope for answers. Now her lack of homework felt like foolishness, even cruelty. But it was too late to turn back. The woman had spotted Erynne standing in the driveway and was heading toward her with a smile.

"You're looking for the estate sale, right?" She spoke with a soft southern accent. "I've been getting a lot of that this morning. I'll never understand why they would name adjacent streets such similar names, but this is Meadowlark, not Meadowbrook. You're one block south of where you need to be." She pulled off her gloves and pointed toward the back of her house. "It's around that way. I was there earlier this morning. It looked like a good sale."

Erynne grasped at the excuse to leave. "Thank you," she said, backing away. "I'm sorry I disturbed you."

"It's no trouble. In fact, why don't you just leave your car here and walk through my backyard? There's a green belt between my house and theirs. As long as there aren't any golfers out there, you can walk straight across without any trouble."

"Okay," she said, "if you're sure."

"My pleasure," the woman said, offering her hand. "I'm Joy Green."

"Erynne O'Keefe."

She shook Joy's hand and followed her around the side of the house. She had no interest in an estate sale, but Joy seemed nice, making it difficult to imagine unloading Sidney's letters in her lap, ruining her day and possibly her marriage.

Why didn't I think this through? Erynne asked herself again. But she knew the answer. If she had let herself imagine this scenario, she would not have come at all.

Reaching the back patio, Joy placed her hat and gloves in a basket and smoothed her hair.

"Do you mind if I tag along? There were a few pieces of Franciscan Ivy I saw this morning at the sale, but they were asking too much." She laughed softly. "I'm a real bargain shopper."

"Of course."

"Just let me run in for my handbag."

Erynne waited while Joy headed into her house, wondering what, if anything, she already knew about her husband's relationship with Shannon. Joy returned quickly, locking the back door behind her – the action of a woman who lived alone, Erynne thought. As they crossed the greenbelt, it occurred to Erynne for the first time that Sidney might not be alive anymore.

They walked through the sale slowly. Erynne watched Joy go from item to item, examining everything carefully.

"My girlfriends and I hit these sales a couple of times a month," she said. "It's amazing what you can find. Are you looking for anything in particular?"

For a moment Erynne had forgotten that she was supposed to be shopping. "Vintage fabrics," she said, saved when she spotted several bolts of brightly colored material stacked haphazardly on top of an old sewing cabinet.

Joy looked surprised. "Do you sew?"

"A little," she said.

"How wonderful."

By the time they reached the cashier, Joy's hands were filled with small treasures. "Would you mind, dear?" she asked, transferring her load to Erynne while she searched for her wallet.

A few moments later, they were walking back across the greenbelt.

"I wonder where I'll put it all," Joy said. "My late husband would have teased me mercilessly if he saw me dragging all this into our house."

So Sidney is dead, Erynne thought.

She saw a fleeting flicker of pain cross Joy's face and wondered if her loss was recent. There seemed no decent way to ask.

Joy insisted Erynne come inside.

"This heat is miserable," she said, switching on a ceiling fan in her sunroom and pointing Erynne toward a chair. "I can't send you out again without something to drink first. Maybe some lemonade? I just made it this morning."

"Yes. Thank you."

Erynne didn't sit, but looked around the room instead, finding a large collection of family photographs on one wall. She moved closer, focused on a portrait of a young couple who must have been Joy and Sidney some thirty years ago. Joy hadn't changed much, Erynne thought. Sidney drew most of her attention. His hair was trimmed short – unusual in that era. Perhaps he was a military man? Erynne scanned the wall and found it – another photo showing him in uniform, looking dashing, but serious. He may have served in Vietnam, then, toward the end of the war. He was a handsome man. Erynne felt oddly ashamed, imagining him through her mother's eyes. What kind of man had he been to betray a lovely woman like Joy?

She moved quickly over the other photos. Sidney was in them more often than Joy, suggesting she was always the one with the camera in her hand. There were shots taken at the Grand Canyon and in front of a baseball stadium. In one, he wore a

JENNIFER FROELICH

fishing hat and posed with two dirty boys proudly holding their catch.

"You're examining my most prized collection," Joy said, handing Erynne her lemonade. "That's my husband, Sidney, and those are my boys: Colin and Glen. Glen is married and living in Trenton. He and his wife have two little ones."

She pointed out two cherub-cheeked girls posing for the camera in velvet dresses. A more recent shot was unframed but tucked in front of the glass, showing Glen and his family in front of a Christmas tree.

"What a lovely family."

Joy nodded, smiling. "I wish they lived closer, but I'm blessed to have Colin here in Phoenix." She frowned slightly, searching the wall. "I guess I don't have a current picture of him. That's his senior picture from high school. I would guess he's just a bit older than you."

Erynne nodded, wishing she could find a tactful way to refocus on Sidney. Social situations had never been her strong suit. Blurting out indelicate questions would certainly kill the friendliness Joy had shown so far. But Joy was still talking about her son, whom she described in glowing terms.

"He's so helpful," she said, casting an expectant glance toward the door. "He should be here any time. He promised to fix my leaky faucet."

Erynne quickly finished her lemonade. It was time to go. The subtle change in Joy's voice could only mean she was ready for Erynne to leave or, worse, that she had matchmaking in mind. A bolder woman might stay and use them both to learn more about Sidney, but Erynne's nerves were shot. She wasn't cut out for this kind of deception and she certainly didn't want to meet Joy's son.

130

"I really need to get going," she said. She stood up and grabbed her purse, trying not to react to the fleeting look of disappointment that crossed Joy's face. "It was really nice meeting you. Thanks for your company at the sale, and for the lemonade."

"My pleasure, dear," Joy said as she walked Erynne to the door. "Come back and visit me anytime."

Erynne's hand shook as she unlocked the car door and tossed her unnecessary fabric purchase on the passenger seat. She could blame adrenalin for the symptoms, but when hot tears sprung to her eyes the moment she pulled away from the curb, she had to acknowledge her deep sense of disappointment.

What did you expect?

She shook her head. Not this.

She drove mechanically, retracing her path to the hotel. Guilt gnawed at her conscience, as if she were complicit in her mother's relationship with Sidney.

She blinked her eyes, clearing the tears. Disappointment was giving way to anger.

How could they do that to Joy? To her father?

There were no answers. She had come without a plan and was leaving just as confused as ever.

Chapter 16

    Erynne was back in Sun City at the estate sale. It was nighttime and she was searching for something with a flashlight, something important that she had left behind. Every surface in the small house was stacked with objects for sale. They towered over her, threatening to topple: furniture, house wares, clothing. Junk.

    "Where are you?" she called. There was no answer.

    She turned a corner, passing into another room. The clutter was shifting around her and multiplying, making it difficult to get through. A light was shining around the edges of a door at the end of the hall, beckoning. Erynne turned sideways, squeezing through a narrow gap between two tables to reach it. They shuddered as she passed and several picture frames tumbled from the top, landing at her feet. She kicked them away and pushed the door open.

    She was in a small room, flickering with candlelight. Erynne rushed forward, dropping her flashlight as she reached the room's lone occupant.

    "It's you!" she said.

She touched his face, drinking in every detail. It had been too long.

"I'm here."

Her companion spoke in a whisper. His eyes darted over her shoulder, fierce and wary. She understood. There wasn't much time.

"Why is this happening?"

"I don't know." He pushed her hair away from her face. "I just wish..."

"...We could stay like this."

"Yes," he said.

Their foreheads touched and then he was gone.

⚃

Erynne woke with a start. The morning light was offensive as it peeked through the gap in her hotel room curtains. She lay still for a moment, trying to savor the last few moments of her dream, but it was already starting to fade. By the time she turned on the shower, the details were all but gone, trying to recall them as difficult as keeping water from running through her fingers.

"I can't remember his face," she told her reflection. But it faded too, in the steam from her shower.

A few minutes later, Erynne was drying her hair and thinking about scrapping the rest of the weekend. She could come up with an excuse for not keeping her meeting in Sedona and try for an earlier flight to San Jose.

But did she really want to explain her truncated "getaway" to Gretchen? No. That was reason enough to make the best of the next three days.

Erynne had been hoping for a deeper sense of comfort than a few days away from work could offer. Finding out more about Sidney and her mother would have been far more therapeutic than a dozen days poolside, especially if they had shed light on her dreams. She wouldn't return to Sun City, she had already decided that. If Joy knew nothing about her husband's relationship with Shannon, Erynne wasn't willing to be the one who told her.

So I'll play the tourist, she told herself. *I'll lie by the pool. I'll visit museums.*

She went to the Botanical Garden that morning, finding design inspiration in the colorful flowers and succulent gardens. Walking among the alstroemeria, gladiolus and freesia made her wish she could commission a fabric to mimic nature, seamlessly blending from one rich hue into another like the delicate petals she saw. Her visit to the Heard Museum that afternoon was enlightening as well, providing even more information about the Hohokam whom Professor Enrich loved so well, and showing countless examples of American Indian artwork.

Monday, Erynne spent the day shopping in Scottsdale. After eating lunch at a small deli off Fifth Avenue, she browsed through several boutiques. She bought a delicate turquoise and silver necklace for Gretchen and, impulsively, a Kachina for Mark's office, though she wondered if he would accept it. They hadn't spoken in weeks.

Erynne was heading back toward her rental car when she came upon a small art studio featuring a large painting in its window. It depicted a Navajo mother and child walking hand in hand through a grassy meadow. Towering red mountains perched along the horizon and sunlight filtered through painted clouds to light the child's face as she looked up at her mother with adoration. The mother's eyes twinkled with delight as she considered her child, clearly more beautiful to her than their breathtaking surroundings.

The painting made Erynne think of Mary Cassat, who had captured the same kind of mother and daughter intimacy on canvas. But even more, it reminded her of a day she had spent with her mother on a beach when she was very young. They, too, had walked hand in hand, the hems of their rolled up jeans wet with the sea and their bare feet crusted with sand as they searched for seashells and sand dollars.

It was the last memory Erynne had of true contentment – that feeling that everything was right and safe in the world. They had stayed the entire afternoon and evening at the beach, eating a picnic lunch, building a sandcastle and listening to her father play his guitar at sunset while she and her mother snuggled kangaroo-style under a blanket next to the fire. The very next morning was different, the tension between her parents palpable, the arguments more frequent as the days passed. The nightmares had come again, irritating the festering wound between her parents and bringing on more shouting matches.

Then one day it was over. Erynne woke to strange silence and emerged from her room to find her mother huddled in the corner of the couch under a threadbare afghan, her eyes dry and red. Her father was out at the curb, loading the last of his belongings into his beat-up yellow pickup truck. He had hugged Erynne fiercely before leaving, offering a parting shot to her mother and careless promises to her. There would be lots of visits and trips together, he said. Erynne stood in her nightgown and bare feet on the front sidewalk watching him drive away, not understanding that she was creating a memory that would stay with her forever.

How many days, months, years had she spent pushing aside the living room curtains, hoping to see his truck pull to a stop in front of the house? She had imagined it so many times: her father would hold out his arms and swing her around, then take her away from that house where life had grown more difficult every day.

Shannon's nightmares raged on as Erynne passed from childhood into adolescence, leaving most of her nights punctured by the sounds of groaning, sobbing, screaming. She occasionally cleaned herself up enough to get a job and pay a few bills, usually just after receiving a final disconnect notice from the utility company. Erynne learned to forge her signature on checks, budget whatever money they had, prepare simple meals, take the trash to the curb and quietly gather empty bottles after one of her mother's more difficult nights.

By the time she was eleven, she had stopped looking for her father through the front window. Her dream that he would still return was shattered when she came home from school one day to find a telegram clutched in her sleeping mother's hand.

"Daniel O'Keefe killed in car accident."

The harsh simplicity of the words printed on crumpled yellow paper struck Erynne like a fist. She lowered herself to the floor next to her mother's bed, reading that first line again and again, as if doing so would change its meaning.

Shannon woke moments later. Disorientation soon gave way to recollection and she turned her face to the wall, giving in to more tears. Confusion mingled with Erynne's sorrow as she watched her mother grieve. She couldn't remember affection between her parents, only anger and bitterness. She climbed up on the bed, hugging her mother from behind as her body shook, wanting to give and receive comfort. But Shannon waved her out of the room like an irritating fly, oblivious to her daughter's pain. She had already indulged in her favorite brand of comfort –

evident by the wine bottle that clinked hollowly against the leg of her nightstand as Erynne pulled away and obediently stumbled out of the room.

Pitching herself on the sagging couch, she stuffed a pillow against her mouth, her desperate sobs silent and painful. She had never felt so alone. Her mind sought urgently for a soft place to rest, some trustworthy soul whom she could call, someone to share her burden. Hours passed as she sat that way, the house filling with shadows and her stomach beginning to rumble with hunger, a rude reminder that *her* life was not over.

During the darkest part of the night, Erynne dried her swollen eyes and pushed damp hair away from her face. Shannon had finally fallen asleep again and the silence around her was welcome. She could only hope that it would remain undisturbed by nightmares. Listening to the rare silence, Erynne wished for a thousand quiet nights: solitude, isolation – to embrace the abandonment that was already so much a part of her – knowing that it would never leave, wishing to turn it into something useful.

Life was safer when lived without attachment. Tomorrow would bring even more responsibility, not pardoning her for her youth or frailty. The only person she could rely on was the one who stared back at her in the mirror the next morning, looking so much older than the girl she had been the day before.

Helping Shannon make arrangements for the funeral, she had stumbled across statements for unknown bank accounts in her grandparents' name. Being named their secondary beneficiary for a small inheritance was bittersweet for Erynne, but the funds provided enough for a decent funeral and – when she was old enough for full access – seed money for *EOK Designs*.

That was a seed first carried to her by the wind during high school, thoughtlessly dropped by her spoiled classmates who openly mocked her out-of-date fashions, which were pulled from her mother's closet or purchased at a thrift store. Anger was a ready weapon and Erynne had welcomed it, hating the girls for their vanity, yet becoming more aware of the truth in their observations.

With a forced air of idle curiosity, Erynne began flipping through fashion magazines at the library once her homework was done. Her interest grew and she began studying more than current trends and styles. Digging into fashion icons and the workings of an entire industry, she was soon more knowledgeable than the lemmings from her school, who responded quickly to the latest advertisements in *Seventeen* but knew little about *haut couture*. Using art and home economics classes as a springboard, Erynne proceeded to soak up everything she could learn about dressmaking, silk-screening, weaving and pattern design. Her teachers became willing allies to her passion, having so few students who actually cared. A few allowed her to spend time after hours in their classrooms, trying different color combinations on the looms or screens, or designing costumes for school plays.

Erynne began wearing her own designs to school, undeterred when her improved wardrobe did little for her popularity. At the age of fifteen, she took a job altering dresses for a local bridal shop. She loved the feel of satin, taffeta, silk and lace flying through her industrial sewing machine and spent her break times pouring through fabric and pattern catalogs, her head already filled with ideas. The other ladies in the shop spoke little English and willingly taught Erynne a smattering of both Spanish and Chinese, impressed by her work ethic and enthusiasm, so unlike other girls her age. Worrying over her quiet, reserved demeanor and even more over her sometimes gaunt appearance, they often brought Erynne plates of food, which she shamefully accepted, knowing there would be little to eat when she returned home.

On free nights, she spent her time roaming the Boardwalk, wishing the money she earned could be spent on a caramel apple or bag of Marini's taffy instead of paying her mother's past due bills. Boys her age paid little attention, her self-imposed isolation creating a boundary they readily avoided. She interpreted their attitude differently, assuming there was something inherently distasteful in her appearance – as if the stigma of her mother's mental illness were visible on her skin. She quietly suffered through one or two unrequited crushes, too shy to seek out male companionship, too wounded to believe any such relationship would last.

Advertisements for design schools beckoned Erynne from the back pages of magazines as her senior year approached. She often lay awake at night, listening to her mother's restless movements, desperate to plan her escape. She dreamed of attending a school far, far away. But when her favorite art teacher sent samples of her work to a friend at San Francisco's Academy of Art, Erynne was offered a scholarship based on her talent and financial need. She gratefully accepted.

As it turned out, living just seventy miles away from her mother proved to be a whole new world for Erynne. She loved the city, and embraced her education with enthusiasm. She pushed herself hard to balance her class schedule, a job at the San Francisco Theater Company's costume department and frequent trips home to check on her mother. The visits assuaged the guilt she felt for leaving – the guilt she came to hate for its boomerang quality.

It had been a pure collision of rebellion and opportunity that propelled Erynne to accept her invitation to study in Scotland during her final year, coming on the heels of a bad weekend trip home when she had found a strange man in her mother's bed.

"I'm a lonely woman, Erynne," Shannon said after watching in silence as her daughter removed the man from her house.

"He was a transient, Mother! High on who-knows-what. Why don't you stop to think?"

During her flight overseas, Erynne had wallowed in her sense of justification. She had taken too prominent a role in helping her mother all these years, never allowing her to stand on her own feet.

I'm doing her a favor, she told herself.

But her anger cooled as the semester progressed and she found her thoughts often tinged with worry when they rested on her mother. It had not occurred to her before that allowing anyone into the house was out of character for Shannon – her paranoia making her suspicious of even the postman. Erynne began to recall other changes in her mother's behavior and was left with a nagging sense that a shift had occurred in her mother's mental health, brought on by something far more substantial than bad dreams. The Early-onset Alzheimer's diagnosis had come a year later, but Erynne always related it to that weekend. Why was it that every time she tried to pull away from her mother, guilt brought her back?

○8

Erynne returned from her shopping trip early. Rethinking plans to visit the art museum that afternoon, she chose instead to lounge by the pool with a favorite M.M. Kaye mystery, hoping to put her dismal memories out of her mind. But several hours later after she had eaten dinner at the hotel's restaurant, she was ready to admit that her sense of melancholy was complicated and would not be easily laid to rest.

It's a good night to get some extra sleep, she told herself.

After dressing for bed, she stood on her balcony, welcoming the desert wind that passed over her hot skin. Sprinklers were on below, watering the stretches of grass that wove through the desert landscaping and dampening the concrete walkways leading toward the pool. The water made the air smell different, and Erynne wondered if anyone else noticed. She felt as if her senses were heightened tonight, perhaps from the onslaught of memories. She hated herself for remembering. Reliving the past would never change it, so what was the point? But today she was forced to admit that since her mother's death, she had been drowning in her guilt and resentment. The only thing that kept her from sinking below the surface was her time spent with the man in her dreams.

The irony didn't escape her, but she was afraid that he had – whisked away as quickly as he arrived, her grieving mind having reached a place that no longer required his comfort.

The few seconds she had spent with him last night did little to ease her fears. The brevity of the dream and especially its vaporous quality supported them, if anything.

Her dreams of him had always been so *real* – despite their settings. He had become real to her too and Erynne wasn't ready to let go of him yet. That knowledge alone scared her, going against everything she thought she knew about herself.

Allowing herself a deep sigh, she went back inside her room and drew the curtains tightly across the balcony door before turning off the light. As she fell asleep, she yearned to see him again. If nothing more, she wished for another shared moment so that she could say goodbye.

As the familiar cobblestone street came into focus, Erynne was filled with uncertainty rather than comfort. Her nightgown was the same – crisp and white – and her bare feet were damp from recent rain. She had never felt self-conscious wearing the gown on this street before, but tonight she felt undressed and cold.

Black gaps yawned at her from between the trees while the branches hanging over the street scraped against each other in the wind. Crackling twigs and leaves disturbed by the unknown beyond the walls increased her discomfort.

When goose bumps rose on her bare arms, she hugged them to her chest. The rain still clung to the air, turning into a swirling mist that was thickening against the street like a dark layer of smoke. As it slowly climbed up to surround her, Erynne felt her throat constrict with irrational fear. Soon, she could see nothing in front of her and the darkness of the night beyond invaded her thoughts. She turned in circles, searching the mist in vain, wondering where he was. It had never taken this long for him to appear at her side.

And then it was clear. He was not coming.

An unfamiliar prickling sensation on the back of her neck caused Erynne to turn on her heels and search the misty street. With the footbridge behind her, she squinted, making out a dark figure emerging a few yards from where she stood. Though she couldn't see his face, she knew this wasn't her companion. The figure's massive stature eliminated any doubt.

For a moment they considered each other: Erynne warily, her heart pounding at the base of her throat. Still, she flinched when he moved, walking toward her with slow, purposeful steps.

Raw fear burned through her chest.

Run, it told her.

Erynne turned to obey, but her nightgown was now heavy with rain. Struggling to gain traction on the slippery cobblestones, she moved in slow motion toward the bridge, finally breaking into a run as her pursuer closed in behind her. His heavy strides rocked the very earth beneath them.

He's coming after me!

They were her mother's words. The memory of them sent blood rushing into her ears, blocking out the sound of her feet striking the road. She knew what came next, her own screams of terror as she felt him gaining on her. She opened her mouth, but no sound emerged. Slipping on the wet pavement, she went down hard, scraping her arm and bruising her hip. She scrambled to regain her footing. Every second counted.

Erynne was no closer to the bridge. It loomed ever in the distance, an unattainable goal that had never before seemed so important. Frantically she searched her periphery for her companion. Where was he now?

Momma, wake up. It's only a dream, Momma. Please wake up.

Erynne heard the childlike voice and recognized it as her own, uttered in desperation the first time she had heard the nightmare overtake her mother.

"Wake up. It's just a dream. Wake yourself up!"

The voice was shouting, loud and strong. It was the voice of a grown woman, her own voice.

Suddenly Erynne was hurled back into the darkness of her hotel room. Gasping for breath and covered with sweat, she quickly turned on the light and searched the corners of her room. Disoriented from the nightmare, she was convinced for a moment that he had followed her through.

The bed covers were in shambles. Moaning deeply, Erynne slid to the floor, the rough feeling of the carpet burning against her knees and forehead, feeling comfortingly real. Her arm and hip ached from her fall on the street, though there was no scratch, no bruise.

Slowly her heartbeat returned to normal as she lay curled in a ball, vacant eyes staring at the air-conditioning vent directly in front of her. The tears she had shed in her sleep evaporated on her face. She was too exhausted to cry anymore.

How many years had it been since she last lay in this same position, just outside her mother's bedroom door, praying quietly that the nightmare would end soon and release her mother from its hellish grip? Artlessly composed with childish perfection, Erynne's prayer had been fervent. She was sure that God would hear her, despite how her mother felt about Him. When the nightmares continued, she worried she was saying it wrong. Eventually she gave up altogether. Erynne had not prayed since.

Not until tonight.

Unbidden, a similar prayer passed through her parched lips as she sought desperately for help, for comfort, for protection from her mother's curse.

Chapter 17

Protect her.

Colin woke with a start, his heart beating wildly. His alarm clock told him it was one-thirty in the morning, but it seemed like days had passed since he fell asleep. Whatever he had been dreaming about was gone with consciousness. Only those two words still echoed through his head.

Putting his feet on the floor, Colin sat on the edge of the bed and rested his head in his hands. A thin sheen of sweat covered his bare torso and yet he felt chilled. A shiver passed down his spine.

What was I dreaming?

He tried to focus, but failed. His head swam through murky water. Whenever his thoughts came close to grasping some kind of memory, he was pulled away in a riptide, back to the empty darkness of night. Something had left him with a sick feeling in the pit of his stomach. Now he was fully awake, anxious, and restless.

Turning on the light, Colin blinked until he could see again and picked up the picture that he'd left on his nightstand. As many times as he had studied the woman's face, it still confused him.

How could I possibly have dreamed about her?

There was never a reasonable answer.

He had told himself it was just a bizarre coincidence: two unrelated women who were merely similar in appearance. But each time he returned to the photo he was disappointed, more convinced than ever that his first reaction to seeing it was genuine. *She was the one.* Her image had been permanently etched in his memory, it seemed, from the moment she had first said those words while lying in his arms.

Protect her.

Colin couldn't explain it, though he had sought desperately for a simple, pleasing answer that would placate his mother.

"It doesn't mean anything, Mom," he had assured her after finding the picture. "It could be an old friend from school. Or maybe Dad didn't put it there. Maybe it's someone Glen knew."

Joy had only shaken her head and left the room, too upset to notice the way Colin's hand shook when he held the photo. He had taken a moment to compose himself before following her, worried that she would see how unsettled he was. She couldn't know he had dreamed of the woman too, he decided. It would be too confusing – and probably feel like a second betrayal.

"I'll be fine," she had told him an hour later, shooing him out the door. "I don't want you to fuss over me."

Her smile was tight, but Colin understood her words as a kind dismissal. She needed time alone.

He had called to check on her too many times during the week, something she didn't hesitate to point out to him. Still, he had only been felt better after talking to her on Saturday. She had finally sounded like herself again, telling him about some woman she met at an estate sale, who, of course, would have been Colin's perfect match had he only had the sense to show up while his mother was holding her hostage with tart lemonade.

"I'm sure she was lovely, Mom," he had said absently, paying more attention to the Diamondbacks game on TV than the details of his mother's dream daughter-in-law.

Tonight Colin acknowledged that he seemed to be having a harder time getting over the photo than his mother had. He couldn't stop thinking about the woman, her relationship with his dad and how he fit into the picture.

Why would I dream about a woman I have never met?

That question always led him to the younger woman he dreamed about, further confusing him and leaving him almost desperate for answers. It only intensified in the loneliness of night. Colin tried to walk away from it, plodding to the kitchen for a drink of water and then back to his room where he turned off the light and lay heavily against the damp sheets, pounding his pillow into a more comfortable mound.

Protect her.

The words seemed to blow through his open window and hang in the air above him. Spent from trying to make sense of the photograph, Colin's thoughts settled instead on his beautiful dreamtime companion. His last dream of her had been vague and fleeting. He couldn't remember what either had said, just that he was worried about her.

Could she be the one who needs my protection?

It wasn't the first time the though had entered his thoughts, but that didn't make Colin feel any better.

"I'm losing my mind!"

He sat up again as his words echoed through the darkness of his room, snapping him back to reality. He was making too much of everything, seeing connections where there were none, finding fantastic answers where simple ones surely existed.

He wouldn't be tormenting himself like this if not for the photo.

Perhaps he *had* met the woman at some point in his life. Maybe what he told his mother was true. She may have been one of his father's business colleagues, or even an old girlfriend whom they had run into at the grocery store. Even if he had never met her, it was possible he had seen the picture during his childhood and simply forgotten about it. For whatever reason, her image had stuck in his mind and somehow gotten mixed up in his dreams.

Repeating those thoughts like a military cadence, Colin lay back down. Slowly he began to relax. He closed his eyes and listened to the cars pass in the distance on Central Avenue. His sleep-deprived mind compared the sound to the rise and fall of the tide, reminding him of the moonlit beach he had shared with the beautiful woman.

Floating in the place between inertia and true sleep, Colin saw her pale face stained with tears and her hazel eyes staring at him blankly. His heart ached to see her that way, and he reached out to touch her, sensing that she was closer than she had ever been before. But his fingers groped hopelessly through thin air and before he could decide how to find the place where she was, his mind spiraled down into the deepest blackness of sleep.

Chapter 18

Elevator doors on the Plaza Park Tower's sixteenth floor did not open quickly enough for the silver-haired man who passed through them. Everything had made him wait this morning: trash collectors in front of his driveway, red lights at every half mile, construction zones on the freeway and a fender bender blocking the entrance to his parking garage. Now Kendall Markham breezed past the wall-to-wall view of downtown Sacramento without a glance and ignored the bright good morning offered by his pretty receptionist.

It wasn't a good way to start the week, but then again, anything had to be an improvement over the lousy weekend he'd had. His wife's trailer-trash relatives were visiting from the muggy climes of deepest Mississippi, and had literally taken over his lavish Folsom home. When she had asked about the visit, she only mentioned a sister and some cousins. He hadn't realized their quantity until they arrived in droves, filling up every spare room, pull-out couch and square foot of carpeting. Avoiding them had been almost impossible, though he'd tried at first, staying holed up in his bedroom until the banging, thumping, slamming and shrieking became too much to ignore.

"What's going on out there?" he demanded of his wife. But she had just shrugged, urging him to join in on the "fun." He grudgingly agreed, tending the bar and the grill and trying to stifle their most destructive tendencies. He'd suggested a shopping expedition on Saturday, hoping for a few hours of peace. But the men had stayed behind and made a general nuisance of themselves in the game room. They had invaded his box at the Pavilion that night – not to watch the Kings game, but to make sure he couldn't – and dragged him down to the lake on Sunday, despite his heated protests, leaving an absolute mess of his boat. Late night performances on a karaoke machine were the worst of all. Sleep had been impossible.

He had never been so thankful for Monday in his life, irrationally tying each traffic delay to the disaster at home, where the clan was surely now finishing off the contents of his refrigerator before heading out on another ghastly outing. He planned to work very late tonight, even if he spent those last precious hours throwing pencils at the ceiling while the janitorial crew vacuumed around him.

But as it turned out, Markham never gave his wife's family another thought once he saw the *Sacramento Bee* spread across his desk. Senator Reardon was pictured at a charity ball standing next to the governor and two state representatives in his first public appearance since Margaret's unfortunate attack. If his expression had been simply blank, morose or distracted, it would have been forgivable – even understandable under the circumstances. But the photographer had caught something entirely different in Reardon's eyes: an expression that looked pointedly evil and seemed to rise from the page, causing Markham to shudder and shift in his seat.

He pushed the paper away in disgust. Perhaps it had been a mistake to insist on Reardon's attendance, but the recent polls had caused him to panic. Once upon a time, the senator would have been up to the task, despite his wife's condition. He would have easily taken advantage of the opportunity, milking sympathy from a public who would later remark on his humility and marital devotion with fervent ignorance.

"So you saw?" Bernice quietly gathered the paper up and stood in front of his massive desk, waiting for a response.

"Hmph."

Bernice Glenn was the most efficient secretary Markham had ever had, but her keen eye for such things bothered him. She was a stout woman with prematurely gray hair and deep lines running along the edge of her mouth where her atrocious pink lipstick had a tendency to settle. Smart and shrewd, she was essential to Markham's success, but lacking the people skills and deceptive personality necessary for commandeering political upheaval. If she had been even mildly attractive, he knew she could take over his job and do it better. He suspected she knew it too. It was unaccountable how content she was to remain in such a low position, arriving early every day to pour over information gathered from a clipping service, confirm his schedule, make his coffee.

"I need a print out of Senator Reardon's itinerary for the week."

Before the words left his lips, Bernice laid the document in front of him.

"I also took the liberty of checking on Mrs. Reardon's status. She's stabilized, but still heavily sedated. The senator's flight should have reached Reagan an hour ago. He'll be on his way to the hospital."

At least he can play the attentive husband now, Markham thought desperately. Aloud he asked, "Any word yet on a suspect? Surely they've arrested someone by now?"

Bernice shook her head.

"She still hasn't been able to give the police a description, what with her broken jaw being wired shut." She winced and then paused expectantly. "There was a nice editorial in the *Post* calling for more police on the streets and heavier sentencing for muggers." She handed him the clip. "If you think the senator's up to it, I can arrange an in-depth interview and encourage the west coast papers to pick it up. People have a tendency to look at things differently when personal tragedy is involved." Bernice glanced pointedly as the senator's folded image in her hands.

"Thank you, Bernice," Markham clucked, managing to look sympathetic. "Terrible. Terrible tragedy."

As Bernice closed his office door, Markham swiveled his chair toward the window, for the first time noticing the bright blue sky beyond. Margaret Reardon's attack during a morning jog just over a week ago had come at a bad time during the campaign, pulling the senator away from some key fundraising activities. Markham had shamelessly held her responsible, telling himself that she should have known better than to go jogging near the crime-ridden capital.

Why couldn't she join a gym like normal people?

But after hearing the details of her attack, he had managed to feel a small prick of remorse for his attitude. In truth, she was lucky to be alive, beaten so viciously that she had remained unconscious for days. She might not be alive at all if the senator had not gone looking for her. He found her behind a row of shrubbery in a small park near their Georgetown home. Reardon carried her home himself and dialed 911, sounding appropriately shaken, Markham had noticed with approval, when listening to the report for the first time on the evening news.

Hoping to capitalize on the public's sympathy, Markham's sails were deflated when brush fires in Southern California had pushed Margaret's accident to the back pages of the papers and the last segment of the evening broadcasts. While it was still being covered in D.C., that did little good in California where Senator Reardon's image needed the most help. Now that the fires had died down, Markham wondered if a more aggressive attitude might rally voters around his distraught senator. Looking over the stack of clips that had painted Reardon in a less-than-perfect light over the past few months, Markham knew they needed all the help they could get.

When he had agreed to manage Mike Reardon's first senatorial campaign, Markham believed he had landed a gold mine. Reardon had been the perfect politician – a publicist's dream. Wealthy, handsome, a former athlete. With a lovely wife at his side, he'd been everyone's image of the model American: fighting for truth, justice, and all that. This was a man who never had to be told to smile for a camera. Never.

But this time, Markham could fill a scrapbook with photos, quotes and sound bites that didn't fit the perfect Reardon image. His focus was slipping and though Markham had prodded urgently for answers, he had received none. The handful of months stretched out between this moment and Election Day now seemed fraught with pitfalls, leaving him with an uneasy sense of foreboding in his gut.

Markham had formed big plans for Senator Reardon, perhaps even bigger than the senator realized himself. It was something he had been invited to pursue by the senator's late father: a man who shrewdly knew the business and understood what it would take to win the biggest prizes.

Markham had imagined it all, like watching news footage from the future. First, there would be a respectable tenure in the senate. Reardon would win positions on the most influential committees, be vocal about the popular bills, and even more vocal about the unpopular ones. Favorable media contacts would soon be sliding his name in the mix with other presidential hopefuls.

Coffers would be padded by the right PACs, slick advertising would brand Reardon as the candidate of hope or vision or some other such nonsense. Men had gained the White House with less – why not Reardon?

To say that his candidate's recent change in focus was a threat to Markham's dream was understating it mildly. If it was a mid-life crisis, a troubled marriage, gambling addiction or threatening mistress – those things Markham could handle. He certainly had in the past with more than one respected statesman. But if Reardon was dipping into forbidden waters, Markham needed to know, needed to be prepared with plans, alibis and diversions.

There was always the threat of dirty laundry being uncovered from the senator's past, adding to Markham's anxiety, though he felt fairly confident he had covered those trails. The media had generally been favorable to Reardon, not pushing too hard or too deep. But his shaky attitude during this campaign had certainly not gone unnoticed. Markham predicted a changing wind in some of their supporting publications when it came to endorsement time.

Their opposition during this race was a nightmare: no dirt, no scandal, barely a flaw from head to toe, though Markham had searched fervently. They would attack on strict party lines, but voters were unpredictable. More and more it seemed that candidates found themselves crossing their fingers until the last vote was recounted.

Oh, how Markham wished he could retrace the course of Reardon's first senatorial election! That had been his sweetest victory in two decades of campaigning. They had been fighting a well-respected incumbent who was falling victim to an economic slump. Though Reardon was up a few points in the polls, the outcome was still up in the air. Beating an incumbent is always an uphill, not to mention expensive, battle. But one day Reardon had whispered something in Markham's ear that had forever changed the course of the campaign. The scandal was too good to be true – and damaging to the sitting senator in an all-encompassing way. Markham had leaked the information and watched with delight as a man's world crumbled. It was the victory blow that insured Reardon's win.

Even now, Markham could not understand how Reardon had come across that piece of information. It was something he could have only heard directly from the source, but why would the ousted senator have shared a personal secret like that with his opponent?

He wouldn't, and that was the stinger. Somehow, Reardon had just *known*.

Over the years, Markham had quietly witnessed the senator's extraordinary gift in action. He admired Reardon's subtlety most of all, keenly aware that exposure would mean disaster for them both. Their unspoken understanding worked well. Reardon passed along helpful information from time to time and trusted that it would be used for their mutual benefit.

Markham stopped pacing and looked out at the city below him. Just beyond the dark mirrored building his teenage son had dubbed "Darth Vader," he saw countless treetops surrounding the prominent domed tip of the state capitol building. In his mind he was seeing the larger version in Washington where he wanted to see Senator Reardon continue to spend many profitable years. But his fears were real and justified, and it was time he started doing something about it.

A genuine smile tugged at the corner of his mouth as Markham imagined his wife's disappointed expression. It was almost too bad that he wouldn't see it.

"Bernice," he barked, striding from the window. "Arrange for that interview with the *Post* and get me a flight into Reagan or

Dulles, something leaving this afternoon. I'm going to visit the Reardons in the hospital."

Bernice's pencil flew over her steno pad as her boss continued to issue commands. If she was surprised that Markham wanted her to pick up his suitcase from Folsom during her lunch hour, she managed not to show it.

Chapter 19

Colin stood near the level three escalators at Sky Harbor's Terminal Four. Twenty minutes early to greet a temperamental client, he wished for the freedom to pass through the security checkpoint and wait at the gate. At least from there he could watch the planes take off and land, something he had enjoyed with his father when he was a kid.

"What's that one, Dad?"

"A DC-9. See how the wings are way back on the body and how high the horizontal stabilizers are? It looks like it has a longer nose, and there's one engine under each side of the tail."

Several commercial and military models had adorned plank shelving in his childhood bedroom, pulled often from their perches to traverse the mountainous folds of his quilt for treacherous takeoffs and landings. He'd always believed he would be piloting them one day. But childhood dreams were made to be broken, he guessed. Why else would he be working as an accountant, waiting for a client who was likely to rake him over the coals for his own poor money management skills?

Colin shook his head and glanced at his watch. Still plenty of time to wait. Victor Lyon's flight would arrive at eleven o'clock, giving them just enough time for lunch at Kincaid's and a cursory trip to his office, where he would once again try and explain Victor's dismal profit and loss statements. It wouldn't matter of course – Colin had come to accept that accountants are blamed for everything. Victor had not hired his firm to analyze his overhead, high rent payments, inconsistent wage and bonus disbursement or poor product placement – just to keep the books. He was glad, at least, that the weather was cool enough for golf, insuring that Victor would lose interest by two o'clock and head off to the Boulders for tee time.

He hoped Victor would have no trouble finding him amid the chaos of another terminal renovation. Abandoned skyjacks, roped off walkways, bare concrete floors masked with yellow tape and floor to ceiling plastic sheeting hid any progress. Colin had already glanced at the artist's rendering of what the concourse would look like upon completion, but saw little that he felt justified the heavy price tag – especially in this economy. Maybe he was just in a bad mood, aggravated by his restless nights.

Colin resisted the urge to stand in line at Starbucks for some black coffee. Instead, he circled the escalator bank and idly watched travelers pass by. When he first saw her, Colin blinked twice, suspecting that he had become delusional.

It's not possible.

Yet even from behind, her figure was familiar to him as she wove her way through the crowd.

Had he fallen asleep?

No. She wasn't wearing a white nightgown like in his dreams, just a simple cream-colored business suit that grazed her legs as she walked toward the departure monitors. Colin drank in every detail in a heartbeat. Her black hair was loose, falling down her back as she looked up at the monitors, revealing her white neck and simple diamond earrings.

Feeling ridiculous and weak-kneed, Colin moved toward her, tripping over a bank of chairs in the process, trying to find an inconspicuous place from which to see more than her profile. While the dominant part of his brain *knew* she was the one, his sensible side fought it, trying instead to confirm that she was someone else entirely. But from his new position near a weary-looking potted plant, he could see her face clearly. All doubt left his mind.

Colin's brow creased as he studied her. She was pale and thinner than he remembered. Her pretty eyes were rimmed with dark circles, suggesting sleepless nights and arousing a quick surge of fierce emotion in him. He wanted to cross the five steps of bare concrete that separated them and pull her into his arms before launching into a barrage of questions that could surely never be adequately answered. Instead he checked himself, imagining that such a spectacle would end badly.

Would she even know me?

He wasn't sure that he wanted to know the answer to that question. Still, as the woman readjusted her purse and grasped the handle of her carry-on luggage, Colin knew any opportunity to talk to her would soon be lost if he didn't do something now. She turned toward the B Gates, leaving him no other option than to follow.

Security checkpoints were located at the entrance of each walkway, the lines leading to them stacking up considerably as federal employees confiscated toothpicks, nail files and embroidery scissors from partially disrobed passengers, patiently allowing them time to reassemble themselves before heading on to the moving walkways that would carry them to their gates. Ignoring signs warning that a ticket was required to participate in the process, Colin moved through the converging traffic, managing to take a place in line only one person behind her. The passenger between them happened to be huge – at least six foot three and 250 pounds -- making Colin suspect he had once been a football player. Colin was forced to rise onto his toes or bend at the waist to glance surreptitiously at her as the line inched forward. A continual barrage of inadequate openings passed through his mind, each rejected with good cause.

Was there really any good way to tell a stranger that you've been dreaming about her?

Even if he came up with the perfect phrase, the problem of cutting in front of the Lineman loomed large. Though interminably slow for the travelers, the line moved too efficiently for Colin, who was afraid he would soon lose his opportunity.

A sudden, loud movement from the back of the line made Colin turn around, along with everyone else, to see a large woman pushing her way through the crowd, clutching her ticket tightly and dragging an enormous suitcase. Red-faced and puffing hard, the woman was clearly late for her flight. Persuaded that her need was greater than that of better-prepared travelers, she was determined to reach the security checkpoint ahead of them. One or two passengers were content to mutter under their breath about this injustice while one man wearing a Yankees hat yelled, "Get in line with the rest of us!"

Shamelessly offended by the remark, the woman decided she could spare a moment to swivel and glare at her detractor, but lost her balance in the process, tottering into the crowd and upending her luggage. The ensuing domino bumping game quickly reached Colin and the Lineman, who had picked that unfortunate moment to lean over and unlace his shoes. He tried to correct his mistake with some dexterous footwork, but momentum was against him and he collided with the pretty woman in front of him.

She gasped sharply. Her pallor deepened. Her eyes wild with fear, she tried to back away, tripping over her carry-on bag in the process and spilling the contents of her purse.

The Lineman looked horrified.

"I'm so sorry!" he said.

He stooped to help her collect her things but then checked himself, backing away when he saw her flinch.

Colin moved swiftly around him and began grabbing for rolling lipstick and a packet of tissue, thankful for the opportunity to be near her but confused by the fear that emanated from her like a heater. Her hands shook as she struggled to push her belongings back into the bag and he could see that she was trying to control her emotions. By now her face had reddened and the panic in her eyes had been replaced with disconcerting flatness.

She looked briefly up at the Lineman, her eyes apologetic, but her shoulders were rigid, defensive. Colin again had to suppress the instinct to gather her in his arms. His fingertips brushed hers as he handed her the cosmetics, electrifying him. Lifting his eyes to her face, he desperately wanted her to return his gaze, but instead saw that she was actively avoiding it.

"Thanks for your help," she said quietly as she rose to her feet and tugged on her bag.

"Anytime," Colin said lamely through a strangled voice. He watched her walk to the security gate, wanting to follow, but instead obeying a voice in his head that urged, *Let her go.* The Lineman took his place a good distance behind her in the newly formed line and Colin heard throats being cleared behind him.

"Sorry," he said, stepping to the side and allowing the crowd to move past him. By now she was walking through the gate and gathering her bags without a backward glance.

Disappointment settled in his chest, replacing the adrenalin that had abandoned him. She had barely looked at him.

But surely she would have recognized me if...

Colin did not finish his thought. He looked down, rubbing the back of his neck and saw that he was standing on a crumpled business card that still bore his shoe print. He picked it up and read:

Erynne O'Keefe, EOK Designs, 1901 Pacific Garden Mall, Santa Cruz, California.

Colin turned the card over in his hand as he walked toward the east window, catching a brief glimpse of her as she disappeared onto the moving walkways. His meeting with Victor Lyon was all but forgotten as he considered the card and dared to hope. Glancing up at the departure monitors, he noticed a flight leaving for San Jose in forty minutes at Gate B12. Santa Cruz was near San Jose, wasn't it?

"You're reaching," he muttered to himself. Still, he tucked the card carefully into his pocket before turning back toward the concourse.

Chapter 20

"Erynne, over here!"

Erynne turned around to find Gretchen waiting by the luggage carousel. After a quick hug, she pulled back to examine her face.

"How was your trip?"

"Nice."

"Really?" Gretchen's eyes narrowed. "You look tired."

"I am." Erynne smiled faintly. "Vacation can be more exhausting than work." Spotting her suitcase sliding down the luggage ramp, she stepped around Gretchen to grab it. "Are you ready?"

Gretchen led Erynne toward her car in the parking garage, grilling her with a constant stream of questions. Erynne's answers were mostly monosyllabic. Where she added detail, she sidestepped the substance of her trip. Gretchen knew nothing about her true purpose for visiting Arizona. There was no need to drag her into its disappointments.

"We're stopping to get you something to eat," Gretchen said firmly, closing her trunk lid. "You're supposed to come home from vacation with a little meat on your bones – you look like you've been starving yourself!"

Erynne bit back a denial and nodded. She really just wanted to go home and hide under the covers, forget her recent failures and humiliations. The embarrassing incident at the airport's security gate came quickly to mind, but she stifled it and hoped Gretchen did not notice her cheeks redden.

Perhaps it had been foolish to expect more from her trip – to come home with answers if not with peace, well-rested, if not worry free. Instead she was more tired and confused than she had been when she left, feeling her grip on the world she knew slipping away.

Erynne's nightmares had returned every night during her stay in Arizona, the dark hunter finding her on the street and on the beach, even chasing her through an unknown city that throbbed under rose-colored street lamps. Each time, he had gotten so close that she could feel his hot breath against her neck, only to awaken shivering in the darkness, sure that he had followed her into her hotel room like some friend of Freddy Krueger. Perhaps most disturbing of all was the feeling of defilement he left with her, as if his presence on her pristine street and endless beach had sullied them forever, ruining the beautiful sanctuaries they had once been.

"How was Sedona?"

"Beautiful. The red rocks are almost beyond description."

Gretchen shook her head wistfully as she pulled onto the freeway. "I've always wanted to see them. Did you visit the Grand Canyon?"

Erynne shook her head with genuine regret. "I ran out of time."

It would have been only a two and a half hour drive to the canyon from Sedona, but Erynne had been too exhausted to consider it. When she checked into her hotel, she had been hopeful that the change from Phoenix would relieve her of the nightmares. But only the view out her window was different when she awoke breathless and drenched in sweat. She managed to successfully conduct her business with the Navajo weavers on Tuesday, but hadn't enjoyed it like she might have, going through her fabric selection in a rote way that belied her true interest.

On the last night of her trip she had eaten at a quiet restaurant with a view of the breathtaking red rocks: taking her time, dreading the night ahead. By the time she paid her bill and headed back to the hotel, she was determined not to sleep at all. Instead, she sat on her private patio as long as possible, enjoying the sound of Oak Creek bubbling below and watching the sun bleed into the canyon walls until the sky was left bruised. Finally she ordered a carafe of black coffee from room service and cracked open a thick paperback purchased at the gift shop. Reading with every light on and the patio doors open, she managed to stay awake until dawn. After a long cool shower, Erynne checked out and headed back toward Phoenix. Exhausted and bleary eyed, she had at least avoided another nightmare.

But then she'd gotten spooked at the airport.

"Are you alright?" Gretchen asked, glancing toward the passenger seat.

"Fine." Erynne's cheeks were flushed again with the embarrassing memory. "Just a little warm."

The man behind her in line had been massive – just like the hunter who had chased her on the cobblestone street. When he bumped into, her illogical panic combined with sleep deprivation had caused her to bolt stupidly and overturn the contents of her purse. Looking up, she had found herself facing a horrified overgrown puppy rather than the raving monster she had mistaken him for. Shame filled every pore as she gathered her belongings and stuffed them back into her purse, wishing she could disappear into thin air – or at least get through security as quickly as possible. Other travelers must have stopped to stare, wondering at her ridiculous reaction. One man helped gather her things, but she had been too embarrassed to do more than mumble her thanks to him before bolting through the gate.

Gretchen exited the freeway in Los Gatos, pulling into a small restaurant that she praised as one of her favorites whenever she and Len traveled over the hill. Erynne did her best to eat, mindful of Gretchen's watchful eyes. The food was good, but still felt unwelcome in her stomach.

"My treat," she said when the bill came. Gretchen protested, but Erynne was firm. "You picked me up at the airport – and dropped me off last week. It's the least I can do."

It was dark by the time Gretchen pulled to a stop in Erynne's driveway.

"I can come in and help you get settled," she offered, but Erynne was firm in her refusal. She was tired and working on a throbbing headache.

"I just want a hot bath and my own bed," she said. "I'll tell you more about my trip tomorrow. I promise."

Erynne waved goodbye from her back porch and then dragged her suitcase to her bedroom. A quick check told her there were no messages on her home phone from Mark. Was their friendship over then? Just because it couldn't be more?

She couldn't think about that tonight. Instead she ran a bath and swallowed two Tylenol. It was only seven o'clock and yet her new prayer was already starting to play through her mind.

Please, no nightmares tonight. Please.

Settling into the warm bath water, she tried to relax, floating on nothing, but her mind wouldn't cooperate. She couldn't seem to get the incident at the airport out of her mind. Something about it was bothering her – like a memory just out of reach. She tried to resist, but couldn't shut it off, feeling the strangest desire to return to the airport.

For what? Something she had missed?

She shook her head and settled deeper into the water. She was just embarrassed, she decided. It was a feeling that would pass when the memory faded. Or maybe something had fallen out of her purse that she hadn't retrieved. She promised to check as soon as she dried off.

So why did her cheeks burn again at the memory of the helpful man's hand touching hers? What she felt was stronger than embarrassment. Sudden tears were stinging her eyes, but she didn't know why.

I'm a mess, she thought, remembering that tears had threatened when she boarded the plane too. When the refreshment cart passed shortly after takeoff, she had found herself tempted by the small bottled liquids she had actively avoided all her adult life. Erynne had always seen poison where her mother found comfort, but today the desire for escape had been almost too strong.

But I'm not my mother, she told herself.

Erynne pulled the plug in her drain and toweled off, trying to dismiss her lingering melancholy. She was exhausted, she reminded herself, and there was no possibility of avoiding sleep tonight. After blow drying her hair and unpacking the necessities from her suitcase, she put on her favorite nightshirt and turned out the lights.

CB

Erynne slept deeply, dreamless for some time before she found herself sitting alone on the endless beach, watching a bank of fog rolling in across the bay. It approached slowly and then stopped, lingering over the horizon. She watched it suspiciously, as if it were a manifestation of the turmoil in her life. Even when there wasn't a black mist swirling around her, there was always a threatening fog in the distance, waiting for an opportunity to descend.

She heard him approach from behind, his footsteps a steady heartbeat against the sand. She knew it was her companion and not the hunter, but she didn't look back. He stopped and waited, close enough so that she could feel his warmth. She closed her eyes, stubbornly resistant, even while knowing that he brought safety with him.

"Where were you?" she asked, finally turning to look at him.

Her voice sounded hostile, even to her own ears. She felt betrayed, she realized, caught without him on their street, helpless in the face of a merciless stalker. Hot tears stung her eyes but she blinked hard, forcing them down until they became a hard knot in the back of her throat.

He considered her warily.

"I don't know. I knew you needed me, but I couldn't find my way." He searched the horizon for an answer, swallowing hard, his hands curled in fists that he thrust deep into his pockets. "I wanted to be there, but…"

He stopped abruptly as she shot him a look brimming with bitterness. A torrent of emotions welled inside her, many that were irrational and unfair. She hated the way he was looking at her, as if she might shatter into a million pieces.

"Are you okay?" he finally ventured, his eyes dark with concern.

"I'm fine," she said flatly, turning away. "You should go."

It's inevitable, she told herself. Abandonment. Maybe even for the best – especially if she could control the question of when.

"I'm not going anywhere," he said, his voice softly defiant.

Erynne rose and walked toward the ocean. She crossed her arms, wishing she could turn everything around and make it the way it had been before. Instead she felt helpless, out of control – just like when she was a child and her parents raged, oblivious to her pain. It wasn't safe to rely on others. There was always collateral damage.

And who would be swept into the storm this time? Erynne or this man who had been nothing but kind?

The waves were rising in sharp peaks now, beating the shoreline and stirring up the wind, which tugged at Erynne's hair and nightgown. She swayed but did not move, digging in with her heels, watching the sea.

Her companion crossed the sand to stand in front of her. Refusing to look at him felt childish, but Erynne didn't care. She ducked her head, fighting the tears that threatened.

"Oh no, you don't," he said. He moved in closer, a firm hand against her back as he lifted her chin, searching her face until she had no choice but to return his gaze.

"Tell me what you're thinking," he said.

"It's a curse," she said. Tears were welling now and she couldn't stop them from spilling onto her cheeks. "It destroys lives – whomever it touches."

"You're talking about this place?" he swept his eyes across the landscape. "What can happen here?"

"It's more than that."

"Your mother, you mean. You think this is her fault?"

She must have told him everything, then. She didn't remember. For a moment the knowledge terrified her, as if she were dressed in nothing but her fears, her secrets.

He knows, but he doesn't understand, her mind insisted. *If he did, he wouldn't still be here.*

"I can't outrun it, but you can." She pulled his hand from her face, squeezing it. "You need to get as far away from me as possible."

"I'm not going anywhere," he repeated, pulling her to his chest. "You don't have to handle this alone."

For a moment, Erynne closed her eyes, her resistance lost in the warmth of his arms. His heart beat against hers, so real and strong. If it could only stay like this. If there was no morning light to grab him away – no dark hunter to take his place.

"But it's not real." Her words were lost, muffled against his shirt. She pulled away and immediately the cold air enveloped her, steeling her resolve.

"It ruined my parents," she said. "It will ruin us – ruin this."

He shook his head. "You need to stop thinking that way."

"I can't just will it away," she said. "You think I've never tried that? It's impossible."

"You've only tried to handle it by yourself," he insisted, frustration creasing his brow.

"What choice did I have? She made everything impossible! Even my father knew that – that's why he left her."

"Just stop it." His frustration was giving way to anger. "I'm not letting you do this."

"What am I doing? Telling the truth? Facing the inevitable?"

"Pushing me away, molding your life into some kind of self-fulfilling prophecy that mirrors your mother's."

Erynne laughed. It was a deep, mirthless sound that she couldn't repress.

"I've been working my whole life to avoid it," she said. "But it's all been for nothing. It's happening anyway."

"Do you even hear yourself? Twisting everything to match what you already believe?"

She shook her head. "You don't understand."

"Your father left *her*," he said, his voice tight. "That's what you said just a minute ago. When are you going to get angry with *him*? Do you even realize that he left you too?"

The wind was picking up, struggling against them, lifting her hair into his face – a mask of pain that surely mirrored her own.

"You don't know what it was like," she insisted, shouting to be heard. "He must have hated it, day after day. It was unbearable. He couldn't take it anymore."

"But he could have taken you! He left you alone to deal with her by yourself." He groaned and turned away, passing his hands through his hair. "I'm not telling you to hate him, just to see things as they really were. Your mother was difficult, but she was sick, she couldn't help it. He could have done more. You've got to stop making her the scapegoat."

Erynne's anger flooded through her, white hot and blinding. She could think of nothing beyond making him stop.

"A few ill-advised confidences on my part don't make you an expert in my life," she snapped.

"It's the life you've lived, and you're not an expert in it either," he said, his voice rising above the wind. "Can't you drop that shield for one minute and open your eyes? You're so busy protecting yourself, you keep missing what's right in front of you!"

She had heard enough. Twisting away toward the ocean, Erynne was immediately engulfed in a blinding mist. The fog bank had found its opportunity at last, swooping in from the sea as if beckoned to smother their argument. She whirled around to look for her companion but the fog was too thick, swallowing her whole.

"Where are you?" she called.

He did not answer.

Stumbling through the fog, she groped the thick air in front of her, repentant, wishing to take it all back. But it was too late. The fog was pushing into her lungs and she was gasping, overwhelmed by its black depths.

Erynne awoke with sharp, stabbing sobs erupting from her throat, a torrent of pain that was finally proving too strong for the dam she had built. She cried again for her father, finally for her mother, and shamefully for herself as she recalled her companion's final accusation, recognizing it as a double-edged sword. She had let go of him only to chase a reality she didn't want, giving up her dream for something as intangible as the fog that had taken him away.

Closing her eyes, Erynne lay back against her pillow, trying to remember her companion's face. Only his words remained sharp in her mind, his frustration and anger. As always, his image eluded her, restricted to dreamland, a list of features without a composite image.

You keep missing what's right in front of you.

His words rang in her ears, inviting a fresh wave of guilt, as if he knew that his image had never survived until daylight, even when his voice and touch did.

Groaning in frustration, Erynne brushed the last of her tears away and got out of bed, heading to the kitchen. It was a dark morning, gloomy and promising rain. It suited her mood. She put on the tea kettle and noticed the pile of mail that needed sorting and the bills that needed to be paid. Her refrigerator was empty, which meant grocery shopping, and she needed to water her plants. A week's backlog of work waited at the studio and a Post-It note stuck to her cabinet door reminded her: buy stamps!

Grabbing a pen, Erynne listed each chore on a steno pad. The little task felt important, holding her firmly in the reality of her life, taking the sting away from her dream.

Whatever was happening to her – through the dreams or the nightmares – it was time to face it logically. She had been stupid to go chasing after Sidney. She was reading too much into his letters, attaching herself too much to the necklace, and allowing herself to feel way too much for a man who did not exist.

She still didn't know where to find answers, but she knew of a place to start. Picking up the phone before she could change her mind, Erynne dialed Mark's office number and listened impatiently to his answering machine before leaving her message.

Chapter 21

The following Monday started badly for Evelyn Madison Reardon. It was rainy and her hands were swollen with arthritis, she dropped her favorite teacup and watched it shatter to bits on the hardwood floor, and to top things off, her computer crashed and she had failed to back up the last chapter of her manuscript.

But none of these things would normally have dampened Evelyn's spirits. She had always been described as feisty: a characterization she liked. She had lived with arthritis for years, what was one more day? It was a shame about the teacup. It was a gift her editor had sent after *Sweet Harmony* went into its second publication. And her manuscript? It was a romance novel, like the rest. She could reproduce it fairly easily from memory. She may be getting older, but her mind was still sharp.

No, Evelyn realized her disposition today had little to do with her own life, and everything to do with her son. Michael had visited this weekend – something she used to look forward to. But now he always came with an entourage. She particularly disliked his campaign manager, Kendall Markham, a pompous man whose solicitous manner was as genuine as his perfectly-coifed hair.

"He's all about spin and image, Michael, not substance," she had once told him. "You need to give people an honest glimpse of your potential to lead, not pad your accomplishments or disparage your opponent."

But of course he hadn't listened. He and Markham had spent the whole weekend with their heads together, whispering in the corner as if the housekeeper or gardener were likely to sabotage Michael's next public appearance. With an unwelcome arm around her shoulder, Markham had even dragged Evelyn into the conversation at one point, asking her to comment on Michael's image.

"Our strategy is to offer voters a new American paradigm with a Reardon vote," he said with enthusiasm. "Something organic."

Evelyn frowned. "But surely organic means that there can be no artifice," she said.

Markham laughed as if she had told a joke.

For the next half hour, he had tried to explain his plan, including the positive impact of greenlining Michael's office and adding more facetime with a selection of sympathetic journalists. Markham used so many buzzwords that Evelyn began to suspect he had a "vogue word" app on that fancy cell phone of his. When she could stand it no more, she stood to leave.

"Mr. Markham," she interrupted, "just how many situations can possibly be win-win during an election campaign?"

For a moment his glossy smile faltered. Evelyn seized the gap, excusing herself to the kitchen.

It would have been amusing if it wasn't so nauseating.

There was no doubt that Markham was a weasel, but Evelyn knew she couldn't really blame him for the disquiet she was feeling this morning. So, were her fears about Michael's marriage responsible?

Margaret was still recovering from a terrible mugging. When Evelyn flew out to see her last week, she was shocked by the bruised and swollen face that bore little resemblance to her beautiful daughter-in-law. It was a great wonder she hadn't lost her life. And yet Michael was here on the west coast – and had not, as far as she could tell, even called to check on her.

"Why aren't you at her side, waiting for her to wake up?" she asked.

"Margaret's in good hands, Mother," he said, his eyes dark.

"But Michael…"

His cell phone rang and he had turned away, but not before patting her arm in dismissal, a campaign smile already forming on his face.

Evelyn spent much of the weekend watching him from across the room with a frown creasing her brow. She didn't like the changes she saw in him lately. In the past, she had always succeeded in burying her most worrisome fears. This time something was different. The darker side of his character was taking over, she feared, evicting those few bright spots that reminded her of the child he once was.

It still amazed her that this handsome, powerful man was the same cherished boy who often clung to her shoulder in the middle of the night after having a bad dream. Back then she had been so in love with him, knowing every mark on his body, every expression on his face.

Her fear that Michael wasn't like other children had started on one of those nights, when she had rocked him back and forth, singing endless lullabies while he sobbed into her neck. Evelyn tried to tell herself that all mothers watched for atypical behavior, but her nerves had perhaps been more sensitive than most. Her husband's nightmares had been chronic and particularly violent during those years, leaven for fears that had taken root before Michael's birth.

My son won't be like him, she had vowed. *Not in the daytime, not at night.*

But Michael's nightmares had seemed like a bad omen, giving doubt a foothold in Evelyn's heart even then.

A strong gust of wind billowed against the house, redirecting the rain that now beat at the kitchen window. Evelyn set her teacup on the countertop and sighed, remembering how things had been long before Michael was born.

It seemed like an eternity had passed since she was an awkward college graduate, so different from her well-to-do friends. In the years since, she had made great strides towards accepting her individuality, but she still struggled with it. That was one of the reasons she wrote her novels under a pseudonym. She was somewhere between amused and horrified when she thought about how her wealthy family would react if they knew that she and Violet Trumaine were one and the same.

Evelyn's family had never understood her. Born among the elite members of San Francisco society, she spent her entire youth feeling like a misfit. All the careful grooming, country club parties and private schools hadn't helped. By the time she was twenty-two and still unattached, her mother's desire to see her well married had reached a fevered pitch.

"Well of course you're going to the party tonight," she had told Evelyn on the afternoon of her Uncle Robert's annual gala. "Every eligible young man in San Francisco will be there!"

But Evelyn's idea of eligible varied strongly from her mother's. She desperately wanted to avoid the kind of life her mother led –societies, parties and charities – the constant struggle to be among the who's who, the fears that a family scandal would make the papers. Instead, Evelyn wished she was like the girls on television. She wanted to go to a public high school and state university, live in a dormitory and order pizza on Friday nights. She wanted the romance of impromptu beach parties and the chance to ride on the back of a motorcycle with a rebellious boy.

It was that last desire that got her into trouble.

She first saw Patrick Reardon that night at her uncle's party. Her mother had won their argument, of course, but Evelyn had been determined to make her regret it. She had been sulking in the dining room when she saw him standing in the entryway. He had been watching her, but she didn't know for how long. His brilliant blue eyes seemed to bore through her, making her feel like Scarlett O'Hara looking down at Rhett Butler for the first time.

Patrick had come to the party as a guest of his college roommate, a young man whose blue blood made him infinitely more suitable in her parents' eyes. Reardon came from new money. His father had started an import-export business from the ground up and, with remarkable business sense, had amassed a fortune that he used to wisely thrust himself into the fringes of San Francisco society.

Over the years, Evelyn had thought back to that night many times, recognizing how ripe for the picking she had been for someone like Patrick. They had stolen away from the party within an hour of learning each other's name. To her delight, he had a new Harley Davidson just waiting to be broken in on the San Francisco hills.

Their romance had blossomed overnight. Patrick was charming and clever. Even her parents were taken in by his magnetism. Evelyn couldn't have been happier. Somehow Patrick offered her the best of both worlds – excitement without alienation from her family. He promised to take her to Tibet, Singapore and Africa.

"You name it, baby. We'll go."

After a respectable courtship, they were married with all of San Francisco's elite in attendance. It didn't occur to her how much Patrick gained that day. He already had wealth, now he had married into prestige and power.

As Evelyn and Patrick boarded the plane for their European honeymoon, everything seemed perfect, and when they returned one month later, Evelyn was already pregnant, and finally feeling as if her life had purpose.

Patrick's father had demonstrated his delight with the marriage by giving the newly-weds an extravagant gift – a new home on the Monterey coastline. Evelyn had been dazzled. Pebble Beach was as exclusive as Nob Hill to be sure, but far enough from her family to give them the privacy and independence she wanted. They had moved in right away and spent their weekends choosing furniture and house wares, paying particular attention to the nursery.

During the next nine months Patrick was a doting husband. At first, Evelyn relished his attention. But as the months passed, her anxiety grew. His interest seemed to take on an obsessive quality. He looked less at her face and more at her swelling belly. She struggled against the feeling that she was disappearing into the wings as the baby took center stage in his life.

When it came time for the baby to be born, her labor was long and hard. By the time the nurse handed her Michael, Evelyn understood what no one would say out loud. The delivery had harmed her body in an irreversible way. Michael would be her only child.

The night they brought him home, she remembered looking down at him, so tiny and perfect in his bassinet, and wondering how on Earth she was ever going to know all the right things to do for him. She wouldn't ever get another chance. She had to do it right with Michael.

Patrick showed even less interest in Evelyn after the baby's birth. At first she challenged his detachment, but she might as well have been addressing a brick wall. Their relationship became perfunctory. Updates on Michael's development were the only subject of conversation he would tolerate from her.

At least I can't fault his devotion to Michael, she used to tell herself.

But as Michael grew, Patrick's attention continued to bother her. The look in his eyes often made her heart contract fearfully. She stifled her instinct to shield the baby from his gaze.

What's wrong with me, she wondered?

Time and again she convinced herself that jealousy or despair over their decaying marriage was to blame for her feelings, but the strong sense of foreboding always returned at night when she heard her husband thrashing in his bed. His nightmares continued and Evelyn began watching him carefully, seeing things she had missed before. Patrick had a gift for knowing things, she realized. Things he couldn't know by natural means. She came to wish she had never noticed. As soon as she did, he *knew*, of course. The antipathy he'd shown her since Michael's birth turned to violence.

Evelyn raised a withered hand and touched her cheek, just where Patrick first struck it almost forty years ago. Was it her imagination that made it still tender, the memory of a blow that had bruised the deepest part of her heart?

She would have walked out that day and taken Michael with her, but after a short conversation with her mother, Evelyn learned she had nowhere else to go. Marriage was a responsibility, she was told, and a lifetime commitment.

"Whatever you did to make him mad, darling, don't do it again. Men have such nasty tempers."

Evelyn had hung up the phone, the knot in her throat stinging more than the bruise on her cheek. Deep in her heart, she knew she would never escape. He would find her wherever she tried to hide – unless she left Michael behind. And that was out of the question.

From that moment, her son had been the only bright spot in her life. She was delighted to find him intelligent and creative, showing a special talent for art and music that she hoped to cultivate. She carefully avoided her husband. It wasn't difficult since he spent most of his time in the city at work – a position in her father's law firm, no less. When he was home, he gave all his attention to Michael, and she usually was able to avoid the physical side of his temper. She often heard rumors about his affairs, but the pain of that betrayal faded over time. If it hadn't been for Michael, she feared her heart would have turned to stone.

Of course, her greatest fear was that she would lose Michael too.

It began to happen when he was about five years old, at the park where Evelyn and some friends met for a play date. Michael was building sand castles with Jason, the son of her closest friend, Emma. They'd only been playing for a few minutes when Michael came running toward Evelyn with a worried look on his face.

"Mommy, who am I going to play with after Jason dies?"

A cold hand gripped Evelyn's heart.

"Michael! That's not something to joke about. Why would you say that?" While Evelyn chided her son, Emma looked stricken.

Michael shrugged his shoulders, his brow furrowed with impatience. "He's gonna die, and I want to know who I'm going to play with."

Evelyn had apologized profusely to Emma.

"I don't know what's gotten in to him," she said lamely. She quickly gathered their belongings and rushed Michael home, lecturing him during the short car ride about what he had said. He looked out the window while she talked, his chubby face emotionless and unconcerned. He wasn't listening.

The next afternoon, Evelyn got the call. Jason had been hit by a car while riding his bicycle. He was in critical condition. She raced to the hospital, where she found Emma rocking back and forth on a chair in the waiting room. Her cheeks were dry but she was pale and in shock. When she saw Evelyn, the flood gates opened.

"How did he know? He's just a little boy!" Emma turned her eyes upward. "Oh, dear God, please help my baby!"

All Evelyn could do was cry with her and wait to see if surgery would repair Jason's broken little body. He died that evening at ten o'clock and she couldn't help feeling guilt and horror on top of her sorrow. The next day when she explained to Michael that Jason had gone to Heaven, he took the news with unsettling serenity.

"I told you," he said.

As Michael got older, things got worse. Patrick's influence compounded while Evelyn found herself being pushed further away. She tried to be a good role model for Michael. She took him to church and taught him about right and wrong. But it all seemed futile. Patrick's influence was too strong.

When Michael was a teenager, his father often pulled him into his study for a closed-door lecture. Only once had Evelyn dared to listen in.

"You are destined for greatness, son," Patrick had said. "Don't let anything make you forget it. Don't let idealism stand in your way. My life has been about putting you in a position to succeed. It's what your grandfather wanted more than anything too. You won't disappoint us. Use the gift to your advantage."

Evelyn shuddered and turned from the door, unwilling to hear more. All her doubts were gone. Her husband was systematically removing the conscience she had worked so hard to foster in Michael, replacing it with narcissism.

In the months that followed, Evelyn rarely slept. Instead she lay awake, trying to think of ways to counteract Patrick's destructive example. In the light of day, she was never brave enough to act on her plans, her fear of retribution holding her paralyzed. As Michael passed from high school into college, rumors of his bad behavior began to reach her. With her last thread of influence being pulled out of Michael's life, Evelyn turned inward. She pushed her head under the sand: ashamed, but unable to challenge the living demons in her life.

With Patrick's sudden illness and death, Evelyn finally gained the freedom she had wanted so long ago. A brief hope that his influence over Michael had died with him flickered and faded as she watched her son surrender to the power of politics. Patrick had gotten his wish, it seemed, leaving Evelyn with nothing but the faintest glimmer of hope for Michael's future.

She kept the Pebble Beach house but remodeled it, emphasizing the Moorish influences in the Spanish Colonial design and removing every trace of her late husband. Traveling was her solace now and she was finally grateful for the wealth that made it easy. When she was home, she wrote passionately – novels filled with the romance and intrigue she had been denied, with love that never failed.

Australia was next on her itinerary. She was leaving in a few weeks and had been looking forward to the trip before she heard about Margaret's accident, before Michael had visited and so carelessly set her world on edge again.

No more, she thought.

The weekend she had just endured made her feel violated. That was something she wouldn't stand for, not anymore. Evelyn picked up the phone and dialed, waiting patiently until her son was on the line.

"I only have a few minutes, Mother," he said.

"As it happens, that's all I need." His brusque tone made it easier. "You and Margaret are always welcome to visit me, Michael, but your entourage is not. I won't suffer through another weekend like this."

Michael hung up without comment. For a moment, Evelyn felt that familiar pinch in her stomach – the one that reminded her she wasn't being pleasing, like her mother had trained her to be. Funny that it was still there, after all these years. She sighed and stood up. Tension was already starting to evaporate from her shoulders. Her call had been the right decision, no matter how Michael responded.

Maybe it's never too late to be a good influence, she thought, *to do the right thing.*

She would hold out hope. Maybe someday soon she would see a change in Michael for the better.

Chapter 22

The medical plaza's courtyard was cool and damp on Monday morning. Fog had crept in from the San Francisco streets, adding to the chill in the air and clinging to the lush plants that encircled a bubbling fountain. Erynne loitered nearby, shivering despite the warm pea coat she wore over a black turtleneck and jeans. She knew it was silly to stay out here when she could be in the warm waiting room reading a magazine, but she couldn't bring herself to go inside yet. Her appointment with Mark's friend from the Northern California Sleep Clinic would come soon enough.

Erynne's dreams over the past few nights were beginning to overwhelm her, even during the daytime. Those featuring her comforting friend were thready, remembered only in a pulse of desperate images. Her nightmares, though, seemed to be growing stronger: both those in the dark forest, where the cries of a baby rang in her ears, and those of the monstrous man who was toying with her now, surely strong enough to strike if that was his wish.

It took every ounce of her courage to tell Mark she was suffering from nightmares like her mother's. His initial silence on the phone line had not been encouraging.

"I need answers," she said, despising the tremor in her voice. "I remembered you once mentioned a friend – a doctor who had some interesting theories about dream-related sleep problems."

"Yes. His name is John Peterson," he said, his voice quiet and clipped. "Let's see how soon we can get you in to see him."

Erynne thanked Mark and hung up the phone, wishing he had at least offered some token resistance. She had hoped he would tell her that an appointment with his friend wasn't necessary. Not yet, anyway. She was even more unsettled by how quickly he called back with a time and directions.

"His clinic is highly regarded," Mark told her. "I think you'll like him. He's easy to talk to. Almost like a dad."

Erynne didn't find his analogy particularly comforting.

After glancing at her watch again, she took a deep breath and went inside, checking in with the nurse at the front desk. She took a seat in the waiting room and skimmed through a pamphlet about the clinic. Dr. Peterson and his partner had both spent most of their careers involved with clinical studies at UCSC and Stanford. Five years ago, they opened this private clinic specializing in dreaming disorders. Dr. Peterson's focus was neuroscience. Erynne would meet him first to learn the basics about the clinic and what they hoped to do for her. His partner, Dr. Holly Leitch, was a psychologist. Erynne had an appointment with her this afternoon.

At Dr. Peterson's request, she had visited her primary physician in Santa Cruz late last week, enduring her prodding and poking with barely concealed impatience. She carried her doctor's notes and a lab report with her, something Dr. Peterson needed to rule out any medical conditions that could explain her nightmares. Despite her grumbling, Erynne acknowledged a faint glimmer of hope in the process. A medical explanation would be welcome – and likely – she tried to tell herself, considering that the dreams had affected two, maybe even three generations of women in her family.

"You must be Erynne O'Keefe."

Deep in thought, Erynne hadn't heard Dr. Peterson's approach. She stood to shake his hand. In his late fifties and bald except for a salt and pepper ring of hair around his head, he did remind her of a father – at least one from television.

"Thank you for seeing me," she said.

"Of course." His smile was bright, crinkling the skin around his eyes. "Anything for Mark. He's a good friend. How's he doing these days?"

"He's well."

Dr. Peterson led her to an elevator, telling Erynne a story about Mark's residency and another about his golf game. For the first time, she wondered how close the two men were and how much he knew of their truncated relationship. They quickly reached his third-floor office, where he pointed Erynne to a pair of club chairs by the window.

"I only spoke to Mark briefly about your situation," he said, leaning on the arm of his chair, "but he warned me that getting information from you might be harder than pulling teeth."

"I'm not that difficult," she said defensively. She sat down and handed him her file.

"Our techniques here do involve a lot of Q and A," he said. "But our questions are far from gratuitous. Are you okay with that?"

Erynne didn't answer. Instead, she looked out the window. The fog was holding its own, offering no diversion from what was happening inside. A sudden desire to throw open the windows and invite the gray obscurity inside passed through her thoughts. Steeling herself, she turned back to Dr. Peterson and nodded.

"Great," he said, springing to his feet with the agility of a man half his age. "In that case, why don't you take a few minutes to relax while I get us some coffee? Cream or sugar?"

After Dr. Peterson left, Erynne rose and walked around the office. A collection of family photos sprinkled the wall behind his credenza: graduations, marriages, tiny infants, vacation shots by a lake, a cruise ship, Disneyland. Framed alongside the photos were several samples of childish artwork.

What was it like to be part of a family? Erynne rarely allowed herself to think about it. But would she be sitting in this office today if she had that kind of support to fall back on?

The concept was so foreign, she almost couldn't imagine the answer. She closed her eyes and thought of curling up on a couch with a sister and a cup of tea, explaining the details of her dreams without restraint and then enduring the inevitable teasing that would follow.

"You're dreaming about an accountant?" the sister would ask with a look of mock disgust. "If you're going to start fantasizing, pick someone more interesting – someone who looks like Matt Damon!"

Serious giggling would follow and Erynne would sleep easier that night, surrounded by her own collection of photos, well secure in the knowledge that whatever happened in her dreams (and no matter how crazy she was) her family would love her anyway.

Erynne opened her eyes, blinking back to reality. *Do families like that really exist*, she wondered?

"Here we go," Dr. Peterson said, coming back with two steaming mugs. They both returned to their chairs. "Are you okay with using one of these?" He wiggled a digital recorder in the air.

"Fine," Erynne said. She cleared her throat and fidgeted in her seat while he switched it on.

"I don't know how much you know about dreaming," he began. "It used to be that we all fell in line with traditional Freudian/Jungian theories about dreams and their psychology. But a number of us are pulling away from those ideas. We believe, first of all, that there is continuity between our waking thoughts and our dreams. Modern cognitive dreaming theory suggests that our dreams embody our thoughts: draws pictures of them, if you will. They give us a subjective and revealing image of what is really on our minds.

"For the most part, dreamers report that they are completely immersed in their dream landscape, unable to detach themselves or even recognize that they are, in fact, dreaming. Not until they wake. A handful, though, report cognition during dreaming: an awareness of the surreality of their landscape, if you will. Dreamers like these often report taking advantage of the limitless nature of their minds. They might take off in flight, for example, slam dunk a basketball or sing an aria.

"Do you identify with either group, Erynne? Do you know you're dreaming while you're still in the dream state?"

"Rarely," she said, clearing her throat. "It's happened a couple of times. Toward the end of a nightmare, I have been able to talk myself into waking up."

"So perhaps the intensity of your fear stimulates your consciousness. Yes, we see that often. Can you make decisions about your dreams? Can you change your environment or control your conversation for example?"

"No," she said. "Not consciously. But when my emotions are heightened, my dream environment sometimes responds." She laughed, embarrassed. "The weather – that sort of thing."

"Interesting. What else?"

"I talk about things more freely than I ever would in life," she said, thinking of the comforting stranger. "I go places I've never been: places that probably don't even exist. If I could control my dreams, I would ask different questions. I would say different things."

I would ask who he is, where he lives.

She shook her head, forcing the thought away.

"Why don't you go ahead and tell me about your dreams. Start anywhere you'd like."

Erynne nodded, feeling strangely breathless as she began with her mother's nightmares and progressed to her own. Her voice was low and emotionless as she spoke. She wondered if it all sounded as bleak to him as it did to her. Concluding with her nightmare from the night before, she explained how the hunter seemed to relish his role, as if stalking her were part of a sick game. Dr. Peterson listened quietly with a slight wrinkle across his brow and his hands crossed easily in his lap. He didn't speak until she was finished.

"Your recollection is remarkably strong," he said, shaking his head in sympathy. "It sounds like you've been having a rough time."

"Are my dreams in any way similar to those of your other patients?" she asked, ready to move to a more clinical discussion.

"They have a repeating pattern, which is typical of nightmares, but their frequency and imprint is unusual," he said. He opened her doctor's report, flipping through it quickly and tapping his fingers against the pages.

"No prescription medications?" he asked, looking up for confirmation.

"No. Could something like that affect my dreams?"

"Some prescriptions have been found to cause bad dreams. Rezulin always come to my mind. It was once a popular drug used to treat diabetes, but nightmares were reported as a side effect. It's off the market now, but there are others. A new smoking-cessation drug, varenicline, also has unusual dreams listed among the possible side effects."

"I wouldn't have thought of that," Erynne said. "But unless my mother and I were taking the same medication..."

Dr. Peterson shook his head. "It's unlikely in your situations, yes. But we don't want to rule anything out – or necessarily infer a connection between your dreams and hers just because they seem to be the same. In truth, there's a lot we don't know about dreaming and nightmares. We have found that somewhere between five and seven percent of adults report problems with nightmares. Of course with some folks, you have to consider their abuse of alcohol or drugs. That still leaves a pretty good chunk of people who – just like you – have chronic bad dreams."

"Drinking makes it worse?"

He considered her over his glasses. "Heavy drinking, yes. Is that a consideration?"

Erynne shook her head. "Not for me, no."

"Your mother?"

"Unfortunately."

"I'm sure it exacerbated the problem," he said, his eyes sympathetic. "That kind of escape is too great a temptation for many to resist. But she would have been better able to cope with a clear head."

Erynne nodded, wondering how many of her bad memories could have been prevented. She pushed the thought away.

"What about my other dreams? They're not disturbing like the nightmares – almost the opposite, in fact – and different than anything I've ever experienced. When I wake up, I almost expect to have sandy feet, to be wearing that nightgown. The taste, smell and feel of the dream is still with me." Erynne couldn't repress the wistfulness in her voice.

"Again, the strong imprint of your dreams is unusual, but your mind may simply be responding to the trauma of losing your mother, creating a safe place for you to grieve."

"For this long?"

"I don't mean to easily dismiss your concern. It's certainly understandable and we can explore several options for analysis and treatment. But a quick fix isn't likely. As much as we study dreaming here, there is still so much we don't understand. It amounts to much more than we know, despite our years of study.

"Dreams are mysterious. They have plagued people for centuries. Most cultures, ancient and modern, have theories about dreams and what their purpose may be. Modern scientific thought has rested on the belief that, while dreams can be very revealing about our personalities, interests and fears, they are devoid of any problem-solving function, which basically means they have no specific purpose." He paused. "But I've never been sure I agree. Our cultural experiences tell us differently.

"For example, American Indians have sought visions in dreams for centuries," he said, shifting in his seat. "There are many legends about dreams of birds or animals lending warriors wisdom and bravery. Likewise, ancient Celtic culture placed great importance on dreaming. Druids were often called in to interpret the dreams of their kings. In fact, Druids were so fearful of where the mind went during sleep, they had guards watch over them through the night to ensure that they would not slip away into the Netherworld."

Erynne nodded. *The Netherworld*. Was that where she went each night?

"Dream lore can be traced even farther, though, into civilization's most ancient stories," he continued. "Did you ever go to Sunday School?"

"No."

"The Bible is filled with stories about the importance of dreams. Joseph and Daniel interpreted dreams as instruments of God, accurately predicting the rise of empires, famine, and even the destruction of Babylon. Even Jesus' earthly father, Joseph, was visited by an angel in a dream, warning him to escape to Egypt to protect the Christ from certain death."

"It's all interesting," said Erynne. "But also very ... mythical."

"Do you think so?" He smiled, turning toward the window. Erynne followed with her eyes, noticing that the landscape was beginning to appear under the softening fog. "I once would have agreed with you, but I see things differently now. The point is, we can speculate and theorize for centuries without learning a lot. Anecdotes, theories, stories, and histories – they mean different things to different people. But the one thing we know for certain is that dreams happen inside your head – invisible to all others, only open to interpretation once revealed by their owner."

Dr. Peterson paused for a moment. "I still find it fascinating," he said quietly, as if astounded by his own words, "but not much to go on when it comes to my work. Instead, my job is to find quantitative data. I need something tangible to solve your dream problems."

"That sounds like exactly what I need."

Turning away from the window, he gestured toward the door. "Come on. Let's take a walk."

Erynne followed him down a long carpeted hallway painted in a pleasant shade of yellow, noticing the carefully placed artwork, mirrors and potted plants.

"This looks more like a hotel than a medical office," she said.

"We try to make it as comfortable as possible for our patients who spend the night," he answered. "Making someone spend such personal time in a sterile office doesn't mesh well with our philosophy. Since we take up the whole third floor of the building, we have been able to create a contained, secure environment for our patients. I've personally spent the night here, looking for things to improve."

As he spoke, Dr. Peterson led Erynne down a second corridor and into a small room full of computer and medical equipment. One wall of the room was covered with a mirrored window. On the other side she could see two separate rooms, each with a bed, night table, lamp and closet. The walls were covered in wallpaper and decorated with more art.

"It's nice," Erynne said. Still, she didn't want to spend the night there.

"We're proud of it," Dr. Peterson said. "We try to keep the technology and machinery out of sight and mind as much as possible. For example, those closets provide more than just space for clothes. They house the EEG, audio and video recording equipment that we use to monitor our patients."

"An EKG monitors the heart, and an EEG monitors ... the brain?"

"That's right. An EEG is a visible record of amplified electrical activity generated by neurons in the brain. We measure this by placing electrode patches – just like those used for EKGs – on different parts of the head. The electrical activity is recorded by a state-of-the-art computerized data acquisition system. Individual patient readings are run through complex computer software that provides quantitative analysis of the EEG mapping. From these programs we get important spectral and coherence analysis, as well as clinical polysomnography.

"Of course, we don't rely on the computers to do all my work," he added with a smile. "I personally examine every report looking for patterns, anomalies – really anything that might give us a clue into what is happening during sleep."

Erynne turned her attention back to the mirrored window. "How many rooms like this are there?"

"Only two others."

"Why so few?"

Dr. Peterson laughed, "My accountant asks, 'Why so many?' The truth is that for years we performed the majority of our studies in sleep labs. But we also consulted sleep journals: a place where patients could document their dreams under natural conditions, in their own beds. We have found that information recorded in these journals can be used just as effectively to study dreaming. In fact, it was a couple of researchers at UCSC who designed a unique coding formula that creates an objective, valid way to record an individual's dream information."

"Will that be my homework? To keep a sleep journal?"

Dr. Peterson crossed his arms and considered the quiet rooms beyond the mirror for a moment. "Actually, I was hoping you would spend at least one night in the lab."

Erynne looked at the rooms with a new perspective. "Is that really necessary? I've booked two nights at a hotel, hoping to take care of some business while I'm in the city."

"Well, how about we split the two. You spend tonight here and tomorrow there – when you'll start using a sleep journal. I'm just concerned because of the suddenness of your symptoms and the extreme violence of your nightmares. I want to see what that looks like on the EEG. It might give us faster results. What do you think?"

Erynne didn't tell him what she really thought. She didn't want to stay the night in the lab, but his suggestion of faster results was too tempting to ignore.

Dr. Peterson led her back to his office. Through his window she could see that the fog had burned off, leaving a beautiful view of the city between the treetops. Her desire to leave the clinic and escape to the obscurity of the city's streets was strong, but she steadied her nerves and returned to her seat.

"Where do we go after exhausting all possibilities here?" she asked.

"The mind is an incredible mystery, Erynne," Dr. Peterson said, sitting down again. "It has fascinated people for centuries. Scientists are still trying to understand how it works, what its limitations are. I'm sure you've heard that humans use only about ten percent of their brain. That's a myth, by the way, with no basis in science. But how much of the brain do we understand?" He wrinkled his nose. "I can't give you a percentage. It's growing, but still low, I believe."

"Someone like me doesn't give it much thought – until something like this happens," Erynne admitted.

Dr. Peterson nodded. "Have you ever heard of genetic memory?"

"No, I haven't."

"It's a fairly recent field of study – and highly theoretical – that suggests a person can hand down not only their physical and mental qualities to their descendants, but their actual memories as well."

"That sounds like science fiction."

Dr. Peterson laughed. "It does, doesn't it? The idea is that our very experiences in life are seared, as it were, on our genes. That those experiences – as genetic memories – can be passed down to our children. I find it fascinating."

Erynne was silent for a moment. "If that theory were true, my dreams could simply be inherited as memories of my mother's dreams?"

He shrugged. "It's not my area of expertise, but if you accept the theory, there's logic in that."

Erynne frowned. "But then, wouldn't the children of Van Gogh, Michelangelo, Einstein all have been greater geniuses than their fathers?" she asked.

"The theory does present some problems, doesn't it?" he responded easily. "As do most. But then, when it comes to science, we often start looking for a particular result, only to find something much better in the process."

Dr. Peterson escorted Erynne down to the courtyard. "It was a pleasure meeting you," he said, shaking her hand. "I'm very hopeful that we can help you with your dreams."

"Thank you, doctor. I'm counting on it."

"I'll have your notes transcribed and sent to Dr. Leitch before your afternoon meeting with her. Don't be surprised if she questions you more thoroughly."

Erynne grimaced. "I was afraid of that."

⋈

"This won't hurt."

Erynne lay still while a nurse named Kate attached the EEG patches to her head. She wore comfortable scrubs covered with sleepy lambs jumping randomly-placed fences. Erynne smiled at the irony.

Kate squeezed her arm before leaving the room. "If you need anything, just press the buzzer."

Erynne turned off the light after Kate left and blinked into the blackness. She had been offered a nightlight but refused it. Such a childish crutch seemed unnecessary – no matter how frightening her dreams had become. Instead, she reasoned that the darkness was best. It would be easier to forget where she was and just pretend she was sleeping in another anonymous hotel room.

But as she settled against her pillow and closed her eyes, the gentle pressure of the EEG patches on her head became more pronounced. She wondered who would be sitting behind the double-sided mirror tonight. How would they see her in the darkness? The thought of a techno-geek outfitted in white lab coat and night-vision goggles made her giggle for a moment. She wondered if she was succumbing to a slight case of hysteria.

Just relax, she told herself. After a few minutes, she succeeded, in part, falling into her more typical bedtime pattern, reviewing her day.

After her morning appointment at the clinic, Erynne met a client for lunch in Chinatown. It felt both good and strange to switch tracks – listening to local society gossip and discussing fashion trends instead of nightmares. She smiled and laughed, fully engaged as far as Becky was concerned, while part of her mind did not stray from the clinic and her dreams.

After lunch she visited a popular new boutique in Union Square.

"Erynne! It's so wonderful to see you!" The owner had greeted her with enthusiasm, wasting no time in moving on to her favorite topic. "When are you going to let me sell EOK here in the city?"

They had gone back to her office and discussed the merits of a joint venture. Exclusivity was Diane's major sticking point, while Erynne worried about the problems involved in opening another production studio.

"It would be necessary if I were to broaden my label," she said. "A daunting undertaking. I'm not sure I'm up for it, honestly."

"But it has merit, right?" asked Diane. "Expansion, growth. You could produce overseas, or in Mexico."

Erynne frowned. "And lose my base, perhaps. My *own* exclusivity. You know my clients love it: the whole experience of visiting my boutique in Santa Cruz, wearing originals."

Still, she promised to give it more thought and said goodbye, hoping that once she solved the mystery of her troubled nights, she could focus more clearly on career decisions.

With more than an hour to kill before her afternoon appointment, Erynne went by her hotel and changed her reservation before stopping by the garment district to say hello to a friend from school. It certainly wasn't the nicest part of the city, but Erynne had always felt perfectly safe in the past. Perhaps it was the pending night that made her suddenly edgy, bustling past a group of harmless transients with a sense of purpose. One, it seemed, had given her a hard look before quickly turning down a shadowed alley.

Probably more afraid than I am, she tried to tell herself.

By the time Erynne returned to the clinic, she was relieved that she would not be venturing out again that night.

But Erynne's visit with Dr. Leitch had been ultimately frustrating. The doctor was astute. Erynne would certainly give her that. She had not wasted time, narrowing her focus to two areas: Erynne's attitude toward her parents and her feelings for the man in her dreams. Erynne had resisted her gentle prodding, but eventually described her last dream with the stranger, including their argument and how angry she had been.

"Have you considered that the stranger serves two valuable functions, Erynne?" Dr. Leitch asked. "He comforts you, yes. But perhaps he also voices your own buried thoughts – those that you have refused to acknowledge yourself. It's fascinating really: a subconscious personification that is changing with your needs."

Erynne crossed her arms, her eyes narrowing. "Fascinating isn't the word I would use. I'm not a case study: I'm dealing with this every night – trying to make sense of it."

"Of course," Dr. Leitch said. "I'm sorry – that was a thoughtless choice of words. I don't like such confrontations in my life either.. I just want you to consider the possibility that the stranger was simply saying what you already know to be true in your heart."

Erynne nodded, turning toward the window. It had been so easy to make her mother the villain, letting her father remain free from responsibility. But had it been fair?

Lifting herself up on her elbow, Erynne punched her pillow into a more comfortable mound. She swallowed a hard lump and lay back down. Letting go of her father's blamelessness was like tasting his death again.

A distant clap of thunder rolled against the sky beyond the heavily-curtained window. Rain began to fall softly only moments later, finding a rhythm that calmed her frayed nerves. Slowly, the stress of Erynne's day began to relax from her muscles and the fog of sleep approached.

Remembering Dr. Peterson's story of the Druids who were guarded in sleep, Erynne realized she felt safer than she had all week. The modern scientists with all their equipment were her sleep guardians, she decided, protecting her from the Netherworld that was drawing her farther from reality with each passing night.

Chapter 23

"Coffee, Peter?"

Kate stuck her head in the doorway and smiled, rousing Peter from semi-consciousness. He quickly took his feet off the desk and rubbed his eyes.

"Yeah, that would be great." Straightening his glasses, he looked at the digital clock above the door as she placed the steaming mug in his hands. 2:54 a.m.

Kate let the door swing shut behind her while Peter retrieved the textbook that had fallen from his lap. He remembered reading chapter sixteen. Evidently he hadn't found molecular biology particularly riveting. He hoped his students found it more so on Monday morning.

"Ouch!"

The coffee sloshed over the rim and landed on his wrist. He put it aside impatiently and turned his attention to the sleeping patient beyond the two-way mirror. The hard copy of her brain mapping had spilled into a wire basket, and he scanned it, looking for areas of active sleep.

So far, her sleeping patterns had been predictable. The progression of low voltage, fast frequency readings that indicated wakefulness gradually increased in amplitude until stage one sleep, where he saw sharp waves and scattered spikes. As with most sleepers, she had spent the majority of her time alternating between stage two and REM sleep.

"Anything interesting tonight?" Kate stepped back through the door, a clipboard in her hand.

Peter bravely reached for the coffee.

"Nothing to report. Dr. Peterson thought she might display prominent physical signs of nightmares, but nothing so far." He looked back at the monitor. "Looks like she's just now heading back into stage two. I'm guessing it will be about ninety minutes before we see any more REM."

Sudden movement through the window caught Peter's attention. The patient was moving her head from side to side.

"Looks like you might have been wrong." Kate put her clipboard down and walked out the door. Peter watched her enter the patient's room to check the monitors. She quickly returned

"Well, she definitely has the physical symptoms. Blood pressure and heart rate are up, her breathing is heavy. You can see for yourself how her reflexes are responding."

Peter had stopped listening, his attention diverted by the activity on the paper in front of him. Kate leaned over his shoulder.

"What is it?"

"Right here." Peter pointed to sharp spikes on the paper, still wet with ink. "It looks like a K-Complex ... but not."

"I don't understand."

"I don't either. That's the point," he said, straightening in his chair. "K-complexes are sharp, upward waves followed by a drop below the tracing line. Only the amplitude on these ... well, they're too high for stage two sleep, like delta waves. Yet the frequency is too fast for stage three, and she's obviously dreaming."

Kate looked back through the window. The patient was still thrashing, but now she was moaning too. "Do you think we should call Dr. Peterson?"

Peter didn't know what to think. He'd been monitoring patients for a couple of years now, since he entered graduate school. He'd never seen anything like this.

"Yeah," he nodded his head. "You better get him on the phone."

Chapter 24

Jack ignored the loud argument his neighbors were having, even though he could hear every word through the thin walls. Instead he stared vacantly out the window. Raindrops mixed with dirt and grime combined with the light from a Michelob sign in the bar across the street cast a strange glow across Jack's face, making his eyes flicker like fire.

He drummed dirty fingernails impatiently on the cracked Formica table and stared at his cell phone. It rang almost as if on demand. He picked it up immediately.

"Yes?"

"What do you have for me?"

Jack knew the voice. An eager smile crossed his face.

"I saw her today, sir. Just like you thought."

Jack heard a sharp intake of breath. The caller cleared his throat.

"Have you learned her name?"

Now why was he having her followed if he didn't even know her name?

"No." He swallowed. "I tried to hear it, but you told me not to get too close. If you'd let me lift her wallet..."

"Stop whining, Jack," the caller said. "I told you, no. Where is she staying?"

"She checked in at the Hilton, but hasn't been back tonight."

"What? I told you to keep an eye on her!"

"Don't worry," Jack licked his lips nervously and tried to keep his voice steady. "She dropped off some luggage. She has to go back for it sometime, right? When she does, I'll follow her."

"Don't mess this one up." There was a pause. "And Jack, be discreet. You're out there on your own if you get caught."

"I understand. You got nothing to worry about."

Jack slid his phone shut and wiped sweaty hands on his jeans before reaching into his pocket for the drawing. He unfolded it carefully. Still, it was beginning to show signs of wear. He couldn't help it. She was so pretty – so clean compared to the girls he knew.

But he had been doubtful when he'd first seen the sketch.

"Don't you have a photograph?"

"That will have to do."

The man had talent, he'd give him that. And when he'd seen her in person down near the garment district, it was all he could do not to reach out and touch her.

But that's what had gotten him into trouble before.

No, this one had to go by the book, like the man said. Still, even the thought of scoping out her hotel again sent a rush of anticipation through his veins. He would have to be more careful from now on. She had looked right at him this afternoon. He'd had no place to go but the alley, but what else was he going to do? Go strike up a conversation?

"Easy, Jack," he told himself, carefully folding the drawing and grabbing his jacket. "Don't blow it again."

Chapter 25

I conceive the notion that we live, each one of us, a double life ... sleeping and waking.

– Gerald Bullett

Erynne read the quote the day before on Dr. Leitch's office wall. Tonight it ticked like a clock in her mind – sleeping and waking, sleeping and waking. Sighing, she walked toward her hotel room window and pushed aside the heavy draperies, staring out at the lights of San Francisco. Union Square was pulsing with life down below, but Erynne felt far removed from it all. She had in fact made a point of avoiding it tonight, ordering room service rather than visiting one of her favorite local restaurants.

Turning back toward her table where fabric samples and sketches were pushed to the side to make room for her dinner tray, she tried to will herself to focus on one or the other. Eat or work. Surely she couldn't go wrong with either. Instead her thoughts vacillated between sleeping and waking: her nightmare last night and her discussion with Dr. Peterson this morning.

She wished she had handled things differently. She wished she had shown more reserve, held her emotions in check. But the nightmare had unsettled her more than any other: a mosaic of themes twisted together to strike at the very core of her fears.

Dr. Peterson had been at her bedside the moment she woke, apparently called in by the technician during the middle of the night.

"Can you tell me about your dream?" he asked.

Erynne's initial response had been an almost violent denial. Still shivering and paranoid, she curled into a knot at the head of her bed and stayed that way until the gray dawn offered her nerves a welcome reprieve. Dr. Peterson waited patiently until her breathing was measured, her heartbeat normal.

"I was in the forest," she finally said, her voice flat. "The trees were dense and I was moving fast, almost floating. I couldn't feel my feet. I couldn't feel much of anything because I was bound somehow and unable to turn my head. In past dreams, this was when I would panic and try to scream, but I didn't last night. I wasn't alone. I was with an old woman who wore a thick wool shawl. She tried to comfort me. She gave me my necklace," Erynne touched her throat. "Then she led me through the trees, down a hillside and toward a cottage where three lights burned in the window."

She shuddered, drawing her knees closer to her chest.

"As soon as I saw the lights, I pulled back, panicked. She urged me forward, telling me I was safe, but I knew it wasn't true. I knew what waited inside the cottage – death for her and worse for me. I shook my head and tried to pull her away. I opened my mouth to speak, but words would not come. The baby started crying then and I covered my ears, spinning around. We had to find the baby. We had to hide her – she was in danger.

"But it was too late," Erynne said. "He heard the baby crying. He must have. He threw open the door and rushed out, flanked by others. They all wore robes, like the Druids you told me about, with hoods that covered their faces. But I knew who he was, even without seeing his face. The way he always moves toward me, the slow purpose of his steps. He knows he'll reach me someday. For now he seems content with the chase, and I never disappoint him."

For a moment, Erynne couldn't continue. The doctor waited.

"I turned and ran, pulling the woman along with me," she finally said. "But she was so old, and I knew she was terrified. She thought she had planned it all so well – that she had eluded them. And then suddenly they were surrounding her. I couldn't keep her hand in my grasp. She was just gone."

Erynne shook her head and tears began to fall. "I didn't try to leave her behind, but I knew it would happen. She never escapes. She sacrificed herself so that I would have a chance.

"He didn't stop, though." Her face twisted in pain. "He pushed past them, letting them do his dirty work as he continued to chase me through the trees. I started to climb a hill, pulling myself up by my hands, it was so steep. I was bleeding, cutting myself on the sharp rocks, but I didn't stop. I couldn't. My lungs were burning for air, but I kept climbing. And then I heard another voice calling from a distance. I couldn't see him, but I knew he was just out of reach – my friend. Maybe if I just kept going, I would find him."

This time Erynne paused for so long that Dr. Peterson was compelled to prompt her.

"What happened then, Erynne?" he asked softly. "How did it end?"

"I kept climbing and the hunter kept chasing, but my friend never found me. His voice faded until it was nothing. I could feel the hunter's breath on my neck when I woke." She shuddered. "He was so close – and I know it sounds crazy, but I can't help wondering..." her voice trailed off.

"What, Erynne?"

She looked up, meeting his eyes. "What happens after I disappear from the dream? Does it go on? Because right before I woke up, it felt like – no, I was *certain* that after the hunter caught me, he would go looking for my friend."

Erynne's last words hung in the air just as the sun broke over the horizon, peeking in through her window with happy curiosity, at odds with her black memories.

"You've never dreamed about the old woman before?"

"No."

"But you spoke with expectation, as though you knew her story."

"I did. It was like a story my mother told me as a child." She shook her head. "But this was different. *I* was in the story and the hunter from my dreams had become the villain."

Dr. Peterson left her to shower and change, asking her to meet him in his office whenever she was ready. Erynne took her time, trying to focus on each task, but the dream continued to cling to her. The baby's cries, her stalker's pursuit and the stranger's frantic voice were impossible to wash from her memory. She'd never dreamed of them all at once. It felt like an ominous crescendo, dragging her toward an inevitable and dreadful climax.

"I'd like you to stay another night or two, Erynne," Dr. Peterson said as soon as she had taken a seat in his office.

"No." She shook her head. "I can't."

The idea of spending another night was impossible to fathom. To Erynne, the nightmare was tied to the clinic. Discussing her dreams yesterday had been like stirring them together in a Petri dish and setting them under a microscope.

"But, Erynne," he protested. "I don't think you understand what we recorded last night. We don't even understand it. We can't identify the meaning of the irregular spikes on your brain scan. In truth, I haven't been able to produce one example of a similar situation. I need to call in some favors, get some help. The genetic memory idea seems a lot more likely today than it did yesterday. We need more time to understand what's happening to you."

Erynne closed her eyes and put her head in her hands. She knew she should be pleased by what he was telling her. It was strong evidence that there was a reason for her dreams after all. She wasn't crazy. She wasn't delusional. But it didn't matter this morning. She felt drained and defeated.

"I'm not ruling out more study. Make your calls, figure out a plan and get back to me." She shook her head again. "But I can't do it tonight. I can't."

Shouldering her overnight bag, Dr. Peterson walked Erynne down to the courtyard. The sun was still twinkling against the dew-covered foliage, another stark contrast to the bleakness Erynne felt within.

"Use your dream journal and make a follow-up appointment with Dr. Leitch," he said. "And Erynne, don't forget that what you are experiencing is very real. The EEG data doesn't lie."

But does it make any difference? Erynne thought, looking away.

"You can't lose hope," he said, as if she had spoken out loud. "And please, don't go through this alone. I can see that you're independent. You're obviously used to shouldering heavy burdens without help. But it sounds like you've got some people who are willing to be there for you – Mark, for one, and your other friend – the one who likes to mother you. They want to help. I'm sure of that."

Erynne tried to imagine carrying this to Gretchen, but instead she thought about the comforting stranger from her dreams, and then about her father's death and how she had suffered alone.

"I don't know how." This time she was startled by the sound of her voice, even though it was barely a whisper. She hadn't meant to speak out loud.

"Hope for brighter days, Erynne – and have a little faith. When well-placed and willingly sought, faith can be a great comfort. Prayer is always a good place to start."

Erynne thanked the doctor and walked away. She wouldn't admit that she *had* been praying: silently, artlessly – ever since her first nightmare. But she had yet to see the benefit that Dr. Peterson promised. Instead, she now believed more fully in evil than ever – maybe because it seemed to be seeping through to her daylight hours.

She felt it today as she moved around the city. Whether meeting with a textile representative in Russian Hill or placing an order for notions and supplies South of Market, she felt like she was being watched, as if the monster from her dreams had learned to find her not only on the cobblestone street, but on the streets of San Francisco.

Weary of looking over her shoulder, Erynne had retreated to her hotel room early and spent the better part of her afternoon attending to e-mails, phone calls and paperwork. After finally forcing herself to eat a few bites of her cold dinner, she had switched on the television and watched part of a taped stage performance of *Turandot* on PBS. Aside from the expectedly impressive *Nessun Dorma*, the opera wasn't interesting enough to hold her attention. She flipped absently for a while, pausing for Rachel Ray and a local weather report, breezing past reality that wasn't real and music television that featured no music.

Impatiently, she switched off the TV and rose to double-check the security latch on her door. With nothing else to do, she brushed her teeth and climbed between the covers.

Waking and dreaming. The clock didn't rest. Twilight and dawn kept coming whether she was ready or not. But would tonight be blissful or horrific?

Erynne had tried throughout the day to be hopeful. Dr. Peterson would find others to confer with and she would steel her nerves and submit to more nights at his clinic, more tests. But what would they learn that could change her reality? She still had to sleep every night, and wake up each morning. And even if there were a magic pill or special therapy that made the dreams vanish as quickly as they had arrived...

Then I would never see him again.

The thought triggered an ache so deep in her heart, it made her breath catch in her throat and her eyes fill with tears. She was becoming more entangled in her dreaming world with each passing night, each tick of the clock. And as Erynne drifted off the sleep, she wondered: was she more terrified of getting lost there or of never going back?

Her dream came well after midnight, giving her a few hours of restful sleep before she found herself once again sitting on the beach, staring out at the untroubled sea. Her companion approached from behind and sat beside her without a word. The wind picked up just then, bringing with it his distinctive scent: not cologne, but a mixture of soap and aftershave that she had come to love. Erynne's heart fluttered happily at his presence, at the way his warm arm brushed against hers.

221

This is the way it should be, she thought, hardly able to recall the painful emotion she had greeted him with during their last visit.

"Forgive me?" she asked, turning to look at him. He leaned close and kissed her softly on the lips, smiling as her eyes widened in surprise.

"Forgiven," he said, curling his arm behind her back and stroking her hair. "I'm sorry I haven't been here for you."

"But you tried, didn't you? I could feel you there, somehow." She leaned against his shoulder, repressing a shudder.

His arm tightened around her.

"I knew you were in trouble, but I couldn't reach you. Every time I got close, you were farther away."

Erynne pulled back and looked at his face, searching his eyes for comfort. "What if he comes back?"

He drew her back into his arms, but not before she saw his eyes darken with frustration. For several minutes he said nothing, then he lifted Erynne's hand and threaded his fingers through hers.

"I've been looking for you all my life, even though I didn't know it," he said, his voice a whisper. "If I get nothing more than these brief encounters with you in the night, it will still be more than I ever dreamed of. There's something between us that can't be chased away by monsters. And no matter what happens, I'll always find my way back to you here."

Erynne closed her eyes and squeezed his hand, for a moment unable to speak. The raw emotion in his voice echoed the silent wishes of her heart. He didn't promise to be there every time she needed him or threaten vengeance on her stalker. But his simple statement of unity made her feel safer than ten thousand words of bravado. He was hers, and she was his. Time, distance and the darkest intentions of a black heart couldn't take that away.

"I have never been able to put my faith in anyone," she said. "I've always been strong – too strong to rely on others, but too weak to trust anyone either." She shook her head. "I see that now: how I've pushed everyone away. But not you. Because I can't – or maybe because everything felt safe in this place before he came. I don't know which. But I need you to know: I trust you. I love you."

Tilting her head back, she found his eyes, looking back at her with intensity and understanding. Then he was touching her face, wiping away tears she didn't know had fallen.

"He can't change us. He can't change this." His words were just a whisper as he drew her once again to his lips. Everything else melted away.

They sat together until dawn, Erynne leaning against his chest with his arms around her, warm and comforting, strong and real. She wanted to stay in the safety of his embrace forever, but the sky was growing lighter. She turned often to look at him, to study his face, determined to remember every detail once daylight dragged her back to reality.

Still, as the dawn crested the horizon, panic crept in.

"What can we do?" she asked.

"Be careful," he whispered, kissing her temple. "And please: stay safe until I find you."

Chapter 26

"I just don't understand this, Colin."

Joy stood helplessly by the foot of the bed as Colin pushed another pair of jeans into a duffle bag. He paused for only a moment to shoot her a look of frustration.

"What are you going to do? Walk in and tell her that you've been dreaming about her, even before you saw her at the airport?"

Colin wiped his hands over tired eyes. "I don't know, Mom. But what else can I do? I can't ignore this."

Colin had not planned on seeing his mother before he left. He would have called to tell her he was out of town, but her unexpected visit had changed those plans – along with the careful words he would have used to explain his trip. In a hurry to leave for the airport, he had been in no frame of mind to put off her pointed questions, especially after she saw the photograph that still sat on his night table.

In a disjointed and hurried fashion, he had told her about his dreams, seeing the woman at the airport and finding the business card that he hoped had fallen from her bag.

"I think this was her mother," he said, handing the photograph to Joy before digging in the night table drawer for his wristwatch.

"What? Why would you think that?"

"Because I dreamed about her too. Just once. Before I started dreaming about the woman at the airport."

Joy's breath caught audibly in her throat.

"She was older," Colin said. "But then suddenly she was young again – that's the only reason I recognized her. She told me: 'Protect her.' I didn't understand." He pushed his hands through his hair. "I'm so dense sometimes. But I finally figured it out. It's her daughter – the woman I'm dreaming about now. And she's in some kind of danger."

"Colin, would you listen to yourself? You're not making any sense. It's scaring me."

"I'm sorry I didn't tell you about it, Mom, but I have to do something." Colin's voice pitched, pleading. "You understand that, right? If my dreams are anything like Dad's, we can pretty much bet they won't go away on their own."

Joy sat down on the foot of Colin's bed, her face ashen.

"Mom, I'm sorry."

Colin dropped the photo on top of his open duffel bag and squatted in front of her. He was such an idiot, bringing up his father's dreams – reminding her of the woman in the photo. "I wish I could spare you this. I would have figured out a gentler way to explain – if I had my head on straight."

Joy took a shaky breath, squaring her shoulders. "You're so much like your father," she said thickly, putting her hand on his right arm where a dark patch of skin was half concealed by the edge of his polo shirt. "Even down to your birthmark. He always regretted hurting me too. I saw it in his eyes, but I was always so stubborn. I don't think I wanted to know the truth. Now I wish I had. It would have been easier for him. Easier for me too."

Colin put his hand over hers. It had to be so difficult for her to watch him leave like this, chasing the woman from his dreams.

"I'll be back, Mom. But this is something I have to do."

"But she didn't recognize you at the airport," she said.

"She didn't look at me," he said with conviction. "Not even a glance. She was embarrassed about spilling her purse. She was scared of something too – another reason I need to go."

"Can't you just call her?" his mother asked. "Or e-mail, text…"

"Can you imagine that, Mom? Getting that message? If she's not already freaked out by what's going on, that would certainly do the trick."

"So why can't you just ask her," Joy grimaced, "you know – during a dream – if it was her?"

"It doesn't work that way," he said wearily. He rose and walked toward the closet, where he began searching among an untidy pile of sweatshirts on the top shelf. "Believe me, if I had any control over what I said or did during these dreams …" his voice trailed off.

Colin's sleep habits had been erratic ever since he saw the woman at the airport last week. Somehow he had managed to stumble through his meeting with Victor Lyon, but his concentration at work had been shot. It had been even worse after losing her in the fog after their argument. Why had he insisted on picking a fight?

The forest nightmare had only made things worse. His desperation to find her had not dissipated when he woke, but rather hardened into an irrational knot of panic. Last night's dream had eased his discomfort only slightly, and settled the question of whether he would do anything about the business card he found at the airport.

She said she loves me.

His heart lurched at the memory – as clear and strong as if it had been said in the light of day. And he knew she needed him too. The fear in her eyes had been palpable. Even he had felt its validity, pulsing along the edge of their dream world – an evil lurking beyond the shadows, obscured by the darkness.

Colin called his boss first thing this morning to ask for a few days off, citing a personal emergency without elaboration. Logic and rational thought were thrown to the wind. He was determined to go.

"Are you ready, Amigo?"

Colin heard Hector's voice calling through the back door.

"He's taking me to the airport," he explained to his mother as he zipped his bag and headed through the house with her trailing behind.

"Colin, maybe you're just lonely," she said with a trace of desperation in her voice. "Give it a few days to settle in your mind. If you still feel the same, then go. Oh, hello Mr. Garcia."

"Mrs. Green," said Hector, nodding. "Nice to see you again. It's good to see our boy taking some time off finally, huh?"

Joy offered a vague smile, but said nothing else as they walked to the driveway. Colin stowed his bag in Hector's trunk while she looked on, her arms folded across her chest.

A brisk breeze had picked up, carrying purple and yellow blossoms from Colin's Jacaranda and Palo Verde trees across the driveway. Vague thoughts about Mays past crossed his mind.

Allergy season, blossoming trees, Bermuda grass and the onset of Phoenix's hot season. He had once thought about planning his pool this month. How could the mundane realities of life be so important one spring and yet so inconsequential the next?

"I have to go, Mom, or I'll miss my plane."

Hector got into the driver's seat and started the engine.

"I don't want you getting hurt. Please, Colin. Consider."

"There may be only one chance in a million that this is the woman I've been dreaming about, but I've got to take it." Digging the business card out of his pocket, he looked at it again, reassuring himself that it was still there.

"Colin, wait ..." she protested. But he was already opening the car door.

"Don't worry, Mom," he said with a parting smile – the first one he'd worn today. He flicked the card with his fingers. "Let's just hope that Erynne O'Keefe really is the woman of my dreams."

"Wait! Did you say Erynne O'Keefe?" Joy asked sharply.

But Colin didn't hear her. The car was already pulling away. Joy was left standing alone in the driveway with a look of astonishment on her face.

Chapter 27

Erynne stood in her studio, examining the skirt on her dress form. It wasn't draping well and she was beginning to suspect the integrity of the wool.

"I don't have time for this today," she told the empty room. Putting down her pincushion, she walked back to her work table and made a note to call the mill. Looking over the list of designs still needing attention this week, she saw that all of them were in some stage of development, but most were waiting on issues to be resolved outside the studio, outside her control.

It doesn't matter. Keep busy. Stay focused.

She'd been repeating that mantra to herself since dawn, but her work load wasn't cooperating, leaving gaps and stops, giving her mind too much time to wander. She looked at the telephone on Gretchen's desk, fantasizing about an emergency call from Genevieve's – maybe a favorite client needing a custom wedding gown – anything to keep her too busy to think. But the phone didn't ring.

Stifling a sigh, Erynne walked toward the window and watched people pass by on the mall below. Sam was tuning his guitar on the other side of the street. He looked up as she opened the window and waved before starting a song that sounded vaguely familiar. Dave Matthews maybe. It was an unusually warm day and Erynne inhaled deeply as a breeze passed through the room, bringing with it the smell of the sea and, once again, the memory of her dream. She blushed, remembering details. Twisting her necklace around her fingertip, she leaned against the window frame, bothered that for all she could recall, her companion's features continued to be unclear, as if she were looking at him through a blurry window.

"I'll find you," he had whispered in her ear.

She closed her eyes, fighting the memory, the way it felt like a string tied to her heart – either tugging it sharply or lifting it like a balloon. It didn't matter what he said, she reminded herself, or what *she* had said in return. It was only a dream.

The sound of Gretchen's voice on the staircase made her jump, startling the birds that were perched on the window sill. Had the lunch hour really passed so quickly? She checked her watch. Yes, in fact it was much later than she thought – nearly a quarter to two. Frowning, she turned back to her work table. She didn't want to be caught daydreaming. Gretchen didn't need another excuse to frown at her from across the room.

She grabbed a pen and sketchpad just as Gretchen entered the room with Len at her heels.

"How was lunch?" she asked.

"Good," Gretchen said. "Gabriella's – it's one of my favorites, of course."

Erynne put down her pen. Something was wrong. Gretchen was standing awkwardly in the middle of the room while Len stood just inside the door, holding several old books in his hands.

"What is it?" Erynne asked, her eyes volleying between them.

Gretchen took a few steps toward Erynne's work table, her expression difficult to read. She pulled a familiar book from her purse.

"I have your mother's journal," she said. "I'm sorry I kept it so long. The story was so interesting – so sad. Your mother was a good writer. It read almost like a novel, don't you think? I don't imagine she told it like that when you were a girl."

"No, but she was a good story teller," Erynne admitted.

"There's a talisman mentioned in the story, do you remember? The one the old woman thought would protect the baby from evil."

"Yes, I remember."

Gretchen turned through the pages of the journal and began to read aloud.

"Here it is:

'*The princess was asleep, bless her soul, and oblivious to the wind, cradled snugly in the sling the old woman had fastened under her shawl. Still she worried about having her out in the cold. Knowing that the talisman was securely fastened around the child's swaddling gave her some comfort.*'"

Erynne shifted in her seat. Hearing her mother's story made her uncomfortable, reminding her of the dream she had at the clinic. "What's this about, Gretchen?"

Gretchen glanced at Len, who had inched his way toward them. He piled his books onto the edge of the table with a resounding thud and began searching through them.

"Last night I read your mother's journal to Len," she said. "He thought the story sounded familiar."

"Really?" Erynne frowned. "I always assumed it was a family thing."

"Yes, well that's what I would think too. I certainly had never heard it – but then Len started doing some searching this morning and he found something. Something we just had to show you."

Len had opened his largest book, which Erynne now gave her full attention. It looked very old, its pages yellow and brittle and mostly filled with text, some of which appeared to be in an unfamiliar language. Len was tapping his finger underneath a pen and ink drawing that was labeled: *Sacred oak talisman, eighth century Ireland.*

"That's my necklace!" Erynne said. She reached up instinctively and fingered the stone as she scrutinized the drawing. The artist had portrayed it lying on the folds of a piece of delicate fabric, which served to accentuate its weight. Lines and shadows were carefully contoured and shaded, mimicking the reality of Erynne's necklace down to the placement of the hole, through which a dark cord, rather than a gold chain, was drawn.

"Len saw the necklace at your house and thought it looked familiar," Gretchen explained. "When he read your mother's fairytale, it triggered his memory and he went searching through his books."

"It took me a while to find it," Len said, "but there's a legend that goes with that necklace."

"A legend?"

Len nodded. "In essence, it's the same as your mother's story."

"And the talisman in the story... that's your necklace!" Gretchen added.

"Erynne, what you have around your neck could very well be tied to a story that goes back eleven hundred years, maybe more."

"You really think it's that old?"

"You would need to have a mineralogist help date it, but ... well, yes, I do."

Erynne leaned back in her chair, her head filled with images from the story, from her dream. "Can you tell me about the legend? Where it came from?"

"It's Irish, for one thing. Irish literature dates from the sixth century, largely based on oral tradition. We call it Irish, but it's actually Gaelic. Most Gaelic stories were similar to the Arthur tales, dealing with mysticism and supernatural elements, much like your mother's story. Even though the Druids – a class of pagan priests, if you will – began to disappear in the sixth century, the oral tradition of storytelling went on long after that."

Pulling another thick book from the middle of his pile, he flipped through its pages.

"Anyway, the point is that the legend about the talisman probably originated from the ninth or tenth century. The story says that there was a Druid who was an adviser to the ruler of a small kingdom, or *tuatha*. He would be the villain from your mother's story. His name was Modranhe, sometimes written as Modrahein. Even though he came from a long line of vision seers, or *tabshears* -- well-respected nobles who used their abilities to help solve problems for the kingdom – he was more interested in gaining personal power.

"Some versions of the legend – probably those transcribed by monks, who would have put a Christian slant on things –

indicate that Modranhe made a deal with the Devil to gain more visionary power than he came by naturally. Others say he got his power by visiting the Netherworld and stealing it from an evil spirit. Either way you look at it, Modranhe added the gift of mind reading to his arsenal and began to use it to manipulate regional nobles. He quickly gained a fair amount of control over them, which weakened the power of several kingdoms.

"The kings knew what Modranhe was doing, but found it difficult to rally many supporters to their cause. Even though he was known for cruelty and mercilessness among the villages and *tuathas*, his power of manipulation was almost impossible for people to fight."

"Are we still talking about a legend?" Erynne asked skeptically. "Which part is history and which is just a story?"

"Hard to tell the difference," said Len. "Remember the King Arthur legends? He was probably a real man – perhaps even the round table was real – but what else? We know that not *all* of the Arthurian legends can be true, but how many are? That's how these oral traditions go – like fish stories that get exaggerated and changed, but have some essence of truth."

"So the trick is figuring out where truth ends and legend begins?"

"Or maybe it's just about what you choose to believe," Len said.

Erynne shook her head. "So what happened next with Modranhe?"

"While he was in the middle of gaining all this control, something not too short of miraculous happened. The legend says that one day, at the same hour of the day, two babies were born to queens in neighboring kingdoms – one boy and one girl. After the births, a well-respected *tabshear* named Cruithne de Magnal prophesied that the children had a natural bond between them. They were soul mates, if you wish. She proclaimed that the betrothal and eventual marriage of the two babies would one day have the mystical effect of removing Modranhe's special powers, thereby giving the kingdoms back their sovereignty and freedom."

"That's just like Mom's story," Erynne said.

"Yes. Cruithne de Magnal was well known since her own childhood for *da shealladh*, the gift of two sights," Len said. "She would be the old woman from your fairytale."

And the one who gave me my necklace in the dream, Erynne remembered. She suppressed a shudder.

"Of course other translations of the tale – the ones that rely less on folklore and superstition – suggest that the betrothal of the babies was a political decision, showing a united front of power against Modranhe and his growing forces."

"That sort of thing happened all the time during feudal societies, right?"

"Absolutely," Len agreed. "And naturally when Modranhe learned about the union, he mounted an offensive. Both royal families feared for the safety of their children until a secret plan was executed, one which would remove the children from their kingdoms by night on *Samhain* – All Hallow's Eve. They were to be hidden until the threat had passed, or until they were old enough to rule a united kingdom."

"According to Mom's story the vision seer devised the plan."

"That matches the legend. Cruithne would hide the princess and another trusted servant of the king was to hide the baby prince. Only a handful of people knew about the plan."

"But the babies were not hidden successfully, were they?" Erynne asked.

Len shook his head. "Unfortunately, no. They all underestimated Modranhe's skill in reading minds – or perhaps he had a spy within their trusted circle. When he learned of their plans, he laid a trap for them at the rendezvous point."

"A cottage in the woods," Erynne said, "...*hidden in a thick glen of trees at the foot of a hill.* In the fairytale, that's where the princess was taken."

"Yes. Modranhe and his soldiers killed Cruithne and another loyalist guard and took the babies. Neither child was ever found. Modranhe eventually gained control of the entire region.

"Folklore says that his special powers were passed down through his bloodline, giving his descendants the power to continue with his brand of oppression. Stories about Modranhe, his son, Corthel, and other descendants disappeared around the end of the eleventh century. They go from one end of the spectrum to the other in terms of believability."

Erynne closed her eyes, imagining the story as Len had told it, merging it with the fairytale images she had carried since childhood.

"If any of the story is true – it's so heartbreaking," said Gretchen. "It would be hard enough to give up your child, but to learn that the plan meant to save her had brought about her destruction?"

"That's not how these stories usually go," Len said. "Think of Sleeping Beauty or Baby Moses."

Gretchen shook her head. "Cruithne would have been filled with guilt, knowing she had failed. Death was probably a mercy."

The baby's pitiful wails echoed across the ravine and returned to her ears like daggers.

"Erynne? Are you okay? You look white as a ghost."

238

"I'm okay," she said, rising to her feet and walking to the window. "I just need a little air." She leaned against the sill, inhaling the cool sea air until her heartbeat returned to normal. The shadows were beginning to lengthen across the pavement below and only a handful of shoppers passed by, reminding Erynne that the afternoon was almost gone. She reached up and touched her necklace again, the contact reconnecting her with reality.

"What about the talisman?" she asked, her voice hallow. "It certainly didn't protect the baby, did it?"

"No, you're right, of course." Len was sorting through his stack of books again, pulling out several rumpled pages that looked like they had been printed off the Internet. "But it is significant. Your mother's story ended with the babies' abduction – but the legend goes on, telling us that Cruithne was not yet dead when loyalist soldiers found her the next morning. One of the soldiers reported that she was chanting, and that she was drawing a symbol in the dirt floor where she lay bleeding to death. The symbol was like an oak tree, narrow at the bottom, ballooning out into an uneven cluster at the top."

Erynne felt a surge of adrenaline. "Like my necklace," she said.

Len nodded. "By piecing together what the soldiers saw and what the queen knew, it seems that Cruithne had fastened a talisman around the baby just before they made their escape from the castle," he said. "It was a piece of *Connemara* stone cut in the shape of an oak tree. She told the queen it was sacred – that it would bring luck to the child."

Erynne unfastened the necklace and held it up to the light, trying to imagine it with sharply cut edges rather than smooth curves, worn down by years – perhaps centuries – of handling.

"Is this *Connemara?*" she asked, holding it out to Len.

"That's what it looks like in pictures, but I'm no rock expert."

Why did it feel as if the stone were suddenly pulsing in her hand, brought to life by the words of a history professor? Erynne pushed the thought away, but her mind couldn't escape the story – the inevitable conclusion.

"So Modranhe had the babies killed," she said.

"Maybe, maybe not," Len said.

"But why wouldn't he?"

"I don't know for sure. There are some obscure stories that conjoin with this legend, adding an entirely new dimension to the story." Len tapped on his print outs. "Some of it's rather Oedipal, really. There were reports that the man who carried out Modranhe's orders to kidnap the infant boy was hesitant about killing him. On his deathbed he confessed that he had abandoned the child in a field, allowing providence to decide whether he would live or die. From there it became hearsay and conjecture – some saying the child was carried away and raised by fairies, others claiming he was found and sold to a wealthy family who left Ireland soon after – no one knows the truth."

"And the baby girl?"

"It's impossible to know for sure. There were rumors linking her to a servant girl who was raised in a brothel not too far from where the kidnappings took place. She would have been about the princess's age – raised by a woman who was ... less than maternal, shall we say. When she was twelve or thirteen years old and her duties at the brothel changed for the worst, she stabbed a man sent to her room. One of Modranhe's henchmen, incidentally. They didn't find him until morning. By then she was long gone."

Erynne rubbed the necklace with her thumb. "This piece of rock has never brought luck to anyone," she said quietly.

"No, but it does appear to be special. How else would it have survived for so long?"

"If it is the same stone. I'm not convinced."

"Erynne, you told me you dreamed about the fairytale," Gretchen said. "That's not the only strange dream you've had, is it?"

Erynne looked up sharply. "Mark ..." she said slowly. "He told you?"

"No! Honey, of course not." Gretchen moved toward her, grabbing her hands. "You fell asleep on the way home from San Jose when I picked you up from the airport. You were talking in your sleep ..."

Erynne flushed and pulled away, crossing her arms over her chest.

"And, of course, I saw the business card for the sleep clinic in San Francisco." Gretchen smiled apologetically. "I didn't mean to pry, but you left it on the corner of your worktable."

Erynne rubbed her fingers over the bridge of her nose. "I've been having strange dreams – nightmares even," she said after a moment, her voice flat. "My mom had them too." She looked up at Gretchen, her expression dark. "Any more questions you have – ask me directly, would you?"

"Erynne, it wasn't like that..."

"Never mind," Erynne said wearily. "What does any of this have to do with Len's history lesson?"

"It has to do with Cruithne's tree – the one she drew in the dirt while she was dying," Len said, looking anxiously between the two women. "She may have been trying to use *da shealladh* to create a blessing for the children – spurred on by her failure to protect them from Modranhe."

"Just think how frantic she felt while she lay there dying, wishing for a way to help the them," Gretchen said.

"What kind of blessing would have helped at that point?" Erynne asked.

"One that strengthened the bond that already existed between them," Len said. "A blessing that connected their spirits, not just during their lifetimes, one monk wrote, but one that would be handed down through their descendants – like the blood bond Modranhe would share with his children. Such a blessing might survive longer than the two children themselves, assuming they were given the chance to live – to grow and have children of their own. Cruithne wanted to give them a chance to right her wrong: to challenge Modranhe with a blood line of pure and innocent origins. It was a last-ditch effort to put a stop to the evil he had unleashed."

Bloodlines. A thousand years of lives not intertwined, but still connected. But how?

Erynne closed her eyes. Blood pounded in her ears.

"How did she do it?" she whispered. "How were they connected?"

A draft of air caught Len's notes and pulled them from the table. Slowly, they floated to the floor, unnoticed.

"Through their dreams, Erynne."

Moments passed. No one spoke. Erynne stared unseeing at the papers on the floor in front of her. She ignored the tears in her eyes. They fell on fists that were now clenched together around the necklace. She closed her eyes again, willing away the story, the stone, the knowledge. Instead she was met again with the pounding of feet against the forest floor, the mournful cries of a baby. The kisses of a comforting stranger.

"No."

She pulled herself to her feet and walked toward the coat tree, jerking free her jacket and purse.

"Erynne ..." Gretchen began.

"Just stop," said Erynne, holding out her hand. She shifted her eyes between the two of them. "You expect me to believe that this necklace managed to stay in one family for hundreds of years? No one sold it or lost it? It was never stolen?" Her voice was high and breathless.

The usual sounds of chattering seamstresses from the workroom across the hall suddenly stopped, but Erynne didn't care.

"It's unbelievable," Len agreed nodding his head. "A chance in a million. But, perhaps ... the talisman doesn't *want* to be lost."

"I'm not even going to respond to that!" Erynne said hotly, looking at Gretchen. Why did she just stand there? Surely she saw the lunacy of this.

"What about your mother's love letters, Erynne?" Gretchen asked quietly. "What if that relationship wasn't as – illicit as you thought?"

"But how?" Erynne continued to fight. "How could all of that have happened in Ireland when my mother ... and Sidney ...?"

She couldn't continue. Feeling Gretchen's gentle hands guiding her, she allowed herself to be lowered into a chair next to the desk.

"I don't know. Immigration, perhaps? Ireland suffered a terrible potato famine in the middle of the nineteenth century," Len offered. "More than a million people left Ireland as a result. Many of them came to America."

"More than a million of them died, too," she said. "But none of that gives credence to the suggestion of mystical forces at play!"

"Your last name is O'Keefe. That's Irish, right?" Len asked.

"O'Keefe is my father's name," she said, struggling to control her temper. "My mother's name was Kelly."

She stood up again, her anger adding stability to her movements this time. She pushed her purse firmly on her shoulder and walked toward the door.

"Erynne, don't go!" Gretchen pleaded. "Please. Len and I only wanted to help."

Erynne stopped. Long shadows filled every corner of the studio, but no one had bothered to turn on the lights. How could words from a book have such effect? How could an old necklace left to rot in the bottom of a closet give meaning to the chaos of her life? Erynne gripped the doorknob with one hand and the talisman with the other, thinking of the two lost children, forever apart, forever connected.

"I appreciate your concern and the information you've shared," she finally said, her voice void of feeling. "It's just ... too much to believe."

"Or too much to hope for?" Gretchen asked quietly.

But Erynne didn't answer. Instead, she walked out the door and quietly closed it behind her.

Chapter 28

The sun was poised just above the horizon, bathing Erynne's front porch in its watercolor hue: blue bleeding to purple and pink as she turned the key in the lock. Inside the house was dark and the shadows were long, reaching beyond the confines of the small rooms, holding in the gloom.

Erynne shut the door with force and leaned back against it, letting it support her weight. She didn't bother turning on the light, content to allow the dark silence to engulf her. Her short trip from the studio had been filled with thoughts of Len's story and the arguments she should have stayed to make against his absurd suggestion.

But as her eyes adjusted to the shadows, she found herself looking around at the everyday things in her life – the small desk with stamps and pencils and bills to be paid, the stack of magazines on the coffee table, the new chenille sofa she had bought at the beginning of the year and the oil painting of the French countryside that she had found at an auction last fall. Everything in this room had once held meaning for her – objects that were an expression of her personality, a tribute to her accomplishments.

245

She had come so far since her years as the girl in ill-fitting hand-me-downs who scraped peanut butter from an empty jar for her supper. But her feet were still planted firmly on the ground. It seemed unfathomable that she could be tied to something cosmic and eternal, something from which neither time nor distance could separate her.

But she *was* considering it – combining what she had heard today with the things Dr. Peterson had said. She couldn't separate these revelations from her own experiences either. Her nightmares. Her dreams.

Deny it all you like, she told herself, *it will not change what you feel*.

The legend resonated in her heart, returning home, it seemed, confirming something imbedded in her very being. But she could only follow the possibilities and ramifications for so long before they crashed against each other inside her mind, leaving her confused and reeling.

Erynne left the solid feel of the door against her back and walked toward the dining room where she had laid and forgotten the fabric she purchased in Sun City. Joy Green had remarked on how pretty it would look made into a dress.

"Funny how styles come and go," she had mused. "That type of print was popular back in the late sixties – now I'm seeing it everywhere again."

Erynne had smiled and followed her inside, drinking lemonade and showing polite interest in her family photos, completely oblivious to the explosive information that had been there, hanging behind yellowing glass and aging frames.

Now she put her hand on her pulsing temple, thinking of Sidney and her mother, doing the math.

Was his picture on that wall?

The thought sent daggers into her stomach. She closed her eyes again, vainly searching the deep recesses of her memory for some hint of his face. Joy had mentioned two sons, but Erynne couldn't remember their names. One lived in Phoenix and the other lived somewhere else and was married with children.

Please. Not him, she thought.

She leaned against the table, trying to find reality again. The shadows lengthened while more reasonable explanations failed to present themselves.

"This is insane," she said out loud.

She had to do more than just stand in the dark, accepting the accumulating evidence, succumbing to a fit of fancy. In two strides she reached the dining room wall and snapped on the light, erasing the dark corners of the room and removing some of the madness. What she needed was something tangible to consider rather than hours of lonely speculation.

It took only a few minutes for Erynne to turn on her laptop and look up Joy Green's phone number on the Internet. Determined as she was, her hand still shook as she punched the number into her cell phone. Part of her would be relieved if she reached the wrong number, she realized. But there was no time for second guessing once she heard Joy's lilting southern drawl, distinctive and clear as she answered the phone.

"Joy? This is Erynne O'Keefe." She cleared her throat. "I met you a few weeks ago at your house...we visited an estate sale together. Do you remember?"

"Yes, Erynne, I remember."

"I hope I haven't disturbed you," Erynne said.

"Of course not," Joy said. "I'm glad you called. I've been rather anxious since Colin left. He doesn't seem to have his cell phone on." She paused. When Erynne didn't fill the silence, she went on quickly. "I'm sorry – I hope he hasn't alarmed you."

Erynne frowned. "Colin?" Suddenly her eyes widened in understanding. "Your son!"

"He isn't there?"

Erynne's heart began to pound. "Here?" she asked. "Why would he be here?"

"I've had all day to consider that question, and I'm still not sure I understand it," Joy said. "He saw you at the airport, Erynne. Here in Phoenix. There was some kind of disturbance – do you remember? And he helped you collect your things?"

Erynne leaned against the table again, feeling light headed. Someone *had* helped her at the airport, but she had been too embarrassed to look at him properly.

"It was quite a coincidence, wasn't it? I met you in Sun City, he saw you at the airport..." Her voice trailed off.

"Joy, I can explain."

"It wasn't an estate sale that brought you to my door, then?"

"No, it wasn't," Erynne said quietly, flushing with shame. "I'm sorry, Joy. So sorry. I didn't intend to deceive you."

"Life is strange," Joy said after a moment. She sounded more tired than angry. "I suppose if you had been straight with me, I wouldn't have thought much of you. But as it happened, there was something about you I liked right away. I suspect that something is what kept you from asking what you came here to ask."

Erynne cleared her throat. "My mother died a few weeks before I visited Arizona. You're right – I came looking for answers, guided by letters that I didn't understand. I'm only starting to understand now."

"Letters?" Joy's voice was thick with heartache. "From Sidney to your mother?"

"Yes."

They were both quiet for a moment. Erynne hardly knew the woman who was grieving on the other end of the phone line, but she admired her strength. She looked across the room at a snapshot of her mother that sat on a bookshelf. Words from one of Sidney's letters poured through her mind.

"Joy, I know your husband loved you. He wrote as much to my mother. He said he would choose you over and over again. I don't think any of it was his choice – or hers, though I'm sure there were mistakes – and secrets that shouldn't have been kept, no matter what the costs."

"Well, it was all a long time ago, wasn't it?" Joy said, brightening her voice with what seemed like an extreme force of will. "I think it would be best if we concentrate on the future."

Erynne's thoughts snapped back to Joy's son. "You said Colin was coming here," she said, loving the sound of his name on her lips. "How can that be?"

"Yes, he left this morning, despite my ignorant objections," Joy said.

Stay safe until I find you, he had told her.

"He found your business card after you separated at the airport. I never would have understood the connection if he hadn't mentioned your name."

Her business card. He must be at the studio.

"Joy, I need to call the office and see if he's there."

"You go ahead, Erynne. I won't hold you up," she said. "But have Colin check his phone, won't you?"

"I will. And thank you."

Erynne hung up the phone and dialed the studio. It rang only once when her doorbell chimed, making her jump.

Colin!

Her heart began to thud as she walked toward the door. She quickly glanced at her reflection in the oval mirror by the coat closet. Her eyes were slightly wild, but her hair seemed to be in place.

"Hello?... Hello?"

For a moment Erynne had forgotten about the phone in her hand. Now Gretchen's voice on the other end of the line brought it back to her attention. Hurriedly she raised it to her ear.

"Gretchen? It's Erynne."

"Are you okay? I almost hung up on you."

"I know, I'm sorry." Erynne took a deep breath. "Listen, Gretchen: I'm sorry for everything. I can't explain it all now, but I think you were right – you and Len. I think he's at my front door."

The doorbell chimed again.

"Slow down, honey," Gretchen said with a trace of alarm. "Who are you talking about?"

"His name is Colin Green," Erynne swallowed hard. "He's the man from my dreams. I have to go. I'll call you later."

Before Gretchen could ask another question, Erynne flipped her phone closed and set it on the coffee table.

I can do this, she told herself. Taking another deep breath, she opened the door.

"Hello."

"Hi."

Erynne looked closely at the man standing on her porch. He wore khakis and a blue Oxford shirt. His hair was blond and his eyes were blue. Small lines around his mouth suggested that he smiled often, although the expression he wore now more closely resembled wonder than amusement. She studied his face without another word, trying to picture him alongside her on their street, their beach.

He seemed to be examining her too.

"You're even more beautiful in person," he said, almost under his breath.

Guilt caught in Erynne's throat. He recognized her, but she still wasn't sure about him. Pushing aside her doubts she smiled and reached out, taking his hand.

"Colin Green," she said softly. "It's nice to meet you."

Chapter 29

Gretchen had been trying to concentrate on EOK's monthly accounts payable report when Erynne called. Now she was pacing. The sudden sound of the glass door rattling made her jump. She whirled around to see Len walking into the studio, his cell phone in his hand, his eyes quizzical.

"You should really keep this locked after dark," he said. "What's up? I thought we were meeting at home."

"I know, but Erynne just called." Gretchen pulled him toward her desk, noticing for the first time that he was carrying another large book under his arm. "You won't believe this, but she said that the man she's been dreaming about just showed up on her doorstep."

Len looked up sharply. "When did this happen?"

"Just before I called your phone. She didn't say much, just his name – Colin Green."

Gretchen continued her pacing. Erynne's call made her uneasy. Though she had certainly never seen Erynne behave irrationally, she worried that the recent upheaval in her life might cloud her judgment, making her vulnerable.

There was so much about Erynne's experience that Gretchen still didn't know – gaping holes about her mother, her dreams and nightmares – none of which were likely to be filled in by their owner. Gretchen had only meant to help Erynne by showing her the picture of the necklace. How could she not share the legend – almost identical to her mother's bedtime story? But Erynne's reaction had made those unknown parts of her life seem blacker, more troubling to Gretchen. She worried that their meddling had done little more than create a barrier to further confidences.

"Oh, Len, this has me really worried," she said. "What were we thinking? She's been through so much lately. We should have thought this through."

Len nodded absently, patting her hand as he sat in her chair and began leafing through his smelly old book. Gretchen had been only too willing to let him go when he suggested a quick trip to the library and then to their storage shed, where boxes of similar tomes were molding. He had been eager to check a few more sources, and with all the computer work Gretchen had piling up, it had seemed like a good idea to let him go.

"She didn't sound like herself on the phone," she told him now, remembering the unfamiliar lilt in Erynne's voice. Was it hopefulness? Gretchen had always wanted Erynne to let her guard down, to lean on trustworthy friends in times of sorrow. But who was this person that had shown up at her house? Even if Erynne and he were connected by some eternal bond, that didn't necessarily make him the best person to put her faith in.

"Do you think we should call her back? Or go over there?" Gretchen asked.

"Hmmm?" Len looked up from his book. "It might be a good idea. There's more to that legend, Gretchen. Right here. It might explain her nightmares."

"Are you sure we aren't putting too much weight into these stories, Len?" Gretchen asked, looking uneasily at the night beyond the windows. During the daytime, the Irish legend had seemed exciting and romantic. Now she wondered if they weren't both letting their imaginations run wild.

Len shook his head. "I don't know, Gretchen. It's all mind boggling. More so for Erynne, I should think. Still, you'll want to hear this – even if we decide not to share it with her right away."

"Okay. Tell me."

"This historian wouldn't be considered as reliable as the others," Len said, tapping the dusty book with his fingers. "But according to his account, Modranhe's son, Corthel, learned about Cruithne's final blessing late in life and tried to undo it with dark magic of his own. He tried to find the children and finish the job his father left undone."

"I don't suppose he had any luck," Gretchen said.

Len shrugged. "Evidently not. The trails had all gone cold. Following through on every rumor of their whereabouts wasn't an option. So, of course, he turned again to the only weapon he had – witchcraft."

"Since Cruithne had linked the children by their dreams, he decided to give chase the same way. It was his contention that if he could invade their dreams, he would learn enough about their whereabouts to find them and kill them."

Gretchen shuddered. "But he couldn't have succeeded if we're to believe that Erynne is a part of this. Otherwise she would have never been born."

Len shook his head. "No, you're right. Corthel never succeeded. But do you remember what I said earlier about Modranhe's bloodline? The legend says that his powers were passed down through the generations – like a genetic trait."

"That's not the kind of heritage I would want."

"No, perhaps not." Len paused, looking out the window. "But what if you inherited it anyway? The power to see people's thoughts – the power to invade their dreams? What do you think that would do to a person?"

"It would drive him crazy," Gretchen said. "But … it would also make him extremely powerful, wouldn't it?"

They were silent for several minutes, considering.

"Are we talking about reality here, Len?" Gretchen finally asked, shaking her head. "Or just a crazy story?"

"I don't know."

Gretchen moved quickly past Len, powering down her computer and grabbing her purse.

"Let's go," she said. "I have a bad feeling about this guy showing up at Erynne's house. Maybe getting a good look at him will set my mind at ease."

Len nodded and helped Gretchen put on her sweater as they walked to the door. Footsteps on the staircase below stopped them both.

"Maybe that's Erynne," Gretchen said hopefully. She pulled on the doorknob and stepped into the dark hallway, only to step back again when she saw a man standing at the top of the stairs. It was an unusual time of day for a stranger to be in the building.

"Can I help you?" she asked.

The man stepped into the light and Gretchen breathed easier. He didn't look threatening, just tired and slightly rumpled. Looking first at Gretchen and then at the name painted on the glass door, he pulled a business card out of his pocket and examined it before responding.

"I'm looking for Erynne O'Keefe," he said.

Gretchen frowned. "She's not here tonight," she said. "It is rather late."

"I'm sorry." The man grimaced. "I should have been here earlier, but my plane was late, and I had trouble with the car rental agency." He swallowed hard and looked over her shoulder, where Len was standing with his arms folded across his chest. "Can I find her here tomorrow morning?" he asked hopefully.

"You can leave your name and a message," Gretchen said. "And I'll see that she gets it."

"Thank you," the man said quietly. "My name is Colin Green."

Chapter 30

There were no lights flashing on his telephone and no nurses paging his name over the intercom system. He had finished his evening rounds, and now Mark sat quietly in his office, looking beyond his wooden shutters to the last colors of twilight as they disappeared, leaving a clear, star-lit sky in their wake. As the darkness settled around him, he heard the structured movements of the nurses along the hallways making their rounds. They were on a tighter schedule now, ever since Shannon O'Keefe's death. He tapped his fingertips on the police report that sat on his desk but didn't read it. The detective's call had been enough – Mark and Cypress Care Center were not deemed negligent in her death and the investigation had been closed.

Closed.

Mark wondered what else was closed. Erynne's heart, maybe. But perhaps he was fooling himself to imagine it had ever been open in the first place. Not for him anyway.

When was it that he first suspected he was in love with her?

Mark had been struck by Erynne's solitary beauty from their first meeting. She had been so difficult to read, all business about finding a place to take care of her mother. Her eyes had been deep and stormy even then, obscuring the signs of a traumatic life – he understood that now. But he had instinctively wanted to brighten them, like some dopey poem about how love can turn gray skies to blue.

Over the course of Shannon's stay at Cypress, Mark had tried to draw Erynne out little by little. Each truth he learned was a cherished blessing, a moment of triumph. But it had all amounted to so little. She had never laid down the burden of her painful past. Her eyes had never lost their wariness, even when she finally accepted his invitation to dinner. Perhaps it was during one of their few dates to follow that he had allowed himself to hope for more. From across a table, or the next seat in a theater, she would allow him to hold her hand without resistance, but without passion. Her kisses had been the same. He had told himself love grew slower in some hearts, especially those that have never felt trust. But by that time, she had already begun to quietly extract herself from his life without explanation.

Erynne's withdrawal had not changed his feelings. He had interpreted it as habitual – the expected self-protection of a wounded bird. He had loved her even more. Betting on patience to beat out persistence, he had stopped calling, talking to her at Cypress only about her mother's care until she seemed ready for more.

And then Shannon had wandered from his care home and stepped off a cliff to her death.

Mark ached inside as he watched Erynne drop clods of dirt on her mother's grave. He was responsible, no matter what the police report said. He knew she might never forgive him, much less find a way to love him.

Inviting her to join him for dinner on the wharf had been a mistake. He knew that now. He had pushed too soon, if not too hard, and had seen her eyes flash with anger and grief before darkening in confusion.

In the weeks that had passed since, he had been willing to retreat to his corner again, to allow the police to finish their investigation, to give Erynne space as she grieved. It had not been easy, but he had deserved no less in the way of penance. While he waited he had foolishly hoped that grief would push her to lean on someone.

Even if it isn't me, he told himself.

But it should have been him, shouldn't it? He seesawed between guilt and hope.

When Erynne's call for help had finally come it had taken him off guard. He had wanted to see her, to hold her hand while she unburdened herself, but the phone line had been a barrier he was forced to respect. So he had listened quietly as she chose her words, so careful to reveal only what she must. She was having dreams and nightmares, just like her mother's. She needed help finding answers.

The information had shocked Mark, though he hadn't said as much. He had always assumed the simplest explanation for Shannon's nightmares. Erynne suffering in the same way couldn't mean mental illness like her mother's, surely. He was quick to recommend John Peterson, hoping to allay her fears and his own. But she had not called him since returning from the sleep clinic, John had. He hadn't said much. Of course, he couldn't.

"Tread carefully, Mark," was all he had to offer.

Mark wasn't sure he could take his friend's advice. Something she said on the phone had been burrowing a hole in his subconscious ever since, festering like a disregarded wound.

"Nightmares could be a simple sign of stress and mourning." It had been his first statement when she called him last week.

"It's not only nightmares," she said. "There are other dreams too, strange and different than anything I've ever known." He had heard longing in her voice, despite her carefully controlled tone. "Wonderful dreams. Dreams I don't want to leave."

Mark had focused on the nightmares, arranging the appointment, wondering about the connection with her mother. Later he remembered the change in her voice, the soft, lilting note that spoke of something private, something cherished that she did not wish to share.

What happens during those dreams? he asked himself.

Something that offered happiness, peace. Something that Mark had failed to give her. He found himself bitterly jealous.

Mark toyed with his pen, turning it end to end on top of the police report, carelessly allowing dots of ink to create a random pattern. He thought about the placement of people in life and how it shifted by chance or providence, allowing them to meet and befriend others, to share the same air, the same space. Circumstance had led Erynne into his life. He chose to see it as meaningful instead of arbitrary, like a careful drawing rather than ink splattered on paper. His love and faithfulness had more substance than the sweet vapor of dreams, which would only abandon her by morning, leaving her very much alone.

Mark dropped his pen on the desk and stood up, grabbing his jacket from the back of his chair.

"I won't be scared off by a dream," he said as he walked out the door.

Chapter 31

Who was Colin Green?

Jack didn't care. He quickly stuck out his sweaty palm when Erynne reached for it, hoping she didn't notice his dirty fingernails. Instead she searched his face, making him squirm. He needed to play this part long enough to get in the door, after that it wouldn't really matter who she thought he was.

A fantasy flashed through his mind of pushing her hard against the wall, seeing her eyes contract with fear. "You can call me whatever you want," he would say. A quiver of fear would pass through her body, kindling his senses.

Jack shook his head. *Steady.*

He had been waiting restlessly since watching her check out of the San Francisco Hilton. Though spoken softly, her name had carried across the lobby to where he hid behind a potted Ficus tree. He had repeated it eagerly to the senator just a few minutes later.

"Erynne O'Keefe," he had murmured into his phone.

"Good work, Jack."

The senator had sounded eager himself, promising to call soon with more instructions. Jack had shot out of the city like a bullet when he'd finally gotten the call. But he had almost blown it completely when she opened the door, looking so much like the sketch folded in his back pocket. He didn't know what the senator wanted with her, but he hoped he could be part of it.

Jack licked his lips and looked from side to side as he moved to enter the house. To his disappointment, Erynne instead directed him across the porch toward a pair of cushioned patio chairs. Hanging ferns might partially obscure them to passersby, but the porch light was bright and being outside made him nervous. He hoped she didn't notice the way he angled the chair before sitting down so that his face would not be visible from the street.

He swallowed a knot in his throat and resisted the urge to squirm, tap his leg, or check his pocket for the knife. He wished she would stop examining him that way, but was glad at least that she wasn't one of those women who filled every second with chatter. If he could keep up the charade until complete darkness descended, it would make his job a lot easier. She seemed nervous too. Maybe this guy, Colin Green, was some kind of blind date.

"I just got off the phone with your mother," she said, watching his reaction. He lifted his eyebrows in mock surprise, hoping that was appropriate. She smiled for the first time and he struggled to choked down some air and steady his heartbeat. She was so pretty. Her ignorance of the trouble she was in made her even more desirable.

Settle down, he told himself. The senator said no monkey business.

"Really?" He cleared his throat, searching for a safe question. "What did she have to say?"

Erynne's face turned serious. "We have a lot to talk about," she said quietly.

It seemed a strange answer, making Jack squirm again. He rubbed his sweating hands against the leg of his pants, thankful that he at least had the good sense to shower and change into these preppy clothes before he came. He'd actually been surprised by his reflection in the mirror. "You clean up nice," Momma would have said. It was a good thing – he had a feeling Erynne wouldn't have believed he was Green if he had shown up wearing a leather jacket and an Aerosmith T-shirt.

"Could I have a glass of water?" he asked. It seemed like a good way to get inside the house. It only now occurred to him that since she had been expecting Green, he was likely to show up any minute and expose him as a fraud. He needed to make his move soon – before he could be interrupted.

"Of course."

Erynne went inside. Jack wasted no more time on the porch, but quickly entered the house behind her and softly closed the door, standing with his back to it as he watched her retreat toward the kitchen. He quietly assessed her home: a small living room and dining room with the kitchen in the back, where another door led outside. A short dark hall to his right led to bedrooms and a bathroom. *Just two ways in or out, then.*

He heard the tinkling of ice and the water faucet being turned on and off. He remembered to flip the front porch light switch off just before Erynne returned to the living room, holding his water and frowning slightly. Was she concerned about the way he had followed her into the house?

"Thanks," he said, smiling as she handed him the water. He drank greedily, realizing she was scrutinizing him again. The focus of her concentration was starting to change – a pattern Jack recognized from past experience – placing her on the precipice of alarm. She wasn't conscious of it yet, but had nonetheless crossed her arms over her chest and backed away, putting the sofa between them.

Jack swallowed the last gulp of water, realizing it was time to act. She was obviously confused about Colin Green, but she seemed like a pretty smart lady. He remembered how she had stopped and looked right at him when he was tailing her in San Francisco. He expected recognition to register in her eyes at any moment.

He smiled and set down his glass, reaching for the door to allay her fears.

"Do you mind if we get out of here?" He blew air through his lips, hoping to appear nervous – the way a nice guy might on a first date. "I could really go for some fresh air."

Erynne uncrossed her arms, the crease between her eyes disappearing. "I'll get a sweater," she said, crossing to a coat closet near the front door. Jack rubbed his hand across his jawbone, trying to press away a smile.

Too easy, he thought.

But nothing ever turned out easy in Jack's world.

As he waited for her to pull on her sweater and grab her purse, Jack heard the unmistakable sound of footsteps on the front porch, closely followed by the chiming doorbell.

Green, he thought. *Time to act.*

Erynne's brow creased again and Jack stepped courteously away from the door, allowing her to move past him. Shifting his feet until he was concealed by the shadowy closet alcove, he pulled out his knife as she turned the knob.

Light from a table lamp illuminated the visitor's face. "Hi," he said, stepping through the door like a friend would. His smile was timid, but his eyes never left her face. He obviously thought they were alone.

Jack acted swiftly once the visitor was clear of the door. In one fluid motion, he grabbed Erynne from behind and kicked it closed. She gasped, feeling his knife against her throat.

"Careful," he hissed, tilting it until it pressed into her flesh. She stilled then, all but her heart, which hammered against his forearm like a bird desperate for freedom.

Her fear surged through Jack, beating any drug he had ever tried. He smiled wickedly at the visitor, who stood with eyes widened in horror, ping-ponging between Erynne's face and Jack's, clearly out of his element.

"I'm not Colin after all, am I?" he whispered against Erynne's ear, tightening his grip as he felt the effect of those words pass through her body. His knife didn't move.

"You have bad timing," he said, addressing the visitor whose gaze swept from the door to the room. He was shifting his position. Needlessly, thought Jack, who was amused by the way he held his hands out in front of him, as if he might coax the knife away like a chocolate bar from a child.

"What do you want?" The man cleared his throat, his voice tinny and weak. "There's no need for anyone to get hurt."

"Shut up!"

Jack needed to think. The senator wanted this quick and slick. This unexpected visitor was making things messy, and time was running out. With the grace of a street thug, Jack pushed Erynne roughly toward the closet and lunged at the newcomer with his knife.

The open edge of the closet door struck Erynne forcefully, knocking out her breath as her body ricocheted. She landed on the floor, striking her head on the edge of a table.

Jack had underestimated the man's strength. They struggled with the knife, tripping over each other's feet and landing hard against the floor, just inches from the coffee table. Jack was on his back, his unyielding grip on the knife the only advantage he held. With adrenalin-laced force, he kicked with his legs, setting his opponent off balance. It was just the window he needed.

"Like I said before, you have bad timing," Jack said, breathing hard as he pitched forward, his knife blade gleaming as he slashed the man's throat.

Jack turned to face Erynne, but she was unconscious, a trickle of blood running down her temple. She was breathing, at least, and wouldn't put up a fight. Wiping his blade on his jeans, he took a moment to peer through the front curtains before picking her up and opening the door, glad there was no streetlight nearby, no moon.

He took one last look at the man whose blood was staining Erynne's rug. His eyes were still open, staring as his mouth moved wordlessly, making gurgling sounds as his blood continued to spill. Jack moved quickly through the door without giving the man another thought. It didn't matter whether he lived or died. He wouldn't be telling anyone what he saw.

Chapter 32

"*You're* Colin Green?"

Gretchen took two steps backward and looked him up and down, still spooked by her recent premonition of danger.

"Yes," he said, watching her carefully. "How do you know my name?"

"From Erynne," she said. "She said you were at her house."

Colin looked startled. Color began to creep into his tired face. "But how? I haven't even...I only have this," he said, holding up the card. "I don't know her address."

Gretchen stared at him, blinking. She felt Len step behind her and rest his hands on her shoulders.

"Erynne knows my name?" Colin repeated quietly, seeming mystified. "How could she? She doesn't even know me."

"Len?" There was fear in Gretchen's voice.

"Can you tell us why you're here?" Len asked.

Colin put his duffel bag on the floor. "I saw Erynne at the airport in Phoenix and ... and I recognized her. She dropped this

269

business card – that's the only reason I know her name." Colin held out the tattered card as proof of his story.

"You flew all the way from Arizona to see a woman you don't know? Why?"

Colin looked away, deepening Gretchen's concern.

"I don't know if you'll believe me," he finally said, "but I dreamed about her before I saw her at the airport." He raised his eyes. "That is … if Erynne is the woman I think she is."

Gretchen turned to look at Len, wondering if his thoughts were following the same line as hers. If this man *had* seen Erynne in his dreams, was he the one she was linked to by Cruithne's blessing? Or Corthel's curse?

Colin reached into his pocket and pulled out a snapshot, fingering it carefully before handing it to Gretchen. "Can you tell me … do you think this might have been Erynne's mother?"

Gretchen looked at the photo carefully. She had never met Shannon, but had seen a photo of her when she was older. Still, there was something around the eyes and mouth that looked like Erynne. She handed it back to Colin. "I don't know. I didn't know her."

Colin raised his hand, rubbing the nape of his neck. Despite her suspicions, Gretchen found herself feeling bad for him. They were getting nowhere it seemed.

Suddenly she drew a sharp breath.

"Len, look!"

She pointed at Colin's arm where his shirt sleeve had raised to reveal a dark patch of skin – narrow at the bottom, ballooning out at the top, like a tree.

Colin rubbed it self-consciously. "What is it?"

"Is that a birthmark?" Len asked sharply.

"Yes, my father had one just like it." He was beginning to sound irritated. "What's this about?"

Gretchen ignored him. "Len, we have to go. To check on her."

"It was probably just a salesman at the door," Len said.

"But how did she know his name?" Gretchen asked, pointing at Colin again.

"Look, I know that I'm the stranger here," Colin said, "and that all of this is weird – really weird. But I came all this way, not just to meet her, but to make sure she's alright." He tapped Shannon's photo against his fingers. "This woman told me to protect her."

Gretchen was shaken to hear this stranger echo her fears. She was beginning to believe that he was the good guy in their scenario – either that or a really good actor. Crossing to the desk, she picked up the phone and dialed Erynne's numbers – her house first and then her cell phone.

"Both went to voice mail," she said, grabbing her purse. "We need to go check on her. Now."

Len held the door open and looked at Colin. "Why don't you come with us?" he asked. "I'd like to tell you a story."

Chapter 33

Mark heard the phone ring like he was awakening from a dream. Blood was everywhere.

Dear God, my throat!

He grabbed a pillow from the couch and pushed it hard against his neck. The phone rang again. It was just out of reach, resting on Erynne's side table. With considerable effort he dragged himself toward it, leaving a trail of blood behind him. It rang a third time, just as he reached the table, knocking it from its base and onto the floor.

He tried to focus enough to see the numbers. The knife must not have gone in too deep. If it had, he would already be dead. Still, his blood was everywhere and he felt light headed.

Dialing 9-1-1, he hoped fervently that he reached an experienced operator, one who would recognize that the constant beeping in her ears was a distress signal. If he tried to speak again it would only come out in a sick gurgle – and add to his danger of bleeding to death.

"If you can hear me, an ambulance has been dispatched to your location. I'll stay with you until they arrive." Mark heard the calm voice over the phone and closed his eyes, praying they would get there in time. He continued to apply pressure to his throat and continued to pray, this time for Erynne.

God, protect her from that butcher.

Chapter 34

Erynne woke when a gust of frigid Pacific air passed over her face, accompanied by a strange mechanical noise. She opened her eyes, but quickly closed them again as sharp pain shot through her head, making her feel sick to her stomach. Forcing herself to stay still, she took in what she could without sight – the rumble of tires against pavement, the smell of an old sputtering car engine and the feel of torn vinyl beneath her hands.

She opened her eyes again, moving slowly this time. A dashboard came into focus – then a windshield and a clear moon-lit sky above. The sound she had not recognized was a convertible top being lowered, giving riotous passage to wind that curled around her body, easily finding its way through her thin sweater. Her temple continued to throb and she remembered falling and hitting the table. She could feel a lump and the tightness of blood drying along her hairline.

A furtive glance over her left shoulder confirmed what she feared most. The imposter who had shown up on her doorstep was driving the car. He hadn't noticed her stirring yet but was focused on the road, singing along with the Police on the radio and tapping his fingertips against the steering wheel. Erynne peered over the passenger door and saw the ocean beyond the cliffs and dunes. They were traveling south on Highway One.

I'm not Colin, am I?

Erynne shuddered, remembering more clearly her last moments of consciousness. This man had held a knife to her throat and Mark ... Oh! Where was Mark now?

She pushed herself up, gulping air and gripping the seat as a stronger wave of nausea pummeled her stomach. Her kidnapper had finally noticed her movements and was eyeing her warily now, his song forgotten.

"You're not going to throw up, are you?"

Erynne sucked in more air and pushed it out slowly through her teeth.

"Where's Mark?" she asked, surprised at how strong her voice sounded.

The man didn't answer. Instead he glanced sideways at her through lowered eyelids, wearing an expression that shaped a knot of fear in Erynne's throat. He turned his attention back to the road.

"I'm glad you're awake," he finally said, adjusting his grip on the steering wheel and cocking his head like a nervous dog. "That's one less thing for me to worry about."

Erynne closed her eyes again, trying hard to ignore her throbbing head, her twisting stomach. She wanted to demand more information from her abductor. Why had he taken her, and, more importantly, what had happened to Mark?

But somehow she knew. The look in his eyes spoke of violence, swift and merciless. Her helplessness made the knot in her throat swell. Hot tears formed behind her eyelids. She steeled her nerves, forcing the feeling away.

"Who are you? Where are you taking me?" Her voice cracked.

He licked his lips. "You'll find out soon enough."

For the next ten minutes, Erynne considered a plan of escape. But the highway was relatively barren tonight, and those cars they did pass were occupied with travelers too concerned about their own plans to focus on her abductor's dilapidated convertible, or to understand the pleading eyes of its passenger. She considered asking him to stop so they could use a restroom but she knew he would refuse. The only other option was to wait and see where he was taking her. She would take any opportunity to run. In the meantime, she studied his profile, hoping that she might later be able to describe him to the police.

Sudden recognition dawned when her captor turned in her direction, momentarily allowing his face to be bathed in moonlight. She *had* seen him before, but not in any dream. It had been somewhere in San Francisco, within the last few days. Had he been following her even then? And why?

Erynne tried to keep her mind away from Mark but found that she couldn't. Fresh guilt flooded over her. She should have known better than to allow this stranger in her house. Brief and unfamiliar hope had led her to cast aside customary caution. She had quite literally opened her door to the enemy – not only putting herself in danger, but Mark as well. How could she have ever allowed herself to believe that this thug was the man from her dreams?

Erynne's teeth began to chatter, adding harmony to her thumping headache. She tried to think back to her conversation with Joy Green and test the accuracy of her assumptions. Instead she could only recall what she had hoped for, what she felt to be true. Joy's son, Colin, was the man she had been dreaming about all these months. And he was on his way to find her.

Colin.

Somehow he had believed – had allowed himself to hope, to take a leap of faith and follow through on his dreamtime promise.

Stay safe until I find you.

She had not even been able to accomplish that. Instead she had jumped from arrogant denial to careless belief in the space of a few minutes – the exact minutes when she should have been cautious, moved slowly.

Erynne closed her eyes again. She pulled her sweater tightly across her chest and held it there with shaking arms. Maybe she had not been able to remember Colin's face because she refused to believe, turning her back on something deep and primal. Their dreams together were as real as anything she had ever experienced. In them, she had been free to exist without the weighty garments of self-protection and isolation. To be loved that way – as she really was, stripped of pretense – had been the most genuine experience of her life.

She wanted it back. She wanted Colin. She wanted to believe.

His image came to her then, somewhere along Highway One, playing like a reel of film on the inside of her eyelids. His smile, his eyes – the cut of his hair and the stubble that often dusted his jawline. Every expression spoke of truth and love, reminding her that he was out there somewhere, still looking for her. That knowledge comforted her as nothing else could.

Erynne opened her eyes and carefully straightened in her seat. The highway was curving away from the ocean now and they were traveling through farmland. They passed the exit toward Castroville and hundreds of acres of artichokes. Soon the scenery changed, the fields giving way to sand dunes as they again curved back toward the bay. A good fifteen minutes passed before Erynne could see the water again. They sped past Marina and Fort Ord. With each signpost, Erynne glanced toward her captor, wondering if they were getting close to their destination.

By the time they reached Seaside, Erynne could see the lights of Monterey leading a path to the right and out to the bottom of the bay. Just two blocks from her home in Santa Cruz, she could see these same lights on a fog-free evening. They had always comforted her as a little girl when she had imagined another child on the other side of the bay, looking north and wondering who might be looking back. But tonight as she drew closer to those lights, she felt nothing but dread, wondering what would happen when they reached their destination. Struggling with the horrible possibilities and the increasing pain in her head, Erynne again succumbed to a black cloud of unconsciousness.

The change under the tires from smooth pavement to a cobbled driveway stirred Erynne from sleep for a second time. They pulled to a stop and her captor cut the engine. She straightened and opened her eyes, taking in their surroundings. Her hopes of a heavily populated area were quickly squelched.

The Pacific air was still cool, but the wind had died out, allowing a low fog to move in while she slept. The large house in front of her was only partially visible. She first made out a garage, dimly lit by wrought-iron wall sconces that did little to shed light on the rest of the property. Still, she squinted in every direction, looking for an avenue of escape. Her eyes adjusted to the soup and more of the house took shape. It was a Spanish colonial with ivy climbing its walls, reaching up to a second floor balcony. A gate on the side led through a copse of Cypress trees that disappeared into darkness. The sound of the surf crashing against a cliff confirmed that they were close to the ocean.

Her captor got out of the car and, after stretching briefly, came around to the passenger side, opening the door and offering Erynne his hand. He seemed unconcerned about any escape attempts, making no threats, offering no warnings for silence. She ignored his hand, instead choosing to steady herself on the frame of the car as she rose from her seat. The murky world spun around her as she stepped onto the driveway, bringing with it a fresh wave of nausea. But something else was causing the hair on her neck to rise and a jolt of fear to run through her blood like an electrical current.

His footsteps were barely discernible as he approached. His face was shadowed, but his size greeted her like a signature, unmistakable in its girth and height. The sconce lighting that struck him from behind magnified the impression: a stark, silent silhouette. He managed to exude a sense of euphoric triumph.

A sharp cry of panic escaped through Erynne's lips, ascending from a place deep inside that knew this man, this figure who was as familiar as the pillow she slept on every night. He was the one who had stalked her again and again until she woke up sobbing, clutching her sheet, waiting for her waking world to remove the terror of her dream.

Erynne backed away slowly, feeling for the edge of the car as her cloudy mind fused this waking moment with the horror of her nightmares. Her kidnapper stood to the side, silent and forgotten. Whether words passed between the two men, Erynne would never remember, only the way the world had begun to spin and the fog had closed in. Like countless times before, she turned to run, searching for unknown avenues of escape while he slowly began his pursuit from behind.

Erynne stumbled over a raised planter, wishing vainly for the moon's assistance. The estate was large, the grounds circling the house and extending in unknown darkness, but she pushed herself to keep moving, to ignore her burning lungs and the dizzying headache that threatened to conquer her with each step. Still, it seemed she was gaining no ground in the mist.

Her stalker followed – drawing closer, like always.

Erynne reached the north wing of the house without knowing it. She slowed only slightly as she turned to avoid colliding with its curved wall, searching for a hiding place. A grove of ghostly Cypress trees covered this part of the estate, only dimly visible through lighting that escaped from the windows. Their branches danced in the rising wind, bringing the trees to life as Erynne stumbled onward. They reached out to embrace her, grabbing her with raised roots, bringing her down hard.

"It's just a dream," she whispered hoarsely, trying to crawl toward a dark space, ignoring a new sharp pain in her ankle and the slow but steady approach of her stalker.

Just a dream. It's just a dream. Wake up, Erynne.

But she could not wake from reality. Instead, she turned to face it, pushing herself backward until she was pressed against the tree that had brought her down. The dark hunter was coming. There would be no escape this time. Raising muddy hands to cover her eyes, Erynne screamed, "Colin!"

Darkness enveloped her.

Chapter 35

The unmistakable sight of red and blue strobe lights greeted Colin and the Martins when they turned onto Erynne's street. From the backseat, Colin craned his neck to see three police cars and an ambulance blocking the road in front of a gray shingled house with a wide front porch. Gretchen gasped and reached for Len's hand, confirming Colin's fears. The house was Erynne's.

Tugging on the door handle, Colin jumped out of the car as soon as it rolled to a stop at the curb. Gretchen and Len were only moments behind as he pushed his way through a crowd of neighbors gathering on the sidewalk. Two paramedics were carrying a stretcher out of the house just as he reached the front steps.

"Mark!" Gretchen said, peering around his shoulder. Colin expelled a heavy breath as he made out a tuft of short brown hair above the mask. It wasn't Erynne.

Gretchen started to cry. She turned to bury her face in her husband's sleeve as the paramedics wheeled Mark toward the waiting ambulance.

Colin was the first to turn away. He climbed the steps of the house, only to be barred entry by a plain-clothed detective on the front porch.

"Where is she?"

Colin's eyes swept through the room beyond the open front door, taking in the chaos. Furniture was awry and a Persian rug was stained with a wide circle of blood.

"Who are you?"

"Colin Green."

"Detective Daniels. You looking for the homeowner?"

"Yes." Colin's heart was pounding. "Erynne O'Keefe."

"Where is she?" Gretchen asked as she and Len joined him on the porch.

"She's not here," Detective Daniels said.

"She was here about an hour ago," Gretchen said. "She called me and was interrupted by someone at the door. I'm Gretchen Martin – I work for Erynne."

"Is she the one whose mother jumped from West Cliff a few weeks back?"

Colin drew a sharp breath.

"Yes," Gretchen answered, her eyes narrowing. "Why?"

"Sometimes a trauma can affect the way people behave," Daniels said, looking meaningfully at the ambulance as it pulled away from the curb.

"You don't think Erynne did that!" Gretchen shook her head. "No – whoever hurt Mark has taken her somewhere."

"What happened to Dr. Osborn?" Len asked.

"Someone slashed his throat with a knife," the detective said. "You know him well?"

Gretchen swallowed hard. "He's a friend – of ours and Erynne's. Her mother was a resident at his clinic."

"Yes," Detective Daniels looked up. "Any disagreement going on between the two of them?"

"No! Absolutely not," Gretchen said.

"Was she upset, by any chance, that his clinic was just cleared of negligence in her mother's death?"

Gretchen shook her head emphatically. "She didn't hold him responsible – not even in the beginning. Erynne is a victim in this – just like Mark."

"You say she just called you?"

"Yes, just a little while ago."

"Can't you try locating her by her cell phone?" Colin asked.

"It's in the house," Detective Daniels said, jerking his head back over his shoulder. "She left her purse too."

"Surely that proves what I'm saying," said Gretchen. "You've got to find her!"

For the next several minutes, Colin listened with barely controlled patience as Gretchen gave the detectives a description of Erynne. A recent snapshot was taken from the house and handed over to a uniformed officer who carried it to a squad car. A few minutes later, another officer brought something out of the house and handed it to Detective Daniels.

"You recognize this?" he asked, showing Gretchen something inside an evidence bag.

"It's Erynne's necklace," she said, her voice shaking. "She was wearing it when she left work today."

Colin looked over Gretchen's shoulder at the stone. Instinctively he reached up and touched the birthmark on his arm. The shapes were identical.

"Where was it found?" Colin asked the detective.

"It was near the table by the door, right?" Daniels asked the other officer.

"Yeah. There's blood on the edge of that table. We got samples."

Daniels followed the officer inside, leaving Colin and the Martins alone on the front porch.

Gretchen stepped close to Len, turning her back to the front door. "What should we do?" she whispered.

Colin's eyes narrowed. "What's going on?"

"Not here," Len said, his eyes on the door. "They won't believe us."

"Won't believe what?" Colin said, his tone low but sharp. He wasn't sure he should trust Len's discretion. Whatever they were hiding, surely it should be divulged if there was a chance it would help the police find Erynne.

"They won't believe why *you're* here, for one thing," Len said. He jerked his head toward the front door. "You understand, surely. Do you want to explain your relationship with Erynne to the police? It would probably do more harm than good."

Colin rubbed his hand over his eyes. "You're right. They would think I'm crazy."

"At best. Or a suspect."

He nodded, swallowing a hard knot.

"Erynne's mother is dead?" he asked after a moment, latching on to something tangible.

286

"She had Alzheimer's," Gretchen said. "She wandered from her care center and stepped off a cliff several weeks ago. Erynne saw it happened – but she couldn't reach her in time."

Colin felt his face drain of color, imagining her death – understanding more of the conversations he had shared with Erynne and the heartache that was so often behind her eyes. Unshakable fear for her safety had brought him here, set in motion by words that had echoed through his dreams.

Protect her.

The words of a dying mother whose last, desperate wish had been the safety of her daughter.

His thoughts returned to Mark Osborn – the doctor who had cared for Erynne's mother. A friend, too. Perhaps more? Battling emotions set Colin's jaw on edge as he imagined the attack he had suffered here in Erynne's home, presumably trying to do the job Colin had failed to perform. Colin didn't know if he would have fared any better, but he was convinced of one thing: it should have been *him* who was with her when the danger came.

ଓ

Two hours later, Len and Gretchen insisted that Colin accompany them home. At first, he refused.

"No. Thank you, but I can't sit around while she's out there. I need to do something – look somewhere!"

But even as he said it, he knew that taking such action would do little more than keep him busy – and perhaps from losing his mind. He was in a strange town. He had no leads to go on and no good starting place from which to search. Erynne was outside his reach, just as if she had only been a dream after all.

Len seemed to understand Colin's frustration. He squeezed his shoulder, steering him toward the car. "We'll go out at first light – I promise. Detective Daniels has your cell number – and ours too. He'll call if they hear anything. In the meantime, there's something you can do to help. But not here. Come on."

The drive to their house was brief. As they climbed Bay Street in the fog, Colin could see little but trees and rooftops. Several short turns later, they pulled to a stop next to an ancient Nissan pickup in front of a two-story redwood house. Silently they climbed from the car. Colin's own weariness was mirrored in their faces as he followed them through the front door, where an excited Labrador greeted them.

"This is Bart," Len said, patting the dog's head. Colin put down his bag and held out his hand for inspection. The dog's wet nose felt comforting and Colin let out a ragged breath, blinking his eyes rapidly as he knelt and scratched Bart behind the ears.

"I'm going to call the hospital," Gretchen said, heading down a short hallway toward the dark kitchen. "Marge is on duty tonight. She'll tell me what's happening with Mark."

"Come on," Len said, turning on lights and motioning Colin to follow. "I'll make some coffee and we'll talk." He pointed Colin to a table and chairs while he opened a cabinet and started measuring coffee into a filter. Bart padded softly into the room, circled Len's legs and then came to lie down at Colin's feet. Gretchen was leaning on the counter, twisting an old spiral phone cord around her finger as she offered monosyllables into the receiver. After a few minutes, she hung up the phone.

"Mark is in stable condition," she said. She pressed her lips together. "He'll be in ICU for a few days."

"Did he regain consciousness?" Len asked. "Has he been able to tell anyone what happened?"

Gretchen shook her head. "They don't know yet how much damage was done to his vocal chords, but there's a lot of swelling." She looked at Colin. "He won't be able to tell them anything."

"All the more reason for you two to tell me what's going on," Colin said, a muscle twitching in his jaw. "What are you withholding from the police?"

"It's about your dreams, Colin," Gretchen said, sitting beside him. "Yours and Erynne's – otherwise we wouldn't be holding back. We just think the police would find it all too hard to believe."

"It's decaf," Len said, putting a steaming mug on the table in front of Colin.

"Sleep is the last thing on my mind," he answered, ignoring the coffee. "I want to hear your story."

"Okay, but you need to sleep soon, Colin," Gretchen answered, covering his hand with her own. "You need to dream. It may be the only way to find Erynne."

⁓

It was well past midnight by the time Len finished telling Colin about the legend. His coffee was cold, his eyes unfocused as he listened, drawn into the past like Erynne had been earlier that afternoon. Bart stayed at his feet, a comforting sentry.

"Do you mean that for more than a thousand years, all of my ancestors – my great grandfathers all the way back to the Middle Ages – had dreams like this that connected them to Erynne's great grandmothers?" Colin shook his head. "That's ... incredibly unlikely."

"That's what Erynne said," Gretchen said. "She was so angry when she left the studio. But something changed her mind when she got home. Someone gave her your name. She opened the door expecting to meet *you*."

Colin rose and walked toward an arcadia door that led to the backyard. He searched the darkness beyond the glass for a logical answer, but only found his own befuddled expression staring back at him. The weeks he had spent wandering strange streets in the night, waking breathless, as if someone had been searching for him – was that evidence of the truth in Len's story? Were they the same dreams that had tormented his father, from which he had only found comfort in the phantom arms of Erynne's mother?

Colin turned back toward Len and Gretchen, who sat silently while he wrestled with the truth.

"The man who has her – do you think he knows about this story?"

Len shrugged his shoulders. "If it was handed down to him – like Shannon's fairytale? Maybe. But if not, I wouldn't think so. This isn't the stuff of Irish History 101. The books where I found information are pretty obscure –the information from the Internet is sketchy at best, only providing fragments of the whole story. And I had the necklace as a starting place."

"Colin, try to get some sleep," Gretchen said. "Please? Erynne has always been a strong woman, but what she's gone through already, and now this ..." her voice trailed off, her eyes pleading. "We need to find her."

"I'll sleep," Colin said. "I'll try anything – but I'm not sure it works that way. I've never been able to make myself dream of her. The dreams come as they will – both the bad and the good. And we always meet in surreal locations – a foreign street, a desert river..."

"Never any place real?"

He shrugged. "The beach, maybe. She said it looked like Carmel – but she wasn't there in reality, was she? Not while she was dreaming."

Len shook his head. "It may not work then. I was hoping for more."

"But it's worth a try, right?" Gretchen asked.

"Of course," said Colin, now eager for sleep and the chance to see her tonight. He couldn't wrap his mind around the legend, the forces at play or the odds of anything he had heard being true. But he would find her. That was a promise he intended to keep.

He turned toward the stairs with Bart at his heels, his tail wagging in ignorant pleasure.

"Whatever this is – a blessing or curse – it pushed me to come here searching," he told them. "One way or another, I'm going to find her. I refuse to lose her now. Not when I have come this close."

Chapter 36

The thick fog that had settled over Evelyn Reardon's estate parted noticeably for just a moment, allowing the moon to cast a glow over Erynne as she lay unconscious against the Cypress tree. To Michael she looked like a broken doll, thoughtlessly discarded by a spoiled child. But she wasn't a doll. She was a living thing – right here in front of him. He was finally moving beyond pursuit to capture.

His limbs trembled as he squatted down to examine her. Reverently, he picked her up and carried her inside. Finally holding her in his arms produced an indescribable combination of desire, fear, and violence that intensified his tremors, threatening to overwhelm him. He placed her carefully on his mother's sofa, relieved to break the connection of his skin against hers.

His mother was out of town again – a stroke of luck coinciding perfectly with his need for a safe place to keep Erynne. Was it Australia this time? Or maybe the Orient? Michael could never keep track of his mother's travels, but he hated the strange treasures she brought back with her. They filled the corners and shelves of her home: Kachinas, totem poles, carved figurines, drums and oddly-shaped stones –all potentially dangerous if treated lightly. He had adopted his superstitions from his father, who had something to say about such things when Michael was a child. He wished he had listened better, wondering if that knowledge would have added strength to his craft.

He had surprised himself this week, stretching the known boundaries of his gift to find Erynne. The information came on one of those nights when he had drawn close, penetrating her thoughts, mapping his course. That's when he finally broke through to a new level of sight – something his father had whispered of in the bowels of this very house – a heightened connection to his power that allowed him to track her in a vision, not just in her dreams. The knowledge had been almost overwhelming. She was walking along the streets of San Francisco. She had been so close all along!

But being privy to her thoughts had been a strain, both mental and physical. She was always focused on the intruder. Her longing for the man enraged Michael – as had his unexpected presence in the forest, his voice echoing against the hill and ruining the thrill of Michael's pursuit. Together, they would be too strong for him. This was something he knew without a doubt.

His fatigue when he woke the next morning only reinforced that conviction. He had been too weak to rise from bed, too weak to attend an important fundraising event, much to Markham's chagrin. Too weak to visit Margaret and make sure that her fear continued to motivate her silence.

Walk away. It's not too late to change.

That day, he heard his mother's voice in his head, urging him to step away from his chosen life. As usual, it took him a while to shake her off, to harden his heart. What did she know about him anyway? His father had always insisted that only he understood Michael's gift. Michael had fought against that logic long enough, just like he had fought against their connection. He didn't want to consider his mother's sense of morality anymore. It was too much of a struggle.

He had only started feeling strong enough to sit up in bed late that afternoon. Grabbing a pad from his bedside table, he had sketched the dream woman's face from memory, carefully moving his charcoal against paper, paying special attention to her eyes, the line of her jaw, the full curve of her lip and the way her hair fell away from her brow. When he had completed the sketch, he held it up, admiring its perfection. He hated to share it, but knew he must.

Jack had kept his eyes open for Michael in the past. Never before had it paid off so quickly.

Having his vision confirmed gave Michael back his strength. He knew he needed to take her – knew it the first time he heard her name. The days that had passed between Jack's phone call and tonight had been agonizing. Strong enough now to meet lobbyists, kiss babies and placate the press, Michael had been ever mindful of the clock, which seemed to hold still at times. All the while, fantasies of Erynne O'Keefe had been growing in his mind.

Tonight, part of those fantasies had come to life. Instead of seeing his wife's eyes widen in terror, he had seen Erynne's – as she cowered against the tree, waiting for him to strike.

Of course, the strike hadn't come. Michael had learned something valuable from the rage that had sent him after Margaret. He should not have allowed himself to lose control that way. He should have savored the moment, drawing out her fear until her pleading voice was nothing but a soft whisper, filling him with shuddering waves of euphoria.

Still trembling, Michael backed away from the couch, from Erynne, and wiped the back of his hand against his lips.

With Erynne, I'll take my time.

Jack slammed the front door, shattering Michael's mental reverie. He scowled and turned to face him.

"What happened to her head?" he demanded.

"She hit the corner of a table. I was taking care of an unexpected visitor."

The scowl deepened. "Who?"

Jack shrugged and transferred his weight from one foot to the other. "I don't know, some guy who showed up at her house just as we were getting ready to leave." He smiled at Michael. "No one you need to worry about anymore."

Michael turned back toward Erynne's sleeping figure, folding his arms across his chest. Using Jack had been an unavoidable risk. He could not have approached her on his own, not with his recognizable face. But Jack could be an incredible liability, and Michael had spent the past few hours pacing restlessly, waiting for the sound of tires on the driveway.

Jack stepped away from the door and entered the living room. He looked over Michael's shoulder at the motionless figure on the couch.

"What do we do with her now?" he asked.

Michael did not miss the eager tone in Jack's voice, but he didn't answer him. His thoughts had returned to Erynne's visitor.

What if it was the Intruder from his dreams?

Violent anger surged through him at the thought of them together: an instant headache across his wide forehead.

Turning swiftly, Michael grabbed Jack by the collar of his shirt. "Never mind about her. She's not your concern anymore. Is the man dead? Did you kill him?"

Jack gulped air and shifted his gaze between Michael and the doorway. "I think so," he stammered. "I mean, I slashed his throat. He was bleeding like crazy – but he was breathing when I left."

Cursing, Michael pushed Jack roughly toward the door.

"Go back and find out. If he's dead, call me immediately. If not, don't bother coming back until he is."

He turned back to Erynne as Jack hurried out the door. His thoughts were once again solely occupied by the sleeping figure in front of him. He was fascinated by the rhythmic motion of her chest, rising and falling like the tide, the only indication that she was alive. Giving in to temptation, he reached out and gently touched her black hair, smoothing it from her face. She was his now. How could the Intruder ever find her here?

"No need for worry," he said softly, kneeling by her side. "No need to concern yourself with him ever again. From now on when you dream, you'll only dream of me."

Chapter 37

Erynne opened her eyes and saw nothing. Silent blackness like she had never known filled every inch around her, thick and oppressive. She gasped, a sound that echoed in spirals, circling high above her head. Wherever she was, it felt both confined and voluminous. The inconsistency added to her confusion.

Was she awake or dreaming?

She sat up slowly, waiting for her eyes to adjust, but the darkness would not soften. Feeling with her fingers, she found the edge of a bed and carefully swung her feet around. She winced in shock as they came in contact with a cold concrete floor. Minutes passed, but she still saw nothing. No shadows, no movement, no light from under a doorway. The only sound was her quickening breath and the blood raging in her ears, pulsing with a memory just out of reach.

It suddenly cracked open, releasing her last waking moment. The dark hunter from her dreams was chasing her through the fog. She was trapped with nowhere to hide.

Panic followed the memory and Erynne sprang to her feet. With outstretched arms, she began feeling frantically in front of her face. A moan rose from her throat and echoed back from the walls she could not see. She inched forward, a half step at a time.

In seconds she was touching the cold texture of a curved stone wall. The room was a cylinder, then – an old silo, a medieval tower. Her pace increased as she followed the wall, feeling for a door, stairs or ladder. Any means of escape.

More seconds passed. An eternity. When she finally found a change in the wall's texture, her heartbeat quickened. Her fingers moved greedily, tracing a groove, making out the edge of a steel door – *a doorknob!* She gave it a swift tug, instantly bathing the cell in brilliant sunlight.

Erynne stepped out of her black prison and onto a small beach. She shielded her eyes with one hand, waiting for the spots to go away.

What kind of prison cell leads to a beach?

She turned around to examine the door from the outside, but found that it had disappeared. Nothing was behind her now except the sheer wall of a cliff that climbed up until it disappeared into the cloudless sky.

Looking down, Erynne saw that she was wearing her long white nightgown, the one she only owned in her dreams. Her heart began to thump against her chest. She searched the beach in both directions, dreading the sight of the man who had stalked her in her nightmares before following her into reality. But there was no sign of him – not him or anyone else.

The beach was small, a narrow strip of sand that began and ended where the stark cliff walls curved out into the sea. Erynne traveled from one end to the other, searching for a footpath or stairs that might lead her to the cliffs above. She found nothing but a deeper sense of isolation. Hugging her arms to her chest, she wished for Colin's comforting presence beside her. But this wasn't anything like one of their meeting places. It was another prison, prettier than the dark cell, but just as confining.

The clouds seemed to agree. They gathered quietly over the ocean, urging the wind to pick up along the shoreline. It lifted her hair and tugged at her gown. The sun had been high in the sky just moments before, but now it was setting too quickly, falling fast below the horizon in a beautiful and terrifying wash of color. The frigid tide steadily marched forward, reaching out tenaciously to grab her hem. The narrow beach was growing smaller by the minute.

Panic welled in Erynne's chest. It wouldn't be long before the waves reached the cliffs and she would be dragged along too – beaten mercilessly against them. Or the strong undercurrent would pull her out to sea.

Now desperate for anything that would lift her out of the tide's icy reach, she climbed on top of a wide, flat boulder and searched again for any foothold, any kinder entrance to the steep cliff. But nothing was there.

Then something moved in her periphery. She turned quickly, peering along the cliffs.

There it was again. Her heart skipped a beat.

This time, her eyes moved more slowly, turning to rest on the southernmost point of the cliff where a ghostly tree perched precariously above the sea. It was the Lone Cypress, postcard perfect – a sentinel silhouetted against the angry backdrop of crashing waves and blackening sky. But it hadn't been there a moment ago. And while Erynne stared, a man stepped away from the tree to look down at her on the beach. Even at a distance, she recognized his movements.

"Colin!"

Her cry carried on the wind, resounding with fear and relief. The waves continued to rise. Colin was her only hope.

Erynne pressed her body against the cliff as the water slipped over the top of the boulder. It moved at an alarming rate – reaching her knees in seconds, tugging violently on her sodden nightgown.

"I'm coming, Erynne!"

Colin's words carried down to her ears in agonizing echoes. He was so close, yet so far away. She watched with hope and fear as he tried to make his way down the steep edge of the cliff, needing his help but afraid he would lose his footing and fall into the ragged rocks below. For several agonizing minutes, she watched his precarious descent only to realize that he was making no progress. Each time he found a lower foothold, the cliff would swell unnaturally, lengthening the distance between them.

The frigid water was now swirling around Erynne's waist. With each pull of the tide it weakened her wet grasp on the slippery cliff. She continued to search for something to hold on to, desperate to fight the inevitable sea.

"Colin." It was a whisper now. The water was tugging at the ends of her loose hair.

"I'll find you," he shouted. "I won't stop until I find you!"

But it was too late. A final wave struck Erynne, forcing her to release her grip on the cliff. Water enveloped her. Colin's final words echoed as the foaming water pulled her out toward the sea and then down, deeper and deeper into its black depths.

Chapter 38

Jack's shoes squeaked on the linoleum floor as he entered Dominican Hospital and walked briskly past the unattended volunteer desk. It was late, too late for volunteers, too late for visiting hours. Still, he turned left, guided by signs hanging from the ceiling, and continued down a carpeted hallway.

What am I doing here? he asked himself, rubbing his stubbled jaw.

During his drive north on Highway One, he had been racking his brain, trying to come up with a plan: something that would satisfy his boss and not land him in jail. He could end up behind bars either way. He knew that. If the senator had not come to his rescue last time, he wouldn't be breathing fresh air now.

If only I had stuck that knife in deeper.

His victim had obviously had enough life left in him to call the police. Or a nosy neighbor had seen something. Maybe Colin Green had finally shown up. Jack heard a report on the radio shortly after passing Watsonville naming his victim as Dr. Mark Osborn. The information was sketchy and reported by a newsreader who sounded much too cheerful when she spoke the words: "stabbing," "victim" and "manhunt."

Manhunt. Imagine that.

At least they had not provided a description of him on the news, meaning they probably didn't have one. Still he worried. This was what he got for messing with a high-up doctor. "A community leader," the reporter had called him.

"With bad timing," Jack had muttered, turning off the radio.

He had to be crazy, heading back toward Santa Cruz now. He had at least borrowed a different car this time – a sweet ride parked at a Seaside golf course, probably left by some drunken semi-pro.

Idiot rich people, he thought, picturing the senator with his upper class nose held high in the air. Jack had delivered the girl, as promised. What did he get in return? Nothing but grief. Oh, and one more dangerous job to do.

What would have been the harm in letting Jack have a little piece of the action? Reardon wouldn't have even found her if it wasn't for him!

Jack punched the elevator button and jammed his hands into his pockets. The senator should be thanking him. It had taken an incredible amount of self-control to keep his hands off her while they were in the car. She had looked like a fairytale princess in the moonlight. Snow White maybe, with that pale skin and dark hair. Was it a kiss that had awakened her in the story? Yeah, but a kiss would have meant suicide for Jack. The senator had about torn him apart just because of a little bruise on her head.

The elevator doors opened and Jack stepped out and turned left. The ICU nurses' station was at the end of the corridor behind a sliding glass door. Red letters on the glass warned Jack to check in before attempting a visit. He hovered there for a moment, examining all he could through the glass. It didn't take him long to determine which room Osborn was in – there was a dozing police officer sitting outside Room 254.

Jack turned around and entered a nearby waiting room. It was empty but recently used as evidenced by the full trashcan, scattered magazines and blaring television. Digging for a dollar bill, Jack walked toward the Coke machine and gave his predicament some thought.

His first instinct was to find hospital scrubs, a lab coat or janitor's uniform. But reality quickly set in. Without an ID badge, he would be no less noticeable than if he decided to enter the room by rappelling down the side of the building.

"This is a lot of trouble for a pretty woman," he muttered under his breath. Jack shook his head, wondering how he could possibly succeed.

Cut your losses. Run.

Why not? He could grab the first Greyhound to L.A., give the acting career a second chance. He had fooled Erynne O'Keefe for a while today. The senator could find another lackey to do his dirty work.

Jack reached for the doorknob but stopped, feeling an eerie sense that someone was watching him from behind. He turned around and almost jumped out of his skin when he saw his reflection in the black glass of a floor-to-ceiling window. Genuine fear shone from his eyes.

"He would find me," he told his reflection.

He shuddered, knowing it was true. It might not happen right away. Probably wouldn't, seeing as the senator had his hands full at the moment. No, it would be when Jack least suspected it. He could see himself walking home from the liquor store with a brown bag stuck under his arm. He'd have just gotten a part in a commercial and things would be looking up. Suddenly he'd be pulled into an alley and watch forty bucks worth of amber liquid shatter on the asphalt.

"You disappointed me, Jack," the senator would say. "You won't ever do that again."

And that would be it.

The senator's talent for knowing things had always been helpful to Jack in the past. If he jumped ship now, he had no doubt that it would be used against him in the future.

"So I have to do this," he told himself.

He walked toward the window and leaned against the metal frame, hoping for a miracle. Instead, he saw a priest walking through the hospital's entrance below.

That'll do, he thought.

Jack had played a pretty good preacher in a high school play once. No reason he couldn't do it now. Using the window as a mirror again, he licked his fingers and pushed them through his hair, tucked in his shirt and straightened the collar of his corduroy jacket, again thankful for the preppy attire. Satisfied with his appearance, he turned back toward the room, scanning it quickly until he found a tattered Bible under an outdated copy of *Field and Stream* in the corner. Before he could talk himself out of it, he opened the door and headed toward the nurses' station.

"Excuse me, Ma'am?" The southern accent sounded good, he thought. "I'm Brother Bill Udall from the Unity in Peace and Light Church over on Pacific Street. I just learned about our Brother Mark Osborn's terrible ordeal tonight and have come to pray with him. Which room will I find him in?" Jack looked around in what he hoped appeared to be eager ignorance.

The nurse frowned and looked at the Bible clutched in his hands.

"Visiting hours are over. If you're not an immediate relative…" Her voice stopped abruptly. An alarm was beeping and she looked down at a flashing light on her switchboard.

"I only mean to lift his spirits," Jack pressed on with a dopey smile. "I'll be in and out, quick as lightning."

For a moment it looked like she was going to continue her argument, but suddenly several more blinking alarms sounded on her desk. She rushed toward a room in the opposite direction and dismissed Jack with a quick, "Over there, room 254. You'll have to clear it with Officer Jacobs."

"God bless you," Jack called after her for good measure. He turned and walked toward the uniform.

One down, one to go.

The officer turned and looked at Jack drowsily as he approached the door. Jack held the Bible higher against his chest and nodded at the man with a smile, hoping to reflect both sympathy for the wounded and that inner peace that preachers always have pasted across their faces.

"Is Dr. Osborn resting?" he asked in a stage whisper. "I'm Bill Udall, here to pray with him."

The uniform didn't answer, but shifted in his chair and waved him toward the room. Jack walked past, holding his breath.

Osborn was asleep, his neck covered in a thick layer of gauze bandages. The room was filled with whirring equipment, each machine connected to the extremities of his body with colorful tubes and wires. Jack shivered in spite of himself, wondering what it was like to feel the edge of a knife pass through the delicate skin of your throat. He had never been forced to revisit an adversary like this, to face what he had done in a moment of violence.

Jack sighed and laid the Bible on the foot of Osborn's bed before pulling out his knife. He figured if he could reopen the wound, only sticking the knife in deeper this time, Osborn might just lie there and bleed to death without anyone being the wiser.

At least he can't scream, he told himself.

Jack's hand shook as he pulled inexpertly at the gauze. The wound beneath made his stomach turn. It was swollen, bruised and stitched back into place with purple thread the pressed heavily into the angry flesh. Jack looked at his switchblade, wondering if it carried germs that had given Osborn an infection.

You're being ridiculous, he told himself. *It hardly matters now.*

Steadying his hand, he switched his blade open and aligned it with the purple thread.

A sudden scream from behind made Jack jump. He turned around, swinging his blade in a careless arc that missed Osborne's damaged skin by mere centimeters. A nurse stood just inside the door. At the sight of Jack's knife, she dropped her bandage tray and turned around, yelping like a small dog for the officer.

Jack moved quickly, scooting around the foot of the bed and causing the Bible to fall to the floor with a heavy thud. He searched desperately for a second avenue of escape, but found none.

This is the price you pay for using the Word of God as a means for murder, Jack. It was his mother's voice he heard in his head, reverberating from the sterile walls and finding acceptance somewhere in Jack's chest.

The uniform came running in seconds later, his gun drawn and aimed at Jack's chest.

"Drop it, dirt bag!" he shouted.

He's awake now, Jack thought, smirking in spite of himself at the cop's cheesy line. He dropped the knife and raised his arms high above his head, imitating a center on the basketball court.

For some reason, he felt strangely relieved.

Chapter 39

Kendall Markham arrived at his office well before dawn. Snapping on the overhead fluorescent lighting, he scowled at the empty reception area and the cold coffee pot in the corner. Where was Bernice? More than an hour had passed since he called her.

"Get down here ASAP," he had hissed into the phone.

Of all the unthinkable things to happen, Senator Reardon was missing! Markham hadn't heard from him in more than forty-eight hours – not since he had called to back out of yet another fundraiser. He had left messages on Reardon's phone, had someone knock on his door, look for his car and check all of his usual haunts – but there was no sign of him. Even the senator's mother was getting worried, leaving Markham several messages from Australia to complain that her son wasn't returning her calls.

"Get in line," Markham muttered miserably after he hung up the phone.

Meanwhile Margaret was finally home, under the care of a private nurse, though her recovery from the accident was going slowly. *Too slowly*, Markham thought. He suspected her of milking it for sympathy. Didn't she realize that the public was no longer interested?

Markham switched on his desk lamp and sat heavily in his chair. He should have seen this coming. Over the past two weeks, the senator's mood swings and erratic behavior had only increased, making it more and more difficult for Markham to cover for him.

"I understand what's at risk here, Markham," Reardon had said darkly when they had their last heart to heart on the subject. And yet he had turned around and missed three more scheduled events. Three! Including the most important fundraiser of the year.

"Yes, I should have known," Markham muttered. He was the player who had been played, a victim of false promises, just like those he had been spewing for years. Part of him wanted to retaliate, drop Reardon and spill his secrets. Ruin him, punish him.

But then the truth always hit. The boomerang effect.

Bernice bustled into the office like a bulldog, interrupting his fleeting fantasy of revenge. Stray gray hairs were falling haphazardly from her hastily fastened bun and her face looked flaccid and powdery without makeup. Markham wished again for a prettier secretary until she set the early edition of the *Examiner* in front of him along with a *venti* Americano from Starbucks and a hand-written list of countermeasures to the article on page one. She waddled out of his office without comment, leaving Markham to face the headline alone.

"Reardon a No Show," it read. There was an unflattering picture beneath taken at the senator's last public appearance. In it, he was wagging his finger in the face of his opponent with his lip curled in ugly contempt.

Markham pushed the paper off his desk and listened to the muffled thud it made hitting the carpet. Reardon's rise to greater power had been a picture that he had been carefully putting together in his mind. Now he was watching it come apart, like a jigsaw puzzle hastily gathered up and thrown back into its box.

"Mrs. Madison-Reardon is on line one," Bernice said, sticking her head in the door.

Markham could see by her expression that Reardon's mother would not be put off again. He smiled as he lifted the receiver, hoping his false confidence would travel through the phone line.

"Evelyn, I'm glad you called ..." Several excuses were on the tip of his tongue but Markham was tersely interrupted.

"Save the pleasantries. I want to know where my son is."

Markham pursed his lips and tilted his chin toward the ceiling. This woman had a way of setting his teeth on edge. Didn't she understand that he alone was keeping this campaign afloat? Neither Reardon nor Margaret were pulling their weight, though they would certainly be the ones receiving adulation from a cheering crowd should they eke out a win. Markham considered saying some or all of this, but instead he mustered his last ounce of patience and took a deep breath.

"Actually, I don't know where he is," he finally said. "I haven't been able to get a hold of him in two days."

"Have you called the police?" Even from thousands of miles away he could hear the scorn in her voice.

Markham chortled nervously. "He could do without that kind of publicity right now." *To put it mildly.*

"Forget about the publicity. We're talking about my son. You find him and have him call me within the next few hours, or I'll call the police myself. Do I make myself clear?" The line went dead.

Markham dropped the phone into its cradle and sighed. For the first time in months, he swiveled toward the window and watched the sun rise over the city. Exhaustion enveloped him. While the orange light blazed against mirrored glass and polished granite, he had an epiphany, finally understanding why some people retreat into themselves without warning. Shutting out the world, content to be locked up in asylums – they were the ones with the guts, or maybe the good sense, to give up. Sunrises and sunsets could be their priority. No need to waste another moment on vain ambition, doomed from the start.

Bernice cleared her throat in the doorway and Markham turned to find her looking at him oddly. He recovered from his moment of insanity and leaned forward to gather the scattered newspaper from the floor.

"Get phone numbers for anyone who might know where the senator is. *Anyone*. If we don't find him – and I mean soon – that woman is going to have his disappearance all over the news."

Chapter 40

Michael did not dream about Erynne, perhaps because he knew she was sleeping under lock and key only a few doors away. Instead he was beckoned from his bed by cloaked men – his ancestors, he believed – who escorted him to the basement. Once again, it was transformed. Red candles flickered against curved walls. They chanted a cadence and fed him steaming broth. His strength revived, Michael was ready to hunt. Not for Erynne, but for the Intruder – the one she still cried for in her sleep.

He caught his scent the moment he stepped outside. Turning south, he tracked him through the forest. Michael was amazed at how sharp his senses had become. Though it was night, he could see every tree, every rock. Better still, he could sense the Intruder's trail. The air itself seemed to resonate with his parasitic aura, stirring Michael's blood and urging him forward.

How many times had Michael sensed him in his dreams? He had been there from the beginning, he realized. Unseen, unwelcome. Even then Michael had given chase, following him through abandoned cities, pounding wet pavement, ducking through shadows, only to lose him in the predawn hours. It was his first glimpse of Erynne that had pulled him off those dark paths. She had always been a temptation too strong to ignore.

But she's mine now, he thought. *Safely tucked away where he'll never find her*.

Michael saw the Intruder in the distance emerging from the forest. He hesitated for a moment and then turned toward the sea, carefully picking his path over rocky terrain.

Michael smiled in the moonlight. This was too easy.

He continued to follow, keeping to the tree line. His target was passing in and out of site as he moved behind large rocks and ducked between trees. Moving with a new sense of urgency, his eyes were determined and focused on something Michael couldn't see.

Or someone?

His heart began to pound, building into dread as he came around a bend and spotted it in the distance ahead – The Lone Cypress. They were just two miles from his mother's home!

Had he unwittingly led him here?

The Intruder began to run. Michael tried to keep up, but couldn't. Something was wrong. He was losing speed and stumbling on the uneven terrain. Each breath he drew was ragged and his feet felt heavy, as if they had been injected with Novocain.

What was happening to him? Where was the reinforcement his ancestors had provided just moments ago?

But somehow Michael knew. The Intruder was taking his strength, just like he and Erynne would take his power. If he didn't stop them. If he didn't fight.

An unnatural mist rose from the Pacific, instantly swirling around Michael, putting a stop to his halting progress. He could no longer see his enemy, but he heard his raised voice, strong and determined over the roaring waves that crashed against the cliffs below.

"I'll find you!" he was shouting.

He's coming for her, Michael thought. *And I can't do anything to stop him.*

Throbbing pain woke Michael in the murky moments of predawn. He lay still, trying to fight it with shallow breaths, but the headache fought back: waging war, winning.

Staring at the ceiling, Michael remembered his dream with disturbing clarity. He tried to steady his pounding heart, hoping to silence the cacophony in his head as well. Instead it increased in tempo, propelling him to his feet and toward the bathroom. His stomach revolted in cramping pain, barely giving him time to reach the porcelain sink before body-racking heaves overcame him.

Everything was caving in. The fundraiser he missed had been crucial – yet getting to Erynne had seemed more important, overshadowing his better judgment. He should have at least checked in with Markham, but he couldn't stand to hear his admonitions – as if Michael were a child who didn't know what was at risk. To add to his worries, Jack had not returned last night, and the dream made it all too clear that the Intruder was still alive and an imminent threat.

When the heaving stopped, Michael splashed cold water on his face and looked at his reflection in the mirror. His eyes were bloodshot and shadowed with dark crescents. His hair was showing more gray, and his skin was sallow where it wasn't red and angry – blotched from worry and stress. No wonder Markham had been complaining so much about his pictures in the news. Disgusted, he turned away and slumped against the bathroom door.

Is this worth it? Is she worth it?

From his first glimpse of Erynne on the cobblestone street, Michael had recognized the threat she posed. Still, her ethereal beauty drew him in. He had bargained with his fate, always a man who knew how to have his cake and eat it too. If he could just find her and keep her away from the Intruder, surely any danger she posed would be eliminated. She would be his prize, a hidden jewel kept under lock and key. The idea had been intoxicating, but now he was forced to consider that her danger and beauty were one and the same. She was a Venus flytrap, a siren, a black widow.

He closed his eyes, moaning as he passed his fingers over dry lips, remembering the night before. She hadn't wakened on the couch, or when he carried her upstairs and laid her carefully on the bed. Michael's fingers had trembled as he moved them to the buttons of her blouse. The long white nightgown he had purchased lay waiting on the foot of the bed, bathed in blue moonlight so like the light in their dreams.

But what he had longed for as a forbidden and erotic delight, he had instead found terrifying. Contact with her skin had caused a cataclysm inside him – a fight between desire and fear that made the task almost impossible to complete. Still, he had pushed forward, moving carefully but swiftly as he transferred her into the gown, feeling relief coupled with disappointment when he finally pushed himself away from the bed. By then his brow was drenched in sweat.

Weak and uneasy, Michael had lowered himself gratefully into a chair and watched her sleep, fearing he was capable of little else. After a few minutes, he felt strong enough to stand, though he hadn't risked returning to her side. Instead he left the room, taking one last hungry glimpse before locking the door. Michael told himself he was simply tired and overspent. The morning would bring fresh perspective.

A good night's sleep – that's all I need.

But sleep had only made things worse.

As dawn crept through the curtains, he was reminded that time marched on. There were consequences to face now – alternatives he needed to consider to neutralize them. He could lose this election. It was Markham's admonition, but it was still true. Michael didn't feel stronger with Erynne under lock and key, he felt completely impotent.

It couldn't go on like this. He couldn't keep her.

Bitter regret met a violent surge of anticipation. Michael felt the first moments of relief from his headache. The fog that had covered his recent decisions was lifting, giving way to simple truth.

Erynne was responsible for draining his concentration. By keeping him hunting night after night, she had dulled his senses, pulling him away from his campaign. She wasn't a jewel, he realized, but a rare flower, cut clean from its roots, drawing its last hours of life from a source that could not sustain it, but only delay the inevitable.

Just for today, he told himself. *Just one more day.*

It was a sad truth about flowers, Michael knew. They must be destroyed before they have a chance to wilt. Otherwise, their beauty cannot be remembered – only their decay.

Chapter 41

Colin pulled Len's sputtering pickup into a parking space in front of Dominican Hospital. Shivering, he zipped up his fleece jacket and walked briskly toward the entrance. He had left the Martin's house before dawn after hastily scratching out a note and borrowing Len's keys. His rental car was still parked downtown, near Erynne's studio. He had forgotten all about it until this morning, when he'd wakened to darkness, the sick feeling of watching Erynne disappear beneath the black sea rising in his throat.

Like last night, Colin's first impulse was to scour the local beaches, cliffs and marinas for signs of Erynne. But finding the hospital in this unfamiliar setting had been difficult enough. Better to wait for full daylight. For now he could think of nothing better than to come here, hoping that the only man who knew anything about Erynne's abduction might have recovered enough to provide the police with some clues.

The prevailing mood of chaos Colin found in the ICU ward made him glad he had come. Trying to walk briskly toward the group of uniformed officers gathered outside of Mark's door, Colin was stopped at the nurses' station.

"I'm sorry, sir," the nurse said, grabbing his arm. "You can't go back there."

"What happened?"

She glanced over her shoulder before leaning across the desk to whisper. "Someone got into his room early this morning with a knife. Luckily, Theresa interrupted him."

Colin felt a cold coil of fear surround his heart. "Did they catch him?"

"Yes. They took him out of here about an hour ago."

"Did he tell them anything? Have they found the woman he took?"

"I don't know." The nurse looked at Colin curiously. "Are you a friend of Dr. Osborn?"

"No. I've never met him," he answered quietly. "But I would like to. Is he awake?"

She shook her head. "The police keep asking that too."

Colin looked back toward the group gathered around Mark's door and recognized Detective Daniels from the crime scene at Erynne's house. He was interviewing a nurse, presumably the one who had interrupted the second murder attempt.

"Could you tell Detective Daniels that I'm here?" Colin pointed him out to the nurse while pulling a business cards from his wallet. "My name is Colin Green. He knows me from the first crime scene."

The nurse took the card with fresh curiosity on her face. "Sure. There's a waiting room by the ICU entrance doors."

"Thank you." Colin headed back down the corridor.

The view from the waiting room window was dismal. Fog still hovered on the ground in a thick layer that made the street lights look like they were floating in air. Colin turned away and dropped into a chair, resting his head in his hands. He could not shake the images from his dream, or the desperate feeling that his inactivity was compounding. If only he had come sooner – or called ahead to warn Erynne about his premonitions of danger. But would she have listened? Could anything have prevented this?

"Mr. Green?"

Colin jumped up as Detective Daniels entered the room.

"I heard about your suspect. Is there any news about Erynne?"

"No. I'm sorry. He's not talking yet."

"So what happens now?"

The detective walked to the Coke machine and dug in his pocket for change.

"We keep questioning him until he's got something to say," he said.

"Do you know who he is? Anything about him?"

"Yeah," the detective said, popping his Coke open. "His name is Jack Lender. We sent a unit to his address in San Francisco, but it was empty – no trace of your friend. Lender has a record as long as my arm: drug possession, car theft, petty burglary, a few sexual misconducts."

Colin felt a wave of anger hit his stomach.

"And he's been out on the streets?"

"Not just out. For the past couple of years, he's been clean as a whistle."

"Which means…"

"Either he cleaned up his act for a while," the detective shot Colin a doubtful look, "or he's learned to be more careful. Sometimes when a guy like Jack slips off the radar, it means he's gotten himself a mentor – someone with the influence to cover up his crimes."

"Why would someone do that?" Colin asked.

The detective shrugged. "For what they get in return. Someone to handle their dirty work – a layer of insulation between them and the crimes they orchestrate. It's usually someone connected to organized crime."

Colin turned toward the window, his fists clenched at his sides. "In the meantime, there's no telling where he's taken her – or if she's even still alive."

"We'll get him to talk, Mr. Green," Daniels assured him. "And when we do, we'll find your missing friend."

ങ

Colin pulled into the driveway right behind Gretchen, who was clutching a bag of bagels as she got out of her car.

"Good morning," she said softly. "How's Mark?"

"Stable. But someone managed to get into his room last night with a knife."

"What?"

Colin held open the front door and returned Bart's enthusiastic greeting. Gretchen followed, barraging him with questions while Len took the bagels off her hands. Colin quickly brought them up to speed on Mark's second attack.

324

"I would have gone straight to the police station, but I had your truck."

"We'll go with you," Len said.

"But first, tell us," Gretchen asked. "Did you dream?"

Colin nodded, patting Bart absently. Every time he closed his eyes, the dream was there again, tearing at his resolve to stay focused and present. But he was reluctant to share it with Gretchen and Len, despite how hospitable they had been – or how much they cared for Erynne. Describing the scenes out loud would make them too real.

"Please Colin," Gretchen said. "Any little detail might help."

"I was in a forest," Colin said. "There was a clearing and then a bluff in the distance that overlooked the ocean. As soon as I reached it, I knew that Erynne was nearby, so I began running, trying to find her. I ended up on a rocky cliff that jutted out over the ocean. There was a tree there. When I walked around it, I saw a narrow strip of beach below that was almost completely covered by the rising tide. Erynne was there. Her back was pressed against the cliff and the waves were wearing her down.

"She called my name," Colin said. "I told her to hold on. I tried to find a path down the cliff side, but every time I descended by even one step, the cliff would stretch, pulling me farther away. She couldn't hold on any longer. A huge wave pulled her out to sea. That's when I woke up."

"Pulled out to sea?" Gretchen repeated weakly. "But what does it mean?"

Colin shook his head. "I don't know."

"It could mean she's still nearby," Len said. "That he hasn't taken her inland, anyway."

"You don't know that," Colin said, his forehead burrowed in frustration. "Who's to say it's a real place? The cobblestone street wasn't real. For all I know, every place we've dreamed together has just been part of our own Neverland."

"It's our only place to start, Colin," Len said. "Think about what you saw. We need details. Was there anything unusual? Maybe a lighthouse or wharf?"

"I can't remember any landmarks. Nothing unusual except the tree that grew so close to the cliff's edge." His eyes widened. "But that's something, isn't it? I've seen that tree before! It's unique, the way it grows out there by itself."

While Colin was still talking, Len disappeared into the living room, coming back with a large coffee table book titled, *The Wonders of Highway One*. He flipped through the pages, finally stopping and turning the book around for Colin to see.

"Is that what you saw?" He pointed at a picture under the title, *The Lone Cypress, Pebble Beach*.

Colin only had to take one look at the ghostly sentinel, stark evidence of life against the barren landscape of rock, to recognize it from his dream.

"That's it! Pebble Beach? It's not too far from here, is it?"

Gretchen shook her head as she rose to grab her purse and jacket. "No, Colin. The Lone Cypress is only about forty-five minutes down the coast."

Chapter 42

Erynne woke from her dream abruptly and gasped for air, her mind refusing to register that she was no longer floundering in the dark water. Her lungs felt tight and spent as she blinked her eyes against a narrow vein of light that seemed out of place in the midst of the ocean. But the sea had disappeared beneath her and she was lying still on something firm. It was a bed, its sheets and pillows soft and forgiving. The light was coming through a window – dawn, she finally realized – though last night it had seemed impossibly far away.

Sharp pain shot through Erynne's temple as soon as she tried to sit up. The room swayed around her, and she lay back against the pillow, wishing away her memories of the dream. It proved impossible. She shivered, remembering the dark water that had seemed alive, intent on swallowing her whole. She pulled a thick quilt up to her chin, fighting off the chill.

Her room was not the same cell from her dream, although it was similar in shape, with rounded walls that she could just make out beyond the curtains of her bed. Lying back, she was forced to focus on the canopy overhead, which was intricately embroidered with countless creatures – peacocks, hummingbirds, squirrels and dragons. She suddenly remembered them from last night. They had come to life around her in the soft lamplight, moving in a horrible dance and escorting her in and out of nightmares too strange to recall.

Was she still dreaming? Erynne moved her hand from beneath the quilt and touched the bump on her temple. It was tender, but she found no trace of dried blood. Cautiously she pushed herself up to a sitting position again and looked around, though she found no strong evidence of the material world she knew. Her bed was large and the quilt was covered in rich, Asian fabric like she had seen in Hong Kong. Four posts of carved mahogany rose to the ceiling, supporting the canopy overhead and shrouded in thick ruby velvet that draped over the wide footboard, obscuring her view of the rest of the room.

With each subtle movement, Erynne's head swam and her muscles protested, especially her left ankle, which throbbed painfully under the weight of the heavy covers. She tried to ignore it as she leaned forward, catching sight of treetops through the window. She was on an upper floor, then. The air in the room was thick with dust as if seldom used and she could hear no sounds of life beyond its walls.

She pushed back the covers and scooted to the edge of the bed. After waiting for a wave of dizziness to pass, she limped to the window, wincing with each step. Peering over the tiled encasement, she looked down on a lush lawn that spread to the edges of the property. Trees and hedges hid whatever existed beyond. Her mind grasped at fleeting images. She had been down there last night, running in the mist, chased by a shadowy monster.

Or had that been another dream?

Erynne felt sick and sore. A wet, racking cough rose from her chest, pushing through her parched lips and adding to her body aches.

Turning back toward the room, she stopped, startled by a movement in the corner. But it was only her reflection, staring back at her from a full-length antique mirror. She looked like a ghost, pale and lit from behind by the dusty sunlight, and wearing a long white nightgown – one she did not own, except in her dreams. She stared at herself, trying to make sense of it all. Was this another trick of her mind?

Erynne couldn't turn away from the mirror. Her eyes were drawn beyond her reflection to the unexplored side of the room. A scream rose in Erynne's throat, but she was too paralyzed to release it. The hunter sat quietly in the shadows, watching her every move.

Adrenalin coursed freely through her veins, lifting the fog that had surrounded her since waking. She remembered everything – especially this man who had parted the veil of sleep to find her.

I have to get out of here.

Erynne tamped down the hysteria that threatened to bubble over. She moved backward until she felt the mirror pressing against her shoulder blades. The hunter rose from his chair and was walking toward her, rubbing a large hand across his lower lip. The light from the window revealed a haggard face capped with unruly black hair touched at the temple with silver. His jaw was unshaven and his eyes were penetrating blue, but blood-shot and carved beneath with dark lines.

"Where am I?" she asked.

"Shh," he said, reaching out to place a large finger against her lips. The brief touch generated a reaction in both of them. Erynne shrank against the mirror in revulsion, while the man stepped back as if burned. She watched his retreat with confusion, noticing that beneath his unkempt appearance was a familiar face. *Who was he?*

"Let's not spoil this with meaningless questions," he said. "Our time together will be...so brief."

Erynne glanced at the door, wondering if it was locked. He watched her eyes shift past him and smiled, a flash of pleasure flaring in his own.

"Go ahead," he said, leaning so close that she could feel the rise and fall of his chest. His breath was labored with excitement, warm and frightening against her forehead. "It's unlocked."

Erynne cringed against the mirror.

"I'm going to miss our dreams together," he said softly. For a moment his gaze left her face. "Following you on the street, on the beach – it's been so exhilarating." He sighed. "But we have today, don't we? So go ahead, run. There's no one to interfere. I'll give you a head start, like I always do."

Erynne closed her eyes, wishing that she was back in her dream world, as she had so often wished herself awake. There had always been an avenue of escape in her dreams – the light of morning or the determination of her spirit forcing her to reject the nightmare. But the escape he offered now was false, only part of the game he wanted to play.

"You won't get away with this," she said, edging away. "Someone will come looking for me."

"Someone?" he asked quietly. His smile was gone. The color in his face had drained and he began to shake, his hands pumping into fists at his side. "You mean *him*, don't you?"

He took a step away, tore a lamp off the night table, and threw it against the wall next to Erynne's head. She screamed, covering her head with her arms as shards of crystal erupted around her. In an instant, he was back at her side, still shaking in rage as she shook in fear.

"Never mention him again!" he shouted, his voice reverberating against the high ceiling. "He'll never find you here. This place is for us. This day is ours – ours alone!"

A whimper of fear escaped from Erynne's throat. He seemed to find it there, encircling it with his hands and squeezing.

"Do you realize how much I've sacrificed? Do you understand what this day is costing me?"

Erynne felt a cloud of fog descend over her as he tightened his thumbs against her throat. He continued to rant: blaming her for luring him onto the street, for drawing his focus away from his work and then betraying him. But his words were becoming muffled, as if from a far off place. As the room faded away, Erynne's thoughts stayed focused on her only source of hope.

Find me, Colin. Please.

Chapter 43

"Thank you, Ruth. Just concentrate on Margaret. I'll call you if I hear anything."

Evelyn hung up the phone and checked her watch. It was five o'clock in the morning in Sydney, but noon in Georgetown, where her daughter-in-law remained heavily sedated and under the care of a private nurse. There was still no sign of Michael – not even a phone call during the past 48 hours, said the housekeeper.

Evelyn pushed her hands over tired eyes and into her hair, wondering what to do next. Yesterday she had expected her phone to ring at any moment. It would be Michael on the line, irritated by her numerous messages and brusque in his assurance that everything was fine. But as the day lengthened, she had resigned herself to familial obligation – for Margaret's benefit, at least – rescheduling her flight to the states, cancelling a trip into the outback and abandoning concert tickets.

Overnight, her sense of duty had turned to fear, keeping her awake. Three hours ago she had pushed back the covers and followed through on her threat to report Michael's disappearance to the San Francisco Police Department.

"Can you check his home in Pacific Heights?" she asked when Inspector Bridges received her call. "The phone just goes to voicemail – and I haven't been able to raise him on his cell either."

"What happened to his security detail?"

"I don't know. He usually moves with a bigger entourage than seems necessary, but no one's telling me anything." She gave him Kendall Markham's phone number. "He'll press you to keep your inquiries discrete. For the moment, I'm inclined to agree."

"I understand, ma'am," the inspector said. "I'll put out some quiet feelers. But try not to worry. It isn't unheard of for a political figure to slip away from the limelight from time to time – especially during a heated campaign. Mostly likely, you'll hear from him soon."

Unconvinced, Evelyn had thanked Inspector Bridges and hung up the phone. Every moment that had passed since saw her vacillating between anger and worry. Shame trumped them both. That Michael could abandon Margaret at such a time was unforgiveable, lending credence to a suspicion she had refused to acknowledge. But what on earth would make him jeopardize his campaign?

Evelyn watched dawn emerge through her hotel room window. The stars were fading one by one as Sydney's skyline took form. Turning away, she opened her day planner and made a quick note to arrange for a few purchases to be shipped home. None of it mattered anymore, but she wanted to stay busy until time to leave for the airport. Her bags were already packed and stored with the concierge downstairs, she had but to grab her purse before turning her key over to the registration desk.

Fatigue was setting in, but Evelyn fought it. Putting down her pen, she went into the bathroom to splash cold water on her face. She avoided her reflection – the chastisement she would see in her eyes. But it didn't matter. Her shame refused concealment.

She had run away again. Unable to face the responsibility she bore for Michael's character, she had retreated, indulging in the comfort of anonymity and the diverting pleasures of travel. Even the dark shift she had recently seen in Michael hadn't persuaded her to change her plans. Willingly blind, she had refused to face the unthinkable result. It was something she forced herself to consider now.

"Margaret," she whispered.

She could still see her daughter-in-law's battered face, could hear the doctors speak of the vicious nature of her attack. Margaret's need for heavy sedation was rooted in the hysteria she displayed when awake – a reaction that didn't seem to fit her strong character. Unless...

Evelyn closed her eyes, but it was too late to suppress what she imagined: not a nameless street thug, but her son's face, contorted in evil as he extinguished his last flicker of decency.

"No," she moaned, gripping the sink, refusing to let the ugly possibility drive her to her knees. Guilt and sorrow were not useful tools – not now at least. She couldn't fall apart. She'd been selfish long enough. It was time to go home.

Two hours later, Evelyn stepped out of the elevator and walked briskly toward the hotel lobby. With a shaking hand, she dialed Inspector Bridge's phone number and waited impatiently for him to answer.

"Inspector Bridges."

"Mrs. Madison-Reardon calling again, inspector," Evelyn said. "Have you found my son?"

"No ma'am. His housekeeper said he hasn't been home. His chief of security told me the senator had given his team an extended furlough." He paused. "I was hoping that he had been in touch with you by now."

335

"No, he hasn't. I've called everyone I can think of. No one has seen him."

Inspector Bridges paused. "The next step is a call to the FBI and Department of Homeland Security, followed by an All-Points Bulletin," he said. "You understand, I'm sure. A missing U.S. senator can be classified as a matter of national security. Once we do this, discretion will no longer be an option."

Evelyn closed her eyes and pressed the place between her brows. "That's not important at this point, is it, inspector? We just need to find my son. I'm afraid something terrible has happened."

"We'll do everything we can, ma'am."

"Thank you, inspector. For all you've done." Evelyn gave him her flight information and told him she would call again when she landed in San Francisco. She sat still for a moment after closing her phone, her eyes closed and her lips moving in silent prayer.

Michael has done something terrible, she thought. *Dear Lord, help me make it right.*

Displaying more grace than she felt, Evelyn rose from her chair and walked outside. As she stood under the hotel's canopy, she watched absently while her luggage was loaded into the waiting limousine. She remembered those nights, so long ago, when she had patted her baby on the back, soothing away his tears as he woke from another bad dream. He had learned to pat her back as well, and they had cried together, the broken-hearted mother with her tormented son, giving and receiving the simplest comfort.

Evelyn tipped the doorman as she stepped into the limousine, ignoring the tears that were finding a path down her lined cheeks. As any mother, she would gladly trade places with her child at that moment to save him from the dangerous road he was traveling. But she couldn't help wondering: how do you save someone whose greatest enemy is himself?

Chapter 44

Detective Daniels blew on his coffee and watched the steam swirl above the rim of the cup. He risked a sip and burned his tongue. Still it was good. The new station assistant, Melanie, was a treasure. He only wished Phyllis Gates had retired years ago, the old Battle-Ax. Her coffee had been like used motor oil. She had never known where anything was, never even worn a smile on her jaundiced face until the evening of her retirement party when she drank too much punch, kissed him on the lips and invited him to go with her on the cruise to Mexico that she had been talking about for years.

That had been a low point in his career.

Melanie had eased the pain with her youth, efficiency, chipper attitude and gourmet coffee. He would probably propose marriage to her if the difference in their ages wasn't so obscene. There was also the station's anti-fraternization policy to consider.

Daniels took another sip. Behind a wired-glass window in front of him, Jack Lender sat on a cold metal chair, resolutely refusing to answer any questions. In all his years in law enforcement, Daniels had seldom come across a criminal so stubborn about providing information. You saw that sort of thing on TV all the time, but not in the real world. Not when deals are offered regularly and a perp's major concern is how quickly he can get back on the street so he can score again.

But this guy was tough. Or maybe afraid?

"He's protecting someone," he told Detective Phillips early that morning.

"How do you figure?"

"What's he got to do with Dr. Osborn or Erynne O'Keefe, huh? They're both upstanding citizens – not into the drug or party scene. Where would he have even encountered them?"

Phillips had learned early in their relationship not to interrupt Daniels's strung-together questions. They were all rhetorical.

"And what was so important about Osborn that he had to come back for? Would you do that? March into a hospital to finish someone off? Seems to me like maybe he was following orders. But whose?"

Daniels's blood was boiling as he drove to the station this morning, thinking about the possibilities. This could be a case like no other. Santa Cruz had its fair share of murders, and plenty of other criminal activity to keep him busy too. But it was usually domestic stuff or maybe an unexplained dead transient. There was always a clear motive and a positive ID on a suspect within hours. Modern day forensics took all the mystery out of sleuthing these days and truthfully Daniels had become bored with the hippies, mall trolls, and political rent-a-mobbers that usually caused all the trouble.

But this case was different. He had a respected doctor in the hospital whom someone had tried to kill not once, but twice, a missing business woman who had never seen a bit of legal trouble, and now an arrested two-bit criminal who wouldn't so much as blink. Daniels wanted to piece the puzzle together himself – hopefully before the feds got involved. Wouldn't that be something?

"Detective Daniels? There's a phone messages from an inspector in San Francisco, an urgent fax from the SFPD and Professor Martin is here to see you." Melanie handed him a stack of papers and walked away without waiting for a response. Daniels turned around and goosenecked it down the corridor to see Erynne O'Keefe's three friends standing behind the front counter.

"Ah, nuts," he said, not moving out of sight quickly enough. He had caught the eye of Green – the one who hadn't really explained how he knew O'Keefe. Last night he was wound tighter than a spring, with a clenched jaw, wild eyes and hands balled into fists and then jammed impotently into his pockets. Yeah, this guy was about to go off – some kind of knight-in-armor complex. Daniels had seen it before and knew it was time to nip it in the bud. He walked down the hallway and stood in front of him.

"Ms. Martin, Professor Martin. *Mr. Green.*" He ducked his head at each of them respectfully, concern creasing his brow. The look had once been crafted, but now came easily – the appropriate mask for meeting with the families of victims. "You didn't need to come all the way down here without calling. I don't have any news for you."

"Actually we came to give you some information," Professor Martin said carefully, exchanging a glance with his two companions while he rocked back and forth on the balls of his feet. "We think Erynne may have been taken to some place near Pebble Beach."

"And what makes you think that?" Daniels kept his voice monotone as he flipped open a note pad and scribbled, "Pebble Beach" across the page.

The professor hesitated and Green spoke up. "This may sound strange, but it was a dream. I ... I dreamed that she was at the Lone Cypress."

"Uh, huh."

Daniels's expression didn't change, but he put away his pencil. Why should he be surprised? He had crack-pot psychics and voodoo spiritualists in here all the time claiming all kinds of stuff. Green was the most normal looking of this bunch, but that didn't mean anything.

"Listen, the guy who attacked Dr. Osborn is keeping a tight lip for now, but I think we are wearing him down. We have given Miss O'Keefe's photograph to the TV and newspaper people, and are very hopeful that something will turn up within the next twenty-four hours."

Green exploded. "You want to sit here and wait for the media to find her? She's in danger now!"

Daniels frowned. "Please calm down, Mr. Green. We're doing everything we can. Now if you'll excuse me, I've got a couple of matters to take care of. We'll let you know if we hear anything new."

Daniels had just noticed the SFPD fax in his hand. Across the top it read, *APB: Senator Mike Reardon reported missing.* This was going to be quite a day.

As he turned back toward his office, Daniels felt Green grab him by the wrist.

"Detective, please." His eyes were desperate. "Since he won't say anything, what could it hurt to ask him about Pebble Beach?"

Daniels scowled and pulled his wrist from Green's grasp.

"Take care, there, Mr. Green."

"I'm sorry," Green said, backing away with his hands in the air. "I just want to help you get Erynne back safely."

Daniels felt himself caving. What would he do if the victim was his sister? That's what the trainer had asked him last year when they made him attend that seminar on working with distraught families. He'd go ballistic too. Like this guy, he would want things to happen now, not later. No, it wasn't worth the trouble to fight him on it. Besides, if he was honest with himself, he would have to admit that those wacko psychics hadn't always been too far off the mark.

"Okay, don't get your panties in a wad. I'll give it a try." Daniels tapped his fingers against the papers in his hand. "But I've got some other pressing matters I have to take care of first. Why don't you go home, and I'll give you a call in a couple of hours."

Chapter 45

Ross held on to the tree branch with his knees. He wobbled a little while he turned the knob on his binoculars, but he was careful not to fall. He didn't want to lose his favorite hiding place at Grandma's house. It was away from his smelly sister and her baby TV shows, and away from his Grandpa's stupid dog who was too old to chase sticks and so grouchy he couldn't even play cowboys with him.

Today it was cold and windy. Ross wore his jacket zipped to his chin and a knitted hat pulled way down over his ears. Still his cheeks were red and stinging and his nose was running. But just a little bit. Not enough to make him to go inside. Not yet anyways. He didn't get to come to Grandma's house every day, and he didn't want to waste his time away from the tree.

He liked to keep a lookout for pirates on the ocean. He had buried treasure – right down by the tree's roots, though the dog had dug up one corner and chewed on it a little bit. He wished he had a good treasure box instead of the cardboard one. But ships were rare along this part of the coast. Ross had other things to look for. In the other direction, there were hundreds of trees. He would spot Bigfoot some day and then get his name in the newspaper.

But today he saw something at Grandma's neighbor's house that was strange. It made him forget about Bigfoot and the pirates. A man and woman had come out of the house and gone for a walk through the grass. But the lady didn't have anything on but a nightgown and she was bare footed. At first he thought maybe she was sick, like those people he and Mom had visited in the nursing home who wore their pajamas all day. But it didn't make sense that she didn't have any shoes on, or even a robe. Every time he was sick, Mom made him wear thick pajamas, slippers, a robe *and* keep a blanket across his lap while he played Wii.

But maybe she wasn't sick. Maybe they were playing a game. The man was a whole lot bigger than the lady and sometimes he would let her walk off a little bit on her own before chasing after her. But the lady was limping and Ross felt sorry for her. She didn't look like she liked the game at all. The man looked angry sometimes. He'd grab the lady's arm and shake her hard. Ross didn't think he was very nice. He wondered why the lady didn't slap him like people were always doing on TV.

No, she *is* sick, he decided. She stumbled and leaned against a tree whenever she came near one. He hoped she would go back inside soon.

Ross climbed up another branch and twisted his binoculars, this time pretending he was a military commando getting ready to invade the enemy's fort. The neighbor's house looked like a cool fort, too. It had a tower at this end that he had always wished he could see on the inside. That's where the lady in the nightgown had been, he was pretty sure, because he had seen a light up there go out right before they came out onto the lawn.

Suddenly Ross's walkie-talkie squawked and he almost lost his balance trying to grab it.

"Lunch time, Ross."

"Okay, Grandma. Be right there."

Ross descended the tree, muddying his jeans and scuffing his new shoes in the process. Running toward the house, he hoped his Grandma made something good for lunch, like nachos or corn dogs. He barely concealed his disappointment when he got done washing his hands and saw what Grandma had set out for him: a grilled cheese sandwich, tomato soup and two carrot sticks.

"Don't make that face," Grandma said. "If you eat all your lunch you can have an ice cream cone this afternoon when Grandpa gets home."

She ruffled his hair as she walked passed him, reaching for the TV remote while his baby sister gurgled happily on her hip. Ross quickly slurped down his soup and tore into his sandwich, hoping he could be outside again before Grandma's soap opera started. All those soap opera people ever did was kiss or cry. In the meantime a pretty weather lady was telling them it would be cold this evening with a chance of rain.

Ross carried his empty plate and bowl to the sink and filled the bowl with water.

"You ate too fast," Grandma said. "You're going to make yourself sick."

Ross made a face, but didn't let her see it this time. He ducked in front of the television, intent on heading straight back outside, but stopped when he recognized the picture on the screen.

"...Any information on her whereabouts should be directed to the Santa Cruz Police Department," the reporter said.

"Grandma, I saw that lady." Ross pointed to the television. "She's at your neighbor's house and she's wearing a nightgown."

Grandma made a face while bouncing the baby on her knee. "Were you in that tree again? Honey, I told you – it's too windy for climbing trees today."

"But I saw her, Grandma!"

Grandma finally glanced at the TV, but not in time to see the picture. They were showing a dog food commercial now. She turned back to Ross. "Evelyn lives alone next door, honey. And besides, she's off on one of her trips. Is it Austria or Australia this time? I can't remember. But no one else lives there. Maybe you saw the housekeeper."

Just then Grandma's soap opera began and Ross was shushed and told to go play a game in the living room.

"No one ever believes me," he muttered as he walked out the door.

Chapter 46

Jack tapped his fingers on the metal table while he waited for Detective Daniels to return. He hadn't talked to anyone since this morning, unless he counted the cute girl who brought him a sack lunch. Last night clearly wasn't the best night of his life, but he felt strangely relieved to be caught before he had the chance to kill Osborn. Now it was about facing what mattered, and Jack had plenty to focus on.

He obviously had two choices -- rat or don't rat. But the question was: which choice would benefit him the most?

The senator had gotten him out of a lot of tough jams before, but nothing this big. Still, there was always the possibility that he would come through again. That all weighed strongly on the side of keeping quiet. It was something Jack found easy to do, despite the detective's most skillful questioning techniques. His lips twitched. He had frustrated that staunch old windbag – that was for sure.

Of course, everything had a flip side, and Jack had spent the better part of the morning thinking about how the senator had changed over the past year. The last few months had been the worst. Senator Reardon had been distracted, less driven.

Temperamental. There had never been any loyalty between them – Jack knew that. He served a purpose in the senator's plans, for which he had been compensated and protected. But last night Reardon had been really angry about the cut on Erynne's head – and about the guy Jack had failed to kill.

He kept hearing the senator's voice playing like a recording in his head. "Don't screw this up, Jack. If you do, you're on your own."

Would he really leave me swinging in the noose?

Jack went back and forth in his mind, mostly ignoring his surroundings. Better to keep his mouth shut for the time being, he decided. He could always talk later if he wanted to, but he couldn't take back the senator's name once it left his lips.

With this thought fresh in his mind, he looked up and smiled nicely as Detective Daniels came back in the room and took a seat on the opposite end of the table. He sat astride the chair, with his forearms resting on the back. Why did cops do that?

"Have a nice lunch?" Daniels asked.

"Yeah." Jack leaned back in his chair and looked at the clock. "Makes me want a nap, you know? I got nothing more to say right now, so can I go back to my cell?"

"Not just yet, Jack." Detective Daniels adjusted his position. "I just heard an interesting story. You want to hear it?"

Jack's smile spread across his face. *He's got nothing*, he told himself.

"Shoot," he said.

The detective set his clipboard on the table and passed Erynne's photo across its surface once again. "Seems someone saw you near Pebble Beach last night with this lady. Does that ring a bell?"

Jack continued to smile, but his heart began to pound against his chest. He hoped the cop couldn't hear it. "Sounds like a fairytale."

Had his voice wavered? Detective Daniels didn't say anything, just kept eye contact. It was a game cops liked to play. Jack usually won.

This time he faltered and looked down at the table. He didn't even try to keep his smile as he read the name, *Senator Reardon,* upside down from the detective's clipboard. A small note pad covered up the rest of the information, but Jack thought it looked like a fax transmission. His mind raced. *Senator Reardon arrested,* or *Senator Reardon suspected in kidnapping* were both possibilities, neither of which would do Jack any good if he didn't cut a deal right now.

Jack looked up and caught a look of triumph on the detective's face.

"Let's talk about Pebble Beach," Detective Daniels said.

Sorry, senator, Jack thought. *You're on your own.*

Chapter 47

Laura Espinosa tapped her high-heeled shoe against the linoleum floor and sighed deeply, wishing she was down at the courthouse covering a celebrity child custody trial. Instead she was stuck at the police station, waiting for nothing to happen with yesterday's attempted murder and kidnapping. The new producer had just reassigned Laura to this beat a week ago – a producer who clearly did not understand how seniority worked at Channel Five News.

Laura had graduated magna cum laud with a degree in broadcast journalism from Northwestern more than five years ago. Back then, she could not have imagined that all the following years of hard work would gain her nothing more than a police beat at a network affiliate in one of California's smallest markets. Still, she had tried to make the best of it, hoping that diligence and old-fashioned hard work would eventually pay off.

This story could be sensational – or it could be nothing. Laura didn't know, but she suspected the latter. Chances were this missing businesswoman wasn't quite the prim and proper person everyone took her for. She was probably shacking up with the guy in custody. Or buying drugs from him. Whatever. In a small city like Santa Cruz, the story would be juicy enough, but the buzz would die at the county line. That made it low on Laura's priority list.

"And yet, the job must be done," she muttered to herself, spotting Officer John Preston as he passed through a door at the end of the hallway. Laura tugged on her blouse to display more cleavage and tossed her chestnut hair just in time for him to notice.

"Hey, John," she said, smiling. "How are you?"

"Really good, Laura," Preston said, looking her up and down. "And you?"

"Oh, you know. Bored, really. I'm waiting for anything new on the kidnapping case." Laura lowered her voice and moved closer, wrapping well-manicured fingers around his uniformed bicep. "I don't suppose you have any information you could spill, off the record, of course."

She licked her lips and waited. Preston had a weakness for pretty women – something she took advantage of without guilt. Today's seduction act paid off quickly. With a brief glance over his shoulder, Preston leaned in to whisper.

"You didn't hear this from me, but there's a rumor going around that the kidnapping is somehow connected to the missing senator."

"What?"

Laura's voice echoed down the hallway. Regaining her composure, she smiled apologetically and lowered her voice. "Do you mean the person who kidnapped Erynne O'Keefe might have taken Senator Reardon as well?"

Preston looked over his shoulder again. "No. The senator may have been *involved* in O'Keefe's kidnapping."

"John!" she gasped, tightening her grip on his arm. "Who are your sources?"

"Well, the perp in custody finally spilled, although he's holding out on O'Keefe's location." Preston rolled his eyes. "Thinks he's going to get total immunity. His word alone is not much to go on, but there's a cop in San Francisco – I don't know his name – who thinks he remembers a connection from years ago between the senator and this guy. Looks like the senator might have gotten him out of some legal trouble."

"This is incredible," Laura whispered.

"I know." Preston shook his head. "I only hope they find her in time."

"Hmm? Oh, yes. Of course." Laura's head was already filled with the copy she would write.

Preston opened his mouth to say something else when the desk sergeant walked by, eyeing them curiously. "I gotta go," Preston whispered, taking a quick step back.

"Thanks!" Laura said as he strolled past the chief's office, whistling cheerfully.

Laura stared at his retreating form for a moment, her mind trying to grasp the magnitude of what she had just heard. A million questions ran through her mind. How would she get the name of the San Francisco officer? Who else would corroborate the story? Could she get a camera crew to the senator's office in time to air on the five o'clock news?

Digging her phone from the bottom of her bag, she turned and all but ran from the station. This was the opportunity of a lifetime, her best chance to move her career soundly forward. She wasn't about to let anything get in her way.

Chapter 48

Ross played outdoors for as long as Grandma would let him, but when the rain started coming down in fat drops, she called him in. Ross howled in protest when she stripped him down to his underwear in the back doorway, but Grandma told him he was too young to feel humiliated. And where did he ever hear such a word?

By the time he was unceremoniously dumped in a warm tub, dried and dressed again in a warm sweat suit, the rain was coming down full force, making him appreciate the warm fire and hot cocoa waiting for him downstairs.

"Thanks, Grandma," he said, snuggling next to Grandpa on the couch while she went back to the kitchen.

"Dinner will be ruined if I don't get back to it," she said.

She's not fooling anyone, Ross thought. *She just doesn't want to miss* Entertainment Tonight.

Ross sat still for a while, watching Grandpa read the newspaper, but he got bored when the cocoa ran out. Grandpa liked it quiet at this time of the day.

"Let's take advantage of Abby's naptime," he had said, nudging Ross in the arm.

That just meant Ross had to be quiet too. After Grandpa told him to stop squirming three times, Ross squirmed right off the couch and padded toward the kitchen with his empty mug in hand.

He stopped in the doorway when he saw Grandma sitting very still on a kitchen stool with her nose almost pressed against the TV. She had a strange expression on her face and was twisting a dishtowel in her hands. Ross was surprised to see that it wasn't *Entertainment Tonight*, but a news lady he didn't recognize, standing with a microphone under an umbrella in the rain. He wondered why she didn't go inside.

"Grandma?" he asked. "Are you okay?"

Grandma jumped and dropped the dishtowel as she turned around.

"Ross, what you said earlier about someone being at Evelyn's house – were you telling the truth or making up another story?"

"Honest, Grandma. I saw her. The lady in the nightgown."

Grandma turned back to the TV and pointed. "Do you recognize those people, Ross?"

Ross studied the faces on the screen. One was a smiling man in a business suit like his dad wore. The other was the lady he had seen on TV at lunchtime. Ross scrunched up his nose and looked at the man again, then turned away as a commercial for Velveeta came on.

"That's the same lady, Grandma, but I don't know about the man. He was really big, but he didn't look so ... neat. Who are they, Grandma?"

Grandma's face had changed colors and Ross was beginning to worry. Was he in trouble for spying on the neighbors? He was about to ask, but Grandma turned around and ran into the living room. Ross didn't know she could move that fast.

He followed, reaching the door just in time to see Grandma pull the newspaper right out of Grandpa's hands.

"Oh, honey!" she said. "We have to call the police. Something awful is going on over at Evelyn's house."

Chapter 49

Colin shouldered his way through the front door of the police station, letting it bang closed behind him. Overhead the sky was darkening ominously, errant sprinkles already splattered the sidewalk. Len caught up with him at the corner, his grasp firm on Colin's shoulder.

"Colin, wait..."

"I can't wait anymore!" Colin shrugged off his hand. "I'm driving down there to find her myself!"

"Think this through, would you?" Len said. "What's your plan? Because Pebble Beach is a very exclusive area – and heavily monitored. The rich and famous pay a premium for their secured privacy. You can't just canvas the area, knocking on doors, demanding to see the wine cellars and attics. You'll only get yourself into trouble. What good can you do for Erynne then?"

Without answering, Colin turned away and began walking toward his car. Len didn't follow him this time. A hot tide of frustration was coursing through Colin, but he tamped it down, using it for fuel.

Every time he closed his eyes, he saw Erynne disappear beneath the dark sea. Sunset was less than an hour away and he had still done nothing tangible to help her. Instead, the day had sped past while they wasted their time – posting flyers that no one looked at, showing Erynne's photo to people who knew nothing. Gretchen had walked back and forth from the police station to Erynne's studio, providing no-news updates for her staff while Len had fetched never-ending coffee and sandwiches that no one wanted to eat.

Colin had finally returned his mother's calls this morning, shortly after telling Detective Daniels about his dream. He had been stunned to learn about Erynne's visit to Sun City and her call to Joy just moments before Jack Lender knocked on her door.

"Oh, no, Colin!" Joy said, her voice breaking. "It's my fault. I told her it would be you at her door!"

The reality that his father had sent letters to Erynne's mother was enough to make his head reel. Part of his heart leaped at the knowledge. It was proof of his connection to her, a puzzle piece laid into place. But it also increased his dread. He couldn't lose her now – not when they had come so close to finding each other.

Colin had rarely left the police station, reluctant to stray too far from the only person who truly knew where Erynne was – Jack Lender. Only once during the morning had the desk clerk offered Colin more than her sympathy. Crooking her finger, she had beckoned him over.

"Detective Daniels wanted me to pass along a message," Angie said.

"About Erynne?"

She shook her head. "He had California Highway Patrol officers go by the Lone Cypress monument – to look for any suspicious activity. They didn't see anything unusual – just your usual trickle of tourists."

At the time, the information had reinforced Colin's decision to stay near the station. Maybe he had been right last night when he told Len and Gretchen that dreamland settings had no connection with real life. But Jack Lender was real enough. And when Detective Daniels had passed him in the hallway this afternoon, Colin thought he saw a flicker in his eyes – something that meant their interrogation was starting to work.

But nothing was happening now. It might be logical to stay here and wait for the police to do their job, but he had been waiting too long. He had to do something more.

By the time he reached his car, big rain drops were starting to fall. He ducked inside quickly, but didn't start the engine. Instead he pulled Erynne's necklace out of his pocket. He had not allowed himself to dwell on the impossible truth of their shared dreams today. But this object that matched his birthmark was something he couldn't leave alone: a tree with unseen roots that reached back through the centuries, intertwining their lives. He couldn't be whole without her, he realized. He never had been.

Colin's phone buzzed, making him jump. He flipped it open.

"Colin, you need to come back to the station," Gretchen said. "Hurry!"

"I'll be right there."

He jumped out of the car and ran through the rain. Gretchen was waiting for him under the awning by the front door. Together, they rushed back inside. Len was already talking to Angie at the front desk.

"What's going on?" Colin asked.

"Detective Daniels left just a few minutes ago," Len said. "I saw him go out the back. He was running and calling instructions to another officer."

"Where were they going?" Colin asked, reaching across the counter to grab Angie's hand. "Please, I need to know."

Angie glanced over her shoulder and then shrugged. "I don't see how it could hurt anything to tell you. The suspect started spilling the beans a couple of hours ago. Said he was working for someone else. Senator Reardon, if you can believe that."

"Senator Reardon?" Gretchen's face drained of color.

Angie shook her head, her eyes wide. "That's what he said. I guess he's gone missing too, so it might fit."

"Where are they?" Colin asked.

"Lender said that the senator has her locked up in a house near Pebble Beach."

Gretchen squeezed Colin's arm.

"So then a reporter got wind of the story and put it on the afternoon news, just about the same time that Daniels found out that Reardon's mother has a home on Seventeen Mile Drive."

"Any details – an address?" he asked.

"Yeah, he got it and was getting ready to check it out. But just a few minutes ago we got a report in that someone called the police out there. A kid spotted your friend and the senator over a fence or something." Angie smacked her gum. "You're not going to tell Detective Daniels I told you, are you?"

Colin leaned over the counter and kissed her cheek. "Not in a million years, Angie." He turned on his heels and ran out of the station with Len and Gretchen close behind.

Chapter 50

Detective Daniels pulled his Crown Victoria to a stop in front of the Reardon estate and promptly struck the steering wheel in frustration. The place was swarming with local police and worse, the FBI.

And just like that, it wasn't Daniel's case anymore.

He would be allowed to stay on the scene as little more than a courtesy. Any glory in the outcome would pass straight over his head and land on the brass and feds with a great, noisy splat. Of course, if things should go wrong, they would remember him easily enough.

If only it hadn't been a U.S. senator.

Daniels donned his rain gear and stepped out of the car, slamming the door behind him. His brain still wanted to do a double take over Jack's revelation.

"Senator Mike Reardon has her," Jack had said.

In all his years of law enforcement, Daniel's had never been so stunned. He had voted for Reardon: would have voted for him again.

"And why would a senator take Erynne O'Keefe?" Daniels had asked. Jack noticed the way his voice lurched and had smiled unkindly.

"Enough to make you wanna puke, huh?" He had crossed his arms and ankles.

"Just answer the question!"

"Easy, easy! Okay, the senator was obsessed with her or something. I don't know. He had this drawing of her. Told me to look for her in Chinatown. She was there, just like he said, so I followed her. I don't know how he knows her – why he'd risk all this for her. He didn't even know her name."

It had been almost impossible to believe, even after talking to Inspector Bridges in San Francisco, who had been in touch with the missing senator's mother – the woman whose home was now surrounded by cops.

"I had a funny feeling about Jack Lender when I saw his name come across my desk," Bridges told him. "So he actually named Reardon, huh?" There was a pause and Daniels waited impatiently, tapping his fingers on the desk while Bridges flipped through his case files.

"Well? Is it plausible?" Daniels finally asked.

"I'll tell you what, I'm looking at one of his case files from about two years ago. The charge was drug possession. Looks like everything was done by the book – witnesses, signed statements – but then the bagged goods disappeared from the evidence cage."

"Was it your case?"

"No, but I remember it," Bridges answered. "Seems like Lender got himself a lawyer – a real sleaze bag, but better than the public defender. He got the charges dropped for lack of evidence. There's a note here in the file that explains why I tied Lender to Reardon in my mind. I had forgotten about it, but last year someone called me with an anonymous tip. It was a woman. She told me that Lender's lawyer was paid by Kendall Markham up in Sacramento. Markham is Reardon's campaign manager."

"You're kidding." Daniels had looked through the wired window and stared at Lender hard. Could he actually be telling the truth?

"So what did you do?" he asked Bridges.

"I turned it back over to the arresting officer. A few weeks later, he told me there was no evidence to back up my informant's tip. We closed the file again and I forgot about it."

"It's not a lot to go on."

"No, but I decided to call a detective I know in D.C., just to put out some feelers."

"And?"

"Do you remember hearing about Reardon's wife? She was mugged a couple of weeks ago in Georgetown. Beat up real bad. It was in all the papers."

"Yeah, I remember."

"My friend told me he went to the hospital to question Mrs. Reardon after the mugging. She couldn't communicate much – she was beaten so badly that her jaw was wired shut. But while he was there, the senator walked into her room. He would swear that the lady tried to shrink back into her sheets. Her eyes widened the moment she saw her husband. Said she was scared to death, nurses came running. She had to be sedated."

"And you think – what? That Reardon sent his own wife to the hospital?"

"He's a big man, shown his temper a time or two recently in public. It's possible."

367

Daniels whistled softly. "This could be just what we need to get a warrant."

"Good luck," said Bridges.

Everything had gone into motion quickly from the moment he hung up the phone. It hadn't been hard to learn about the Reardon estate. The tip they received from the neighbor had been icing on the cake. Lender would get no deal now – he would go straight to prison.

So let the FBI take the glory, Daniels decided. *At least a violent criminal isn't going to weasel his way around the legal system. Not on my watch.*

Daniels hoofed it over to a group of uniformed officers gathered behind a squad car parked at the end of the long driveway. After identifying himself, he asked for an update.

"Sir, we've taken positions all around the perimeter of the house and the property," a young officer named Finley told him. He pointed toward a tall black man wearing an FBI jacket. "Special Agent Anderson tried to place a call to the residence but received no response. We'll be going in soon."

Daniels rubbed his hands together and blew on them while he waited. Sheeting rain fell from the sky and drizzled down around the brim of his weather-proof hat, making it impossible to see much of what was going on at the house beyond the sloped drive. It still amazed him that Green had been right about the Pebble Beach lead. He shook his head and promised himself to be more open-minded in the future.

Through Finley's walkie-talkie, Daniels heard the command given to enter the house and listened impatiently for sounds of success, wishing he were leading the squad. It was a big house, though, and he knew it could take them awhile to find her.

"Detective Daniels?"

Daniels spun around and scowled as he saw Colin Green running toward him, followed closely by Professor and Mrs. Martin.

"I thought this area was secure!" he barked at Finley. Daniels turned back to Green. "What are you doing here? You need to get in your car and leave the area."

Green ignored him and pushed toward the house. "Is she in there? Is she okay?"

"We don't know anything yet," Daniels said darkly, "and if you don't go back to your vehicle, I'm going to use these and put you in the back of mine." He tapped the handcuffs dangling from his hip. Professor Martin responded quickly, pulling Green back toward the road.

Several minutes passed before the walkie-talkie squawked again. "We've secured the premises. There's no one here, sir."

Special Agent Anderson responded from the other side of the squad car. "Give it a second sweep, just to be sure."

He got away with her, Daniels thought.

He turned around, prepared to remove Green and his friends from the crime scene, but he only saw the older couple, dutifully standing at the curb, huddled under a large umbrella. Mrs. Martin was crying. She had clearly heard Agent Anderson's report.

"Where's Green?" Daniels asked. All three turned as they heard the sound of tires spinning on the rocky roadside. Green's rental car lurched forward and took off in the direction of Carmel.

Chapter 51

Two hours before the police arrived at the Reardon estate, Erynne's captor had finally ushered her back inside and up to the tower bedroom. Despite being soaked to her core and wracked with violent shivers, Erynne felt feverish. The illness she had suspected early in the day was now burning in her chest like a hot ember. Painful coughing spells were compounded by her sore throat, which served as a constant reminder of the dark bruises on her neck. She was lucky to be alive after his brutal attack this morning. But though she was relieved to be out of the rain, she was terrified to be sharing such a confined space with him again.

Leaning against the bedpost, Erynne watched him warily as he stood in the doorway. All day he had behaved as if he was oblivious to the elements or their effect on her, but now he frowned as he watched her tremble.

"Here," he said, grabbing a quilt from the foot of the bed and wrapping it around her shoulders. Erynne flinched, but allowed him to lead her to a wing chair in the corner where she gratefully sank and closed her eyes. Lethargy fought hopelessness in her mind, which had remained murky throughout the day, pulling in and out of focus. She wondered vaguely if it was her fever or his assault that was responsible.

She must have dozed off. When she opened her eyes again, she was alone and the door was closed. She didn't bother wasting the energy it would take to check it. She knew it was locked – knew that even if it wasn't, she wouldn't be able to navigate the stairs and find a way to escape.

He had left her briefly that morning too – long enough for her to fumble with the locked door and search her room for a phone or a weapon. She found nothing, not even her own clothes. Thinking about how she had come to be dressed in the nightgown made her shudder in revulsion.

"Call me Michael," he told her when he had returned. He led her down the spiral staircase, offering her no breakfast and nothing to drink. The thought that he regarded her as something other than human flitted across her mind.

They spent most of the day outside, wandering through the courtyard, around the rose garden and across the lawns to the edge of the cliff. There he had hovered over her, his breath quick, his eyes dark. Each time they returned to that spot, Erynne was sure that he would push her over the edge, forcing her to follow her mother's chosen path of escape. Instead he would turn away, leaving her to retreat on wobbly legs as her adrenalin evaporated.

Erynne had looked for opportunities to escape early in the day – to make a break for the street or a neighbor's house. But she soon realized that was exactly what Michael wanted – for her to run so that he could give chase, recreating their dreams. Moments of panic frequently settled into a conviction that this *was* just another dream, though the worst: the most detailed. Each time truth emerged, she faced her captivity with fresh horror. It didn't take long for her to give up any hope of escape. There was no way to outrun him, not with her sprained ankle or the tightness in her chest. Not in her disoriented state of mind.

As the hours passed, reality continued to twist. Michael was clearly unbalanced, but was she going crazy too? She had finally recognized him this afternoon, looking beyond the unwashed hair, the blood-shot eyes with dark shadows beneath. Could this mad man really be Senator Reardon? A man whose campaign smile was kind, whose track record spoke of compassion and human rights? The thought had caused a bubble of hysteria to burst from her throat in an unnatural laugh. He turned and looked at her sharply, as if she were a doll that had magically been given a voice.

No, it couldn't be, she decided. But her mind wouldn't let go of the possibility – not when the alternative was a crack in her own mental state.

Michael's insanity seemed to work like a coil, winding tightly with increased fervor as he described his voyeurism on the cobblestone street and his subsequent nights spent stalking her. From its tightest place, it would spring violently forward in a burst of anger. She was responsible for the constant headaches – she and Colin, whom he called the Intruder. Michael had seen the way they looked at each other, working together to plot his destruction.

"I won't let you ruin my plans," he said, leaning toward her, his breath fast with rage. Erynne had flattened herself against a tree, sure he would finish the attack he had abandoned that morning.

"Everything my ancestors fought for, the carefully laid plans that rest on my shoulders – do you think I'm going to let you interfere?"

His eyes had bulged wildly. For a moment Erynne had seen fear in their depths.

"It's what my father warned me about – why this can't go on much longer." Michael grabbed her by the shoulders and shook her. "You think you can whisper together and I'll do nothing? You think you can leave me there in the street – inviting that Intruder to places I can't follow? Who's on the outside now?"

He released her and stalked away as Erynne crumpled against the ground. Similar tirades had punctuated the day, each one doing more to cripple her emotions. Terror and survival were all she knew – even now, while she sat alone under a quilt. He would be back soon and all she could think about was his promise: *This can't go on much longer.*

Erynne dozed again, but not for long. This time Michael's key in the door woke her and she sat up, watching him carefully as he entered the room with a steaming mug in his hand.

"Tea," he said as he placed it in her shaking hands. Erynne sipped it greedily, craving its warmth, desperate for something to quench her thirst.

"There's a good girl," Michael said, watching her drink. "Hurry. We have to leave."

Erynne released the empty mug, letting him fumble for it as she pulled the quilt up to her chin. His sudden concern for her welfare tugged at her mind, triggering an alarm that she was too weak to regard.

"I can't go anywhere," she told him flatly, closing her eyes.

"We must!" His voice was suddenly cloying. "He's coming, my sweet, and we can't be sitting here, waiting. If we don't hurry, he'll spoil my plans."

"I need to rest." The words were hardly a whisper. Erynne was giving up, drifting back to sleep.

"I know you're tired," Michael crooned, scooping her effortlessly from the chair. "Don't worry, it will all be over soon."

Erynne was aware of his quickening heartbeat as they descended the stairs, but she did not struggle, her sense of detachment grew as he carried her to the garage, where a black car was waiting.

The rain beat fiercely against the windshield as they pulled out of the driveway. Erynne leaned against the side window, her gaze fixed on the trees that crowded the winding road, blurring into one dark mass beyond the sheeting water. Watching them pass made her head spin. She closed her eyes and felt reality spiraling away.

When the car slowed and turned off the road, she forced them open again. Michael pulled to a stop on a graveled drive and turned to face her. Red lights from the dashboard combined with Erynne's declining sense of balance made his face look distorted and fiendish. When he spoke, his voice was thick and low, adding to the illusion. Erynne shrank against the passenger door.

"I'm sorry it has to end this way," Michael said, reaching out a tentative hand to push her hair from her face. "But I can't risk any more time with you."

He smiled: a hideous grimace of regret. "I wanted something different with you, but this place has been calling to me." He paused as if hearing something beyond the howling weather. "Do you hear it? This is where it has to end – I'm sure of it."

Erynne struggled to decipher his words long after they left his mouth, trying to reform them into something she could understand. Her eyes widened as he leaned toward her, grabbing her tangled hair and covering her mouth with his. Spidery fingers of fear jolted her senses, rushing through her veins as she fought to push him away. Her protest was lost under his greedy lips.

Finally he pulled away, his breath coming fast, his eyes dilated with desire.

"Now, that wasn't so bad, was it?" he asked, amused, it seemed, by Erynne's resistance. "We could have had fun together. This truly hurts me. I comfort myself knowing that the tea will soften the blow. You won't suffer."

The unwelcome kiss had served to electrify Erynne's system. This time she understood the meaning of his words. Michael had drugged her tea and brought her out here to die.

Erynne turned and fumbled with the door handle. Lurching sideways, she fell out of the car and onto the ground, where her lip found the edge of a rock. Blood and dirt invaded her mouth as she scrambled to her feet. Michael's footsteps were slow and steady as he moved through the loose gravel and around the hood of the car. Gathering all of her strength, Erynne lunged forward, neither knowing nor caring what lay ahead, focused only on escaping the nightmare behind.

Sharp rocks covered the ground, cutting her bare feet while the cold rain quickly penetrated her hair and nightgown. From somewhere nearby, she heard the sound of high tide pounding against the cliffs. The drug was working. The earth tilted beneath her, forcing her to her hands and knees. She struggled to her feet again, hazarding only a quick backward glance to gauge Michael's pursuit like she had in so many dreams, absorbing the confidence of his gait, the resolution in his face.

Erynne pushed forward, making out a dark shape in the driving rain. The form was familiar, a symbol that she had worn close to her heart, one that had both comforted and terrified her. Recognition dawned, but it was far too late to change her course.

The Lone Cypress was as stark and isolated as its name would suggest: a sentinel perched on the edge of the rocky cliff. To Erynne it was more like a beacon, bringing her full circle to face the fate that had been set in motion more than a thousand years ago.

It was no wonder Michael was content to keep his slow pace behind her. He knew exactly where she was running. And that this time, there was no way of escape.

Chapter 52

Colin knew where Erynne was. His idle moments that day had been spent memorizing a map of Pebble Beach, imagining himself tracing her kidnapper's path. The moment he heard the all-clear sign at the Reardon Estate, he had jumped into his rental car and sped toward the Lone Cypress. He only prayed he would make it in time.

The rain fell in sheets, discouraging any other travelers on the winding road. The distance was short, but the drive seemed infinite. When he finally spotted the landmark sign in his headlights, he had to turn sharply to make the narrow drive. Pulling to a stop behind a black BMW, he cut the engine and jumped out of the car.

A quick check told him that no one was in the car or the immediate vicinity. Colin knew better than to look for the narrow beach from his dream. The map had already told him it did not exist. It was close to dusk, but seemed much darker. Thick clouds obliterated the setting sun. Wind and rain continued to roar around him, making it difficult to see for more than a few yards. Colin wished he had a flashlight, but wasn't about to be slowed down by nightfall. He ran out along the cliff's edge and toward the tree.

The Lone Cypress grew on the northern edge of the cliff point, some twenty yards from where Colin left his car. Over the years, conservationists had added tiered rock walls around the base of the cypress and descending down the side of the cliff to preserve the tree's root system against natural erosion and the unnatural effects of tourism. Colin kept to the gravel path until he reached the tree, squinting into the torrent in all directions, calling Erynne's name.

His heart lurched when he finally spotted her. She looked like a ghost, shrouded in the white nightgown he remembered from their dreams. Reardon stood close to her elbow with his hand on her back, his mouth moving fervently against her ear.

"Erynne!" Colin shouted, but his voice was drowned out by the sound of the waves crashing against the cliffs below. In one swift motion, he jumped over the low stone wall and began picking his way across the sharp rocks that stood between them. His heartbeat raged against his eardrums, reminding him that seconds mattered. Erynne was only a breath away from disappearing over the edge.

No, dear God! he prayed. *Please don't let this end like my dream!*

"Erynne!" he called again. This time his voice reached them both.

The senator turned quickly and Colin was surprised by the look of twisted satisfaction on his face. He tightened his grip on Erynne. "I told you he would come," he said, kissing her temple.

Rage boiled in Colin's veins, despite the stinging cold. "Let her go," he said. But he felt as powerless as his words, standing on the secure side of the cliff while only jagged rocks and pounding waves encircled Erynne. She looked at him only briefly, wearing a dazed expression that made his heart ache.

The senator ignored Colin's command, his smile widening as he moved his hand over Erynne's shoulder and tightened his fingers around her bruised throat. Colin shifted closer but tamped down his anger. One rash movement was all the senator was waiting for.

"That's right," Reardon said, almost as if he could read Colin's mind. He jerked his head significantly toward the pounding surf over his shoulder. "But after I let her go, you'll be soon to follow."

Colin's anger gave way to sudden, desperate fear.

"Do you even know why you're doing this?" he shouted hoarsely. "This power at work here – this connection – it's something I don't understand. We're all a part of it, but it doesn't have to control us. Please. Let her go! We'll fight it. We'll figure it out together!"

Colin reached out his hand in a gesture of desperation and watched the senator's face change, the confident smile replaced by raw fear. He tightened his grip on Erynne's throat and slapped desperately at the rain that was pelting his face.

"My father warned me that someone would try and stop me..."

His voice trailed off and his gaze shifted to a place over Colin's shoulder, as if he was looking for something in the black night. But whatever he was struggling with passed as quickly as it had come. His fierce grimace returned as he focused again on Colin's face.

"The power you recognize is mine – not yours! Don't pretend you're here to help me. You only want to steal it for yourself – just like you stole her from me, taking my place in her dreams! I'm done playing into your hands. This ends now."

Reardon turned, ready to hurl Erynne toward the white peaks below when she suddenly slumped against him, merciful oblivion having finally prevailed. He was only taken off guard momentarily, but Colin took advantage of it. Lunging forward, he grabbed Erynne's wrist, pulling her toward him and away from the edge, where rocks and pebbles were already loosening and falling to the sea below. Her listless body responded to the tug of war, tottering away from the senator and upsetting his slippery footing. Colin watched in horror as the large man stumbled for balance on the ragged terrain and slipped, crashing to the ground and tottering halfway over the edge of the cliff, all while keeping a tight hold on Erynne.

Colin was jerked roughly to the ground and dragged toward the cliff's edge. Jagged rocks tore his clothing, grating the flesh beneath. He ignored the pain, desperate to maintain his hold on Erynne's arm. Most of her limp form was resting precariously on a large rock, while the senator's legs swung freely below, his grasp on Erynne's bare ankle tenuous at best. He was panicking, trying to pull himself upward, fighting the wet resistance of Erynne's skin. Colin could feel his grasp on her arm loosening.

"Hold on," he yelled, though Erynne remained unconscious, unable to reinforce his grip or to kick herself free of the captor whose weight was threatening to pull her over the edge.

Protect her. Colin heard it on the wind and felt a surge of strength beyond his own.

Clenching his teeth, he used his shoulder for leverage and finally felt the senator's hold on her ankle give way. It was the momentum he needed. Colin rolled, pulling her fully into his arms as Reardon's heavy body succumbed to the powers of gravity and slipped out of sight.

Scooting away from the edge, Colin pushed Erynne's wet hair away from her face and studied her fervently. She moaned and shifted against him – the most beautiful thing he had ever felt. She was alive, but he had to get her help. Soon.

"Help me!"

The senator 's cry was barely audible over the sound of the crashing waves. Laying Erynne gently to the side, Colin rocked forward and onto his stomach again to look over the edge. Just three feet down, Reardon was hanging from the side of the cliff, one hand entangled in the loosening roots of an ice plant, the other bloodied and clawing for a hold.

Colin froze in indecision, staring down at the man who had filled Erynne with fear for months, haunting her dreams. He had kidnapped her and brought her here to die. To fall to that end himself was just what he deserved. But he wasn't dead. He was clinging to life, and Colin didn't know how to simply walk away.

"Hold on!"

Reardon's face remained frozen in fear. Shifting for balance, Colin offered his hand, feeling the senator's massive weight as it was taken. His muscles strained and resisted as he tightened his grasp, determined to maintain his hold, angry with himself for helping at all.

"Slow. Steady!" Colin shouted. Reardon wasn't listening, but panicking. Releasing the plant roots, he was now grabbing at Colin's arms with both hands, clawing his way upward until his feet found pigeon holes in the rocky cliff and his torso was resting on the edge. Colin moved to back away, release the senator's hands and increase the safety of his own position.

But Reardon had other plans.

They were visible for a fleeting moment in his eyes before he pulled roughly on Colin, drawing him halfway over the cliff to again face the crashing sea that pummeled the rocks below.

"One way or another, you'll die here tonight!" the senator growled through clenched teeth.

Colin scrambled for a foothold. Reardon was using his own strength and Colin's body weight against him, dragging him further over the edge until the men were eye to eye, both breathing heavily and locked in a battle that could easily end in death for them both. Colin cursed himself for his faulty sense of honor, considering what it was about to cost him. He could see insanity in the senator's eyes, hinging on his sense of invincibility.

It's going to end this way, Colin thought, panic seeping into his muscles. His body inched further over the edge, tottering on that balance point where another gram of weight would make recovery impossible. The senator saw it too, triumph emanating as he reached forward to deliver Colin's fatal blow.

A blur of white interrupted Reardon's hand, accompanied by an anguished wail that sounded far from human. It was Erynne, lurching herself between the men, pushing against the senator with strength that belied her illness.

"No!" she shouted, her voice hoarse and her eyes wild. They fluttered upward for a moment and Colin thought she would lose consciousness again, dooming them all to the sea below. But it was enough to distract the senator. Colin slipped free of his grip and scrambled over the edge while Erynne fell against Reardon.

Stark fear filled his eyes. His position wasn't as secure as he thought. The pressure of Erynne's attack was too much. Colin felt the senator's grasp give way as he and Erynne began to tumble over the edge.

"No!"

Colin lunged forward, grabbing Erynne by the waist and watching the senator fall. His large body struck the rocks below with a sickening thud before disappearing into the foam. Only his shriek of terror was left behind, echoing against the walls of the cliff amidst an avalanche of rocks and pebbles.

Colin rocked backward with Erynne across his legs, horrified that they would be pulled down as well, caught up by an angry environment that had seen its beauty defiled. His heart beat violently against his chest and his hands trembled as he pulled her against him. Moments later he heard the wail of a siren. They had to move – to get back to the road where they would be seen. He lifted her carefully, adrenalin giving him strength that would otherwise have failed, and picked his way slowly around the tree.

Erynne was unconscious again, her skin so pale that it appeared transparent beneath the blood and bruises. Colin shuttered as he took in her sodden form. The thin nightgown was wet, torn and bloodied where sharp rocks had found her tender skin. He stopped on the graveled walk and dropped to the ground again to remove his soaked windbreaker and wrap it around her. He could scarcely feel a pulse at the base of her neck. Cold fear engulfed him as he scooped her into his arms and held her tightly as the police came running. Colin willed his body heat to enter hers, all the while whispering urgently into her ear.

"Come on, Erynne. Don't leave me. Don't leave me now."

Chapter 53

A bright light surrounded Erynne, warming her like the sun. She stood on nothing, weightless and still. Closing her eyes, she felt the warmth penetrate her, surround her. Something had changed, but something else had shifted back into place.

"Erynne?"

She opened her eyes. "Mom?"

Erynne turned in a circle, searching for the source of her mother's voice, squinting into the blinding light. "I can't find you!"

"I'm here, Erynne. I'll always be here."

Her mother's voice was changing.

"Wake up, honey. It's time to wake up."

Erynne closed her eyes against the brilliant light. Blinking rapidly, she opened them again and tried to lift her hand, but it was too heavy, weighed down by something inside that frightened her. She tried to speak.

"She's coming around," someone said.

Erynne was lying down. Another bright light flashed into her eyes and she groaned, trying to turn away.

"Erynne? Can you hear me?" It was the same voice, gentle and efficient, but not her mother's. The bright light was fading to black as she heard another voice, one that she loved, from further away.

"Is she going to be okay? I want to stay with her!"

"You need to wait outside, sir."

Erynne tried to tell them that she wanted him to stay, but the blackness was swallowing up the light, swallowing her whole.

ॐ

The next time Erynne woke, she was screaming.

"He's here," she said, searching her hospital room while a nurse tried to restrain her. "He's not just a dream. He's coming — he'll find me!"

A chair scraped across the floor and the nurse backed away, replaced by warm, familiar arms that wrapped around her.

"Shh, it's alright."

Erynne trembled in his embrace, holding on for dear life. She was afraid to move — afraid to lift her eyes to his face for fear that he would evaporate like so many dreams. She didn't know how long they stayed that way, crowded together on her hospital bed. Eventually reality refused to be mistaken. She tipped back her head and looked into Colin's eyes for the first time.

"You're not a dream," she said.

Colin shook his head. "It's over." He brushed the tears from her cheeks, blinking back his own. "He's gone, Erynne. And I'm not going anywhere."

Erynne fell asleep in his arms, searching his face, praying that he would not be gone with the morning as he always had been in the past. She slept dreamlessly for the rest of the night and woke early to find him dozing in a chair pulled close to her bed, his fingers still linked with hers. Erynne scooted closer and kissed his hand, relishing the reality more than the dream.

"You're still here," she said when he opened his eyes.

"I told you I would be."

"I didn't know how to believe you."

Colin gently urged her back against her pillows, wincing as he took in her bruises and cuts. Erynne could only imagine how they looked this morning: angry and raw against her pale skin.

"How did you find me?" she asked, still searching his face. Her memories were so hazy. He had been standing on a cliff above her.

But wasn't that a dream? Then it had been real, but she was on the cliff as well and that monster had tried to kill her. He had tried to kill them both.

Colin shook his head. "Let's leave the details for later. I'm here, and I'm not going anywhere." He smiled. "I had to find you. I can't dream without you. It seems I can't live without you either. I love you, Erynne. With everything I am."

Then Erynne remembered Colin holding her in the rain. There were sirens and he had rocked her in his arms – these arms that were still holding her.

"Colin?"

He sighed and put his forehead against hers, his voice thick. "It's so good to hear you say my name."

∞

As the weeks and months passed, Erynne recovered from her injuries, from Michael's drugs and the pneumonia that had almost taken her life. She cried when she first saw a news report about her ordeal and Michael's attack on his wife. She cried again when she was well enough to visit Mark and see for herself that he was truly alive and making his own slow recovery.

But Erynne's nightmares did not stop on the night of Michael's death. They returned vengefully, his ghost finding new ways to terrorize her, a haunting echo of their time together. The doctors called it post-traumatic stress, though Erynne knew they couldn't understand the meaningful differences. Eventually they tapered away and disappeared. She still dreamed of the crying baby now and then, but was learning to see those dreams in a different light, aided by Drs. Peterson and Leitch. Gretchen and Len helped even more, behaving like her parents never had, giving her love like she'd never felt.

Colin was constantly by her side, both in the hospital and when she was able to return home. Revisiting their shared dreams during the quietest part of the night with fingers entwined, sitting by the fire or under the stars, Erynne and Colin fell in love again, more deeply and irrevocably, delighting in the sureness of reality, the constancy of the physical world they shared.

They still dreamed of each other, something that pleased them both – especially when Colin had to return to Arizona. The dreams became only sweeter as their relationship grew, adding a depth to the reality, a measure of their connection. Finding each other changed them both – something that Gretchen noticed in Erynne and Joy in Colin. It was as if they understood each other instinctively, each shedding the fears that had kept them out of meaningful relationships in the past.

No one was surprised when Colin put his house on the market and began meeting with Bay Area accounting firms, though Joy hinted rather strongly to Erynne that Phoenix made a very nice place to settle down and raise a family.

Erynne and Colin actually spent very little time planning their future together. Instead they spent most of their days like today, curled up in each other's arms. Glad to be alive. Glad to be awake.

Acknowledgements

For invaluable research information, my sincere thanks go to Caitlin and John Matthews, authors of the *Encyclopedia of Celtic Wisdom*; Robert Van de Castle, author of *Our Dreaming Mind*; and Adam Schneider and G. William Domhoff at the University of California, Santa Cruz, authors of *The Quantitative Study of Dreams* and *dreamresearch.net*. (It was a delightful coincidence to learn that you were there, right where I had already decided Erynne's dreams would begin.)

To my earliest readers: Dawndi Phillips, Susan Smallen, Lara Russell, Rhonda Burks and Linda Forbes, thank you so much for your support. To Michael Baxter at Baxter Imaging, who took time out of his busy schedule to help me design *Dream of Me*'s beautiful cover art – thank you!

To Josh Groban, for inspiration, album by album, concert by concert, thank you.

To my husband, Bryan, who inspired me without knowing it, and to my children, Drew and Tara: Thank you for your patience, love and support. I love you all so much.

To my sister, Michelle Britton, *Dream of Me's* first reader, who kept me writing, one chapter at a time. To my sister, Christy Ford, my first and last editor, who has supported me with passion at every turn: I love you both. To Dad, for always having a book in your hands, and to Mom, who has loved everything I have ever written – from my sloppiest poetry to my sappiest prose, I love you. Most especially I thank the Lord God of Heaven, who has given me every good and perfect gift – many of them the people listed here. I am truly thankful.

About the Author

Jennifer Froelich is a graduate of the Walter Cronkite School of Journalism at Arizona State University. She now lives with her family in Boise, Idaho.

Find out more about *Dream of Me* and Jennifer's next novel at www.jenniferfroelich.com

Made in the USA
Charleston, SC
27 May 2015